# Praise for THE SEER

"In THE SEER, Raquel Y. Levitt beautifully weaves together a story of visions and betrayals, sisters and friendships, violence and love at the end of the nineteenth century. An impressive debut by a talented new writer."

—Ann Hood, New York Times Bestselling Author of *The Stolen Child*

"THE SEER is an evocative and sharply rendered exploration of a startling inheritance that binds two sisters in 19th century Missouri. With beautiful prose and a masterly emotional reach, Raquel Y. Levitt has written a riveting and heartwarming debut. Extraordinary."

—Danielle Trussoni, New York Times Bestselling Author of *The Puzzle Box*

"THE SEER by Raquel Y. Levitt is a gripping novel of two sisters burdened with a haunting gift: the ability to see the mists that surround people, with the colors revealing the secrets of their hearts. What begins as a mysterious power soon spirals as their visions lead them down dangerous paths. A mesmerizing tale of trust, betrayal, and the devastating consequences of good intentions. I could not put this book down!"

—KIM TAYLOR BLAKEMORE, AUTHOR OF *AFTER ALICE FELL*

"THE SEER explores the essential connection between women and reminds us that the power of intuition, the transformative potential of belief, and the resilience of women transcend time. With vivid characters and a captivating narrative, this is a must-read for those who trust in the extraordinary magic that happens when women come together."

—LEAH DECESARE, AWARD-WINNING AUTHOR OF *FORKS, KNIVES, AND SPOONS*

"In her exquisitely written, courageous debut historical novel, THE SEER, Raquel Y. Levitt takes on the theme of domestic abuse with its terrible violence, shame, and secrets. Interweaving magical realism, Levitt takes us deep into a woman's struggle to support victims and bring their perpetrators to justice during a period when the judicial system provided little protection."

—JANE LOEB RUBIN, AUTHOR OF THE AWARD-WINNING GILDED CITY TRILOGY: *THREADBARE, IN THE HANDS OF WOMEN, AND OVER THERE*

"Raquel Y. Levitt's debut novel, THE SEER, is a first-person narrative of Sarah, a girl whose psychic abilities present a remarkable problem when she encounters serious trouble and must find a way to convince others that her testimony can be trusted. The page-turning plot weaves Sara's personal drama into a tale of loving family on both sides of the grave."

—CAROLYN KORSMEYER, AUTHOR OF *RIDDLE OF SPIRIT AND BONE*

*The Seer*


Printed in the United States of America. For information, address Acorn Publishing, LLC
3943 Irvine Blvd. Ste. 218, Irvine, CA 92602

www.acornpublishingllc.com

Interior design by Kat Ross
Cover design by Damonza



ISBN-13: 979-8-88528-116-4 (hardcover)
ISBN-13: 979-8-88528-115-7 (paperback)
Library of Congress Control Number: 2024921594

# *The* SEER

RAQUEL Y. LEVITT

Helping talented writers publish exceptional books

*For my mother, Olga Diamontina*
*The strongest woman I know*

# Chapter One

*Rolla, Missouri, 1896*

I've never been able to see God through the mist colors coming off everyone at church. Grandma Rose once told me to close my eyes to the colors and *feel* God, but it's hard ignoring the man or woman sitting next to me *Amening* and *Hallelujahing* if their mist is repulsive, like moss green or bile yellow, because it tells me something's wrong in their heart, mind, or body. There's one thing I know for certain—mist colors don't lie, even if people do.

Pastor Garrett constantly reminds us we'll go to Hell if we don't keep our thoughts and our lives clean, yet some people don't seem to care. Not even the pastor. His mist turns purplish red, what Grandma once told me was a "hush-hush" color, whenever he and Mrs. Stanton look at each other. If they haven't crossed the forbidden line, they will soon. But I can't see visions in my mind as clearly as my sister Katherine and Grandma do, at least not yet, so I can't be sure.

"Do you think the pastor needs to reread his own sermon about the weakness of the flesh?" I asked Katherine when the service had finally ended and we were standing under the shade of the cottonwoods.

Katherine nodded. "The pastor and Mrs. Stanton kiss each other in private."

"What did you say?"

I jerked my head toward the voice. Beth Evers, a classmate, was standing closer than we'd realized. Grandma's always telling me to trust my instincts and at that moment, I sure wish I had. I looked at Beth, thinking about the contagion of stories that would spread through town.

I shrugged and shook my head. "We didn't say anything."

She crossed her arms over her chest and raised her chin and her voice. "Katherine most certainly did say something."

Several teenagers gathered around us, probably hoping for a fight.

"I *heard* her. She said the pastor and Mrs. Stanton kiss each other in private."

A collective whoop from the boys startled me. I looked toward Grandma and Daddy and realized all the adults were looking at us.

A few of the boys ran to the pastor, shouting over one another. Mrs. Stanton went limp. Mr. Stanton caught her and carried her back into the church while a couple of the ladies followed with their fans flicking over her face. If it hadn't been my fault, it would have been the most exciting church day ever.

Daddy stalked up to us, grabbed my sister by the arm, and pulled her over to the pastor. My stomach knotted, knowing it should have been me. Children stood wide-eyed and teenagers snickered and elbowed one another, while the adults shook their heads and clicked their tongues at Katherine.

*Hypocrites*! I wanted to scream.

I looked at Grandma Rose when Daddy demanded Katherine apologize. Grandma's mist darkened and she crinkled her forehead. I could tell she wanted to butt in.

Pastor Garrett placed his palm over his heart and closed his eyes. "I don't want to know why you feel the need to soil my and Mrs. Stanton's impeccable reputations," he said to my sister. "I want to remind you that you are setting up your soul to burn in Hell for all eternity if you keep on lying like that. Now kneel down so I can pray for you."

The hair on my arm prickled as Grandma pushed her way to the front of the crowd. I sensed our world was about to shift.

"Hold on, Pastor," she said.

"Keep out of this, Mother," Daddy snapped. Pink splotches were spreading from his neck to his face.

Grandma ignored him. "I will not stand by and have my granddaughter humiliated for telling the truth. If someone's going to burn in Hell for lying, it's you, Pastor."

Daddy's shoulders slumped as the crowd erupted.

He didn't even try to slow the mares as we rode home. His set jaw and the way he sat rigid instead of swaying when the wheels of our buckboard slammed down on a wet rut were enough for me and Katherine to keep quiet. Grandma Rose sat next to him just as angry, though for a different reason. Pastor Garrett had accused her of having an evil mind and forbade her to ever step foot into his house of worship again.

I stared down at the coffee-colored spatter of mud on my dress, stewing with the thought that until this day we'd been able to keep our abilities a secret. Our hides would have been saved if I had kept my mouth shut about the pastor's weakness. Sometimes the right choice becomes obvious only after suffering the consequences of picking the wrong one.

I grabbed Katherine's hand and held it until Daddy brought the wagon to a jolting halt in front of the barn.

"Y'all get inside and wait for me." He jumped down and began unhitching the horses.

Katherine helped Grandma Rose out of the wagon before trudging into the house.

"My goodness, Sarah, look at your dress," Grandma said when she saw the mud.

"I know. Yours too. We've got some wash to do."

She looked at the spattering on her skirt. "Oh, Lordy. We best go on in."

I stood by the open window and watched as Daddy came out of the barn holding a switch.

"There's no need for that, Charles," Grandma said when he came inside.

"You bet there is." He looked at me. "Were you a part of this?"

"It's not Sarah's fault, Daddy," Katherine said.

I glanced at my sister, then down at my mud-crusted Sunday shoes. It certainly was my fault. Katherine had always been braver, maybe because she's a year older, always protecting me whether I deserved it or not.

"Then you get on back there." Katherine and Daddy headed to his sleeping room.

Grandma Rose stood behind me with her hands on my shoulders. We listened to the switch snap again and again, each one followed by my sister's whimpers. My heart gripped at every one of them.

"Damn you, Charles," Grandma whispered.

Katherine sobbed as she walked out of Daddy's room and into ours and closed the door.

Grandma gave me a push. "Go on."

Katherine was lying on her side, sobbing into her pillow. I bent over and gave her shoulders a squeeze. "I'm sorry. I'll wash the dishes tonight." It was the only thing I could think of to make it up to her. I gave her a kiss on the cheek before stepping back into the hall where I stilled and listened to the quarrelling going on in the parlor.

"Katherine is a young woman. Sixteen is too old for that switch," Grandma said.

"She needs to start acting like a woman. She embarrassed

me in front of Emma and everyone else. And if you don't want those girls to be beat then stop encouraging them with that mind-reading nonsense the way you do."

"It's not nonsense. God Himself has given us a gift——"

"You know better than anyone that that gift has cost us more than we've got to spend, so I don't want to hear any more about it."

I think it's a shame Daddy doesn't have the gift like the three of us do. If he did, maybe he wouldn't hate that part of us as much as he does.

Several days after my nosiness caused my sister to get whipped, Daddy stood from his rocking chair and walked onto the porch. We'd heard a horse whinny through the open window. I craned my neck to see who it was and went right back to playing checkers with Katherine.

"It's Tom Clifton," I said, though no one asked. He was our widower neighbor and probably Daddy's closest friend.

"What's the news?" Daddy always asked that when anyone stopped by unexpected.

"I was wondering if you'd heard about Pastor Garrett," Tom said.

Katherine and I looked at one another while Grandma stopped rocking and held her knitting needles still.

"He's got a broken nose and a shiner delivered to him by Roy Stanton. Roy's in jail," Tom said.

I stepped closer to the window, making sure to stay out of their sight. Daddy's jaw was clenched and he looked off at the horizon.

"He walked in on the pastor and Mrs. Stanton acting like they were in a fever over one another, their lips and hands moving all over each——"

"I got young women in there," Daddy grumbled. "Now, I ain't one for gossip so I'd appreciate it if you'd go on home."

"Thought you'd like to know Katherine and your mother told the truth after all."

Katherine kept me up that night with her fretting. "Trouble's coming. I can feel it."

I didn't want to admit I did too. "Don't worry. No one will remember what you said."

I wish that was true, but we both knew I was lying. Gossip around Rolla was like a nasty stomach bug that spreads and infects quickly; especially dirty talk, like what Tom Clifton told Daddy. I knew darn well no one had forgotten Katherine had revealed the pastor's secret first.

# Chapter Two

I woke up with a gnawing in my stomach. By the way she didn't talk much at breakfast, I could tell Katherine had it too. As we walked to school, the feeling grew.

We slowed our steps when we saw a group of our classmates ahead, watching us. Their mists were a mix of dull and bright shades, and the way the colors extended beyond their bodies more than was usual revealed their excitement. I looked at Katherine and noticed her eyes skimming the faces of the crowd.

"They're waiting for us, aren't they?" I asked.

"Yep," she said.

As we approached, the hair on my arms prickled. As soon as I saw Beth Evers, I knew this was her doing.

"Tell us how you and your grandmother knew about Pastor Garrett and Mrs. Stanton," an older boy said. "Are y'all witches? The pastor said y'all have evil minds."

"I was spreading rumors. That's all. I didn't know it was for real," Katherine said.

"Liar!" Beth yelled. "My daddy said you're spawned from the devil. And so is your grandmother."

It was one thing to hurl hatefulness at me and Katherine,

but Grandma Rose was another matter. She was an angel on Earth even if she had been kicked out of church for good. I punched Beth square in the mouth. Blood and spit spewed and a rock hit Katherine on the forehead. She pulled me out of the crowd when more rocks started flying.

"Run, witches! Run away and don't come back!" someone screamed.

"Grandma!" I yelled when we made it back to the property. I was out of breath and sobbing. How I missed Momma, especially at a time like this. Katherine had a cut on her temple that bled down the side of her face and pain shot through my back and head.

"They threw rocks," I cried as Grandma Rose rushed out of the house.

She held Katherine by the shoulders. "Oh, those awful people."

By suppertime, the crescent-shaped cut on Katherine's temple had stopped bleeding and the swelling had turned purple. Daddy kept glancing at it as he ate his smothered roast beef and mashed potatoes. His mist was grayish blue, the color of sadness—not of grief, but a different kind of heartache. Katherine and I didn't dare speak. We knew he was mulling over how Mr. Evers had stormed over here gripping Beth by the arm so Daddy could see what "his monster" had done. Her lips were three times their normal size and the bottom one was split.

After I apologized against my will, I didn't get the whipping I thought I would. Instead, Daddy was stone quiet after they left, which was almost worse. Grandma behaved as if she didn't seem to care one way or another about Daddy's mood.

"I'd love to be in that church on Sunday. *Eww wee*! That would be something to see. You girls fill me in when you get home about how much sobbing and sniveling Pastor Garrett does through his broken nose when he begs everyone for forgiveness. I wonder if Betsy Stanton will be sitting front and center like she—"

"That's enough," Daddy said.

"That man better apologize to Katherine in front of everyone—"

Daddy banged his fist on the table making water slosh out of our glasses.

Grandma shoved a heaping forkful of potatoes in her mouth, then winked at me.

When the pots were scrubbed and the dishes put away, I sought out Daddy in the barn where he always went to think. He was brushing Matilda's mane. She was our biscuit-colored mare he treated special. He looked up when my shadow crossed the lantern light spilling on the ground. I walked over to Jessie. Daddy rode her mostly, though I sensed she was envious of the way he treated Matilda with extra care. I reached up and scratched between her eyes.

"You mad at me, Daddy?"

He looked at me and the crinkle between his eyes deepened. "Why didn't you tell me what you did to Beth? It should have been us knocking on their door to apologize."

*That's why. No one in that terrible crowd deserved an apology.* "She said some awful things about us."

His look was pained. "You can't let people's words or small-mindedness bring out the darkness in you. You've got to be stronger than that."

I had a feeling he wasn't just referring to me, but to Grandma Rose. He grew up having to defend himself from taunts and rocks and blows from people who made fun of him once they found out his momma had what she calls "the foresight," and they called "the devil's gift." It got so bad they had to move from Farmington to Steelville, which turned out to be a good thing because that's where he met and married Momma.

"I know. But Daddy, everyone at school thinks our family's evil."

He stopped running the brush through Matilda's mane and looked down at his boots. "Not just at school."

My breath caught. "You heard something like it in town?"

His jaw tightened and he nodded.

My chest heaved with sobbing I couldn't release. If I started crying, he'd put a stop to our talk and I needed to know more. "Do *you* think we're evil, Daddy?"

His eyes shifted away from mine. "As far as what y'all have being God-given … I'm not sure about that. Knowing other people's business seems like there's no point to it. I don't get why y'all are burdened with it since it's brought nothing but trouble. And I can't protect you from what other people believe or what they'll do to you because of it." When he turned to me, his eyes seemed to plead. "All I ever wanted is for us to live a peaceful life. I can't make that happen myself. You girls *have got* to help me. Ignore that gift of yours. Don't ever talk about it. Don't ever let on that you know about things you shouldn't."

I thought about all the times Grandma told us our gift will someday come with the responsibility to help "deliver the weak from the hands of the wicked," or to stand against injustice if we're called to. And all the times I promised her I would.

But at that moment, the hurt in Daddy's eyes pressed heavier on me.

"All right, Daddy. I promise."

# Chapter Three

Daddy wanted us to prove we didn't have anything to hide or be ashamed of, but after we begged during breakfast, Grandma finally convinced him to let us stay home from school. He gave in when we promised to do an extra book lesson. By midafternoon all our chores and schoolwork were done, so we sat on the front porch—Katherine with her Emily Dickinson poetry book and me with my needlework sampler.

Grandma sat on the porch swing knitting a baby blanket to put in one of our dowry chests. Daddy had made each of us one for our thirteenth birthdays—mine with a swirly *S* painted in yellow, and Katherine's with a *K* in green. Grandma wouldn't tell us who the blanket was for. She was always collecting or making things she thought we'd need later. This was her way of "honoring the future in the present," she'd once said. Momma told her she might jinx our futures by assuming and preparing for it, but Grandma explained it was a way of calling to us what we want. I liked that way of thinking.

We all looked to the road when we heard Jessie's bray. It seemed something bad must have happened while he was in town because Daddy's mist was hazy. We said a pleasant enough, "Hi Daddy," when he alighted and got close enough to hear, but he didn't respond.

Grandma Rose placed her knitting on her lap and stopped the porch swing with the tips of her toes. She crinkled up her forehead.

"Bad day, Charles?" she asked as he came up the steps. He kept right on walking into the house without a word. "I'm gonna make your daddy some coffee. You girls stay put."

Katherine and I waited until she stepped into the house before we scooted closer to the open window. They were in the kitchen, but their voices echoed out into the parlor and the porch enough that if we stayed still, we could make out bits of what Daddy was saying.

"… calling us wicked … devil's bidding … this town … no place for …"

Katherine and I looked at each other.

"Devil's bidding?" I whispered. "Do you think Pastor Garrett told Daddy we aren't holy enough for his church like he did Grandma?"

Katherine shrugged. "Maybe. But it seems to me he's not in any position to say that." She crept into the house being extra careful where she put her feet down for fear of creaking a board. I took her lead and did the same.

We stood in the parlor, both of us leaned up against the opening of the hallway.

"I lost a sale today," Daddy said. "The gentleman said he's afraid of what our cows have been exposed to on this property. He thinks their milk is tainted. He said people are telling tales of what goes on in this house and it ain't Christian. You know what will happen if Bob Buchanan hears about this?"

Bob Buchanan owns the property and the house we live in. Our classmates call us "squatters" and make fun of us for being too poor to own property. I hate it. I tell them a squatter is someone who doesn't pay to live there, and we do, but it doesn't make them stop. At the end of every month, Mr. Buchanan rides over to collect payment, so the day before, Daddy makes us work extra hard to make sure everything inside and out is "tidy enough for royalty."

Grandma huffed. "I could tell Bob a few things about himself that he wouldn't like—"

"That right there is the kind of thing I'm talking about!" Daddy yelled. "You can't be threatening people with your words. Damn it, Mother, you are determined to relive what happened in Steelville, aren't you?"

She didn't answer.

"You remember why we left?" After a few seconds of silence he said, "Well?"

"It was because of people's ignorance."

"That's not the reason I was looking for."

"It was 'cause of me," Grandma said.

I shot Katherine a look trying to figure out if she already knew this story. Her knitted brow told me we'd both been too young to know why one day she and I were happy enough twirling in our pasture, and the next we were crammed into our wagon packed with all it could carry.

"Yep. 'Cause you couldn't keep quiet about your damned suspicions and premonitions and what not," Daddy said. "I don't want those girls going to jail someday like you did."

*Jail?* I widened my eyes even more. I couldn't imagine what Grandma could have possibly done to wind up in jail with murderers and bank robbers.

"I'ma say one last thing," Daddy said. "If these people make our lives hell like in Farmington and Steelville, I'm gonna leave you behind. Understand?"

"I do," Grandma said.

By Saturday evening, I was beside myself not knowing if we would stay home or go to church in the morning. Part of me wanted to go to see if Mrs. Stanton would be sitting front and center, and if so, if her head would be held high or if she'd be looking down at her lap. Thankfully, during supper, Grandma asked what I'd wanted to know.

"Yep," Daddy said. "We've got to show we don't have anything to be ashamed of."

"I'm proud of you, son," Grandma said. "And to prove yourself to this town even more, you should go on and invite Miss Emma to supper finally."

"I don't know about that," he said, stifling a grin.

"She's a good woman, I can tell. And one who won't stay single for much longer."

Daddy stayed quiet as he chased peas around his plate with his fork. It was clear his mind was not on his meal. He'd asked us a couple weeks before, before Grandma got kicked out of church, if it was all right if he courted Miss Emma. Grandma had told him asking our permission was the proper thing to do since we were still grieving Momma. Miss Emma has pretty golden-brown eyes and pale green, or sometimes soft blue, mist. Those colors mean she's a caring and selfless person, so I told him I wouldn't mind it if he courted her. But I sure do miss Momma.

The next morning, I could see Daddy took Grandma's advice, as his dark hair was shiny, his face freshly shaved, his mist bright, and he smelled like a spring rain. I'd never seen him look so handsome.

An uneasiness came over me as our wagon drew closer to the church however, and I was unable to sit still. When we pulled in, my arm hair prickled.

"Something's not right," I whispered to Katherine while Daddy tied up the wagon.

"I know," she whispered back.

I hoped Daddy would choose a pew in the back, but he held his head up and gave no attention to the bold stares as he led us up the middle aisle to an empty space toward the front.

As we waited for the service to begin, I ignored the evil eyes Beth was giving me while she sang with the choir, her lips back to normal size except for the scab on the bottom one. I pretended like the whispers and stares from most everyone else didn't bother me. I sensed Daddy and Katherine were pretending as well.

Mrs. Stanton wasn't in the first row like usual, or anywhere as far I could tell, and Roy Stanton wasn't there to lead the choir. I figured he was still in jail, or maybe Pastor Garrett told him he wasn't holy enough for his house of worship after the beating he took from him.

I was eager for the hymn to end to see if Pastor Garrett would walk out or if his face was too beat up for public view. When the last of the organ notes faded, suddenly there he was, marching toward the pulpit. The bruises under each eye were turning yellow and purple, and he wore a bandage across his nose. The room was still except for a baby crying and its momma shushing it. I could see the colors of excitement rising from everyone.

He looked over the crowd and when he saw the three of us, he held our gazes. "I was hoping I'd have the opportunity to speak to you today," he said.

I looked at Daddy, wondering if he was talking to everyone, or us specifically. The way Daddy's jaw muscle bulged told me it was us. I couldn't wait to hear what Pastor Garrett had to say. Maybe he was going to tell us how sorry he was for declaring Katherine was setting her soul up for Hell if she continued to make up lies about him and Mrs. Stanton. And maybe he'd ask for her forgiveness for having her apologize in front of the entire congregation. How I wished Grandma Rose was there to hear it.

"As the good people of Rolla know, Rose Richardson is no longer welcome in this house of worship due to her sinful mind and her corrupt tongue. And now I must ask that the three of you leave this house of God and not return as well; however, before you do, let me explain to everyone why it must be so."

His cruel eyes made my heart jump like an agitated frog. I looked at Daddy and saw the pink splotches he was prone to when he got angry or embarrassed were flushing up from his shirt collar to his face.

"It never occurred to me to covet another man's wife until your daughter put it in my mind. It was as if, what Roy Stanton walked in on, Katherine Richardson had willed to happen with her words." He pointed at Katherine. "The evil you wield is so powerful, I couldn't fight it. And for that, I am ashamed of myself. Yet, I know I will be redeemed and forgiven by the good people of Rolla, as I have prayed for God's strength to fill me with His glory and fight the devil. Katherine Richardson, you have the devil inside you, like your Grandmother Rose."

Katherine gasped and stood up. Her mist was fiery red.

Daddy grabbed her arm. "Let's go."

"I suggest you change your ways, Richardson family," Pastor Garrett yelled. "Otherwise, there will be trouble in your future, and hell to pay with your souls."

As we hurried down the aisle, the crowd hissed at us. It grew louder until it sounded like the entire church was filled with angry snakes. My heart battered my chest as I looked at all the glaring faces. As far as I could tell, only two people weren't hissing—our neighbor Tom Clifton, and Miss Emma. She stared down at her folded hands as we passed.

"What he said is an out and out lie, Daddy!" Katherine said as we rushed to the wagon.

"Hush it!" Daddy snapped. No one said another word the entire way home.

Grandma Rose came out of the house and stood on the porch with her hands on her hips. It was far too early for us to be home from church service. Her face was grim, her mist dark.

"What happened?" she asked when the wagon came to a stop.

"Oh, Grandma. It was horrible," I cried.

Daddy jumped down. "You girls go to your room."

We did what he said but stood inside the open door.

"Katherine *put it in his mind*? If that ain't the biggest lie of the season!" Grandma yelled.

"Keep it down, Mother," Daddy said.

"That man has been carrying on with more women than Betsy Stanton for the past several months! How *dare* he blame Katherine for *putting it in his mind*! I'll put something in his head all right! I'll—"

"Mother! Shut your mouth right now. I know he's lying about it. That's not the problem. The problem is that the people in this town believe him. Now, it's one thing for us to put up with whispering and finger-pointing. It's another when they stop doing business with me because of it. How am I supposed to pay for everything I owe?"

After a few seconds Grandma said, "God will help us."

"He better be quick about it," Daddy said.

THAT EVENING, Daddy stood up from the dinner table when someone knocked on the screen door. "Stay here," he said. When he stepped into the parlor we heard, "What's the news, Bob?"

Katherine and I looked at each other, knowing the hog pen and chicken coop were a complete mess. It was two weeks before rent was due, so we hadn't prepared for royalty just yet.

Their voices faded as they walked away from the house. When Daddy returned several minutes later, he looked as if someone near to him had died.

"What is it, Charles?" Grandma asked.

"Several congregants had a talk with Bob after service today. They told him they suspect witchcraft or the like is taking place on this property and they will no longer be doing business with me. He's giving us a week to move out."

I looked at Katherine. Her face crumpled.

I walked over to Daddy. "If the town thinks we're evil, then me, and Grandma, and Katherine will leave so you don't have to."

"Oh, Sarah! Where would we go?" Grandma asked.

"Somewhere where people don't know us." I looked down as the tears came. Big, fat ones, making splotches on my bare feet. I grabbed Daddy and held onto him tight. It was my fault. It was all my fault. If only I could go back, I wouldn't have mentioned what I suspected about the pastor's mist. I would have kept quiet like Daddy was always wanting us to. Who would have thought my silly-minded comment would have led to so many terrible things?

"I NEED to make this up to Daddy," I said to Katherine that night.

"He blames me and Grandma," she said.

"I know. And I'm sorry. I guess I need to make it up to all of you."

Katherine sighed. "It's too late for Rolla, Sarah. We both need to do as he wants from now on so it won't happen again. That's all we can do."

"You think we'll have to leave Rolla like we did Steelville?"

She waited several seconds. "Yes."

"Momma?" I whispered. She was buried in Rolla.

"We'll have to leave her behind."

Tears streaked out of the corner of my eyes and pooled in my ears.

# Chapter Four

We were all relieved when Daddy received a wire from Jefferson City a few days later. He'd been offered a grist mill job he'd inquired about, so we spent the next few days packing up and cleaning out. The evening before we were to leave, I went to Grandma's room. What we'd overheard Daddy say to her about what she'd done in Steelville had been gnawing at me for days. I was dying to know what he meant. I knocked on her door and pressed my ear against it.

"Come in."

She was knitting while sitting cross-legged on a straw pallet on the floor, her bed already broken down and tied in the wagon.

"Long day tomorrow. You girls should be getting to bed."

"I'm about to, but I want to know something first. I heard Daddy tell you he doesn't want us going to jail someday like you did."

Grandma tightened her lips, making deep wrinkles form above and below. Finally, she said, "Alright, maybe it's a good time for you to learn from one of my mistakes." She sat thoughtful for a few seconds and I was afraid she'd change her mind. Then, "I seem to have a low tolerance for hypocrisy. By that I mean, when someone sits there and tells me one thing, while all along I know darn well he does or thinks another, I get agitated. And if it happens too often, I have a hard time holding my tongue. So that's what happened one day.

"I got fed up with certain people in Steelville and their nonsense and I told them so. These men sat up there making rules and laws and moral codes meant for punishing everyone except themselves. I stood in a town hall meeting in front of God and everybody, pointing my finger at this one and that one, spilling all their secrets so that everyone could see they weren't as virtuous as they made themselves out to be. Of course, the second I did it, I regretted it."

"Why'd you regret it? It sounds like they deserved it."

"Whether they did or not, I am no judge and jury."

"What happened next?"

"First thing that happened, I was accused of slander and arrested. I stayed in jail for four days before the judge saw me. He was friends with the councilmen, so I'm sure the wait was on purpose. I believe your Momma and Daddy told you I was visiting a sick relative. Do you remember when I didn't come home?"

I did remember that. It's hard to forget when the person you love more than anyone else in the world stays away for days. "How'd you get out?"

"I wrote the judge a letter explaining how I knew the things about the councilmen that I accused them of and proved it by telling him something about himself that only he knew. I reminded him that clairvoyance isn't a crime. He let me go, telling me I best leave town. By then the councilmen had created a posse of our neighbors to run my evil self out of town anyway."

"You're not evil, Grandma."

"I know, honey. And I believe most who say we are don't

believe it either. I think they're afraid we can see things in them they're ashamed of. Everyone's got secrets."

"Even you?"

Grandma looked away. "Even me."

I could tell by her mist that her secret was a sorrowful one. I thought it best not to dig deeper, so I turned the conversation back to something else I was curious about. "Will you tell me what you told the judge that only he knew?"

"Nope. That's between him and me."

My shoulders slumped. "You can't tell me only part of the story."

"I didn't. I told you the most important parts of it. What he and I knew is neither here nor there. The point is, I used my God-given gift to my advantage. Twice. Once to put those men in their place, and the second to get myself out of trouble. And guess what came of it? Your daddy lost his reputation, his business, his home, and it was all my fault."

"So, what happened there is almost the same as what happened here," I said. "That's why Daddy wants us to keep quiet and ignore our gift."

"That's right. I promised your daddy I would never do it again when we left Steelville, then I went back on my promise, letting Pastor Garrett have it when I'd had more than I could stand. That man has way too many secrets to be raining damnation on everyone else."

"Yep, I heard you say he's been carrying on with more women. Like who?"

"Like no one. Never mind. I told you more than I should have. This conversation is over between you and me. Keep everything I've said to yourself."

"I will. I promise."

"Good. No telling what your daddy would do to me if he found out. Now, get to bed and stop worrying about everything."

"I can't seem to help it." If a fifteen-year-old's words can bring about a whole town turning against her family enough to make them leave, suddenly worrying about everything seemed right.

# Chapter Five

We departed as pale orange blushed above the black horizon. I refused to turn for one last look at the house or the pasture, especially when some of the cows bellowed. I'd only heard that mournful noise when their calves were taken from them, and I wondered if they knew we weren't coming back.

I looked up from the wildflowers I held in my hand to watch the emerging sun's glow turning streaky gray clouds into shades of raspberry, apricot, and melon. I didn't chance looking away because the dawn is quick to show her colorful array, and just as quick to fade it all into blue. I'd once asked Grandma Rose if the pale colors of sunrise were God's way of reminding us how we should behave toward one another, and the fiery colors of sunset of what to temper within ourselves. She said that was a fine way to decipher God's messages to us, and even if other people can't see auras like we can, maybe a part of their soul understands.

It'd rained for a few hours overnight and Daddy was doing his best to take it slow, but the wagon swayed every time our wheels hit a muddy rut. I was glad when we finally turned onto the less bumpy Main Street. Not too many people were out, yet those who were stared at us crammed into our buck-board. The back was piled high and things were strapped to the sides while every space between us and under the seats was filled. When we passed the schoolhouse, my heart pinched a little as I wondered how long it would take for our classmates to realize they wouldn't be seeing us again. There wasn't a nice one amongst them so I shouldn't have cared. Yet, for some reason, it mattered.

When we arrived at the cemetery, Daddy helped Grandma Rose out of the wagon. He trudged ahead as the three of us lifted our skirts and did our best to avoid patches of mud or rain puddles. We picked our way around several resting places, trying not to tread on them too much.

When we reached Momma's headstone, we stood in silence.

*Victoria Elizabeth Richardson*
*1860 — 1893*
*Beloved wife and mother*

It had been three years since the Lord took her. It seemed longer. I was ashamed I had a hard time keeping her features fixed in my mind or remembering the sound of her singing voice.

My throat tightened when Daddy sniffled. Tears streaked down and he didn't even try to hide them or wipe them. I looked at Katherine. She was watching Daddy and crying too.

Grandma's lips trembled as she stared at Momma's head-stone. "I hope you've forgiven me," she whispered.

I glanced at Katherine, wondering if she'd heard her, but she was weeping too hard to have heard anything.

Daddy knelt and placed his hand on her headstone. "It might be some time before we make it back here, but I swear you won't be forgotten." A sob broke through, and his shoulders moved up and down as he tried to get ahold of himself.

Grandma leaned in and placed her arms around him. My chest ached as I looked at them.

*I'm sorry*, I said to Momma in my mind as I knelt and placed my flowers down. I hoped Katherine didn't feel as guilty as I did for causing us to abandon her.

That afternoon, the sun's heat and the ground's moisture made the air thick. Katherine and I took off our bonnets and used them to fan our face. We passed the hours trying to ignore the perspiration trickling down our underarms, or our aching backs and bottoms, by listening to Grandma call out the name of this bird or that one, and pointing out different types of trees or wildflowers. At a quiet moment, I looked over at Katherine as she stared at several horses in a pasture. A couple of them had stopped grazing to watch our wagon pass by. I noticed the jagged scab on her temple was leaving a crescent-shaped scar. It would forever be a reminder that what Daddy believed was true: people will tend to want to overcome whatever threatens their notion of normal, sometimes through violence.

WE ARRIVED in Jefferson City on the second evening and made our way to the river to set up camp. It was a calm night except for the pesky mosquitoes. Daddy pulled out his harmonica after we ate and played it by the fire, something he hadn't done since before Momma died. He was good at playing it. Grandma sang while we clapped along, and for the first time in a long time, it seemed everything might be all right.

In the morning, we bathed in the river and put on our Sunday clothes even though it was Thursday, and after a porridge breakfast we headed to the grist mill to meet a man named Donald Bryer who had offered Daddy a job.

"Y'all stay put," Daddy said when we rode up to the mill.

I fanned my face with my bonnet, wishing it was January instead of September. I could feel sweat streaking down so much that I hoped it wouldn't show through my dress if Daddy made us get down from the wagon.

"My, they certainly are busy bees," Grandma said.

Black, white, and brown men in overalls were everywhere, working all sorts of noisy machinery. I wondered how they could hear each other over the noise. There was a lot of pointing and motioning, head nodding or shaking, thumbs up or down going on between them. It's like they had a special language that they used their arms and hands to communicate. I wondered how long it would take Daddy to learn it.

After several minutes, he came back to the wagon with a man who I assumed was Mr. Bryer. I was uneasy even though he wore a huge grin and his mist wasn't too hazy. I looked at Grandma and Katherine, trying to get a sense of what they were feeling about him. Neither of them were smiling.

THE HOUSE DADDY rented from Mr. Bryer wasn't any bigger than the one we had in Rolla. It had three very small sleeping rooms which meant Katherine and I still had to share a bed. I didn't mind it as much as she did, since I enjoyed our nightly talks.

Our journey from Rolla to Jefferson City had taken two long days, and our bodies were sore from sitting on a wooden bench during the day and sleeping on the ground at night. Regardless of how tired I was though, I stayed awake for what seemed like hours, listening through the open window to the coyotes howling in the distance, and the crickets and frogs calling for a mate. At one point I heard an owl and thought of Momma. I wondered if she'd lived, would we be waking up back in Rolla instead? I retraced the road that led us here and decided she probably wouldn't have been able to stop or change anything. She'd be right here in this house, making breakfast for us, and as we headed off to our new school, she'd be standing next to Grandma Rose on the porch, both women waving and smiling while silently being worried sick about us. I remembered what Grandma had whispered at her gravesite about hoping for Momma's forgiveness. I wondered what she meant by it.

# Chapter Six

We were cooking after we'd spent the day washing, scrubbing, and dusting in preparation for having guests. And not just any guests. Daddy's boss Donald Bryer and his wife Mildred were coming for supper. I was sure they'd be pleased when they came in and saw how tidy everything was. I'd even picked two bouquets of wildflowers and placed each in a water glass, one in the parlor and one on the kitchen table, like Momma used to do when company was coming.

Daddy had killed a couple of chickens and Grandma was roasting them in the oven with sweet potatoes, carrots, and green beans on the side, while Katherine's biscuits were ready to go in the oven the second the chickens came out.

Daddy greeted the Bryers on the porch and invited them into the parlor where the three of us stood wearing our second-best dresses. Mrs. Bryer came in and to my delight, she was holding a plate with a cake covered in mounds of buttercream frosting. I immediately noticed her gray-brown mist which told me that, despite her smile, she wasn't a happy woman. When Mr. Bryer walked in, I figured he was the reason. His mist was different from the first time I'd seen him.

It was the color of the slimy moss that floats on top of frog ponds. Grandma once told us a putrid color could indicate a sickness of the mind, and if we ever came across someone like that, to be wary. I hated to think that Daddy's new boss could be one of those people.

I paid close attention to them throughout the evening, noticing every so often that when she tried to talk, he'd talk right over her as if he was deaf to her voice, and the annoyed looks he'd give her if she happened to get a word in.

When we finished eating supper and a slice of cake, Katherine and I cleaned up the dishes while the adults went into the parlor with coffee. We could hear their conversation. Mr. Bryer was talking about stories he'd read in the newspaper. I knew Daddy wasn't interested since he avoided bad news when he could. Grandma, on the other hand, was eager to hear it all.

"And here's a story I thought you'd want to know about, Charles, being that you're from Rolla," Mr. Bryer said. "I figured you might even know this man."

Katherine and I stopped scrubbing and stood perfectly still. He went on to explain that a particular pastor named Patrick Garrett in Rolla was forced to leave his congregation.

"The report said he'd been caught with a married woman by the woman's husband. The second one in several weeks." Katherine and I looked at each other.

"Mm, mm, mm," Grandma replied, probably shaking her head as well. "Shameful."

Katherine and I each placed a hand over our mouth at the same time and our shoulders shook with laughter.

When the Bryers prepared to leave, Grandma Rose had us come out to say goodnight to them. As I stepped into the parlor, the strangest thing happened. Mrs. Bryer looked directly at me with her blue-gray eyes, and I suddenly needed to cry. And not a silent cry. The weight on my heart at that moment was almost as heavy as the day Momma died. Something was terribly wrong with her.

Later, I couldn't sleep. "Say," I whispered to Katherine. I could tell she was still awake by her breathing. "How do you feel about the Bryers?"

"She seems like a good person, but I feel like he reviles her for some reason."

"I kind of thought so too."

"It hurts my stomach to think about it. Like Daddy's always telling us: 'their business ain't our business.' Go to sleep and forget about them." Katherine turned her back to me and put her pillow over her head.

Sometime later I got kicked. Katherine was moaning and thrashing around, trying to fight her way out of the blanket. I shook her awake. She sat up, breathing fast.

"You had a nightmare," I said. "And you kicked me. Hard."

"I'm sorry," she said. "I felt like it was real. Like I was standing right there, watching it all happen." She reached over and plucked her kerchief off the night table and blew her nose.

"Watching what happen?"

"Mrs. Bryer was cowered in a corner. Mr. Bryer was whipping her with a belt."

The heaviness in my chest came back and so did the need to cry. "He hurts her?"

"I think so."

We laid back down and stared at the ceiling, watching moonlight and shadow change shape as the curtain blew.

Neither of us said anything more about the Bryers that night or the following days. I shoved thoughts of them away and pretended I knew nothing about them except what a good cake maker she was, and what a nice man he was for giving Daddy a job and us a place to live. It wasn't until Daddy came home from work one day and asked Grandma

Rose if she'd make a peach pie that they filled my thoughts again.

"Mildred was injured," Daddy said. "Donald told me she had a fall and broke her arm. I think it would be nice if the girls brought it to her as a get-well gift."

The way Grandma's mist dimmed and her lips tightened told me she was thinking what Katherine and I were thinking. None of us said a word.

"I hope he's not home," I said as Katherine and I walked to the Bryers' property the following day. We took turns holding the cloth-covered pie, switching off when our arms began to ache.

"Naw. It's work time. He should be at the mill."

The cows grunted as we passed them on our way toward the two-story white house with a black roof and black shutters. It had a wrap-around porch edged by several rows of primrose and violets. They bordered the stone walkway too. Simple and pretty.

Katherine knocked on the screen door. The main door was open, so we were able to see the kitchen and large dining room to the right, with a chandelier over the table. I'd never seen a real chandelier before.

"Who's there?" Mildred Bryer called out. She was beyond our sight.

"It's Katherine Richardson, ma'am. And Sarah. Our grandmother made you a peach pie."

Mildred peeked around the interior door but didn't come too close. Even through the screen, we could see her eye was bruised. I held up the pie so she could see it.

"That's mighty nice. Tell her I said thank you. Why don't you leave it there and I'll get it? I'm not fit to be seen since I wasn't expecting company."

Katherine gave me a sharp nod. I placed the pie at my feet.

"Is there anything we can do for you?" I don't know why I

asked, or what on earth we could do for someone in her state. The words came on their own.

"No. I took a little spill is all. Donald's always teasing me about how clumsy I can be."

Katherine and I didn't talk as we walked home. There were too many thoughts and wonders and concerns racing through our minds.

"How'd she look?" Grandma asked when we got back.

"Didn't see much of her," Katherine said.

"She stayed behind the screen, but her eye looked bruised," I said.

Grandma clicked her tongue and shook her head. "You girls say a prayer for her tonight. That's all we can do."

That night, Katherine bolted straight up in bed and screamed. She held her arms out like she was trying to protect herself while her legs thrashed around. I jumped out of bed before she could hurt me.

I grabbed her arm. "Wake up," I whispered.

Daddy stomped into the room with Grandma right behind him. "What's wrong?" he asked. Katherine's palms were pressed to her heart. She was breathing fast and hard. Daddy sat on the edge of the bed with his hands on her shoulders. "You're all right."

"No. He's whipping her." Katherine's chest heaved while tears glimmered on her cheeks. She pushed Daddy's hands away and hugged her knees.

I prayed she wouldn't admit she was seeing the Bryers again.

"No one's whipping anybody. You had a bad dream. That's all it was," Daddy said. "You're all right now. Get back in bed, Sarah. Y'all go back to sleep."

I got back into bed and put my arm around her shoulders.

"Katherine? You hear me?" Daddy said. "It was a dream."

"Yes, Daddy."

"You scared the life out of me," I said a few minutes later.

"Sorry. I felt like it was happening to me."

"You think it's getting stronger? Your gift, I mean?"

"Yep. And so is Mr. Bryer's cruelty. Sarah, I think she might be pregnant."

My breath caught. "How do you know?"

"It's hard to explain. It … it was like I was in her mind. As if I heard her thoughts. She kept trying to protect her stomach from the belt so he wouldn't hurt the baby."

I felt like I could throw up. "Does he know?"

"I think he does."

It took a while, but Katherine's breath softened and slowed as she gradually fell back to sleep. I stayed awake, stewing about how out of his mind Daddy would get if he knew it was the Bryers' private business she was seeing, and more, that she was tempted to involve herself in it. I was also frightened about what would happen to Katherine if Donald Bryer got ahold of her. I said a prayer right then, pleading with God to make Donald Bryer stop so we would never think about them again. Afterward, the grip on my heart only tightened.

When Daddy left for work the following morning, I asked Grandma what she thought about the Bryers. "Is Katherine just having nightmares?"

Her mist dimmed when I asked, and she kept her eyes on her coffee cup. "I wish that's all it was." She stood and walked to the sink.

"What should we do about it?" Katherine asked.

"The night before we moved here, I made a vow to your father that I would never again cause trouble with my gift and I aim to fulfill that promise," Grandma said with her back to us.

I looked at Katherine. "I promised him too," I said.

Tears glistened in Katherine's eyes. "Grandma, you've always told us we might need to help deliver the weak from the wicked. I don't think I can ignore it. Especially if she's pregnant."

Grandma hung her head. "God help that woman."

&

"I MADE no such promise to Daddy," Katherine said that night. I could tell she wasn't going to let his anger or threats stop her from doing anything she thought was right.

After she fell asleep, I prayed, asking what I could do to keep my sister out of trouble, Mildred Bryer out of harm, and Daddy in his job. Suddenly, an idea came to me.

I crept out of bed and sat at our writing desk. My hands shook as I thought about what I could possibly say to Donald Bryer that would put a stop to Mrs. Bryer's pain, and therefore stop Katherine's visions about them.

*Donald, I know about you. You have a cruel heart and an evil mind. I am watching you. If you ever again raise your hand to Mildred, or hurt her in any way, you will die.*

I couldn't believe I was threatening a man's life, although I wasn't really. I was only trying to scare him. I thought about signing a fake man's name to scare him even more, but I changed my mind. It sounded more menacing if I left it off, leaving him to wonder if every man he saw could be the one who wrote it.

I lied to Katherine the following morning, telling her I'd forgotten my lesson at home. I told her I'd either catch up with her or see her at school. I made my way to the Bryers' farm, and when I was sure no one was around, I snuck into their barn and placed the note in a spot near the milking area. When they'd come to supper, he'd told Daddy he milked his Jersey every morning before heading to the mill, so I hoped only he would find it.

# Chapter Seven

We'd only been asleep for a little while when Katherine began swinging her arms. I slid from beneath the covers and got out of bed as quickly as I could.

"Wake up," I whispered. "You're dreaming again."

Katherine sat up, breathing hard. "She's fighting him."

"She doesn't seem the type that would."

"She would if she was trying to protect the baby. Mr. Bryer was waving a piece of paper in her face and shaking her. He was in a rage."

My chest gripped. "What paper? Do you know what the paper said?"

Katherine sat quiet for a few seconds. "I'm not sure. She said kept saying, 'I swear I didn't write it.'"

*Oh, God.* I had messed up again.

"I've got a bad feeling. I can't lay here." She whipped the blanket away from her body and stood.

"What are you going to do?"

She slipped her night gown over her head and reached for her school dress. My arm hair prickled like crazy as she laced up her shoes. I watched as she opened the window even more and sat on the ledge. I ran to her.

"Tell me what you're gonna do."

She swung her legs over and hopped down onto the dew-covered grass. "I'm going to the Bryers' place."

My heart pounded so hard it hurt. "I'm begging you not to go."

"I've got to. And don't you dare say a word about this. Promise?"

"Please don't—"

"I've always stood up for you, Sarah. And I've never once asked you for anything. This time you can just stay quiet for me. Promise me."

Something inside me was screaming *no*, but I nodded. "I promise." I watched as she ran into the darkness.

My nerves were so fraught and my pulse so quick I couldn't sit still, so I paced around the room and concentrated on the Bryers, trying to get a sense of how much danger Katherine was headed into. The weight on my heart was getting so heavy, all I wanted to do was cry. Suddenly, the fear for what Katherine was about to face outweighed the promise I made to her.

*Grandma would know what to do.*

I crept out of the bedroom, hearing snores coming from both sides of the hall. Grandma's bedroom door creaked when I opened it, but not so loud it woke her. I had to shake her awake.

She coughed and then reached her hand to her night table and grabbed her spectacles. "Sarah, what on earth?" She asked so loudly, that across the hall Daddy snorted and then stopped snoring all together.

"Shh! You'll wake Daddy. Katherine had another nightmare. She's gone," I whispered.

"Oh, Lord." She sat up. "Hand me my dressing gown."

I plucked it off its hook and handed it to her.

"Did she go on foot?"

Suddenly Daddy opened his door. "What's going on out here?"

I looked at Grandma. She looked at me. Neither of us replied.

"Sarah, tell me what in the hell is going on?"

When I didn't answer, he stalked over to my bedroom and poked his head in. "Where is Katherine? Is she going to the toilet? Getting water?"

"Yes," I said.

Grandma and I followed as he strode into the parlor.

"Why isn't the front door open?"

Grandma stood behind me with her hands on my shoulders. We stayed silent.

"One of y'all better tell me right now where Katherine is." His look and tone were severe.

Grandma nudged me.

"Katherine went to help Mrs. Bryer."

Daddy squinted and then shook his head. "Mrs. Bryer? Why does Mrs. Bryer need help?"

"That dream she had. She had another. Donald Bryer is a bad man, Daddy. He beats Mrs. Bryer with a belt."

"Ga-damn it!" He stalked up the hallway and disappeared into the darkness of his room. He came back buttoning his shirt. "Grab my boots!" he yelled.

"But Daddy, Mrs. Bryer is pregnant. He'll—"

"None of this is our business, now grab my ga-damn boots!"

I snatched them up and placed them at his feet.

"Don't you dare leave this house," he said to me after he shoved his feet into them.

Grandma and I watched through the window after he stormed out. He went into the barn, and after a few minutes he led Jessie out. He placed his left foot in the stirrup and swung his right leg over. With a quick "Ha!" they rode out of sight.

"How long has she been gone?" Grandma poked at the embers, then placed a handful of kindling on them.

I looked at the mantel clock. "Not sure. Maybe fifteen minutes."

"I have a feeling he'll get to her before she makes it to their farm." Grandma placed a small log on the twigs and it quickly caught. She sat in her rocker and stared at the fire as she fiddled with the rose charm on the gold chain around her neck.

"*Rescue the weak and the needy; Deliver them out of the hand of the wicked.* Psalm 82:4," she said. She'd repeated that psalm so often in the past, I could have said it myself. "That's the highest test of our humanity, Sarah. To save another life if we're called to do so. When I was sixteen, I would have done the same thing, setting fear aside and running straight into God-knows-what. Between your daddy's anger and her sense of obligation though, your sister's in a very bad spot. Whether she sits by and does nothing or tries to help, either way she's going to get hurt. Emotionally if she doesn't, physically if she does."

I stared at Grandma while tears slid down my cheeks. My stupid note was the reason this was happening.

Several minutes later we heard Jessie braying in the distance. We stood on the porch listening to her hooves clomping up the road. My eyes strained to see in the darkness as their silhouettes approached. Eventually I made out that Katherine was sitting in front of Daddy, and the closer they came, the more I could see her angry face.

"You go straight to my room and wait for me," Daddy said when they arrived at the barn.

"If anything happens to that woman, I'll never forgive you," Katherine said to Daddy. She marched past me and

Grandma without saying a word. She stomped down the hall and slammed his bedroom door.

"Charles, please don't," Grandma said as Daddy walked into the house holding a switch.

It took only a moment for the switch to snap harder than I'd ever heard it, and the screaming, a pitch I'd also never heard, to start. I sat on the divan and cried for two women who were hurt that night because of me.

$\sim$

EVEN THOUGH I APOLOGIZED, Katherine wouldn't speak to me that night or the following morning. Her mist was so dark and her face so tense, I dared not say anything to her. I had to run to catch up with her when it was time to go to school. When I did, she spun around and glared at me.

"Stay away from me you snitch!" she shouted.

I flinched, as her words seemed to slap my face. She stormed off.

About a quarter of a mile from our property, a classmate named Tommy was waiting for us at the end of the dirt road leading to his family's farm. The way his orange-red mist extended far beyond his body told me he was beside himself with excitement. He ran in our direction, hollering if we'd heard what happened. Katherine and I each shook our head.

"Then you might be the only ones. It's all over town. Mr. Bryer said Mrs. Bryer went crazy last night. He had to fight her off with a butcher knife. She's dead."

Katherine whimpered and I looked at her, noticing her chest heaving as if she couldn't catch her breath. She turned and ran toward home. I told Tommy she hadn't been feeling well, and that I better see after her. I walked home in a hurry, tears streaking down my face and my own chest heaving as I asked God to forgive me for getting Mildred Bryer and her unborn baby killed.

When I walked into the parlor they were sitting on the divan, Grandma with her arms wrapped around Katherine's shoulders, Katherine's head pressed up against Grandma's chest. I sat down in Daddy's rocker, feeling as guilty, scared, and helpless as I was.

"I might have been able to save her," Katherine whimpered.

"Or maybe not," Grandma whispered. "Sometimes we can't change fate no matter how much we want to, or how much we try."

We didn't go to school. Katherine cried off and on and even took a nap like she used to when we were little. Grandma said she was exhausted from the stress. I was eager for Daddy to get home to find out what he'd heard, and curious what he'd say about it. I was also curious what he and Katherine would say to each other. When he got home, his mist was so dark that I stayed quiet, and Katherine went to our room and closed the door. She stayed there till supper.

Grandma asked her to come sit with us and eat something. I was glad when she followed Grandma to the table, though her face was grim and her mist cloudy. None of us said a word, each staring down at our plate until eventually the tension building inside Katherine became too much, I guess. She picked at her bread roll before throwing it down.

"I will never forgive the two of you," she said.

*And I'll never forgive myself.* "I was afraid for you," I said.

She looked from me to Daddy. "All Daddy was afraid of was losing his job at the mill. I don't care if I get whipped for saying it either. You cared more about your job than the life of Mildred Bryer and her baby, didn't you?"

Daddy put his fork down. My whole body tensed, waiting for him to pull Katherine out of the room for a whipping, and then he surprised me. And probably her too.

"How did we know at the time that what you saw in your mind was real? What if you'd been wrong?" he asked.

Katherine's mist turned crimson as her anger flared. "You should have *trusted* me."

"I trusted your grandmother once. And she was very, very wrong," he said.

I turned to Grandma. She stared down at her plate.

Daddy picked up his fork and started eating again. The conversation was over for him.

Katherine got up from the table and went back to our room and shut the door. I had to take a deep breath to release some of the pressure that was building in my chest and stomach from absorbing Katherine's bitterness, Grandma's sorrow, and my own shame.

I LAID awake for most of the night, trying my best to push away the bad thoughts that kept blooming inside me by reminding myself that I had only wanted to help. I wondered if I should admit to what I'd done, to take Daddy's anger away from Katherine and shift it to me instead. My gut clenched at the thought. I realized if I told them, they might expect me to go to the sheriff and confess I'd threatened Donald Bryer's life with the note that led to the fight that killed Mildred and her baby. The thought of being taken away from my family and sent to jail was more frightening than I could stand. I couldn't do it.

# Chapter Eight

A few weeks later, Katherine and I were picking peas in the garden. I assumed that, like me, she was thinking about what must be happening in town. Donald Bryer's trial had started and nearly every adult would be there, including Daddy.

"You think he'll be hanged?" I asked.

Katherine didn't respond. She kept right on picking peas, ignoring my existence as she'd been doing for some time.

"I hope he does," I said. "Although I get the feeling he won't. Maybe he'll be put in prison for the rest of his life." Every so often, I'd have to push away the thought that maybe it was me who should be sitting in a cell for causing him to get angry enough to do what he did.

That night, Katherine snuck down the hall and I followed. We listened to Daddy tell Grandma what happened at the trial that day. I was dying to know if the note would be mentioned. To my surprise, and relief, it wasn't. Daddy explained to Grandma that Donald Bryer's lawyer said Mildred had flown into a rage and he used words like "unprovoked" and "insane," and said "it was an act of God" that Donald had been able to get the butcher knife out of her hand and use it in order to save himself. The curious thing for the prosecution, and for many in this town according to Daddy, was that he used it to stab her four times. Daddy said if she really had been enraged, Donald should have been able to stop her with a heavy hand or two across the face because she was such a meek woman.

A COUPLE OF NIGHTS LATER, we overheard Daddy telling Grandma that even though Donald's claim of self-defense had caused a few snickers in the courtroom since he outweighed his wife by almost a hundred pounds, it was still possible the jury would accept it.

"The doctor who testified in Donald's defense said being pregnant coulda caused Mildred to go crazy," Daddy explained. "He said some women don't take to it right. It sometimes causes hysteria or some such thing." He went on to say Donald broke down and cried on the stand, saying he'll never understand why this had to happen, and that he loved that woman more than his own life.

But we knew better.

THERE WAS no talk and no eye contact across the table as the four of us ate breakfast on the morning Donald Bryer's verdict was expected. The only sounds came from Grandma and Daddy slurping their coffee and all of us slopping spoons into our porridge.

"You girls come straight home from school this afternoon." Daddy pushed his chair back and stood.

"I heard lots of kids say they were heading to town today instead of school. Everyone wants to hear if he'll get hanged," I said.

"You girls best go to school and stay there, you hear me?" He then stormed out.

Grandma began lifting dishes from the table. "Do what your daddy says. That man's fate is in the hands of the jury. There's nothing else that can be done for that poor woman."

I looked at Katherine and noticed dark splotches appearing on the tablecloth. Tears dropped as she stared down at her empty bowl.

"How MANY KIDS do you think will be at school today?" I asked as we walked. I hoped she'd slip up and answer me, forgetting for a minute that she hated me. She stayed quiet. "I figure not many," I said.

Suddenly Katherine turned right instead of heading straight.

"Where—" I started to ask, and then realized it would be a stupid question. *Of course* she was going to town. I hurried to catch up with her. As long as Daddy was inside the court-house, and we stayed outside, it was unlikely he'd ever know we were there.

I was shocked to see the streets filled with so many wagons, buggies, and carriages, and the sidewalks crammed with people.

"They came from as far as Kansas City and St. Louis," I overheard someone say.

There were street vendors selling kettle corn, lemonade, and soda pop. I couldn't believe it. It was like the county fair. Children sat on the curb licking lollipops amidst all the excitement. They were probably thinking it was some kind of celebration, not realizing the reason was because a woman and her baby had been murdered.

It was difficult for me to keep up with Katherine as she wound her way through the crowd toward the courthouse. I assumed she wanted to get close enough to hear what was happening as the word was spreading from person to person starting from somewhere on the inside. When I realized she wasn't going to stop there and was headed up the stairs, I grabbed her dress. She looked over her shoulder and glared when she saw it was me who'd stopped her. She jerked away so hard my fingernails bent backward as I lost my grip.

"Go home!" she snapped, and then slipped into the crowd.

I crouched as low as I could and maneuvered my way through the people, ignoring all the excited energy that was making me feel ill and the headache I was getting from so many shades of mist. When I caught up with Katherine, I stayed behind her, not wanting her to know I was right there. I looked around, hoping Daddy was in the courtroom and not out in the hall like so many others. Katherine worked her way to the door, straightened her shoulders, and pulled the door open. Everyone in the hall backed away from her.

As she strode into the courtroom with her head held high, she screamed, "That man is a wife beater and a liar! He stabbed his pregnant wife in a rage!"

Suddenly two guards grabbed each arm and pulled her toward the door.

"She was the victim, not him! He's a murderer! Find justice for Mildred and her child!"

The judge smacked a gavel down hard. "Get her out of here!"

"He's lying!" she screamed as the guards dragged her from the courtroom.

I hid behind a large gentleman when Daddy rushed out, his hat in his hands, his mist gray-black, and his face and neck covered in pink splotches. He stretched his neck until he was able to see where the guards were taking her, and then he followed. I hurried home.

&

GRANDMA'S MIST turned dark when I told her what had happened at the courthouse. She fingered the gold rose pendant that hung on her neck and slid it back and forth on the chain.

"Your daddy is past the end of his patience."

The truth of what she said caused my arm hair to prickle.

Throughout the afternoon, Grandma and I did our best to keep our thoughts on our chores and making supper, all the while wondering why it was taking them so long to come home.

"Do you think Katherine got put in jail?" I asked as I set the table.

"Probably as a formality. The judge can't let whomever storm in like that spewing out God-knows-what whenever they feel like it. I'm not worried though. I have a feeling your daddy will pay the fine and tell a convincing enough story to get her released with a warning."

And she was right. By six o'clock, Jessie brought Daddy and Katherine home.

"Wash up for supper," Grandma said as they entered the parlor, as if it were any other ordinary evening.

I followed Katherine outside to the water pump. "Are you all right?" I could tell she'd been crying, as there were tracks through the dust on her cheeks.

She nodded yet said nothing. She scrubbed her hands before scooping water into them and splashing her face. She flicked her wet hands in the air and walked back inside.

"After dinner you go straight to your room and don't come out," Daddy said to her.

We ate dinner in silence once again. I was desperate to

know what had happened, not only to Katherine but to Donald Bryer. I hoped Grandma would ask about the verdict, but she kept quiet, probably waiting for us to go to bed before bringing it up.

That night I could feel Katherine's tension and thought I'd say something to lighten her mood. "Both you and Grandma have been to jail. Y'all are outlaws, like Belle Starr."

"Shut up, Sarah," she said. "An outlaw is someone who intentionally breaks the law and runs from it. I did no such thing and neither did Grandma."

I ignored her rudeness and instead inwardly smiled since she'd spoken to me. "Do you know the verdict?" I dared to ask even though I sensed the answer.

She sighed. "The jury believed him. He's a free man."

My chest constricted so tight, it hurt to breathe.

I didn't sleep that night. And neither did Katherine. We listened to each other weep every now and then, for the child who never got a chance to live, and for the woman who'd done nothing wrong, but we didn't comfort one another.

It was so dark, the rooster had yet to crow when I heard Daddy walk out the front door. Through the open window I could hear his boots crunching on the gravel as he headed to the barn. The slight breeze carried Jessie's whinny when she caught sight of Daddy.

I envisioned him saddling up before placing his left foot in the stirrup and swinging his right over. I heard a slight slap of the reins and horse and rider trot away.

I turned and looked at my sister. Even through the gloom I could see her staring at the ceiling. I turned and stared at it myself. We watched a streak of moonlight get wider or thinner as a hint of breeze blew the curtain. Something thick was looming. Something I couldn't name. Finally, when pale streaks of light began to lift the darkness, Katherine turned to me.

"Tell me that if something happens to me, you'll never forget Mildred Bryer."

I looked at her. "What's gonna happen to you?"

"I'm not sure. Maybe nothing. No matter what, promise that if you ever get the chance to redeem yourself, you will. Promise you'll never forget her or her baby."

I wanted to make her happy. I also knew Mildred Bryer and her child would live in my guilty conscience forever. "I promise."

# Chapter Nine

We stayed home from school because of what Katherine had done at the courthouse. Everyone in town had read the papers or talked to someone who'd been there to see her being dragged away. I wondered what would happen to Daddy's job since Donald Bryer would most likely have gone to work now that he was free. Although none of us talked about it, unease hung about the three of us as we draped our wash on the line.

"Do you girls know what that bird is?" Grandma Rose asked in a lilting voice, as if she was trying to mimic a bird's song. I knew she wanted to lift our spirits.

Katherine ignored her and kept right on tugging to free the damp bed linen from the basket.

I looked to where Grandma was pointing. "I think it's a wren. Is that right?"

She gave a slight smile and nodded, but her attention was on Katherine. "For such a little bird, they sure have big voices, don't they? Say, have I ever told you girls about my favorite poem?"

Grandma had always been in love with birds, pointing

them out here and there, trying to get us to identify them by sight or sound, so I had no doubt her favorite poem had something to do with them.

I waited a couple seconds for Katherine to answer. When she didn't, I said, "No ma'am. Is it about a bird?"

"Yes. It's called 'Ode to a Nightingale' by an English poet named Mr. John Keats. It's about a bird's song so captivating, it eases someone's suffering to the point they're able to forget their troubles for a while. Isn't that lovely?"

"Yes, it is," I said. "My favorite bird is the hummingbird. They're so fast and when the sun hits their feathers, their colors—" The sound of horse hooves beating the ground stopped me.

We turned our attention to the road. All three of us quit hanging laundry and looked out to see Daddy riding Jessie up to the house, followed by an unfamiliar horse and carriage.

Grandma stepped out from behind the wash line. Her mist changed from bright to shadowy blue in a blink of an eye. "No, Charles," she whispered.

"Katherine!" Daddy yelled as he alighted Jessie. The black carriage came to a stop.

"Charles, *please*!" Grandma screamed as she rushed over to Daddy. "Charles, don't!"

"It's the only way, Mother," he said. "Katherine! Come!"

I grasped Katherine's hand and held it tight while she stood rigid.

"Katherine, I said come!"

A heavy-set gentleman in a waistcoat and top hat dropped the reins and stepped down from the carriage. He opened the door and helped out two women in white dresses, and then walked over to Daddy. He said something I couldn't make out. Daddy and the man started toward us.

"Run!" I urged as I tried to pull my sister away. As Katherine took a couple of steps the men each grabbed an arm and lifted her off the ground, tearing my hand from hers. "Please don't take her, *please*!" I begged. "Grandma, please don't let them take her!"

Grandma pulled at Daddy's arm and dug her heels into the dirt. He yanked his arm away. When they got close to the nurses, the women held up a white garment with elongated arms and Katherine began to scream. Her body writhed as she wrestled to free herself from their grip.

I ran over and tugged on Daddy's arm. In the chaos, he jerked away from me, causing his elbow to hit me under my chin. I bit my tongue and reeled backward. The fat man's top hat fell from his head as both men and nurses secured Katherine's arms behind her back. One of the women reached into a bag and pulled out what looked like a piece of rolled up white cloth. Katherine's pleading eyes were locked on mine as the woman placed the cloth into my sister's mouth and tied it behind her head. Since she could no longer scream, I screamed for her. It sounded unearthly, as if it was coming from someone else, from *somewhere* else.

I could tell by the tears in his eyes and his gray mist the color of grief, Daddy didn't want to be doing what he was doing. And yet he continued.

Grandma grabbed me and held me so tight I could hardly breathe. We watched as they struggled to lift Katherine into the carriage. I squeezed my eyes shut as my sister's guttural wail filled the air. When she was in, the women quickly entered the carriage and closed the door.

The sweaty, portly man huffed as he bent over and snatched his dusty hat off the ground. He straightened and looked at Daddy. "She'll be all right," he said. He hoisted himself into the seat, took the reins, and slapped the backs of the horses.

I clung to Grandma, begging God to let this be a bad dream as the carriage rambled away. When it was no longer visible, I looked at Daddy who stood motionless and silent. His face was red and his eyes even redder. He swiped the back of his dirty hand across his wet cheeks. The sight of him crying angered me.

I jerked away from Grandma and ran at him, my fists flying into his chest. *"How dare you cry!"* I yelled as I pounded over and over. *"How dare you!"*

"I'm protecting her the only way I can," he said.

I wasn't sure what he meant. I was too angry to ask.

That night, after Grandma and I had calmed down and stopped crying, Daddy explained that he sent her away to protect her from Donald Bryer. I couldn't believe it.

"Donald Bryer called me into his office this morning. He told me someone had left a threatening note in his barn. After what she did at the courthouse, he thinks it was Katherine. He said he'd not only press charges against her for threatening his life, but also for slandering his name in court. So, I reasoned with him. I told him I'd have her committed if he'd reconsider."

*Oh my God.* How could I tell him it was me who should have been sent away?

"You need to quit your job. That man is evil," Grandma said.

"I know. I will. Let me find another one first," he said.

I was grateful Daddy believed his boss was a horrible man. Hate filled me as I envisioned Donald Bryer's self-righteous face. I'm sure he got a lot of satisfaction thinking who he thought had written the note was now the one being locked up instead of him. My stomach knotted and my tears were flowing again. As I tried to work up the nerve to tell Daddy it was me, he went on.

"She'll be safer at the asylum than in jail, and it'll give her time to think real hard instead of rushing into something that could get her in serious trouble or killed. She's too headstrong for her own good." Daddy turned to me. His eyes glistened in the firelight. "And Sarah, I want this to be a lesson for you. I've already lost your momma, and now Katherine. I can't lose you too." His tears let loose, and his hands went to his face.

It was a lesson for me. A damned merciless lesson. I got up and hugged him. "You won't lose me, Daddy." I didn't have it in me in that moment to tell him the truth of what I'd done.

That night, the wind keened as it slipped through the window. I sobbed into Katherine's pillow, thinking about the way Grandma's mist changed in a split second. The way Katherine had no choice but to fight until they overpowered her. If only I hadn't told Grandma that Katherine had left, maybe she would have been praised for saving a life—two lives—instead of being sent away. She would never forgive me. Why should she? God help me, I had to make things right. *Someday I will earn back her love, her trust, and her grace.*

THANKS TO DONALD BRYER trying to save his dignity, he made sure the papers knew about the "crazy" person who'd stormed the courtroom: *Katherine Richardson, the young woman who was dragged out of the courtroom during Donald Bryer's sentencing, is now a permanent resident at the St. Louis City Lunatic Asylum.*

The kids at school made up stories about how she had lost her mind and was sent to a house of horror filled with wrathful ghosts of prior patients who haunted and tormented the living patients, driving them even more insane. Any time the guilt would get too much and I'd think about telling Daddy it was me who wrote the note, I'd have nightmares of searching down long, dim hallways. In my dreams I'd open doors to see horrific conditions in the rooms beyond: doctors and nurses performing bloody surgeries on the patient's brain, or strapping a man or woman to a bed and touching their private places. I'd wake up too frightened to admit to anything. Instead of confessing, I prayed hard Katherine wasn't living like that. Grandma assured me Katherine was doing all right. She knew because they wrote to each other often.

I'd written to Katherine a few times. She never wrote back.

# Chapter Ten

*March 1899. Three years later.*

"I'll be back later this evening to check on her," Doctor Shaw said, before he stepped out of the front door. He'd come earlier than he had the previous two mornings, this time on his way to deliver a baby. He'd sat with Grandma Rose and felt her pulse, listened to her chest, and checked her pupils. He told me it was a matter of hours. She'd been steadily getting worse, to the point she couldn't stomach any food and only sips of water.

I sat in a chair next to her bed. She'd give me a weak smile when I wiped her brow and held her hand. Her gray mist was thinning, and I knew her time was slipping. I was thankful Daddy would be coming home for lunch to check on her. I was also thankful Daddy's wife, Priscilla, gave me all the time I needed to be with Grandma and didn't sit vigil with me. She was eight years younger than Daddy and I accepted her, knowing someday I might be married myself and I didn't want Daddy to be alone, especially after Grandma left this world. Every so often, Priscilla would knock quietly and look in, asking if there was anything we needed.

To put Grandma at ease, I sang to her, talked to her, and read to her. I knew she was happiest when I read, because she gave me a faint smile as I recited her favorite poem about the nightingale. Since I hadn't been schooled much in poetry, it was difficult for me to understand a lot of what Mr. Keats had so beautifully written, although parts of it seemed to make some sort of sense. I figured out the narrator of the poem wishes to be more like the bird since it remains in a constant state of joy. I'm pretty sure it's because the bird is incapable of reflecting on death, or something like that. It made me wonder what Grandma thought of her own approaching death.

I set the book down when I finished reading the poem and grabbed her hand. I decided if I was going to say what I'd needed to for so long, I'd better do it now. Even though I'd gotten pretty good at keeping my shame shoved deep down, it was like a festering wound every time I thought of Katherine. And Mildred Bryer. For months after Katherine was taken away, I repeatedly went over in my mind everything I did, what I didn't do, what I should have done. After that, Grandma and I had stopped talking about our abilities, as Daddy had always wanted. It was as if she and I came to an unspoken agreement to try and maintain what peace was left within and between us.

"Grandma?" I whispered so Priscilla wouldn't hear me. "I need to tell you something." Grandma opened her eyes enough for me to know she'd heard me. "If that note that threatened Donald Bryer is what sent Katherine to the asylum, then it should have been me."

"I had a feeling," she whispered, her throat raspy.

I glanced away as shame heated my face. "I'm sorry I kept it to myself."

"Honey, that note wasn't the only reason. She was too willful for your daddy to handle." She gasped the last word and went into a coughing fit. I brought the water glass to her lips. Most of it dribbled down her chin. I quickly dabbed it with a kerchief.

"I need to make things right with her," I said. "I want you to tell me what to do." We'd all written to her in the past few months, telling her it was safe for her to come home. She wouldn't respond to my or Daddy's letters, but her letters to Grandma said she was doing fine right where she was.

"You need to go to her," Grandma said. "Your lives aren't complete without each other."

I knew that was the answer. I just needed to hear it.

A couple of hours later, her brow was fire to the touch and her raspy breathing was now fast and shallow.

"Mother, it's Charles. Can you hear me?" Daddy was sitting at her bedside, his mist the saddest gray blue. She gave an almost imperceptible nod of her head. "I love you, Mother. I want you to know that." His voice cracked and his face crumpled, causing Priscilla to sniffle and leave the room.

I walked over and looked into Grandma's face. I could tell she was no longer fully with us. "I love you too, Grandma. It's okay to go with Grandpa."

Tears slid from the outer corner of her eyes as she smiled. "He's here," she whispered.

"I know," I replied. I could feel him.

§

I sent word to the asylum informing Katherine of Grandma's passing but received no response by the time we had her memorial service. It was a lovely funeral, attended by several members of the congregation. Afterward, many came to our house and lunched on all the food they'd so kindly prepared and the cakes they had baked.

When everyone had gone, I went to Grandma's room and looked through her desk. I wasn't snooping. I wanted to take a few meaningful items that reminded me of her: a pink seashell given to her by my grandfather after one of his travels, a pale green stone that was nearly heart-shaped, and a yellow feather. I also took the gold necklace with the rose pendant she'd always worn. I would give it to Katherine and tell her that Grandma wanted us to reconcile.

At the bottom of one of the drawers, I was surprised to find a folded piece of paper with my and Katherine's names on it. I sat down and read it.

*Dear Katherine and Sarah,*

*I feel like this is a confession. And maybe it is. More than anything, I want it to be a lesson for you girls. It's about what happened that caused your daddy to lose faith in our abilities. One night, I had an awful dream that your mother died at the hands of a doctor. It was so distressing, I kept it to myself. Days later, she started complaining about a pain in her side. When your Daddy said he wanted to fetch the doctor, I had no choice but to tell him about my dream. I told him I felt sure it was a warning. This scared him so bad, he agreed to let me try and help her pain.*
*You girls might remember bringing her my herbal teas that I made her drink, and holding my warm compresses to her side to ease the soreness. And I'm sure you remember the morning she woke up with a bad fever. I tried everything I knew how to get it to come down, yet it persisted. So, we got her to the doctor. What you don't know, is he determined it was her appendix. He was afraid it had ruptured. When he opened her up, he realized it had indeed, and the poisons had spread throughout her body. She died on the surgery table.*
*So, you see, your mother did die at his hands, though it wasn't his fault. I can't say for sure that surgery would have saved her if he had done it sooner, or if she would have died anyway. As far as your daddy was concerned, it was his mother's poor judgement*

*that killed his wife. Regardless, I've never been able to forgive myself.*

*You've heard me say this before, Katherine, when you desperately wanted to save Mildred Bryer, but it's worth repeating. You both need to know that there will be times when we can't change fate no matter how badly we want to, or how hard we try. Please take care of one another.*

*With all my love,*

*Grandma Rose*

I set Grandma's letter on her desk and stared out of the window. A breeze was moving a branch where a goldfinch held on tightly and sang. The sun lit up his yellow belly making its mist glow even brighter. It was a glorious sight that Grandma would have surely loved.

Tears came despite the beauty outside. I cried for the pain Momma must have endured as she died, and the anguish Daddy had for losing her, and the guilt Grandma had carried with her for so long. I cried for the young girls we once were when we lost our mother, and now the loss of our beloved Grandmother, and for the emptiness left by my sister. I also cried knowing that the day Daddy stopped believing in Grandma, he stopped believing in me and Katherine as well.

I had second thoughts about going to St. Louis to be near Katherine after reading Grandma's letter. It made me realize how much Daddy had suffered all these years, and why he'd been so hard on us. Part of me wanted to stay in Jefferson City and spend the rest of the time he had on this earth trying to make up for all the pain we'd caused him. Yet, another part of me felt an urgent pull to mend my relationship with Katherine.

I went to sleep that night praying about what to do. As my mind drifted in the in-between state, I smelled rosewater and heard Grandma's words. *Go to her so everyone can heal.*

DADDY WAS SPENDING time brushing and tending his horses as he did every evening since I could remember. Matilda and Jessie were no longer with us, having died in the past year. He now had Berta, a rust-colored mare, and Rae, black with a white star between her eyes. When Daddy and Priscilla first got married, she whined and asked him not to spend so much time away in the evenings. He told her it was what he needed to do, and he did it regardless of her pout. She finally accepted, the way we all had, that being with his horses was his way to work out his thoughts and feelings that had piled on during the day.

"Can I talk to you?" I asked.

Seeing him brushing Rae's mane brought back the memory of the two of us in our barn in Rolla, years before. The brief image of my daddy so young and so desperate for things to be different made my chest hurt. His hair was gray now, and the lines on his forehead and face much deeper. *Don't you dare cry*, I told myself.

"Sure," he said as he kept on brushing.

"I'm going to St. Louis."

He looked at me. "All right. For how long?"

"I don't know. It depends on Katherine." Daddy stopped brushing. "I need her forgiveness. And yours. Daddy, it was me who sent that note to Donald Bryer all those years ago, not Katherine."

He stared at me with his mouth open as if he wanted to say something but couldn't. He shook his head. "Why didn't you speak up about it?"

"Because I was afraid. Of going to jail or the asylum. Most of all, of hurting you."

Daddy's face reddened and his shoulders slumped. His body shook as he stifled a sob. As I went to him, he dropped the brush he was holding and grabbed his handkerchief. I put my hand on his shoulder and waited for him to speak.

"I wish our lives could have been different," he said. "I wish your mother had lived. I wish the five of us had found a place where we could've all been happy. I wish…" He broke down again.

I held him and thought about how much pain our gifts had caused us all. "I'm so sorry I let Katherine take the blame. I hope she'll forgive me."

Daddy wiped his eyes. "I'm not sure I would have done anything differently even if I knew. Donald Bryer was not about to let go of the fact she said those things in the courtroom. And I get the feeling she did that regardless of the note."

It was true. She had stormed in there not knowing anything about it. "I'm gonna try and get her to move back to Jefferson City if I can."

"I hope she will," he said. "We need to be a family again."

A few weeks after our talk, I received a reply and acceptance from Digby's Boarding House for Women in St. Louis. I'd heard about it from my former schoolteacher who told me that her cousin had stayed there a few years before when she first moved to St. Louis.

Daddy gave me some pocket change and a wad of bills wrapped in cloth. "It's not a whole lot, but it should hold you for a little while," he'd said.

It didn't take long to pick through my wardrobe since I had so few dresses. Knowing St. Louis was a larger and more fashionable city made me embarrassed by my choices. Only four still had some vibrancy left in their color and wear. Though they were probably out of fashion, they would have to do. Priscilla was kind enough to give me a fairly new bonnet and pair of gloves. When it came to my shoes, Daddy and I both agreed I desperately needed a new pair, so I ordered from the *Sears, Roebuck and Company* catalog in town.

I WENT to Grandma's room before dawn on the day I was to leave. I laid on her bed and closed my eyes, trying to sense her spirit. Her room still had a cozy feel to it, and I could smell her rosewater permeating the air. I thanked her for always loving me as much as she did and asked that she continue to watch over all of us.

As I stood to go, I noticed our dowry chests that Daddy had made us peeking out from under an old blanket. I pulled it off, knelt down, and placed my hands on them both. The temptation to open them was great, but I didn't. I'd wait until Katherine was with me, whether it was on one of our wedding days or not.

Daddy told Priscilla to stay home while he took me to the train station. I could see by the dimming of her mist she was hurt. She gave me a hug and told me to write often. Daddy didn't say much on the way. I sensed his emotions were close to the surface and he was fighting to keep them down. When we arrived, he unloaded my garment bag and carried it to the baggage porter.

"I think about her all the time. I want you to know that," he said as we waited on the platform. He wasn't looking at me, but his pink splotches were telling enough.

"Would you like me to say that to her?" I asked.

"If you think she'll want to hear it. Either way, I'd like you to give her this." He pulled an envelope out of his breast pocket. "I'd understand if she refuses it or would rather tear it up. But please, ask her to read it before she does."

I took his letter. "I will, Daddy."

# Chapter Eleven

I watched large trees, lush grass, farmland, and cow pastures eventually give way to streets, carriages, streetcars, and building after building. Through a soot-covered window, I gazed at all of the mist colors emanating from the people on the sidewalks of St. Louis. As the train slowed, the grip in my chest became more pronounced. The closer to Katherine, the stronger my guilt.

The brakes screeched and my nerves shuddered as we pulled into Union Station. The depot was crammed with travelers and I wasn't eager to become part of the fray. All that energy. All those colors. I took a deep breath, held it, and slowly released. *Be brave.*

I clutched my hat box and stepped into the flow of passengers headed into the Grand Hall. At the risk of being jostled, I stopped and looked up. The numerous arched stained-glass windows created splashes of ruby, orange, violet, and green to creep along the barrel ceiling and walls. I brought my gaze down and saw many of the same colors coming from crowd. It truly was a dazzling sight.

I continued on, stopping only a moment later. I was

awestruck, my eyes drawn above the main entry to a large arched stained-glass window. It was the most soul-stirring piece of art I had ever seen. In the center was a bold woman in an orange-red dress who looked as if she was staring straight at me. To her right was a woman in profile wearing yellow, and on her left a woman in green.

"It's called The Allegorical Window," a male voice said.

When I looked at the dark-haired young gentleman who'd stopped next to me, it was as if the floor shifted and the entire room had swayed. I'd seen handsome men before and never felt as though I'd twirled myself dizzy. I looked away from his blue eyes and back to the window to regain my composure.

"It's exquisite," I said, proud of myself for coming up with a description I'd never used before. It was so unlike me, I nearly laughed.

He pointed to the woman in yellow. "She represents San Francisco, the one in the middle represents St. Louis, and the one in green, New York."

"It looks like St. Louis is proving herself worthy," I said.

"Precisely."

When our eyes caught, his smile stilled and I wondered if he was experiencing the current that was passing between us. It was so strong, how could he not?

After several seconds, he said, "I hope you enjoy St. Louis." He tipped his hat to me and walked away.

As I watched him go, I realized I couldn't see his mist. I glanced around to see if there was anyone else whose mist I couldn't see. His was the only one. It disconcerted me enough to wonder about it, thinking back to a time when it had happened before, and I couldn't remember. I was then bumped from behind, a strong shoulder knocking into my hat. It slid sideways, pulling the bun in my hair along with it. My hand shot up to stop my hat from falling further. I hurried to a clearing to replace the hat pins.

*If I only had a hand mirror*, I thought, knowing I was no longer as presentable as I had been moments before. I shrugged and decided not to fret about it.

"Sarah Richardson," I said in response to the porter's inquiry.

"Where to?"

"Digby's Boarding House for Women, on Audubon and Taylor."

He repeated it as he jotted it down, noting the description of my garment bag and hat box. "You can expect your luggage this evening," he said, handing me a receipt.

I walked over to a large map before the exit and stared at the city that looked like a womb. The route would be a several-minute walk heading west on Laclede, more than an hour by the look of it. I noticed I'd eventually come to Sarah Street, a few blocks from the boarding house. I smiled, feeling it was a sign that I was where I needed to be, doing exactly what I needed to do. Since the weather was pleasant enough and I wasn't expected until late afternoon, I decided to take the opportunity to absorb this unfamiliar city by walking instead of taking the trolley.

A vibration thrummed around and through me as I stepped into the moist heat of the day. There was a cacophony coming from the buzz of electric street cars, the pounding of hammers on wood, and the drone of voices from the conversations from people walking toward and away from me. The thick air stunk of steaming horse manure. More overwhelming though, was the fusty smell of the Mississippi River. Its odor was strong enough to be carried on what little breeze there was even though the river was out of sight and a few blocks away.

I walked past a few buildings under construction and was surprised to see a hand-painted sign in front of one that said "Damn the cyclone. St. Louis is rising again!" It had been two years since the tornado took so many lives, and as I headed up Laclede Avenue, the city's resilience seeped into my skin.

Although the surroundings intimidated me, I tried my best to appear sophisticated, even though the little toe on my right foot was being rubbed raw. It was all I could do not to limp as I chastised myself for foregoing what the *Sears-Roebuck* described as "the comfortable and conservative Oxford." Instead, for a few cents more, I had purchased the fashionable opera boot with a needle-toe and curved heel. I knew the moment I ordered them it was a ludicrous choice, but for once I had given in to the impulse to appear to be refined in more cultured St. Louis.

Eventually, I stood at the foot of the stone steps of Digby's Boarding House for Women. I stared at it, admiring the stateliness of the property that would be my temporary home. *I should have confirmed the price before I requested a room.* It was more opulent than I imagined.

It was a naïve and foolish mistake, probably one of many since it was my first adventure alone. I had fourteen dollars and I would stay as long as it would last, because the thought of having to admit to Mrs. Digby I couldn't afford it for even one night made my face flush. Besides, there was a part of me that was eager to experience the luxury I'd often wished for as a young girl. I would just have to do what I came to do quickly and return to Jefferson City.

It suddenly hit me why I was there and looked around to get my bearings. A pleasant-looking woman radiating a light-blue mist was walking in my direction. It took a moment to gather my nerve. With a bright smile and a discreet tone, I stopped her as she neared.

"I'm sorry to bother you. I was wondering if you could tell me how far it is to the St. Louis City Asylum?"

She turned and pointed into the distance. "It's that way. On Arsenal Street. You might want to take a trolley."

"Thank you," I called out as she strode away.

I looked up again, at the white columned home, and down at my dress, thankful I was wearing my prettiest one. I bent down and swiped at the dust on my shoes that I'd picked up on the walk, and then tucked an unruly strand of hair that had become dislodged earlier behind my ear. I climbed the steps, straightened my shoulders, and knocked.

# Chapter Twelve

Through an oblong leaden glass window, a dusky shape drew near. "I'll answer it, Martha," I heard her say. A tall, large-boned woman with orange mist, the color of confidence, opened the door. She wore a black dress and a mourning broach. Her face had a few wrinkles, and her silver hair was perfectly coiffed.

"Mrs. Digby?" I asked.

"Yes," she replied with a smile.

I followed her to the parlor where another woman sat pouring warm milk into her teacup. Her dark hair had streaks of gray and her face was chubby and kind. She stood as I entered. She was much shorter than Mrs. Digby and her mist was a soft blue. Her name was Gertrude Gaines.

"But call me Trudy," she said. I liked her immediately.

"Please sit," Mrs. Digby offered.

The servant named Martha poured me a cup of tea. The chairs were cream and gold with plush cushions that begged me to surrender to them. Relief rushed to my feet the moment I sat down. I wanted so much to take off my shoes, and if I were at home I would have. I took a sip of tea instead and noticed a large portrait above the fireplace of a heavy-set gentleman with a gray beard and bushy eyebrows. His eyes stared right at me, dark and severe, as if he was not happy with what was happening in the parlor.

"Is that Mr. Digby?" I asked. Both ladies turned to the portrait.

"It is. May he rest in peace," Mrs. Digby replied, placing her hand over her broach. "He passed away two years ago." She looked at me. "Anyway, I must say, I am simply *thrilled* a member of the Richardson family will be staying in my home! So, tell me, how is Percival? He's such a generous man. Very revered in this town. His heart is so charitable."

*Percival?* "Um … hmm. I'm not sure who that is," I said.

"What do you mean?" She looked at Trudy who shook her head and shrugged. Mrs. Digby looked back at me. "I assumed you were his granddaughter. Isn't your mother Constance and your father Jonas Richardson? They have a daughter named Sarah in Jefferson City."

"No, no. You're wrong," Trudy said. "Their daughter's name is Sandra, short for Cassandra. And she lives in Jerseyville not Jefferson City."

Mrs. Digby's mist clouded. She was not pleased. "Why, Jerseyville isn't even in Missouri. How could I have been so wrong?"

"I don't know. You should have asked me," Trudy said.

"I hope this isn't a problem," I said. I had no other place to go.

Mrs. Digby pulled a fan out of her skirt pocket and began waving it in front of her face. "No wonder Percival never responded to my letter telling him how happy I was to invite his granddaughter into my home. I shudder to know what he must think of me."

"I'm sorry for the confusion," I said, unsure as to what she expected me to do or say about any of it.

"Yes, I certainly should have asked more questions before accepting your request so hastily. Who are your parents?"

"Charles and Victoria Richardson. Although my momma died when I was twelve. I was raised by my daddy and my Grandma Rose. Sadly, she's dead now too."

Mrs. Digby stared at me, unsmiling. "I hope you understand that I don't let just anyone stay in my home."

My heart pounded. She was going to turn me out into the street.

"However," she continued, "seeing as it was my fault for making assumptions, I will give you a trial period. Although you must improve your grammar. We do not use words like *momma*, *daddy*, or *grandma*. Being well-spoken is every bit as important as being well-mannered and well-groomed. Do I make myself clear?"

"Yes, ma'am, you do." I was relieved I wouldn't have to start my search for a roof and a bed that very moment.

Mrs. Digby studied me a little longer. "Your letter stated you were looking for new opportunities in St. Louis."

"Yes, ma'am. I've never been to a big city like this. I'm excited to see it."

"I hope you don't mind me asking ... How old are you?"
"Nineteen."

She stared at my face a little longer. "A young woman exploring a big city all alone where she has no relatives is a little unusual. I'm wondering what opportunities you're looking for. A husband perhaps? You're the perfect age for getting married."

Her forthrightness shook me. "Oh, no. I'm not ready to fall in love yet."

Mrs. Digby looked up to the ceiling and back to my face. I'd obviously said something else wrong.

"Love isn't the only reason to marry, nor should it be a priority. There are other expectations a couple must fulfill in the eyes of God and society. Isn't that so, Trudy?"

Trudy hesitated and her mist dimmed. "Yes. Sometimes love must be set aside."

I sensed she had experience with this very thing.

"I'm sorry if I sound naïve or selfish," I said.

"Not selfish. Just … optimistic," Mrs. Digby replied. "You aren't one of those women who march in the streets demanding voting rights, are you?"

"Oh, uh, no. That's something I haven't considered."

"Thank goodness. You'd be better off not associating with that group. That is no way to find a husband or move up in the proper social circles," Mrs. Digby said. "Not to mention that the future of our modest society will be in jeopardy if women insist on getting involved in political matters. Once they achieve that, they'll want to work outside the home instead of tending to their families. The eventual result will be the demise of the sacred family structure. Now, our Laura, whom you'll meet this evening, is the epitome of what every young woman should be. Isn't that right, Trudy?"

Trudy looked up from her tea. "Oh, yes."

"She occupies the room across from yours." Mrs. Digby narrowed her eyes as she tapped her chin. "Yes, now that I think about it, it will be one of my conditions for you to stay. She will teach you proper grammar and etiquette. I will leave it up to her to decide if she thinks you're suitable enough to be introduced to her friends."

I felt a rush of excitement at the thought of meeting young people who were living a lifestyle such as this. Even if it was only for a little while, I could pretend and enjoy.

Later, I thought about the embarrassment Mrs. Digby's audacity had caused us both by assuming I was the granddaughter of a rich man. I unpacked my belongings that had arrived from the depot and hung my dresses, wondering what she would say if she knew that every item of clothing I wore since the time I was born had been worn by Katherine first. If Mrs. Digby only knew how frugal we had to be, or how unusual our lives were, or why I was really in St. Louis, she would have me tossed onto the street.

Laura was eighteen, fair-haired, and her delightful face was even prettier when she lit into a smile, exposing a dimple on her right cheek. Her voice was sweet, and her mist was buttercup yellow. I couldn't help but feel dowdy and awkward in her presence.

"Laura is preparing for future motherhood by volunteering as a governess for the children of one of St. Louis's most prominent families: Dr. and Mrs. Albright. He is the leading medical doctor in the entire Midwest, including Chicago." Mrs. Digby's face was smug, as if the Albrights were a reflection on her.

"How wonderful," I said, trying my very best to sound interested and sophisticated. "How old are the kids, I mean, the children?"

"Getting too old for a governess." Laura cut a roasted potato with her knife.

I noticed how she cut all her vegetables into small pieces, chewed silently, and dabbed her napkin on each corner of her mouth. I was suddenly embarrassed that I'd been using my fork to halve the vegetables and then not-so-daintily chew the hunks.

"I'm ready to move on now that I've learned how to be the perfect mother, which I think is even more important than being the perfect wife." She lowered her voice. "Please don't tell my fiancé." She laughed.

"Laura is engaged to one of St. Louis's most prominent young men," Trudy said.

"And one of St. Louis's most attractive," Laura said.

"Yes, Laura and Justin make a handsome couple." Mrs. Digby looked at Laura. "Sarah moved here to begin a new life, find a husband, and eventually have children. Isn't that wonderful? Perhaps you will introduce her to one of Justin's friends."

My cheeks warmed at Mrs. Digby's blatant lie regarding why I'd come to St. Louis. I thought I'd made it clear those were not the reasons I moved here. Yet, if I told them I came to reconcile with my sister in the insane asylum, they would choke on their braised beef.

Laura studied my face for more than a moment, as if assessing my attractiveness. I was relieved when she finally nodded. "I will arrange that."

"Ah! Laura will have you engaged in no time," Mrs. Digby said.

*I won't be here long enough for that,* I thought. "When is your wedding?" I asked.

"Not soon enough," Laura replied. "In two months. After Justin's graduation. He'll then work with his father who is the president of Farm and Business Bank."

"You look like the future wife of a future bank president," Mrs. Digby said with the annoying arrogance I was getting used to.

That evening, Laura and I sat in the library, practicing what she called *e-nun-si-a-shun*. Or was it *e-nun-ci-a-tion*? I dared not ask.

"You have this … I guess what sounds to me, like a small-town accent," she said. "Enunciation is key to speaking in a more refined manner."

"I'll try my best," I replied.

"See, there. Did you hear yourself say 'tra' instead of tr-*eye*? Subtly stress the 'eye.'"

"I will tr-*eye*."

"Better." She smiled.

Laura was the prettiest and kindest girl I'd ever met. I never expected all of this fuss over me when I came here.

I went to bed that night happier than I'd been in a long time, imagining the handsome man Laura might introduce me to. Suddenly, I remembered why I'd come to St. Louis—to heal my relationship with my sister and persuade her to move back to Jefferson City, not to experience a lifestyle that wasn't my own. Daddy would be disappointed, and possibly hurt, by my indulgence. On the other hand, I was an adult now. I could make my own choices and suffer the consequences if I chose poorly. Really, what could it hurt to enjoy my stay here? I would still do what I came to do, and Daddy would never have to know about my time at Mrs. Digby's. When would I ever have another opportunity like this again?

# Chapter Thirteen

I awoke the following morning from a frightening dream. In it, the sun was setting as I walked up a pathway leading to a large building. As I got closer, I could see people in white gowns behind an iron fence on either side of the path. Men on one side, women on the other.

"Hey. *Psst*." I turned to see a dark-haired woman. She gripped the bars of the fence with her face pressed between. She whispered Grandma Rose's words, "Deliver the weak."

"Who are the weak?" I asked.

"You'll know." She turned her back to me.

As I dressed, I pushed away the heaviness of the dream, telling myself it was caused by the stress of travel the day before.

"I'D LIKE to see you in the library," Mrs. Digby said to me after breakfast. She held an invoice that showed how much I would owe for room and board: four dollars per week, or sixteen dollars per month. "I want you to be prepared. You can pay it all at once, or every Saturday morning. Just know I do not grant extensions or favors."

"Yes, ma'am. I understand." At that price, I would be out of money in three weeks. Everything I hoped to accomplish, including learning how to be more refined, would have to be done quickly.

After I told the ladies I was going on a sightseeing walk, I donned my bonnet and headed to Euclid Avenue. A slight breeze carried with it the smell of fermenting beer from the brewery a couple of blocks away. The scent was as thick as the river, making me wish I'd brought a sprig of lavender. After a few minutes, I stopped walking, intrigued with a woman emitting a bold orange mist like Mrs. Digby's, although she was doing something Mrs. Digby would never do—she was nailing a colorful suffrage poster on the outside wall of a hardware store. It portrayed a long-haired woman in a flowing red dress holding a baby with one arm and an American flag in her other hand. Its caption read: *Without women there would be no men to vote for. Give women the respect they deserve. Give women the power to vote.*

I smiled thinking about the fit Mrs. Digby would have if she saw it.

"Hello," the woman said. "Are you interested in learning about the St. Louis Women's Equality Society?" She reached into her bag and pulled out a flyer.

I took a moment to read it.

*Speak up! Speak out! Let Women's Voices Be Heard! They are strong enough to bear your children, capable enough to raise them, and intelligent enough to vote for the good of home and country!* The small print underneath said: *Join or donate to the sisterhood of the St. Louis Women's Equality Society today.*

I thanked her and placed it in my handbag. I then imagined Mrs. Digby's wrath and tucked it even further toward the bottom. "Am I heading in the right direction to Arsenal Street? I'm looking for the city asylum."

She pointed south. "It's on the hill. You can't miss the dome." She proceeded to tell me which trolley to catch.

I watched the pedestrians and their colorful mists from the trolley window and within moments, the large copper dome came into view. I took a breath to calm myself. No amount of rehearsing what I'd say to my sister would matter if she refused to see me or was still angry to the point of not hearing or caring what I said. She had every right to be bitter since the asylum wasn't where she should have grown into a woman, but I hoped all of her negative emotions would fall away when she saw me and realized how much she missed and loved me.

I stood at the gate staring at the massive building as the memory of last night's dream came to me. There were indeed similarities in the fence, the grounds, and the building itself. A tall guard with a white mustache stepped out of the booth. I told him I was there to see my sister.

"Sign in," he said.

When I handed back the form, he gave me a chain with a small placard that read *Visitor*.

"Wear this around your neck and give it back to me when you sign out," he said, unlocking the gate. He stepped aside so I could pass. "You'll come to the reception area straight through those main doors. The nurses there will help you."

I thanked him and headed up the stone path with my heart pounding in my ears.

The center red brick building had several floors, while the east and west wings had fewer. Every window had bars. I glanced up and noticed a couple of faces peering out at me. The walkway leading up to the steps was lined with trees and edged with vibrant flowers. The iron fence running along either side only slightly repressed the beauty.

I slowed my pace in order to take in as much as I could, noticing several female residents walking the grounds to my right and male residents to my left. As I walked up the tree-lined path, I forced a smile to cover my fear as I passed the patients who had lined up to stare at me. Their whispers were eerily melodic and soothing. Their mist colors shifted and mixed as I walked past; some bright, many hazy or dull. The colors flowed into and out of each other like a kaleidoscope.

Dread filled me as I climbed the stairs, anticipating the horror I'd imagined for so long. To my surprise and relief, instead of cold, gray walls and a maze of hallways when I entered, there was a very large sunlit reception area with a wide mahogany staircase leading to the upper floors with a chandelier hanging above. To the right was a sitting area with a grand piano where a young man was playing what I recognized to be Beethoven's "Ode to Joy," a piece I had learned about in music class during my final year of school. I was immediately ashamed for the unfair judgement I'd made about the asylum and the patients who resided there.

"Can I help you?" a red-haired nurse asked. She sat behind a semicircular desk.

"My name is Sarah Richardson. I'm here to see my sister Katherine."

"I'll need to hold on to that," she said, pointing to my bag.

I remembered Daddy's letter and pulled it out before handing it over.

"Open the envelope, please."

I opened it, pulled the letter out, and showed her there was nothing hiding in it.

"I trust you." She smiled. "It's procedure."

She handed me a clipboard and told me I had to sign in again. Suddenly the man playing the piano hit a wrong note and began pounding violently on the keys with his fists until someone shouted for him to stop. It unsettled me, causing my hands to shake as I signed my name. The nurse then sent someone to find Katherine.

I took a seat in the piano room and watched a middle-aged woman standing behind the young man. She had a light green mist and a lapel pin that read *WCTU Volunteer*.

"Why don't you try something slower," she said. "What about Sonata Number Eight, *Pathetique*? You like that one, don't you?"

The young man nodded.

The notes were calming and beautiful. I smiled to myself, thrilled I would finally be in my sister's presence after three years. But when several minutes passed, my tension returned.

I looked at the clock and realized I'd been waiting for nearly twenty minutes. *What on earth could be taking so long?* As I stood to ask the nurse, a woman descended the stairs. Her mist was hazy blue, her dark hair pinned into a bun. She kept her eyes down, carefully watching her feet. There was a pull in my chest. She was most definitely Katherine.

When she reached the bottom step, she looked at me. Like me, she had grown taller and her breasts larger. The freckles that had once graced her nose and cheeks had faded. Although her face and body had matured, her brown eyes with gold speckles remained the same. I smiled all the while trying not to burst with joy, but the moment was too much. I was so overcome with happiness I cried. She backed away when I stepped forward to embrace her, and a pain shot through me.

I glanced around, looking for some privacy. "Is there somewhere quiet we can go? Maybe outside?" I asked.

Without answering, she led the way out of a patio door, to a marble bench within the fenced east lawn.

We sat in silence watching the women wandering about the yard. I savored the breeze caressing my skin while the sun illuminated the flowers and the butterflies feeding from them. A few of the women stopped and stared at us, at me mostly, as if assessing me or trying to read me. Eventually they continued on communing with the flowers or bees or butter-flies or whatever it was they were truly doing.

"Katherine? Will you look at me?"

She turned her face, her eyes focused on my neckline. Her mist was cloudy.

"You're still angry with me."

She lowered her gaze even more. "I didn't realize how much until I saw you."

Her words caused me to flinch. "Well, I'm very happy to see you. I've missed you so much." As I reached for her hand, she snatched it away. After a few moments of silence I asked, "Did you get my letter about Grandma Rose?"

She looked down at her folded hands and nodded.

"She loved you very much. She's the one who told me to come here." I hoped it would at least thaw, if not melt, her icy manner toward me.

"So that's why you're here. Not because *you* wanted to come but because *she* wanted you to come."

"She said I should come, yes, but it was me who asked her advice on what to do."

"About what?"

"About you and me. I want to fix what broke between us. I want us to be sisters again. Come home to Jefferson City with me."

"I don't have a home. Besides, I work here now."

I glanced around. "Here?" The place itself was lovely. But the patients … I could tell by their mists that several of them were definitely not lovely. "You could have a job anywhere."

"I didn't ask for your opinion."

My stomach gripped. "I'm sorry." I remembered Daddy's letter and pulled it from my pocket.

Her scowl stayed constant as she stared at the letter in my hand.

"Daddy asked me to give you this. He said he thinks about you often."

"I let Daddy go a long time ago." She looked away.

"Will you please read it? You don't have to keep it."

She exhaled loudly and held out her hand. While she read, I sat quietly watching a woman with blue-green mist lying on a blanket under a tree, reading a book. Everything about her was serene. *How could someone radiating such beautiful colors be locked up in here?*

Katherine sniffled. Her face scrunched up as she fought to not cry. She smacked the letter down on her lap and turned away from me so I couldn't see her tears.

I was grateful her mist wasn't the dark colors of anger or hatred. Maybe she could forgive him. When she sniffed again, I pulled out a kerchief from my pocket and handed it to her. She grabbed it and dabbed her eyes. She blew and wiped her nose and handed it back to me.

"You can keep it," I said.

"I don't want it."

I knew it was one more way of showing her unhappiness with me. I took the damp kerchief and stuffed it into my pocket as she folded the letter and slid it into its envelope.

"I bet you're dying to know what it says," she said.

I straightened my shoulders and looked away from her. "No, I don't," I lied. "That's between you and him."

"Right. But your mist tells me otherwise. You probably read it before you came."

"I most certainly did not." And that was the truth.

She ripped the envelope in half and then again, and stuffed it in her pocket.

I took a breath to subdue the anger that was rising up. *You don't have the right,* I reminded myself. After a few seconds, it dissipated. Finally, I got up the nerve to say what I came to say. "Katherine, I'm sorry."

"What for?"

"For everything."

"Be more specific."

*Please don't make me.* I wasn't prepared to admit everything yet. "I'm sorry you were sent here."

"Not because you couldn't keep your promise to keep your mouth shut? Or that your broken promise kept me from stopping a man from murdering his wife and child?"

"Yes. I'm sorry for all of that." *And so much more.* "Katherine, Grandma wanted us to heal. She said we aren't complete without each other."

She stared at me for several seconds, her lips tight and the crease between her eyes deep. She shook her head. "I don't feel that way. On the night Mrs. Bryer was murdered, I realized Grandma Rose was the only Richardson I could trust. Now she's gone." She stood and looked down at me. "The day I was taken from Jefferson City, I was no longer Charles Richardson's daughter or Sarah Richardson's sister. I'm sorry you came all this way."

I sat stunned and confused as she walked back into the building. When I went in after her, she was nowhere to be seen. I certainly didn't want to leave it like this, yet something told me to give her more time. Surely, she would accept that even if she didn't need me, I needed her. Daddy had Priscilla. Who did Katherine and I have except each other?

I stepped out of the main door and watched as men on my right and women on my left lined the iron fence. Once again, their hands gripped the bars, and their faces pressed so that their noses and chins poked through. I looked behind me and ahead, wishing I didn't have to walk this gauntlet alone. But there was no one else.

I kept my gaze on the path while my ears were tuned into the rhythmic flow of h's and s's. Like their colors, their whispers swirled together effortlessly. I exited the main gate and turned back when I sensed a pull toward an upper window. I couldn't be sure it was Katherine looking out at me, but it felt like her.

# Chapter Fourteen

I decided to walk back to the boarding house instead of taking the trolley, wanting time to consider what had just taken place between me and Katherine. I'd known there was a possibility of her being angry, though I truly didn't expect she actually would be after all of this time. What she was angry about, I'd done out of love and concern for her. How could anyone hold a grudge for that?

*Stop here.*

The words came into my mind so clear it was as if Grandma Rose herself had said them. I took stock of where I was. I was on South Kingshighway Boulevard standing at the foot of wooden stairs leading up to the front porch of Larsen's Market.

An elderly man with a blue mist was sitting in a rocker with a pipe between his lips. He was staring down at me. It made me blush wondering what he must have thought about my strange behavior. As I was about to continue on, I noticed movement beyond him. A woman was placing a sign in the window: *Help Needed.*

*A job?* Katherine already had a job, and she certainly

wouldn't want me again suggesting it wasn't where she should be. Suddenly it dawned on me. Because of what had happened with Katherine, my time in St. Louis might be longer than I'd originally thought. The job was for me.

"Hello," I called up to the man in the rocker.

"Hello to you," he called down. He drew on his pipe for a while before pulling it away from his face, all the while keeping his squinty eyes on me. He then blew smoke rings.

He was gregarious, and I liked him.

"Well done," I said, lifting my skirt away from my boots and heading up the stairs.

"Name's John. I ain't seen you here before."

"No, sir. I'm new in town, and I'd like to inquire about the help you need."

"That'd be my daughter. Step inside." He took another puff of his pipe.

A bell tinkled when I opened the screen door and the woman behind the counter looked up. Despite her bristly hair pulled into a severe bun and her dismal slate-colored dress, she radiated a soothing peach-colored mist.

"I saw your sign."

"Oh my! That was quick. Please, come in," she said, waving me toward her. "I'm Rebecca Larsen."

Sun filled the store from the full-length windows, and although the natural light made the setting pleasant, it also made the temperature rather warm. The slow circling fans overhead did little to move the air. A trace of perspiration trailed down my back as I untied my bonnet and lifted it, careful not to muss the pins in my hair. I used it to fan my face.

"It was the walk. I'll cool down shortly."

"Yes. Summer has yet to begin and I already look forward to autumn," she said. "Please, sit down."

We each sat on a stool—Rebecca behind the register, I

behind several large glass jars filled with red and black licorice, brightly colored gumdrops, peppermint sticks, and gumballs.

I told her I was new to St. Louis and staying at the boarding house. "If you need confirmation, I'm sure Mrs. Digby will oblige you."

"Yes, I know Mrs. Digby." She glanced out the window at her father. "Does Mrs. Gaines still live there?"

"Yes, ma'am. She does."

"What about your family? Where do they live?" she asked.

I explained how I left Daddy and his new wife in Jefferson City. "And now, I'm hoping to … to reconcile with my sister. She lives here." It was a relief to be able to speak a little more freely than I could with Laura or Mrs. Digby.

"I hope you do," she said with a smile. "Now, I need someone to handle the register from eleven to two, Monday through Saturday. My father used to stock the shelves and take inventory and do the record-keeping." She lowered her voice. "His unofficial job now is to sit outside and greet people. His eyesight isn't as strong as it was. I've found so many errors in our daily numbers that it's better if I do it all myself. If I can get help on the register, and maybe stocking shelves here and there, that will allow me to get other things done."

"I'm very reliable, and I get along nicely with people," I said, although that was dependent on the color of their mist.

"All right. It pays $3.75 per week. Why don't you come back Monday at eleven o'clock and we'll see how you like it?"

I knew I'd like it very much. I reached out my hand and she shook it.

As I stood to go, Rebecca pulled the sign out of the window. "What a coincidence you happened to be walking by right when I put this up."

It was much more than that. Grandma Rose had guided me here.

&a.

AT DINNER, Martha placed a platter of roasted chicken down in the middle of the table. The smell made my mouth water. I reached first for the mashed potatoes and spooned some on my plate. They were chunky, as I liked them.

"What did you do today, Sarah?" Trudy asked.

"I went for a walk, trying to get my bearings, and the most wonderful thing happened."

"Oh? What was that?" Laura asked.

"I got a job! Starting Monday, I'll be working the register at Larsen's Market." I watched as Mrs. Digby looked at Trudy as Trudy's smile froze. I remembered what Mrs. Digby had said about women working outside the home. "It's only three hours per day," I said.

Mrs. Digby narrowed her eyes. "I hope you find a husband as quickly as you found a job. I'm sure it's only temporary, am I correct?"

*Just until I convince my sister to forgive me and leave the asylum.* "Yes, ma'am."

Mrs. Digby began cutting a piece of chicken. "It's a shame Rebecca Larsen isn't married. Now that she's taken over her father's business, I doubt she ever will be."

"Was John there?" As Trudy spoke, her mist blushed pink.

"Yes, he was. Do you know him?" I was a little surprised, since he didn't seem as sophisticated as these ladies, and even more surprised her mist hinted at an endearment.

Trudy looked down at her plate. "A very long time ago."

"Perhaps when you've been there a little while you can convince Rebecca to modernize," Laura said. "The store is in desperate need of it. Especially women's items. That's why I don't shop there. Not enough cosmetics, perfumes, or creams. If she wants to compete with Newell's and entice younger customers, tell her she must renovate and accommodate us."

"I'll see what I can do," I replied, pretending to be every bit as bold as she was.

As I lay in bed that evening, I thought about Trudy's mist at the mention of John Larsen, and I remembered what she had said about marriage: *Sometimes you have to set love aside.*

# Chapter Fifteen

The next morning was Sunday, and Mrs. Digby expected me to attend church. "It's part of our living agreement," she informed me as we ate breakfast, though this was the first I'd heard of it.

After I finished eating, I quickly changed into my Sunday best, which was the dress I'd arrived in, and met the ladies on the front porch. Laura and I walked a few feet behind Mrs. Digby and Trudy as we made our way to the service. At Laura's insistence, I made up sentences with the words we'd been practicing; words like *delectable* and *splendid*. Anything I said sounded clumsy, to the point it made me laugh.

"Please be serious, Sarah," Laura said. "We must get you used to speaking in a more polished manner so it will sound natural."

I took a breath and tried again. "Everything on the table looks splendid. The desserts look especially delectable."

Laura nodded. "Very good! We'll practice more this evening." She immediately said goodbye and disappeared into the crowd the second we arrived, leaving me confused.

"Where is she going?" I asked the ladies.

"She sits with Justin's family every Sunday, and spends the

day with them, not returning until after dinner," Mrs. Digby explained.

I sat between the two women, our bodies getting closer and closer as the pews became crowded with people sitting shoulder-to-shoulder. I did my best to ignore all of the energy and mist colors swirling around me. When I sat back and looked straight ahead, my attention was drawn to the man and woman sitting directly in front of me. Her dark hair was pulled back in a knot at the nape of her neck, and his was slicked back with corn oil so thick I could smell it.

Based on their profiles, I could see they were a handsome couple, but I was immediately disturbed that their mists were a mixture of mossy green and brown. The more I stared at them, the more I was overcome with heaviness.

I did my best to focus on the sermon as the service wore on, but it was difficult to ignore how stifling the woman's oppression was becoming. It caused my face to flush and my head to swim and my underarms to perspire. When I couldn't stand it anymore, I grabbed Mrs. Digby's silk fan that stuck out of her reticule and vigorously waved it in front of my face, pretending not to notice my companions on either side curiously staring at me. I closed my eyes and took a calming deep breath.

*Ignore her,* I told myself. The slight guilt I had about it compelled me to say a quick prayer, that she'd be delivered from any harm or illness, whether physical or emotional. But the heaviness didn't ease up.

When the service ended, Trudy looped her arm through mine as we made our way down the aisle toward the door. "Are you all right, dear?" she whispered.

"I'm fine." Yes, I would be fine as soon as I stepped out into the fresh air. I knew the woman who caused my affliction would not be able to escape hers so simply.

"Perhaps your corset is a little too tight," Mrs. Digby said as we walked toward the boarding house. "Loosen it when we get home."

"I will." I wished that was all the strange woman needed to do to relieve her discomfort—merely free herself from those constricting ties.

☙

AT TEN MINUTES to eleven the following day, I stepped off the trolley and walked a few blocks to Larsen's Market. John sat on the porch with a newspaper and a cup of coffee.

"You came back," he said.

"Yes, sir," I said, mounting the stairs. When I got to the top, I paid close attention to his mist. "Trudy Gaines gives you her regards."

John stilled for a second, and then smiled.

"You tell her I send mine right back."

I smiled as his blue mist flushed a with a hint of pink, just as hers had.

Rebecca showed me around the store. It had four aisles stocked front and back with dry and canned goods, house cleaning products, and toiletry items. Against the length of one wall was an assortment of fresh fruits and vegetables. In one corner was a narrow table with bolts of oil-cloth and fabrics in an array of solid colors and textures, as well as sewing implements such as needles, thread, thimbles, scissors, ribbons, lace, and buttons. In another corner was a sizeable Acme refrigerator that held cuts of meat and dairy products.

"Every morning, we have an ice delivery and the men empty the water tray," she explained. "Although you won't have to worry about that since you'll be here in the middle of the day." She pointed to the Magneto crank telephone box mounted on the wall. "We get a customer every so often who will make calls from here. It's a penny per minute. There's a timer on the counter."

She showed me to the back room where a few cleaning supplies were kept. There was a desk and chair in the corner with a calendar pinned to the wall next to a hand-written delivery schedule and an inventory roster.

"When you see we're running low on something, come in here and write it down."

I nodded and followed her back to the register.

"Since you won't be staying until closing in the evenings, you won't need to learn how to tally the sales against the cash drawer total. But please, be very vigilant of everything you take in and everything you give out. And if you run short on change, tell me right away. Daddy and I have access to the safe. Oh! That reminds me. I need to get to the bank." We both turned our attention to the doorway as the bell tinkled. John stood inside hunched over his cane.

"Ain't you expected at the bank?" he said.

"Yes, sir. Will you sit in here with Sarah until I get back in case someone comes in? She might have questions."

John gave a sharp nod. "Will do." He ambled to the counter with his cane thumping on the wood floor and sat down behind the candy jars.

After I settled behind the register, I smoothed my dress with my palms and focused on a sweet-smelling tray on the counter that held Adam's rubber chewing gum, Juicy Fruit chewing gum, and Wrigley's Spearmint gum, among others. All the while, I could hear him clicking his teeth on the unlit pipe, and I could feel him staring at me.

"You widowed?" he asked.

I looked at him. "No, sir."

"Spinster then. Like my Rebecca. No, wait—you're still too young."

"What makes you think I'm not married?"

"You're working. Husbands don't like their wives working."

"Ah. You're right. I'm not married."

"I see it in your future though. Not like my daughter. 'Fraid it's too late for her. Her time's about up on that mark."

I despised the whole spinster idea. Men had no problem marrying at any age, so why after a certain age were women considered undesirable? "Perhaps it's in my future, or perhaps not. And who knows, maybe Rebecca will find her true love yet." Although something told me she preferred her independence.

The bell above the door tinkled and a man and woman entered. The dark-haired woman carried a straw basket and kept her gaze low as she hurried toward the canned goods. The attractive man took off his hat and smiled as he walked toward the register.

"Hello there, John," he said.

I stared at him, sensing something familiar.

"Howdy, Nathaniel. This here is Sarah. New to us. She'll be working the register."

"It's a pleasure," Nathaniel said, motioning his hat toward me.

His dark eyes were striking, but his murky green mist caused me to hesitate before responding with a nod and a smile. When I did, I felt queasy. I suddenly realized who they were. He was the handsome gentleman from church and his pretty wife whose misery was so strong, it had caused me to be overcome.

"Gettin' hot out there," John said.

"Yes, sir, it is. My least favorite time of year to be working at the shipyard is coming up."

His wife came around the corner. She placed her basket down and unloaded a small bag of sugar, a can of corn oil, and a spool of black thread.

"Is there anything else you need?" I asked, not knowing yet where to find anything if she did. She shook her head without looking up. "All right. Bear with me for a moment.

I'm brand new at this and you happen to be my first customer."

Nathaniel nudged his wife and laughed. "Aren't we the lucky ones."

I punched the prices on the register keys. "That will be seventy-seven cents." I looked at John for confirmation.

He gave me a nod, so I held out my hand. Instead of placing the coins in my palm, the woman put them on the counter. I scooped them up and counted them, wondering how she could go through life so timidly. I wanted her to look at me so I could put her at ease with a smile. She kept her gaze down.

"Here you are." I held out three pennies.

The woman lifted her coin purse under my hand, and I dropped the coins in. She put the spool of thread in her pocket and placed the other items in her basket before turning on her heels.

Nathaniel smiled. "Y'all have a mighty blessed day."

"Same to you," John said. After the screen door slammed shut, and their steps retreated on the stairs, John looked at me. "She's a little skittish. Like a mouse."

I stood and stared down at them, watching as Nathaniel helped his wife into the wagon. "Do you know them well?"

"Know them enough. Know most everyone. 'Cept you."

"What's her name?"

"Norma. What else you want to know?"

I looked at John. He was grinning. "I'm sorry. It's none of my business."

"Nonsense. Women like to know things. Besides, you're new in town. It's good to get to know people. I should've introduced you. Then again, it wouldn't have mattered. That woman doesn't talk to anyone. Like I said, skittish."

Her behavior may have been skittish, but her presence wasn't. She left me with the same heaviness as on Sunday, and it had something to do with her husband's repulsive mist. I took a deep breath to shed the awful sensation.

AT DINNER, Trudy asked me several questions. I was amused at how eager she was to hear about my time at the market. Every time I'd mention John's name her mist and face brightened. I wanted so badly to ask her directly what had happened between them, and why they hadn't reunited now that neither were no longer married.

# Chapter Sixteen

After my evening lesson with Laura, I finally sat down and wrote Daddy a letter. I was sure he was beside himself with curiosity, if not worry, about whether I'd made it safely and if I'd talked with Katherine.

Excited as I'd been, I started with a detailed account of all the places and people I'd seen on the first train ride in my life. I told him about my impressions of the sights, sounds, and smells of the big city, and very little about prim and proper Mrs. Digby, and even less about her boarding house. I gave only enough information to let him know I was being taken care of, and that I'd even made a friend named Laura.

It was page three before I informed him that I'd found Katherine. Since there was such a lack of acceptance and love from her, I had little to share about our reunion. I assured him she was well and that I would visit her again when the time was right. I ended by telling Daddy that she had read his letter, although I left out what she did with it, and said I hoped someday she and I together would see him again.

The following morning, John was sitting next to Rebecca behind the candy counter. He gave me his squinty-eyed grin, making his unlit pipe bob up and down. Rebecca picked a stack of receipts off the counter and shoved them into a satchel.

"I must leave you with Daddy while I run to an appointment," she said. "I'm meeting our accountant for lunch."

When she left, I sat on her vacated stool. "How are you feeling today?" I asked John.

"Oh, you know. Old, I guess."

I laughed. "And what does 'old' feel like?"

"Achy. Stiff. A little on the tired side. Otherwise, full of spunk and spitfire."

"I'm very glad about the spunk and spitfire part."

"What about you? How are you liking St. Louis so far?"

"Fine, although I haven't seen too much of it yet."

His absorbing look made me feel as if he was reading me. "You plan on staying once you get what you're after?"

"What I'm after? What makes you think I'm after something?"

"I get the sense you came here looking for something. Or someone."

I couldn't believe it. He *was* reading me. "You're right. I came to see my sister."

"And things aren't turning out like you hoped, am I right?"

"You are. How do you know this?"

He hesitated for a while, fumbling with his tobacco pouch. "It's a feeling I got, that's all."

"Do you get feelings a lot? About things you shouldn't know about?"

"Maybe," he said, smiling.

"John Larsen, you are frustrating, do you know that?"

He chuckled. "Yes, ma'am. That, I know."

"If I promise to keep it a secret between you and me, will you tell me an instance when it's happened before? I mean, something you sensed that turned out to be right?"

He looked out the window and I could tell he was thinking

about it. Finally, he said, "There was one time when I was a young boy, I told my buddy Chester to steer clear of a certain area in the woods by a creek we liked to explore. Something seemed downright dangerous to me that day. When he asked me why, I couldn't tell him, so he called me a 'chicken' and he went anyway. Sure enough, a few minutes later I heard him hollering. A water moccasin had bit him. He almost died that day."

"I bet he listened to you after that."

"That he did."

I wanted to hear more, but I decided not to push him. "Thank you for trusting me with that story."

"You bet. Now, you wanna tell me about your sister?"

I internally cringed as all my defenses went up. At the same time, I sensed I could trust John. So, I did. "She was sent to the asylum three years ago."

"Did she belong there?"

"No, she didn't."

He smacked his palm on his knee. "Yep, I thought we had a connection. Sounds like my sister Melanie who had no business being there. Her husband got tired of her and made up some cockamamy story about her losing her mind. He paid a lot of money for a doctor to agree."

"My sister wasn't crazy either."

"What about you?"

"What about me?"

He stared at me for several seconds. "What about your part in it?"

"My part? I'm not sure what you mean." Of course, I knew what he meant, but how much did *he* know what he meant?

The tinkle of the bell interrupted us. An elderly gentleman dressed in coveralls and hunched over a cane was coming through the door. He stopped and strained his neck to see past the brim of his straw hat.

"Who you?" he asked, continuing to make his way to the counter.

"I'm Sarah." The smell of pipe tobacco radiated from his body even though the pipe was nowhere in sight.

"Hmm. Name's Fred. John and I play chess sometimes. Give me some of that Sweet Kentucky behind you."

I plucked a tin of tobacco off the shelf. "Can I get you anything else?"

Fred looked at John as he placed coins on the counter. "Where's our lunch?"

"Rebecca left in a hurry. Forgot to put it out for us, I guess," John said.

Fred looked at me expectantly. "We eat sardines and crackers while we play chess."

"Well then, I think you should have your sardines and crackers," I replied, uncertain as to what he expected me to do.

"I agree," he said, staring.

"Do you want me to fetch your sardines and crackers?" I asked.

"Now you're gettin' it," he said as John laughed.

I stood up and walked out from behind the counter. "It may take me a moment. I don't yet know where everything is."

"Second aisle, top shelf for the crackers. Third aisle, bottom shelf for the sardines," Fred said. "Make sure it's the soda kind of cracker and the sardines are swimming in mustard."

I held up the crackers in my left hand and the sardines in my right. "These?"

Fred cracked a smile. "You done good." He grabbed the items and shoved them into his pockets before steadying himself with the cane. He looked at John. "It's your turn to get the tab, ain't that right?"

"That it is." John looked at me. "There should be a pad of

paper under there with a list of items on credit. Look for my name and write those down."

"Thanks much," Fred said with a wave of his hand. Before stepping out, he looked back at me. "By the way, I like the name Sarah. That was my wife's name. She was a good woman."

John followed but stopped at the door. He turned to me. "What's your sister's name?"

"Katherine Richardson."

He gave me a nod.

I sat there wondering how I happened to meet someone like John with the gift. Someone like me, like Katherine, like Grandma Rose. Then it hit me. I think Grandma Rose led me to where I needed to be at the precise moment I needed to be there, although it wasn't only for the job. I think she wanted me to meet John.

&

A FEW DAYS LATER, I felt like I'd waited long enough to see Katherine again. I left after breakfast, a couple of hours before I had to be at the market, and rode the trolley to Arsenal Street. When I told the nurse I was there to see Katherine, her reply shocked me.

"Katherine Richardson is no longer a patient or an employee here."

"What do you mean? I visited her this past Saturday."

"She left two days ago."

"Did she leave a message for her sister Sarah?"

"No, I'm sorry. She didn't."

It was as if I'd been slapped. "Do you know where she went?"

"It might be in her records, but I'm afraid those are private. I can't give you any more information than what I've already told you."

Katherine was gone and I had no way of finding her.

I walked to the market fighting not to cry. I had no idea if John could see my mist. If he could, he'd see it was hazy and thick. I took a breath and forced a smile as I came up the steps, trying to expunge my sadness, at least for the few hours I was there.

He gave me a sideways look as though he knew I was trying to fool him, but only said a pleasant, "Good morning."

I settled in behind the register and stared hard at all the bright gumballs and gum drops. I closed my eyes while holding their uplifting colors in my mind and smelled the sweetness in the air. *Where have you gone, Katherine?*

As I was leaving for the day, John asked me to sit with him for a minute on the porch. When I did, he asked, "You figure out the puzzle of your sister?"

"Not yet, but it's even worse than before. I stopped by the asylum this morning and she's gone. I have no idea where she is."

"That's a good thing, ain't it? That she's finally out of there?"

"It is, but what am I supposed to do? I don't know how to find her."

"What will you do if you find her?"

"Ask her how I can get her to stop being angry with me."

He flinched and chuckled at the same time. "Why is she angry with you?"

"She asked me to do something for her a long time ago and I didn't do it." I couldn't bring myself to tell him she'd simply asked me to keep quiet.

He stared at me for a few seconds as if waiting for me to continue. When I didn't, he asked, "Are you sure that's the sum of it?"

"What do you mean?"

"I get the feeling there's something heavy in your past

that's impeding your present which means it will impede the future. You need to clear it out of the way."

*There are so many things.* "Do you know what that something is?" I asked.

He stared at me for several seconds more. "Nope, I don't. I'm only telling you the sense I get. I suggest you think on it."

I didn't have to think on it. There was the note, and what a horrible sister I'd been to Katherine by allowing her to take all the direct and indirect punishment it caused. Not to mention the weight of Mildred Bryer and her baby, who were not only buried together in a cemetery plot in Jefferson City but also buried in a dark place deep inside of me.

# Chapter Seventeen

I stared at the slippers on my feet as I reclined in the library chaise. The cup of tea beside me had turned cold, and the book of short stories I'd pulled from the shelf lay face-down on my chest. It was the newest collection by a local writer named Kate Chopin called *A Night in Acadie*. I had read her earlier works and enjoyed them, but my mind wouldn't stay focused on the title story. After four pages, I realized I wasn't retaining anything I'd read. My thoughts were on Katherine, and wondering how to even begin looking for her.

Suddenly Laura walked in. Her pale-purple dress was a perfect match to her lavender scent. She gave me a smile and a curtsey.

"I bring good news. I have decided your lessons are going well enough, that you are demure enough, and that you are pretty enough to meet one of Justin's friends."

I swung my feet to the floor and sat up as my pulse raced with excitement. *I was worthy enough.* "What's his name?"

"Thaddeus Mitchell," she said as she sat. "He's a dream because he's very rich. His family lives on Vandeventer Place. It's one of the most prestigious streets in all of St. Louis. The Mitchells were one of the first in the city to have a telephone in their home and even more impressive, Justin told me Thad's father has an automobile on order! Can you believe that? Perhaps someday the four of us will ride around town, being the envy of everyone. And guess what else? Friday evening at seven o'clock, Justin's parents have offered to treat the four of us to dinner at *Le Fleur*!" She squinted as she looked me over. "First, I'll bring you to Maxine, the woman who coifs my hair on special occasions. And we will shop for a dress and pair of shoes."

"It sounds wonderful." *And expensive.*

Laura grabbed my hands and squealed. "It *will* be wonderful!"

Before retiring to bed, I held my hand mirror while thinking about "rich and smart" Thaddeus Mitchell. My insides gripped at the idea of his status and wealth. I stared at my dark brown eyes, my cheekbones, my dark brown hair. I certainly wasn't as pretty as Laura, but I told myself to believe what she had said, that I was "pretty enough," and set the mirror down.

❧

"Daddy's home because he's not feeling too well this morning," Rebecca said when I arrived at the market the following day. "He woke up with an upset stomach. Probably from all the cookies he ate last night. I tell you, that man could eat an entire dozen if you let him. Anyway, I need to run to a lunch meeting with a couple of members from the Women's Equality Society. That means you'll be left here by yourself for about an hour or so."

"I'll be all right."

"I know you will." She picked up her satchel and headed toward the door. "If something comes up and you don't have an answer for it, tell whoever it is to come back at twelve-thirty. Oh, and while I'm gone, Daddy's housekeeper might come to pick up some bicarbonate. That should settle his stomach."

Later, I heard footfalls on the wooden steps followed by the creak of the screen door. The hats of the two ladies standing in front of me at the counter blocked my view of who had entered. "You ladies have a good afternoon," I said as I handed one her change.

A moment later, Katherine came around the corner holding a bottle of bicarbonate. When she saw me, she jerked her head.

"Katherine!" I rushed out from behind the counter.

She looked perplexed, then irritated. "What are you doing here?"

"I work here," I said, stepping closer. I smiled despite her cloudy mist. "I'm so glad you came. I—"

"I think I understand," she said.

"Understand what?"

"Why John Larsen came to the asylum and offered me a job as his housekeeper. I thought it was because I'd known his sister. It's because you put him up to it."

I shook my head. "I did no such thing. He asked me my sister's name and I told him. I never told him to go to the asylum. I found out only yesterday you'd left. I had no idea where you went."

Despite her displeasure, I was touched, and thankful, that John had gone to such trouble for me.

She lifted her chin. "He sent me for—"

"Bicarbonate. Rebecca told me he has a stomachache."

"He told me to put it on credit." She turned toward the door.

"I need to say something before you go."

She held the screen door open and looked at me. I waited for her to close it and come closer, but she didn't.

"I know you're still angry. The reason I broke my promise to you and told Daddy that night was because I felt like you might get hurt, or worse, and I was afraid for you. I did it because I love you."

She looked out at the street below. "I was willing to get hurt if it meant saving a life. You took that choice away from me. If you had truly loved me, you would have done what I asked you to do despite the consequences, allowing me to do what I needed to do."

"I was *young*, Katherine. Young and foolish."

"Your foolishness came with a great cost. We'll never know if Mrs. Bryer and her baby would have lived if I'd been able to get there, but something tells me they would have. Do you know how much guilt weighs on my heart and mind because of that?"

"I have guilt about it too. I swear I do. And I know Daddy does too."

Her brows lifted. "He told you that?"

"Not directly. But he quit working for Donald Bryer after you left."

Katherine rolled her eyes. "Do you expect me to praise him for that?" She walked out. I flinched when the screen door slammed.

When Rebecca returned, I told her John's housekeeper had stopped by.

"Oh, good," she said. "I haven't had much time to get to know her yet. I thought she might be about your age."

"She's a year and a half older."

"Oh," she laughed. "I guess you got to know one another."

"I've known her my whole life. Katherine's my sister."

"She's your sister? The one you were hoping to reconcile with?"

"Yes. Apparently, your father wanted to help me out."

"Are you upset he butted into your personal business? 'Cause if so, I'll tell him to—"

"Not at all. I'm thankful. I just hope she'll let go of her anger instead of letting go of me."

That afternoon, I sat at my writing desk and wrote Katherine a note. I asked that she try her best to forgive the young girl I was at the time, and to honor Grandma Rose's wish that we be reunited. And to add even more persuasion, I went so far as to ask Mrs. Digby for a piece of ribbon and tied a bow around the box that held Grandma's rose necklace. *I brought this with me as a gift to you*, I wrote. *I know Grandma would want you to have it.*

The following morning, I walked up the stairs to the market, smiling at John as I reached the top. "Are you feeling better today?" I asked.

"Yes, ma'am. I had sugar belly. Ever had that? That's when you can't seem to stop eating cookies or cake or whatever sweetness is before you. It's not till later when the pain starts up you regret your weakness. You vow to never do it again. Till the next time."

I laughed. "I've not had that affliction yet, thankfully."

"You've got self-control. That's a good thing."

"Yes, but not only do you have a sugar weakness, you sure are sneaky."

John chuckled. "Nah. I saw an opportunity to help, and I took it."

I thanked him for giving Katherine a reason to leave the asylum by offering her a job. "Katherine said she knew your sister. Is she still there?"

"No, Melanie died a little over a year ago. Afterward, I went back to thank the staff and the residents that had been so kind to her all those years. Your sister was one of them. When you told me her name, I realized who you've been talking about."

"Whether she decides to forgive me or not, I'll always be grateful to you."

"She'll come around. Give her time."

"Will you give this to her?" I handed him the note and the box tied with a pink ribbon.

"You bet," he replied.

A little later, I heard John say "Howdy" to someone who had walked up the stairs. Seconds later, the skittish Norma Malone walked in with her brown mist and shoulders hunched.

"Let me know if I can help you find anything," I said.

She didn't respond. I stood up and looked out the window to see Nathaniel standing on the porch, talking to John about the "God-awful humidity." I sat back down and waited for her.

I heard a bag being lifted, followed by the shuffle of her soles on the wooden floor. A can was slid from the shelf and set back down, and then more shuffling. From the sound of her shoes, I could tell she wore low-heeled boots; probably the most unfeminine, unfashionable, yet practical shoe. When she rounded the aisle and headed my way, my arm hair prickled. I looked at her feet. She was indeed wearing scuffed and dusty black lace-up boots, the leather so worn I could make out the lines of her toes.

"Did you find what you needed?" I tried to sound cheerful even though my heart was pounding.

She gave me a slight nod but didn't look up. She reached into her basket and took out a bag of dried lima beans, a bag of cornmeal, and a box of soap flakes.

"That comes to a dollar and forty-nine cents," I said after ringing up the items.

She looked at me and quickly looked down again. It lasted only a second, but enough for me to see the pain in her eyes. It was so profound I needed to cry. She opened her coin purse and counted out the money. She slid it over to me.

"Mr. Larsen told me your name is Norma."

"That's right." Her voice was a touch rusty, like she hadn't used it in a while.

"It's a pleasure to meet you, Norma. I'm Sarah."

She glanced at me again, and back to the counter. "It's nice to meet you." Suddenly the bell above the door chimed and she looked over her shoulder. Nathaniel entered. Both of their mists clouded as they looked at one another.

He tipped his hat at me and smiled. "Miss Sarah." He looked at Norma. "Looks like you got what we needed. Let's go." She placed her groceries in her handbasket and hurried out.

I walked over to the screen door feeling every bit of her misery. Norma gave me a fleeting look over her shoulder. As they rode away, an image appeared in my mind, of a small clapboard house in desperate need of painting, an uneven stone walkway, and weeds in the flowerbed. It was their house, I felt it.

I couldn't wait to tell Katherine I'd had my first vision.

# Chapter Eighteen

Laura came to my room that night. "I told Mrs. Digby that your lessons have gone wonderfully, especially the way you've mostly overcome your country accent. Remember, do not pronounce a one-syllable word using two syllables. That's a sign of a poor education."

"Yes, ma'am." I said, careful to pronounce it *mam* instead of *may-am* like I was used to.

"I'm over the moon about tomorrow! Aren't you?"

My stomach had been in knots all evening. "Yes, but I'm mostly nervous."

"You have absolutely no reason to be. Thad is a gentleman. Now get some sleep. It won't do to have circles under your eyes. I'll see you at the market at two o'clock sharp."

I laid awake thinking about the very rich, high-society gentleman who had agreed to meet and dine with me. Me, Sarah Richardson, who grew up living in leased houses, cleaning chicken coops, and wearing clothes that had been worn by my sister first.

*For one evening, you too will be high-society*, I told myself. *And maybe fall in love.*

&.

"That Thad fellow is not for you," John said as the two of us sat on the market's porch. For some reason John was holding a harmonica instead of a pipe and I was knitting even though in real life I don't know how. But that's how dreams are.

"Why isn't he for me?" I asked, keeping focused on my clicking needles.

"There's someone else waiting. Neither of you know it yet."

I placed my knitting on my lap and looked at him. "And who might that be?"

"Can't say."

"Or don't want to say?"

John simply smiled and commenced to play the harmonica.

I lay in bed Friday morning thinking about the dream and the unease it brought about Thad Mitchell. Before I got out of bed, I took a deep breath and said a prayer. *Please let this evening go well.*

The market was so busy it was the perfect distraction. It wasn't until the time came for me to leave that my nerves resurfaced. I said goodbye to Rebecca and stepped onto the porch where Laura was chatting with John.

"Why yes, I will certainly tell Trudy you said hello," Laura said.

John gave a nod and tipped his hat as a gesture of thanks.

*He still loves her.* I smiled at the thought.

"I can hardly stand the anticipation!" Laura said as she rushed over to me. "This evening is going to be magnificent. You two are going to fall madly in love, I just know it."

I glanced again at John who seemed to have given me the most imperceptible shake of the head. His pipe bobbed as he grinned.

"You're pretty certain," I replied.

"Yes, I have confidence in my matchmaking ability." She giggled, taking my arm and leading me down the stairs to the walkway.

We took a trolley to Market and Broadway where we spent an hour shopping for an updated and fashionable dress, as well as a pair of shoes that were not as narrow as my Sunday shoes. Although I loved the lace-covered dress and the heeled shoes Laura picked out for me, I wasn't the least bit happy about the price I had to pay for them. It totaled almost two weeks of income I made at the market.

"Are you sure I need to pay someone to style my hair?" I asked as we headed to the home of a woman named Maxine. She charged one dollar, which would come out of my rent budget.

"This is a very special night and Maxine does fine work," Laura said as we strolled the upper end of Fourth Street. "You like my hair, don't you? She'll be able to style yours much the same. We'll be like sisters. One blonde and one brunette. One with blue eyes, one with brown. Do you have a sister?"

"I do."

"Mrs. Digby didn't tell me you had a sister."

"Mrs. Digby never asked me about siblings," I said.

"I envy you. I'm an only child. I was lonely growing up. That's why I cling so much to my girlfriends. Is your sister older or younger? What's her name?"

"Katherine is a year and a half older."

"She must not live here, otherwise you would live with her instead of Mrs. Digby."

How far did I want to go with my discretion? Would she eventually meet Katherine now that she was no longer at the asylum? "She lives here. Unfortunately, we aren't as close as I'd like to be."

"Maybe I can help you. Introduce us and I'll bring the two of you closer."

I couldn't imagine Laura and Katherine in the same room, let alone enjoying each other's company. Their dispositions were much too different. "Maybe someday."

❧

As I sat in the chair allowing Maxine to twist and pin my hair this way and that, I thought about what Katherine would think of such extravagance. Something told me she would think it was wasteful and shallow.

Laughter brought me out of my thoughts, and I watched Laura conversing with another young woman. I was amused at Laura's exaggerated gestures and facial expressions as she spoke. She was so endearing and her mist so bright, it made me thankful to be in her presence. I'd never met anyone like her. How I wished I was as engaging and beautiful as she was.

When Maxine finished with my hair, she grabbed a compact of face powder. "May I?"

I'd never had an opportunity to wear cosmetics. I nodded. She patted my face with a large white puff causing a cloud of powder to fly in all directions. I sneezed.

"I'm very sorry about that." She grabbed her fan and flapped it all around. She then brought out a pat of lip rouge.

I was pleased it wasn't a shocking shade of red I'd seen a few women wearing lately. It was much more subdued—pale pink. When Maxine finished, she handed me a mirror.

Laura rushed over and squealed. "Beautiful! Just beautiful!"

*Yes, for the first time in my life I feel beautiful.*

❧

"Knock on my door when you change into your dress," Laura requested as we reached the top of the stairs. "And be extra careful not to muss your hair."

"I'll be careful." After closing my bedroom door, I laid out my new dress and placed my new shoes on the bed. The salesman had called them "heeled sandals." I'd never owned such lovely or expensive clothing. I could have stared at them for hours. I unlaced and pulled off my boots and eagerly stepped out of my pale blue dress, leaving it like a puddle on the floor. I carefully slid into my new sea-green gown overlaid with cream-colored lace and stepped into my sandals. I walked over to the mirror and admired my reflection. *Just beautiful.*

Laura caught her breath when she opened her door a few moments later. She took a step back to take in my full form. "Exquisite!" She grabbed my hand and led me into her room. "Hold your breath and close your eyes."

I did what she asked and then heard a whisper of a spray and then smelled the perfume she'd misted. I immediately sneezed and waved my hands to disperse the scent. "Sorry," I croaked, before sneezing again. I then blew my nose as delicately as I could.

"Here," she said, tapping my face with more powder. She stepped back and inspected me. "Lovely. The ladies *must* see you like this. They won't recognize you."

When we reached the bottom step, we heard voices coming from the library. Laura stopped me from following her in with a hand gesture. The women quit talking when she opened the door and stepped in.

"How do I look?" Laura asked. Through the crack in the door, I saw her twirl around once and curtsey.

"Beautiful! The gentlemen must be taking you somewhere fancy," Mrs. Digby said.

"They are. And if you think I look beautiful, just look at Sarah."

I took my cue and walked in. Trudy placed her hand over her mouth and Mrs. Digby stood up.

"Twirl," Laura whispered, making a circle motion with her finger. It seemed silly, but I twirled as instructed.

"Sarah, my goodness. Look at your hair!" Trudy said.

"And your dress! It's breathtaking." Mrs. Digby walked closer to inspect it. She looked at Laura. "Very well done, dear."

"Yes, I do good work," Laura said with a smirk.

"Who is the lucky fellow?" Trudy asked.

"Thaddeus Mitchell," Laura responded proudly.

"Oh!" Mrs. Digby said. "Thad Mitchell is a catch indeed, Sarah. His family is very wealthy. I hope you can make a sound impression tonight."

I looked down at my new gown. "I hope so too."

"We will be upstairs when Justin and Thad arrive." Laura turned to go.

"Wait," I said. "Don't you have something to tell Trudy?"

She gave me a quizzical look. "I don't think so."

"I overheard John Larsen tell you to tell her hello."

Laura swished her hand in dismissal. "John Larsen says hello." She turned on her heels and walked out.

I looked at Trudy. Her cheeks and mist blushed. "Oh," she uttered.

"Let's have some tea," Mrs. Digby said to her.

As we walked back upstairs, I asked, "Why do we have to sit up here? It's more comfortable in the parlor."

Laura stopped at the top and turned to me. "Oh, Sarah. You don't know much about first impressions, do you?"

Heat rushed to my cheeks. I didn't want her to think I was still backward in any way. "Yes, of course I do. I guess I'm not exactly sure how being upstairs when they arrive will impress them more than sitting in the parlor or the library."

Laura clicked her tongue and shook her head. "It's called a grand entrance. You must make a riveting first appearance. Turn for a second." She placed her hands on my shoulders and twisted me around so I could look down at the vestibule. "Imagine Justin and Thad standing below patiently waiting when all of a sudden, the two most elegant and attractive women in all of Missouri appear at the top of the stairs. A vision of two goddesses. They'll think they are dreaming."

A laugh escaped me. It seemed silly.

Laura pouted and swatted me on the shoulder. "Trust me." She continued toward her room. "Come. You'll sit with me until it's time."

Laura perched on the edge of her bed, and I sat in the only chair in the room with my back to her vanity mirror.

"Let's make sure you know which utensils to use for each course of the meal." She once again went over what a proper setting looked like, where to place my napkin, how to delicately dab the corners of my mouth, and how to hold my glass with my little finger extended. "And don't eat too much. It's not feminine to eat too quickly or too much."

I was bored with the etiquette lesson, so I changed topics, choosing one I knew she'd prattle on about until it was time to leave. "Tell me about your wedding plans."

Her eyes lit up. "It will be a royal church wedding like they have in London or Paris. Mrs. Digby is beside herself with excitement over the preparations for the bridal luncheon. I'm the decision-maker, of course, and any little detail has to be approved by me."

I'd never met anyone who was wed in a church. Most people I knew got married in someone's home. "Magnificent," I said, pleased that I sounded as if I used that word often.

"It will be! My wedding dress is a mauve silk overlayed with lace. It's copied straight from a Paris magazine. I wish I had my wedding dress here to show you but my mother thought it best for her to keep it. And she's probably right. I would be trying it on every day if I had it with me." She stood up pretending to hold a bouquet of flowers and began to walk as I assume a bride would, down an imaginary aisle. Suddenly there was a knock on the door. Laura rushed over and opened it.

"The gentlemen have arrived," Trudy whispered.

Laura grabbed my hand and led me to the bed and sat down. I was confused.

"What are we doing?"

"We're waiting," she said.

"Why? They're here."

"I know, but we must make them wait."

"Ah. The build-up to the grand entrance."

She smiled and nodded. "Of course."

It was clear Laura had high expectations and would take it as a personal failure if things didn't go well between me and Thad. I hoped for her sake, and mine, that our attraction to one another would be everything she wished for.

# Chapter Nineteen

<br>

While we waited, Laura made me practice how to gracefully walk, and by how many steps, *behind* her. She insisted I be shielded from Thad's view until the last second when, upon reaching the stairs, I would step around to her left. We would pause for a reaction, and then "gently glide down" the staircase side by side. I had to ask what it meant to "glide." She pretended to lightly touch the banister with her right hand, while elegantly holding out her left like royalty, and took deliberate steps so as not to get her feet tangled in the hem of her gown.

"They will watch in awe as we descend with poise."

I waited for her to laugh but she didn't. So, I did.

She gave me a hurtful look. "Be serious, Sarah. Please. You must."

"Of course. I'm sorry." I followed her out.

My breath became shallow the closer we came to the stair-well. I hoped Thad was as handsome as Laura described. Will he believe I'm as sophisticated as I've practiced to be?

I made sure I was two steps behind Laura and watched her feet very carefully so I would know when to stop. When she did, I lifted my chin and stepped to her left. The only thing she hadn't told me was whether to smile or to look indifferent, so I glanced at her. She smiled and therefore, so did I.

I looked at the men below and my breath caught. The gentleman I'd met under The Allegorical Window at Union Station stood at the bottom of the stairs. Even though I still couldn't see his mist, I could certainly see the color of his blue eyes. He stared at me so intently my heart beat out of rhythm. I knew he remembered me. I was grateful for the handrail because my legs had weakened, and as I walked down the stairs it was as if I truly was gliding. Out of all the men in St. Louis, I couldn't believe Laura picked him for me! There was no other explanation than fate.

"Good evening, gentlemen," Laura said.

"Good evening," they both replied.

The shorter one with brown eyes stepped forward and handed me a small bouquet of daisies tied with a yellow satin ribbon. "I'm Thad Mitchell. I'm pleased to meet you."

His orange-yellow mist told me he was self-assured. A picture of Lady Justice flashed through my mind, followed by an image of him standing on the steps of a courthouse. Another vision. Unlike the one I'd had of Norma's house, I could at least find out if this one was accurate.

I glanced at Laura as her fiancé kissed the top of her hand. A flush of heat overcame me. Why would I have such a strong reaction toward someone not meant for me? I was suddenly thankful for the spritz of perfume Laura had sprayed, as well as the floral scented underarm pads I'd purchased to place in my new dress. I quickly turned my full attention to Thad and smiled in order to regain my composure.

"The pleasure is mine," I said.

Laura chatted ceaselessly the entire way and I was grateful as it allowed me to calm myself, as well as recover from the disconcerting effect meeting her fiancé had on me.

When we walked into the restaurant, I stared up at the

copper ceiling and sparkling chandeliers, the tables covered in white linen and the crystal water goblets. I wondered if Momma and Daddy would have ever imagined me in a place like this.

Justin's parents graciously sat at a table next to ours, allowing the four of us to enjoy each other's company. His father was a handsome man and his mist was sky blue, the color of his eyes. His mother was a striking woman with a lovely purple mist. It made me all the more curious why I couldn't see their son's.

Throughout the meal, I carefully watched and emulated what Laura had taught me earlier, as she held her glass with an extended pinky and delicately dabbed the corners of her mouth after every sip or bite. When I began to feel more comfortable, I stopped paying such close attention and instead watched Justin's facial expressions as he listened to her talk about their wedding. I wondered if he was as excited about it as she was. He smiled a bit, which was a good sign, and laughed occasionally. Every so often though, when his look turned serious, I sensed discontentment.

"You're going to law school, Thad, is that right?" I asked when our main course arrived. As the words left my lips, I realized that what I'd seen in my mind when we were introduced, he hadn't admitted, and neither had Laura, but it was too late for me to do anything other than act as if one of them had.

His eyes widened in surprise. He finished chewing a bite of spinach salad and wiped his mouth before answering. "As a matter of fact, yes, I will be." He looked at Justin. "I've been accepted to Harvard Law."

"How wonderful, Thad! Why didn't you tell me, Justin?" Laura asked.

Justin looked at Thad curiously. "Because I didn't know."

Thad beamed. "I received my acceptance letter today. I was going to make an announcement over dessert."

Justin stuck his hand across the table and Thad shook it. "Well done, my friend!" He picked up his water glass and stood. "Here's to my dear friend, Thad. May Harvard be good to you and may you have a very prosperous future."

"Hear, hear!" Justin's father said from the next table. "Congratulations, Thad. Your parents must be so proud."

As we each clinked our water glasses, the waiter rushed over. "May I offer you something else to drink?"

"Champagne," Justin's father said.

Laura squealed. "Oh! My favorite! You like champagne, don't you Sarah?"

"Of course," I said, although I had no idea what it was.

A few moments later, a silver bucket arrived with a corked bottle wrapped in a white cloth, and six tall, skinny glasses. I watched carefully how Mrs. Conroy and Laura held theirs by the delicate stem and sipped the gold-colored liquid ever so gently. As I lifted the glass to my mouth, the bubbles tickled my nose, and I could feel myself tense up to sneeze. *Please don't*, I begged, as if it was something I could command. Thankfully, the sensation dissipated. I held the cold sip in my mouth, enjoying the almost magical feel of the bubbles snapping and crackling. It burned ever so slightly as it slid down my throat, though it didn't last long, and I was left with a sweet, yet tart, taste on my tongue. I did indeed like champagne.

The conversation switched topics many times during the main course, but Harvard came back around as our chocolate mousse dessert and coffee were set before us.

"Something curious has dawned on me," Laura said. I steeled myself, as whatever she had to say was directed at me. "How did you know Thad was going to study law?"

"Oh, a lucky guess, I suppose," I said, upset for being so careless, yet also curious. What I saw was not only true, but what was to come—a future event. My gift was strengthening.

&

"So, what do you think?" Laura whispered after we said our goodbyes to the gentlemen. The ladies were in their rooms for the night, so we quietly made our way upstairs.

"He's handsome, smart, and very nice," I whispered back.

"Do you want to see him again?"

"I would, but he's leaving for Harvard," I reminded her.

"He's not leaving for several weeks. That's enough time for the two of you to get engaged, for heaven's sake."

When we reached the door to her bedroom, I said, "I think we should leave it to destiny."

She placed her hands on her hips. "Destiny doesn't always deliver what we want."

"Maybe not, but it usually delivers what's best."

I lay in bed that night unable to sleep. I replayed the entire evening in my mind, envisioning the interior décor of the restaurant, the table settings, the delicious food and the almost magical champagne. I was in awe of all of it. Especially that I'd had the most wonderful evening with a handsome and kind gentleman. Although it wasn't Thad I was thinking of.

# Chapter Twenty

When I finished my Saturday shift at the market, I walked onto the porch where John was drinking coffee and reading the *St. Louis Post-Dispatch*. As he looked at me over his newspaper an image of him, young and in a military uniform, flashed in my mind. I then saw a young Trudy writing a letter and crying.

The visions were becoming more frequent and although I'd verified the one I'd had of Thad and law school, I was confused about it. If what I saw of Norma's house was present-day, and Thad's was what would come in the future, what of John being younger? Was it possible to see things in the past, present, *and* future? How I wished I could talk with Grandma Rose.

"Were you ever in the military?" I asked John.

He folded the newspaper and set it aside. "Union army. Can't say it was the best time in my life. I lost more than the hearing in my left ear. Why do you ask? Thinking about joining? You're a little late if you were wantin' to go to Cuba."

I laughed. "No, sir. I don't think the military accepts women."

"You're right. Someday they might, though. If Rebecca and the rest of those marching gals get their way."

I thought of Mrs. Digby's disdain for the Women's Equality Society. I took a seat in the empty rocker next to his. "What's your opinion of the Suffrage Movement?"

"I think it's past time for women to vote and everything else they want to do," he said. "It's shameful it hasn't happened yet. I'd put money on the fact that my daughter is more intelligent than any man who walks in here."

"Even you?" I asked, smiling.

"Even me." He smiled back. "So, you gonna tell me why you asked about my military service?"

I felt off kilter admitting it, but I knew John was safe. "I saw it. In my mind. I saw you in a uniform when you were younger."

He drew on his pipe and stared at me for a few seconds. "A lot of young men fought in the war. Lots of 'em died too. I was one of the lucky ones."

"That's true. If that's all I saw it would be an assumption, I guess."

His forehead crinkled as he raised his eyebrows. "What else did you see?"

I looked down at my shoes. "I saw Gertrude Gaines. She was writing you a letter."

He ran his fingers through his hair. "Did you, now?"

It was clear I'd rattled him. "Yes, sir." I hoped he wouldn't ask me any more than that. I didn't want to admit I'd sensed sadness and saw lots of tears.

"Hmm. How do you like that? I thought you might be a seer."

"So is Katherine."

"I figured as much. Oh, I gave her your note and the little box like you asked. She seemed pleased, if that helps any."

"I'm glad. I have questions for her, but maybe you can help me." I told him about my new ability, seeing images in my mind like Katherine had been able to do since she was young, and asked why it took so long for me.

"I think it might strengthen as you get older, though I don't know all the answers on how this works," he said. "I do know that you have to be open to it. 'Cause you could pray on it to shut it down if you wanted to."

"Maybe that's why it took longer for me. Daddy always wanted me to shut it down and I wanted to please him, but I wanted to please Grandma Rose too. She wanted me to nurture it."

John gave me a serious look. "And how do *you* feel about it?"

I sat for a few moments deciding how I truly felt. "I think I want to embrace it," I finally said. And I meant it.

"Well then, do. Trust yourself and your instincts. But think hard before you act on them."

"You sound like my grandma."

John grinned. "I bet she was a good woman."

"Yes, sir, she was."

He gave me a nod. "Say, how'd it go at dinner last night?"

"Thad and I got along, I think."

"Is that the Mitchell boy?"

"Yes, sir. Do you know him?"

"I know of him. His family seems like decent people. You like him?"

"A little." I noticed a change in John's eyes when I said this, and I remembered the dream where he said Thad wasn't for me. I hoped he'd say something about what he sensed about the two of us, but he didn't. "I'm not sure, though, that we'll see one another again."

"Is that based on a feeling or a particular reason?" he asked.

"He's been accepted to Harvard Law. He'll be leaving soon."

"Hmm. I sure hope he likes it better than I did."

I leaned in. "You studied law?"

"Yes, ma'am. I was a lawyer for a few years. Nearly sucked the life out of me. Almost worse than the war. I don't like to think about it much."

Sensations were flooding me, and I was hit by a wave of nausea. "It's because of your gift isn't it?" I couldn't help saying it. I had to know.

"Yep," he said, tapping his nose. "I'm sure you've experienced the darker side of our ability. Like when you feel other people's suffering or their deceit. It wears you down after a while. There came a point when I stopped seeing the light in anything. That's when I knew it was time for me to quit."

"Being around so many criminals made you sick, didn't it?"

"More than that. It degraded my soul. Being able to sense a victim's fear or to see their last moments in my mind stirred up a hatred and fire in me that I didn't know existed, for those who would do such things. I didn't like it and I didn't want it."

"What about all the good that could have come from you knowing things about the criminals that no one else knew? Couldn't you have used that to prove them guilty?"

The lines on John's face looked deeper and his eyes sadder. It was obvious my nosy curiosity was dredging up misery. "I did exactly that. I thought my gift could make me some sort of savior on a large scale. But when you can see even more than others can of human evil, it starts to affect your heart and your mind. I had to make a choice: to keep delving day after day into the foulness of mankind or save myself."

"You'd still help someone in need, wouldn't you?" I wanted to believe he hadn't completely turned his back on his responsibilities.

John rested his forearms on his knees, cupping his pipe in his hands. "I'd have to think it through first, then I might. I haven't completely let go. We're obligated sometimes, you and me."

# Chapter Twenty-One

As we walked to Sunday Service, Laura chattered on, seemingly oblivious to the humidity that was already quite high at that early hour. All I could think about was how miserable I would soon be, sitting in the church for over an hour with sweat streaking down my temples and my underarms. But more than that, it was the odor of concentrated perspiration from so many people in the room that I hated. The sprig of lavender I'd pinned to my collar would not be strong enough to overcome the fetid odor.

When we arrived, Laura left to find Justin and the three of us ladies slid into a fifth-row pew. I reached for the hymnal sticking out from the holder in front of me and began waving it in front of my face.

Mrs. Digby leaned toward me. "We must get you a fan."

I nodded and watched as Norma and Nathaniel Malone slid in two rows in front of us. He smiled and whispered hello to everyone he looked at, while she kept her dark eyes downward, making no eye contact with anyone. Their mists were the same as the previous times I'd seen them—his murky green, hers brown; his contrasting a jovial personality, while hers, a bleak and perfect match.

"Do you know them?" I whispered to Mrs. Digby. I wondered if her love of gossip would enlighten me more than John's few words about them.

"That's Nathaniel and Norma Malone. She's very shy, although he makes up for it. He's very sociable. And quite attractive too, don't you agree?" I nodded. "But he works at the shipyard."

For such a short word, "but" told me everything I needed to know about how Mrs. Digby felt about them.

"They live in the rural part of town and there are other churches closer to their home." She rolled her eyes and shook her head. "I can only assume the reason they worship here is to try and mix with the upper class."

Throughout the service, I tried to ignore the oppressive sensations that always seemed to nag me when Norma was nearby. It was only when the service ended and I walked out the door, that the heaviness began to dissipate.

As Mrs. Digby, Trudy, and I started for home, I heard my name being called. I turned and saw Laura and Justin making their way through the crowd. My breath became fitful when he smiled at me, the same way it had at the train station and when I looked at him from the top of the stairs.

"I'm glad we caught you," Laura said. "Justin and Thad would like the two of us to join them for a walk by the lake this afternoon. You'll come, won't you?"

"Surely you'll accept," Mrs. Digby said.

"I will," I replied.

Justin grinned and quickly looked away.

"We will see you gentlemen at three o'clock," Laura said to him.

He gave her a nod and tipped his hat to us. "Ladies."

My breathing calmed as he walked away. *Stop it!* I scolded myself. *He is not for you.*

I WAS grateful for the breeze later that afternoon as the four of us strolled along the park's lake. Thad bent down and grabbed a couple of flat stones. He flicked one out toward the water, and we watched as it skipped along the surface.

"Nicely done," I said.

He handed me a stone. "You try."

I threw it sideways, similar to how he had thrown his. It hit the water with a *plunk!* and vanished. They all laughed.

"Show me again," I requested.

He held a stone flat with his forefinger and thumb and flicked his wrist. It skipped four times before disappearing. "That is how it's done," he said with a smile.

I was determined to succeed and after three more tries, I finally made one bounce along the surface a few times.

"That's it!" he said.

Justin and Laura joined in, both successful at every attempt. As I bent down to pick up a stone, my attention was drawn to a large crowd in the distance. It looked as if a parade was coming our way.

As the masses came closer, I could see it was a group of women walking in rows of three, perhaps six rows deep. The ladies in the first row held a banner announcing the St. Louis Women's Equality Society. There were women on bicycles on either side of those who marched. Behind the group were several men. Their mists were muddled and dark.

"Put a stop to this ludicrous show!" one man shouted. A few pumped their fists.

"Get back to the kitchen!" some yelled.

Laura gasped. "They're wearing bloomers!"

The women on bicycles were indeed wearing bloomers. There was a heaviness in my chest as they drew closer, seeing the cloudy mists and sensing the intolerance coming from many who were following. As they passed by, my eyes widened in surprise when I saw Rebecca and Katherine walking side-by-side, their arms linked. They looked at me. Rebecca smiled and lifted her hand to wave. As I tried to wave back, Laura slapped my hand down. I looked at her, horrified. With her lips tight, she scolded me with her eyes and shook her head.

When the parade had passed, I walked to the edge of the water and flicked a stone. I was pleased that it skipped several times before disappearing, but I was still shocked and embarrassed at Laura's reaction. Had Rebecca and Katherine seen our interaction? Had Justin?

"May I?" Thad stood beside me.

I looked into his brown eyes and down at the crook of his arm. I nodded, slipping my arm through his.

"Do you believe the gall of those women?" Laura asked as she and Justin joined us.

"You don't agree with their cause?" I knew what Mrs. Digby thought, but she was old and old-fashioned.

"In our circle, a woman's husband and her children are the most important things in her life. Not voting, not working outside the home or whatever it is they're wanting," she said.

My face heated as I thought of my job at the market, realizing she was harboring a distaste for something I needed to do to get by.

"Our friends refer to those marching women as the Spinster and Old Maid Society," Laura said with a laugh. "That should tell you everything you need to know."

Thad laughed too. My throat tightened. I suddenly wanted to be anywhere else.

"That's not completely true," Justin said. "My mother has a few friends in that society. They are happily married and have children. Their husbands support the effort."

Laura's cheeks reddened. It was clear she wasn't pleased Justin had disagreed with her. "Regardless, you must admit, screaming for equal rights is not at all feminine. And neither are their bloomers, for goodness' sake! Please let us talk about something else. New York, for instance." She pulled Justin's arm and began walking. "I simply can't wait for our honeymoon. Justin and I have a suite reserved at The Waldorf, which is one of the most extravagant hotels in New York City! Aren't you both beside yourselves with envy?"

"Indeed," Thad said. "I was in New York once when I was a child. I remember how fascinated I was with all the tall buildings and how loud it was on the street. And the number of people. My mother kept a grip on my hand, afraid I'd get swept away in the crowd."

"I've never been there so this is a dream come true," Laura said. "And I hope you're ready, Mr. Conroy, because I plan to shop, shop, shop."

Justin sighed heavily while shaking his head but gave her a playful smile. "Whatever makes you happy, Laura."

I wondered which was more authentic, Justin's sigh or his smile.

Laura continued to rattle off a list of her sightseeing musts and as I stared at her profile, amused at her excitement, I noticed her mist darken and turn hazy. I could see sweat beads forming on her hairline and upper lip. She plucked a fan from her dress pocket and began fanning herself as she talked as if it was a minor flush, yet her mist revealed something more.

When she finally took a breath, I said, "Perhaps you should slow down," more teasing than serious as far as anyone else was concerned. "You're going to burst with anticipation before your wedding day even gets here."

Laura laughed. "I guess I can't wait for my new life to begin."

I watched her carefully for the next several minutes, until whatever it was that caused her mist to darken began to dissipate.

"Are you feeling all right?" I whispered to her when we returned home.

Her smile flattened as she looked at me. "Yes. Why do you ask?"

"You seem a little tired," I lied.

"I guess I am a little tired. There are so many wedding plans to tend to."

"I'm sure you had a lovely afternoon," Mrs. Digby said when we walked through the front door. "Thad is a promising catch, Sarah. You should count yourself lucky."

"Yes, ma'am. I do," I said, although his laughter at Laura's remark about the women's society disappointed me. What would he think if he knew my sister was a member, and where she'd been for the past three years?

# Chapter Twenty-Two

On Monday morning, Rebecca brought up seeing me at the park but acted as though she hadn't noticed Laura's rude reaction to my wave.

"I guess you saw how our megaphones and bicycles cause a stir. Our goal is to draw as much attention as we can. If we were demure, our opposers would talk and walk right over us. Maybe you'd like to join? We're having a meeting tonight at my house at eight o'clock."

"I wish I could, but … well, there are a couple of reasons I can't. Katherine and I haven't yet healed our relationship, so I'm sure she wouldn't be pleased if I showed up. Another reason is that Mrs. Digby doesn't approve of the society. I should respect her views even if I don't agree with them, at least until I find other accommodations." It was a truthful answer, but there was much more to my hesitation. I was barely on the cusp of being introduced into Laura's circle and I wasn't yet ready to disrupt that.

"If there's anything I can do to help you and Katherine, please ask," Rebecca said. "And as far as Mrs. Digby, she's set in her ways as many older generation women are. But I have hope that things will eventually change, regardless of their viewpoint."

Her remark brought to mind what Grandma Rose once said when I naively told her I wished I was normal. She said normal can't exist because people and the world are in a constant state of change. If what Grandma Rose said was true, the change Rebecca was referring to might be inevitable.

At two o'clock I stepped onto the porch. "Would you kindly tell me where you live?" I asked John. The urge to see Katherine had been getting stronger all day.

"You gonna visit your sister?"

"Yes, sir."

I walked three blocks to John and Rebecca's residence and held my breath as I knocked.

"How can I help—oh," Katherine said when she opened the door.

I exhaled when I noticed she was wearing Grandma's necklace. "May I come in?"

"I'm busy."

"Maybe I can help you," I said, ignoring her blatant rudeness.

She gave me a tight smile and stepped aside. "I was about to dust the parlor."

I could have picked a better time. Dusting was my least favorite chore and she knew that very well. Despite that I'd rather scrub an endless pile of clothes against the washboard than dust, I took the feather duster from her hand and began as if it was the most pleasurable task I could have offered to do.

She cleared a side table and began wiping it with a rag. "Thank you for this, by the way." She lifted her hand to her neck and gently tugged the rose pendant back and forth along the chain as Grandma used to do. "You could have kept it for yourself."

"I wanted you to have it." I plucked porcelain figurines in

the shape of colorful flowers from a display case. I swished the duster around and began to sneeze. Again, and again.

Katherine laughed. "Your nose is still sensitive."

It was a silly, simple thing to say, but I was pleased she remembered.

"I assume you came by to see what I thought of your note," she said.

I stopped dusting and turned to her.

"I'm not the same girl I was." Her look was serious. "I've changed a lot. And I'm pretty sure who I've become will not fit in with your life. Or most especially, Daddy's life."

"I'm not the same girl I was either, and I think you need to give me the opportunity to prove I've grown up," I said.

"I'm not asking you to prove anything. I'm telling you that I don't need family in order to live a contented life."

Her words stung. "We're sisters, Katherine. Blood-related sisters."

"That doesn't mean we have to be friends."

I turned so she couldn't see my face. I took a breath to summon my courage and then turned back to her. "I won't let you go and I won't allow you to let me go. We may never be friends, but we'll always be sisters whether you like it or not." Suddenly a teapot whistled from the kitchen. We stared at one another while the shrill noise filled the room.

"Tea?" she finally said.

"Yes, please."

"I saw you at the park yesterday," she said as I followed her into the kitchen. "Who was that aggressive young woman you were with?"

"Her name is Laura, and she's not aggressive."

"I saw her slap your hand down. It was unbecoming of someone who looked so well-to-do." She grabbed a rag and lifted the kettle away from the stove and began pouring the tea.

"You happened to catch her at a very awkward moment. She's been very nice to me. And very generous with her time."

Katherine's brow knitted. "What are you talking about?"

"She's teaching me things. Like proper grammar and pronunciation. Ladylike things."

"Like how to hold a teacup?" Katherine said with an English accent. She held her pinky out as Laura had taught me. "And how you must sip instead of slurp? And how you must dab the corners of your lips after every bite or sip?" She performed perfectly.

"Yes! Where did you learn that?"

Katherine rolled her eyes and laughed. "At the asylum. The ladies from the Women's Christian Temperance Union volunteer several times a week to teach us how to behave in proper company, like we'd ever have an opportunity to *be* in proper company. It was absurd."

"I think it's wonderful they teach such things there. I never would have guessed."

"They taught us a lot of things. Sewing, poetry, piano, painting, Latin, and of course, Bible verses."

"I never expected that." I told her about what our classmates had said, and the nightmares I'd had after she'd left, and how I held on to that wicked belief.

"It wasn't a complete holiday, I assure you. There were plenty of dark moments we all endured for one reason or another. It's not a place I want to go back to."

"No. Of course not," I said.

"What does your friend Laura think about me having been committed there?"

I looked at my cup, my thoughts swirling like the tea steam.

"Ah. You haven't told her. Afraid she'd suddenly be ashamed to associate with you."

"That's not true," I said, knowing she was probably right.

"Okay, then. What have you told her about me?"

"That we aren't as close as we used to be."

"That's all?"

I began to perspire. "What should I say? Do you want people to know? I was trying to protect you."

Her mist clouded. "No. It sounds as if you're trying to protect yourself. Unlike you, I don't care what people think of me." She shook her head and laughed. "I can't believe this."

"Can't believe what?" I was frightened by the shift in her tone and her look.

"You. You come here saying you want a sisterly relationship, yet you're ashamed to let people know who I really am."

"I'm not ashamed!"

"You're forgetting I can see your mist."

I left after Katherine got up from the table and headed for the front door. She held it open without saying another word to me. I cried as I walked to the boarding house, angry with myself, and wondering what I could possibly do to fix what I'd further damaged between us. *Please let things get easier*, I prayed to God, to Grandma Rose, to whomever could help make it so.

I laid awake that night thinking of what Katherine said—that I was afraid Laura would no longer associate with me if she knew the truth about Katherine. I was startled by a knock.

"Did I wake you?" Laura asked when I opened the door.

I shook my head and opened it a little wider.

"I won't be long," she said as she stepped inside. "I've just been thinking. Since Thad will be leaving in a few weeks, we need to hasten our plans."

"What plans?"

"The two of you falling in love, silly."

"How do we go about hastening that?"

"You must see each other often. I've already talked to Justin about it."

I wanted to smile at the sound of his name. "And what does he think about it?"

She looked down at the gloves she held in her hand. "He thinks I'm too pushy. I told him love sometimes needs a shove and I'm the person to do it. So … I am going to ask Mrs. Digby if we can host a dinner party. We'll invite the Conroys and the Mitchells. It will be the perfect setting for you to meet his parents."

*His parents?* "What if Thad doesn't want me to meet his parents? What if he isn't at all interested in me? I think this might be too soon."

"Nonsense! Justin told me Thad thinks highly of you and would like to see more of you."

"He did?" I still couldn't believe someone like Thad would be interested in me.

"He did. I have already told Justin to make sure it's all right with Thad before we ask Mrs. Digby. I am more than certain he will say yes and so will she. I'll have all the details settled by tomorrow evening."

*His parents?* I now laid awake with flutters in my stomach.

# Chapter Twenty-Three

John and Fred ate their sardines and crackers while playing chess on the porch. Rebecca was meeting a friend for lunch, so I was alone at the register, feeling uncertain about many things. Katherine for one, but also wondering what Mr. and Mrs. Mitchell would think of me. Laura had informed me that not only did Thad agree to the dinner, but she'd also received Mrs. Digby's approval. At breakfast, Mrs. Digby had been beside herself with excitement at the opportunity "to have such affluence" dining in her home.

I began daydreaming about what it would be like to marry someone like Thad, to be a wife of a Harvard lawyer and the daughter-in-law of one the wealthiest couples in St. Louis. Would he expect to have a church wedding like Laura and Justin? I couldn't imagine myself being the center of so much attention. Daddy wouldn't like it either. I could already see the pink splotches of embarrassment creeping up his neck as he sat amongst several of St. Louis's richest citizens. My heart dropped at the thought of how Thad and his parents might feel about Daddy's lack of wealth and education. Suddenly, shame filled me. It should be enough for all of us that Daddy was a good man.

The bell clinked above the door. I'd been so lost in my thoughts I hadn't heard the footsteps or John's usual "Howdy." It was Norma Malone. I didn't bother greeting her since she didn't look my way for even a second. As she disappeared into the aisles, I looked out of the window expecting to see Nathaniel, but he wasn't there. Nor was their wagon out front.

A few moments later she walked toward me, staring down at what she held in her basket. I noticed remnants of a large greenish-yellow bruise on the left side of her jaw as she came closer. Her bonnet stopped at her cheek bone, and the powder she'd applied to her face wasn't enough to cover it. She set a bag of cane sugar, a bag of flour, and a can of baking powder on the counter.

I rang up her items and asked how she was doing.

She placed a finger in her coin purse and stirred, clinking the coins together. "Just fine, thank you," she finally said.

"One dollar and thirteen cents," I said, holding out my hand. She dropped money in my palm. "Cookies? Or cake?" She looked at me as if I'd said it in Latin. "Will you be making cookies or a cake with the sugar and flour?"

"Oh. Cookies. My husband likes the cinnamon sugar cookies." She swept the items into her basket and quickly walked out.

I stood and watched her from the window, wondering about the woman who had the ability to reach out and disturb every part of me. Even when I could no longer see her, I couldn't shake the unease that absorbing her sadness and pain had caused me yet again. I sensed the bruise on her face wasn't the first, nor was it the only one she was trying to hide.

That evening, I sat at my desk in my night-gown, writing a reply to Daddy. I'd received a letter from him that day. He was thinking about coming to St. Louis. He said he missed me and he wanted to see Katherine so he could make things right. I told him that we hadn't yet made amends, but that I was working on it. I asked him to hold off coming, at least until she and I have had a little more time.

Even though everything I said was true, I felt guilty writing that letter. Because there was an even bigger truth. I knew he'd want to see where I was living and possibly meet Mrs. Digby. What a disaster that would be.

There was a rap on the door. "Sarah?" Laura called. She peeked in. "I'd like to see what you might wear for our dinner party on Friday."

I had nothing she would approve of other than the dress I wore the night I'd met Thad.

She walked to my wardrobe and stared at the four dresses I'd brought from Jefferson City. "Oh, my," she said, disappointed. She pulled out the dress I'd worn to the restaurant.

"It's a shame the boys and the Conroys have recently seen you in this." She placed it back and turned to me. "Stand up." She came forward, lifted my arms, and stared down at my waist. "You might fit into one of mine." She walked out.

I stared at my dresses. They'd been my best ones. I sighed and sat down to my letter. A moment later, she came back with two dresses—one pink, one green—draped across her arms.

"Try these," she said, and laid them on my bed.

I was drawn to the pink one but decided to try the green one first. After I'd buttoned the back as far as I could, I twirled. Laura came up behind me and finished off the buttons, then stood back and scrutinized me. "It's nice. Let's see the other one."

We repeated the steps, although this time she tied a pink sash around my middle. She stepped back and smiled. "Yes! This is the one." She grabbed my hand and pulled me toward the mirror. "You look lovely in it."

I silently agreed. The neckline was a little lower than my usual taste yet still respectable. The bodice was embroidered with a cream-colored thread in a flower pattern, and the straight silk skirt was meant for a single slip instead of a petticoat, making my figure look slim. "Won't the Conroys know this is yours?"

"We'll change the pink sash. I have one that's cream-colored. It will look like a different dress. Besides, I can't remember the last time I wore it. They probably won't remember either."

I looked at my reflection again, very much looking forward to Friday.

Laura quickly sat down in the chair. Her mist was the same hazy shade as it had been at the park and her face was pale.

"What's wrong?" I asked as I rushed to her.

"I'm not sure. I feel faint and my heart is pounding."

I walked her to her room and helped her out of her shoes and dress. While she slipped into her night-gown, I turned down her bed. "Has this happened before?"

She nodded. "A couple of times in the past few weeks. I'm sure it's the excitement." She gave me a worried smile.

It was more. I sensed it. I sat on the edge of her bed and held her hand.

"You're looking at me funny. What is it?"

"I had a dream about you the night after our walk in the park," I lied. "I dreamt you went to see a doctor about your heart." I had no idea if it was her heart or something else. I wanted it to sound urgent enough for her to take me seriously.

She looked frightened. "Do your dreams always come true?"

"No. Although, I don't think there would be any harm in at least paying attention to it. Especially since this isn't the first time you've felt faint. I'll come with you if you'd like."

Laura stared down at our hands. "I … I guess I don't want to see a doctor before my wedding. What if he tells me something I don't want to hear?"

"And what if he tells you after a thorough examination that he's found nothing wrong? At least you can head into your future with Justin without worry."

She stared at me for several seconds. "All right. If you'll come with me. We'll go to Dr. Fisher's. He's known me my whole life. He delivered me."

She went on to tell me more of their history, including her parents' friendship with him. We agreed to meet at the market the following afternoon. As I stood to go, she stopped me.

"Wait. Was there more to your dream?"

I shook my head. "If there's anything more, we'll let Dr. Fisher tell us."

&

Laura wasn't her usual chatty self the following day as the two of us walked with our arms linked toward Dr. Fisher's home. I attempted to cheer her by thanking her for introducing me and Thad, and for organizing our upcoming dinner with his and Justin's parents. My distraction worked. Her mist lightened as she began talking about the dinner menu.

"Mrs. Digby has given me permission to order two bottles of French wine and guess what else? We'll be having soup, and beef croquettes, and roast duck! Have you ever had roast duck? It's delicious. And for dessert an array of scrumptious cakes."

I squeezed her arm against my side. "Our guests will be pleased."

She became quiet and her mist dimmed as we approached the doctor's home. A bronze placard that read *Mark Fisher, Medical Doctor, Please ring for service* was affixed to the red brick, to the left of the front door. Laura pressed the button and soon a servant answered and showed us in.

We didn't have to wait long before a stout nurse in a blue

and white dress asked us to follow her to a room with a padded wooden examination table and a chair. She told Laura to sit on the table and wait for the doctor. As for me, she said that I would have to step out of the room once the doctor arrived. Laura looked at me, frightened.

"May I please stay with her?" I asked.

"No, you may not." She looked at Laura. "She'll be right outside the door."

I held Laura's hand until the doctor came in. He was elderly with white hair and beard and bushy eyebrows. He wore crescent spectacles on the end of his nose. I was pleased that his mist was a lovely shade of green, the color of a healer.

When I stepped out of the room, I worried that Laura wouldn't feel comfortable enough to be honest with the doctor about her symptoms. She'd admitted she was anxious about what he might say. After making sure no one was near, I pressed my ear to the door.

She explained what had been happening to her in detail—dizziness, difficulty catching her breath, sudden and extreme tiredness—and how often each occurred, which was more often than she'd admitted to me. I was thankful she was at least being honest with the one person who mattered. "And a few days ago, I woke up with my heart beating so fast it frightened me."

He told her he needed to listen to her heart. Seconds later, he asked her to breathe in deeply and exhale completely. He repeated it a few times.

"What is it?" she asked, her tone worrisome. "You hear something, don't you?"

"I can't be completely certain yet. I would like to check one more thing." A few seconds later, he said, "This is a Sphygmomanometer. I place this cuff around your arm. Hold still."

"Oh! It's tightening."

"Shhh." After a few moments, he said, "Laura, because I

have been your family's doctor for so long, I know about your family's medical history. Your grandmother was thirty-five when she passed. Your aunt, twenty-four. Are you aware of what took their lives so young?"

My arm hair prickled as I waited for Laura to respond.

Her voice was high-pitched and panicked. "Their heart?"

"That's correct. I'm concerned that your pulse is not as strong as it should be."

Laura gasped, as did I.

"I'm putting you on bed rest. Is that clear? You are a very busy woman taking care of Dr. Albright's children and planning your wedding. You must hand over your work responsibilities to someone else."

"I'll quit the Albrights today if I must, but let someone else plan *my* wedding? I will not!"

"Laura, I'm afraid you don't understand. The symptoms you have been experiencing are trying to warn you of something possibly dire. I must insist on bedrest immediately."

"For how long?"

"For one week. And then I'd like to see you again."

"I have so many things to do," Laura sobbed.

"I know it's difficult, but you must stay calm. Getting upset will only make things worse. I'm sending a wire to your parents. They should be informed."

"Oh, doctor, please! My mother will make me come home. I don't want to go to Edwardsville! My fiancé is here!"

"They are old and dear friends of mine and I owe it to them to tell them their only daughter is in need."

"Why is this happening to me? God is punishing me. Please don't punish me too by telling my parents."

"I don't believe people are afflicted as punishment. Sometimes certain conditions run in families." There was silence for several seconds, then I heard him sigh. "We can't be sure right now if you have a weak heart. That is why, after proper rest, I want to check it again. I will wait to tell your parents then if you haven't improved. That means you must hold up your end of the bargain this week and rest. Agreed?"

Laura sniffled. "Agreed."

An ominous feeling came over me as I stepped away from the door. His tone revealed how truly concerned he was about her.

Laura's lips were tight and her face rigid as we started home. I pretended as though I'd heard nothing. "Is everything all right?"

"Oh, yes. He said I simply need more rest," she said with a smile.

"That's all?" I tried to keep my voice steady.

"Yes. Now, I must ask that you do not tell a soul about this. I don't want anyone worrying and fussing over me. I especially don't want Justin to know." She gave me a stern look.

I nodded.

"That won't do. I need you to promise."

"I promise." At that moment, I prayed she would be all right and that there would be no need to tell anyone anything.

# Chapter Twenty-Four

I watched Laura closely for the next few days whenever I was around her, which wasn't very often. Instead of the bedrest I'd heard Dr. Fisher order, she continued on as usual, although she came home earlier in the evenings and would retire to her room immediately after supper.

On Friday, she was beside herself with anticipation, as was Mrs. Digby who had hired Janine, another servant, to help Martha prepare and serve the dinner for the Mitchells and Conroys. Trudy, the only one in the household whose presence had the ability to calm me, was absent, having made arrangements to dine with her daughter. All of the bustling of Martha and Janine trying to keep up with Mrs. Digby's orders made my nerves even more frenzied. Not only was I concerned about the impact Laura's excitement would have on her heart, I was worried sick about the impression I would make on Mr. and Mrs. Mitchell.

I sat in my room combing my hair while staring at my reflection, trying to recognize the young girl I'd once been in Steelville, Rolla, and Jefferson City. The young girl who was brought up milking cows, beating dust out of rugs, hanging laundry on the clothesline, and calling loved ones "Grandma,"

"Daddy," or "Momma." It was so strange to be sitting in a place like this, wearing an expensive dress, in anticipation of dining with some of the wealthiest people in St. Louis—and they were coming here to meet me!

I wondered how Thad had described me to his parents and what his answer had been when they asked about his feelings for me. I shifted in my chair. How did I feel about him? Justin came to mind and my stomach fluttered. *Stop it!* I chided. *Not now. Not ever!*

I pulled the comb through my hair and then lifted a lock from my temple and twisted it. I picked up a hair pin and secured the twist. As I did the other side, there was a soft knock at the door. It was Laura. She looked lovely in her lavender dress. Her blonde ringlets cascaded over each shoulder.

"Would you like me to help you with your hair?" she asked. I was confident enough to have managed it on my own, but I nodded. She took another section of hair from each side and twisted and secured them with a pin in the back. The rest of my hair flowed freely.

"Stand up," she requested. She stood back and looked at me wearing her pink dress with a cream-colored sash. "Beautiful."

"I hope Thad thinks so too."

"He will. And so will Mr. and Mrs. Mitchell."

"Have you ever met them?"

Laura nodded and went on to explain that Thad was the oldest of three children, a brother Samuel who was two years younger, and the youngest, their sister Marianne, who died of scarlet fever when she was four years old.

Mrs. Mitchell had lost her daughter, and I, my mother. My nervousness shifted into compassion. Could she love me like a daughter someday?

Mrs. Digby made sure to correct my posture as we waited for our guests to arrive. I was now standing with my back straight, shoulders back, and chin up.

"And when it comes time to converse with them, emulate Laura's behavior," she said, although that would be impossible.

Laura was like a honeybee, talking and moving so incessantly and swiftly that it was difficult to keep up let alone anticipate what she would say or do next. Besides, her gregarious personality was almost the complete opposite of my timid one.

"Tonight is very important for me as well as you," Mrs. Digby informed me. "Therefore, whatever you do this evening, please make us proud." Her words had a bite. I knew she was hoping this opportunity would improve her social standing.

The Mitchells arrived first. Thad's reaction to my appearance when he walked in made my heart sing. His smile widened and his mist brightened. His whisper in my ear of, "You look beautiful," gave me gooseflesh.

All eyes were on me as his mother stepped forward. She wore a string of pearls and her mist was a very bright lemon yellow, the color of dignity and control. Mr. Mitchell's mist was blue, like his son's, and he had gentle brown eyes and a kind, round face. I'd been practicing my curtsey in this slender dress and attempted my best one as I greeted them.

A moment later, Martha announced the Conroys' arrival. I could tell the Mitchells considered them friends, as their mists brightened when they walked in. My breath became shallow as Justin's gaze sought me out, even before Laura, and he seemed taken aback when he saw me, as Thad had been. I suppressed a smile and looked away before he noticed my blush.

Laura and I sat with Justin and Thad in the parlor while Mrs. Digby offered to show the Conroys and Mitchells around. I wasn't sure how typical it was to do such a thing, but apparently Mrs. Digby couldn't resist after Mrs. Mitchell said, "I've always wondered what it looked like in here. I don't know why these places fascinate me."

"I assure you, I don't take in just anyone. They must meet particular requirements aside from their prominent family name. They must be well-spoken, well-mannered, and well-groomed. I've had to turn away quite a few who didn't meet my considerable standards." Mrs. Digby continued talking as they walked down the hall toward the library.

I was uneasy at her mention of the "prominent family name." Although she'd originally thought I was related to the Richardsons of St. Louis, I had corrected her. I only hoped that her words weren't misleading the Mitchells. It made me wonder, yet again, how accepting they would be if they knew my true upbringing.

The conversation at dinner started out about Laura's engagement to Justin and her outstanding wedding plans. Mrs. Mitchell even went so far as to compliment Mrs. Conroy on her "most bright and delightful future daughter-in-law."

"The two of you make such an attractive couple," Mrs. Mitchell said to Laura and Justin. "You are the envy of young St. Louis society. Isn't that so, Thaddeus?"

"It is. Our fraternity brothers have always been jealous of Justin."

"Why do you think I chose him?" Laura asked with a laugh.

*How lucky you are, Laura, that he chose you*, I thought as I looked at Justin. His lips had formed a tight, shy grin and his handsome face was flushed.

"All I know is that I am going to have the most beautiful grandchildren," Mrs. Conroy said. "And lots of them, am I right Justin?"

"Yes, Mother, of course. Laura and I have agreed on three. And we will do our best to make sure their gender is whichever you decide, in whatever order you decide," he teased.

Everyone laughed.

"I won't go that far, I promise," she said. "Except to say that three is not enough."

Everyone laughed again.

"Your grandchildren will indeed be beautiful." Mrs. Mitchell turned to me. "Sarah, tell me how you are related to Percival Richardson and his late wife? Thaddeus wasn't exactly sure. Mr. Mitchell and I had been meaning to write to Percival to ask about you before tonight, but time has gotten away from us."

My throat caught as I looked at Mrs. Digby and watched as her mist dimmed.

"Sarah isn't exactly certain either," Mrs. Digby said, her smile strained. "A distant relative at least, we're sure." My pedigree was important enough for her to lie.

"I will ask my father the next time I write to him," I replied, hoping there might be a connection in our bloodlines somewhere in history.

"What brought you to St. Louis if not relatives?" Mrs. Mitchell asked.

*What do I say?* I thought of Katherine's words, about how I was ashamed of her. I looked down at my plate as sadness filled my chest. I missed my sister. I missed Grandma Rose. I missed Momma and Daddy. What I wouldn't give for all of them to be sitting around this table with me instead of these people who knew absolutely nothing about me. I lifted my head and looked straight into Mrs. Mitchell's hazel eyes.

"It was a relative who brought me here. My older sister, Katherine."

Everyone at the table seemed interested in hearing more as all heads turned to me. Mrs. Digby looked surprised, and then squinted, as if she was warning me to choose my words carefully. I took a sip of water to buy some time to think about what I should say. What could I tell them? Any part of the truth would upset the rest of the evening, and more.

"Katherine? Her name isn't familiar, so I don't think we know her. Who is she married to?" Mrs. Mitchell asked.

"She's not married," I said.

There was an awkward silence and it was clear they were expecting more. My stomach knotted. The scent of rosewater suddenly wafted through the thick smell of roast duck. I whole-heartedly knew speaking the truth would disappoint, if not distress, everyone at the table but regardless, I felt compelled to speak it.

"Then what does she do if she's not married?" Mrs. Mitchell asked.

"She's John Larsen's housemaid." Thad's mist clouded considerably, as did his parents'. Mrs. Digby cleared her throat. She was not pleased with my revelation. I looked down at the half-eaten dinner on my plate, my appetite gone. It was several seconds before someone spoke.

"Oh, I just love Larsen's Market," Mrs. Conroy said. "You've reminded me that it's been too long since I've been there."

I looked up at her bright smile and purple mist and my spirit lifted. "I work there. Part-time. On the register."

"Temporarily," Mrs. Digby interjected.

"How wonderful!" Mrs. Conroy said. "Please tell Mr. Larsen and Rebecca I said hello."

"Why didn't you tell us Sarah worked at the market, Thaddeus?" Mrs. Mitchell stared at her son. Although her tone was light, her look and her mist were not.

Thad looked at Laura. She was staring down, moving vegetables around with her fork.

"I'm sorry, Mother. I didn't know," he replied.

Nothing more was said for several seconds as everyone at once began to take an interest in what was on his or her plate.

The air was so thick with embarrassment and unease, I wanted to run to my room and weep.

"You won't believe who I ran into at the university library," Justin spoke up. He was looking at Thad. Before Thad could reply, he said, "Mrs. Chambers."

Thad laughed. "Is she still angry with us?"

Justin looked at me. "When Thad and I were in grade school, he dared me to draw on the chalkboard a picture of our teacher, Mrs. Chambers, before she came into the room. When she asked who drew it, everyone remained silent. She threatened to keep the entire class after school until 'the culprit who had drawn such a grotesque image,' confessed to doing so. Thad replied, 'It's a picture of you,'" Justin laughed, and then continued. "Needless to say, we both received a paddling from Mrs. Chambers as well as a note to our parents." His gentle eyes stayed locked with mine as the mood lifted in an instant when everyone around the table laughed at his story.

"As I recall, you were both extra nice to Mrs. Chambers after that," Mrs. Conroy said.

"Being paddled for a second time when we got home encouraged it," Thad replied.

"I'm so sorry our son was such a terrible influence on yours," Mrs. Mitchell said in jest. "I'm grateful you both grew out of it."

Although the conversation moved on to other things for the rest of the evening, I was aware of how most had cooled toward me, including Laura. When it came time for goodbyes, the Mitchells barely looked at me, and Thad's "Goodnight" was nowhere near as intimate as his hello had been. The only thing that kept me from feeling completely wretched was Justin's gentle look and sweet smile as he said goodbye to me.

*Thank you,* I wanted to say to him, for dispelling the awful pall that had descended earlier. I knew he'd done it purposely, for me.

"Why didn't you tell me you have a sister in St. Louis?" Mrs. Digby demanded as she and I stood in the foyer with Laura. Before I could answer she went on. "And I am certain tonight wasn't the proper time to disclose her occupation or your ties to John Larsen. I don't believe he is someone the Mitchells would associate with."

"Trudy knows him and she's your best friend." *And she loves him.*

"Not every connection is as important as others. What they think of *you* is. I only hope you haven't ruined your chances."

I looked at Laura, hoping she would defend me. She simply stared at me, her mist dim. Mrs. Digby stalked off toward the dining room. Laura walked away without another word. I watched as she ascended the stairs and disappeared into her room. Since I was too agitated to go to bed, I went into the dining room and began helping Martha and Janine clear the table of the tremendous number of dishes.

"*Really*, Sarah. You must learn how to become a proper lady if you expect to marry someone like Thaddeus Mitchell," Mrs. Digby scolded. "I assure you, he will not allow his wife in the kitchen. The Mitchells have paid servants for this kind of work. Do you think Laura would feel compelled to pick up a dish and wash it after a dinner party? She most certainly would not."

"They'll be up all night clearing this away and cleaning. Honestly, I don't mind. I always helped my mother and grandmother prepare and cook meals and clean up afterward."

"Yes, and that's another example of something else you shouldn't mention."

I looked at Martha and saw her mist dim at Mrs. Digby's remarks. "It's all right, Sarah. Janine and I can take care of this. Thank you," she said.

After giving her and Janine my appreciation for everything they had done, I went up to my room wishing to stomp my feet on each step to release my anger. I gritted my teeth instead.

I closed my door and stepped out of Laura's dress. I sat on the edge of the bed in my slip and draped the dress across my lap, rubbing its smooth silk between my fingers. Clearly Laura's parents spared no expense when it came to their daughter's attire. Even if my parents could have afforded to buy me clothes like this, they would not have dreamed of it. *Wasteful*, they would have thought, as I'm certain Katherine would.

I hung the dress on the outside of my wardrobe and stared at it with irritation. The evening had gone miserably, and why? Because I am not related to the right people and work to support myself? Why couldn't Thad be more like Justin, and Mrs. Mitchell more like Mrs. Conroy? God, how I envied Laura.

# Chapter Twenty-Five

When I arrived at the market the following morning, my spirits were still low. I did my best to fool John by smiling and being as chatty about the weather as I could stand, but I felt awful knowing that neither he nor this place were good enough for Mrs. Digby and the Mitchells.

As I headed inside, John said, "Hold on a minute." He was eyeing me closely. "It seems you've got something other than the weather on your mind."

I looked away. There was no sense in trying to hide anything from him. "I'm ... confused. Like I don't know where I belong."

He pointed to the rocker next to him. "Afraid you'll have to be more specific."

I sat, wondering if I could, or should, explain what had happened at dinner, and quickly decided to focus on the broader issue. The urge to cry hit me. It mattered more than I had realized. "I sort of feel like I'm stuck between two places. Where I want to be and where I am."

John stared at me for several seconds, his eyes softening.

"You believe the place you want to be is better than where you are?"

I needed to be careful not to hurt him. "I don't know. Parts of it seem better, and other parts … I'm not sure."

"I get the sense you're not talking about a place on the map."

"No, sir."

His grin caused his eyes to glisten. "Let me tell you a quick story."

I looked inside the window to make sure Rebecca knew I was there, as it was already a few minutes past eleven o'clock.

"She knows we're talking, not to worry. Now, I knew this girl one time who was madly in love with this fella. The problem was, he didn't run in the same circles as she did, and her parents didn't like it. When they were old enough, he joined the military and then asked the girl to marry him, and although he knew she wanted to say yes, she said no. And the reason? Her parents had already arranged for her to marry a much richer fella, one who could give her anything she wanted and make the rest of her life comfortable."

An image of Trudy crying while she wrote a letter flashed in my mind again. *So that's what happened.* "If she truly loved the first fellow, why would she choose the other one?"

"She told him it seemed like a better choice for her being that the other fella had affluence that appealed to her. That, and she didn't want to upset her parents."

"Was it a better choice?" I knew the answer, or at least I thought I knew.

"She wrote to the first fella years later telling him that she was living with the biggest mistake of her life."

I had the urge to give this man with a gentle soul a hug. His heart had been broken because Trudy had been caught between two places, like me. "Trudy still loves you."

John grinned. "I know."

"Thank you for that story, John."

"Search your heart for the answer. It'll never lie to you."

"Hello, there," a female voice called from the street.

We both turned. I caught my breath. Mrs. Conroy was walking arm-in-arm with Justin. He smiled at me as they made their way up the stairs.

"Mother insisted on taking a walk on this lovely day and when she told me she was coming here, I thought I'd join her," he said.

"Yes, when you reminded me of Larsen's Market last night, it brought back memories of my mother. She used to shop here. It's been too long," she said.

"It has been a while," John replied. He grabbed his cane and stood. "I believe I left my tobacco pouch on the counter. I'll escort you in." He gave his arm to Mrs. Conroy and walked her inside.

I knew he'd intentionally left me and Justin alone on the porch because I'd seen him tuck his pouch in his breast pocket when I first arrived. That's where he always kept it.

My nerves fluttered as Justin held his hat in his hands and ran his fingers through his hair. "It was very kind of you to escort your mother here," I said, trying to keep my voice and my heartbeat steady.

He gave me a timid smile. "I thought it would be a nice opportunity to spend time with her. I've been so busy with school and Laura—" He paused.

I stared at his profile. His jaw was tight, and I sensed aggravation. Was it because of school or Laura?

"Your wedding day is only a few weeks away," I said, as if he needed reminding.

He nodded but said nothing.

"Although, your graduation comes first, doesn't it?"

His mood lifted. "Yes. I'm very much looking forward to that." We looked at one another and our gaze held until a burst of laughter from inside broke the spell.

"Justin!" his mother called. "Come in here a moment. I want you to see this."

We walked in and saw them looking at a catalogue of specialty items for order.

"I asked Mr. Larsen and Rebecca if they carried dark Belgian chocolate. You remember the chocolate we had at Christmas-time at the Peterson's? Anyway, Mr. Larsen showed me they can order it from this catalogue. Look at all the things for sale these days! 'Strong beauty pills for weak, ugly women.' Can you believe the nerve," she said, laughing.

"I assume they make those pills for men too," Justin said.

"They do! For baldness, obesity, breath odor, flatu—goodness me!" Her face was flush with laughter. "Although it's tempting, I think we'll just place an order for the chocolate. How much do I owe?" she asked Rebecca.

My admiration for this woman increased even more. She could have walked into any of the uptown markets and purchased Belgian chocolate. She wouldn't have to wait at all.

"You can pay when it arrives. It'll take a few days since it ships from Chicago," Rebecca informed her. "I can send a courier to deliver it."

"No need for a courier. Ring us when it comes in," Justin said, pointing to the Magneto wall phone. He looked at me. "I'll drop by for it."

I had a difficult time suppressing my smile well after they had gone, and I was still elated when it was time for me to leave.

"I haven't seen two people's mists match up at the sight of one another in a very long time," John said when I walked out on to the porch.

"You saw his mist?"

"You bet. Yours too. Pink. Both of you."

*The color of love?* I walked over and sat down. I was suddenly sweltering. I tugged at my collar and waved my hand in front of my face. "Is that why you left us alone to look for the pouch that was already in your pocket?"

He tapped his nose. "Not sure you're aware of how much that boy admires you."

"I can't read him, John. I sure wish I could see his colors."

He pulled his pipe away and exhaled a stream of smoke. "That's not unusual. I can't see everyone's. And thank the good Lord. I'd be overwhelmed every minute of the day if I could. I'd say you not being able to read Justin could be a blessing."

"Why is that?"

"You get to learn about him, from him, instead of figuring him out yourself. Besides, things being unpredictable and mysterious can be good for a relationship. Staves off boredom."

My shoulders slumped. "Unfortunately, there's no point in Justin and I having feelings for one another. He's marrying Laura."

The bowl of his pipe glowed. He blew out the stream of smoke slowly. "Yeah, I got the sense there was some kind of barrier. Wasn't sure what though."

"I guess he and I will have to pray that our feelings disappear."

"If praying is all it took, there'd be fewer heartbroken people walking around. I'm afraid it don't work that way," he said.

# Chapter Twenty-Six

I wondered if Thad and his parents would seek us out at church the following morning to at least acknowledge Mrs. Digby's hospitality, if not the pleasure of meeting me. I couldn't resist glancing in his direction. Every Sunday since we'd met, we'd exchanged glances and smiles from across the church. On this day, Thad refused to look my way. When I realized Mrs. Digby was craning her neck to see past those who were blocking her view of the Mitchells, embarrassment flooded me.

I turned my focus ahead, expecting to see Nathaniel and Norma Malone like every Sunday, but they weren't sitting in their usual area, within the first three rows. Part of me was relieved they weren't there, since it saved me from coming away emotionally exhausted. And maybe it would allow me to appreciate the reason I was there, to listen to the preacher. He spoke softly most of the time, and when he was about to lull people to sleep, he gradually raised his voice as if climbing a steep mountain, until he reached the pinnacle of his sermon and began shouting. This snapped the congregates out of their sleepiness. Suddenly everyone sat up straight, nodded their heads, and shouted "Amen!" with their hand over their heart or in the air.

When the service ended, Mrs. Digby stood and looked around. "I'm certain the Mitchells would like to thank me for the other evening," she said, scanning the crowd. "Maybe even extend an invitation to their home." Trudy stood and craned her neck as well, while I sat, pretending to search for something in my handbag.

"Sarah?" Mrs. Digby waved her hand for me to stand up.

"Just a moment," I said, my concentration focused on finding nothing in particular at the bottom of my bag. How I wished Mrs. Digby wasn't so eager, but from my side view I could she and Trudy straining, looking through the flow of people while I dawdled.

By the time we slid out of our pew, we were at the tail end of the crowd. I was relieved to see the Mitchells' carriage riding away from the church as we stepped out of the front doors. Mrs. Digby looked deflated as she frowned, but just as suddenly, she straightened her shoulders, lifted her head, and marched homeward. Trudy and I had to rush to keep up.

Martha greeted us when we returned. She was holding an envelope. A courier had delivered a note while we were at church. Trudy and I stood silent while Mrs. Digby ripped it open. Her mist clouded as she read it.

"What does it say?" Trudy asked.

Even though Mrs. Digby smiled, her disappointment was clearly written in the deep lines of her face. "It's from the Mitchells. It says *Thank you for a lovely evening. The roast duck was especially good. All the best, The Mitchells.*"

"That's all?" Trudy asked. "They aren't reciprocating the invitation?"

"Apparently not," Mrs. Digby said, staring at me.

❧

ALTHOUGH THE SUN was shining that afternoon and I could hear birds chirping outside my bedroom window, it was the most wretched day. Mrs. Digby's mist and attitude toward me were dim, Laura was with Justin, and I couldn't seem to do anything except stew over every difficulty in my life. The one in the forefront of them all was Katherine. I had to repair our relationship. I had to. And maybe once that happened, every-thing else in my life would somehow become easier.

*Grandma Rose, I know you can hear me. I need your help.* After several seconds, I closed the book I'd been holding and swung my legs off the bed. I grabbed my bonnet.

"CAN WE TALK?" I asked Katherine when I entered John and Rebecca's house. Rebecca had answered the door, surprised and happy to see me, as was John. Katherine didn't smile, however.

"I need to get started on supper," she said.

"No, no. You go ahead," Rebecca said. "I'll make it. You two go for a walk."

"Yeah, take your time," John said.

Katherine gave them a nod, snatched her bonnet off its hook, and went out to the porch. "There's a park a couple blocks from here," she said, and headed off.

I hurried to keep up. "I told everyone a little about you at dinner the other night. That you work as a housekeeper for John and Rebecca."

"Am I supposed to care about that?"

I flinched. "I guess not." I realized she had no idea what a big deal it was for the people I'd told. "It's just … that I want you to know I'm trying. That's all."

She stopped walking and looked at me. "Why is it so diffi-cult? What is it you're trying to hide, Sarah?"

*Everything. Every single thing about my past. Even from you.*

"Whatever it is you want to talk about better be more meaningful or I'm going home and making supper." She sat down on a wooden bench that faced a water fountain.

"I think it's about time we talked about Mrs. Bryer." I was torn about whether discussing Mrs. Bryer with her would be a good or a very bad thing. However it turned out, I sensed it was what Grandma Rose wanted: for me and Katherine to finally talk about what ripped our family apart. "There's something you don't know about that night."

She stared at me expressionless, her mist cloudy.

"I had tried to scare Donald Bryer so bad that he'd quit hurting his wife. I did it for her, and I did it for you. I didn't want you to get involved in something that might put you in danger or anger Daddy again."

"Daddy? Daddy only cared about himself, his job, his reputation. He didn't care about Mrs. Bryer, or her baby, or me."

"That's not true."

"Sure it is." She crossed her arms against her chest. "Now what do you mean you tried to scare Donald Bryer?"

"I wrote a note threatening his life. I told him he'd die if he didn't stop hurting Mildred."

Katherine sat so still it was as if she'd stopped breathing. "That was what he was waving in her face the night he killed her." She shook her head. "Sarah, he thought *she* wrote it."

I knew what she said was the truth. I'd always known it. "And then he thought you did."

Her chest heaved as her breathing quickened. "Oh my God. How do we know the note wasn't the reason he killed her? How do we..." She looked around wildly, as if searching the park for answers.

"I'm sorry. I'm so very sorry," I said, my hand on her shoulder.

She shrugged it away and looked at me, her eyes red. "Does anyone know about the note?"

I nodded. "Donald Bryer told Daddy he was going to have you arrested for threatening him. That's partly why Daddy sent you here. To protect you from jail."

"So, you never admitted it was you who wrote it and not me?"

I looked down at my lap.

"I see you had no problem keeping quiet about that!"

"I told Grandma the morning she died. And I told Daddy before I came here."

She shook as she spoke. "So all these years they thought it was me? I paid heavily for what you did! Three years of my life! I don't think I can forgive you for this."

"I didn't march into the courtroom! If you hadn't done that, Donald Bryer would have probably never suspected either one of us wrote the note."

"No, he would have kept on believing Mildred wrote it and you would have let him believe that. And all I did when I marched into that courtroom was speak the truth, Sarah! Unlike you. You hid the truth. You hid it because you're a—"

"Coward."

Katherine stood. "Yes. You are."

I watched her walk away from me. I sat there until well after the sun set, until the lanterns were lit, until my back ached. Walking to Mrs. Digby's after dark wasn't the safest choice I could have made, but I felt being frightened and uncomfortable is what I deserved.

# Chapter Twenty-Seven

❧

At breakfast, I was still miserable and couldn't help mulling over what Katherine had said to me the previous afternoon. But when Laura came in and sat down, my attention went fully to her. She looked awful. She had no idea I knew of her second appointment with Dr. Fisher, and I wondered if she would mention it.

After we finished eating, I followed her up to her room, hoping she'd ask for my company again, but she didn't say a word about it. When I asked her how she'd been feeling lately, her mist darkened.

"Oh, much better," she said, but the purple circles under her eyes, her pale skin, and her dull hair were telling.

"I know you have another appointment with Dr. Fisher this afternoon. I couldn't help but hear him say that when we were there."

Her smile dropped. "Is that the only thing you heard?"

"Yes."

Her shoulders relaxed. "He wants to make sure I haven't had any more fainting spells. Which I haven't."

I didn't believe her. "I'd like to go with you to your appointment."

"There's no need."

I grabbed her hands. "You're my friend. I want to be there for you."

She grimaced and looked away, then looked back at me. "All right. I will be honest with you. I'm not as well as I pretend to be. So, if I let you come with me, you must promise to keep it a secret. My appointments, my diagnosis, everything. Am I clear?"

"I promise," I said. We agreed to meet after I left the market.

ʒ₪

"YOU MAY SHUT THE DOOR, Dr. Fisher. Sarah is staying. I insist," Laura said when he came into the room.

He did as she said, and pulled a wooden tool off a shelf. It was several inches long with a flared opening on one end, and a much smaller flare on the other. He placed the wide end against her chest, bent toward it and placed his ear on the smaller end. His mist clouded and his face turned serious. He looked at her eyes, her tongue, and her nails. He brought out a contraption that had a mercury vial encased in glass with numbers and dashes on either side. It had a rubber tube with a strap he called an arm cuff extending from it, as well as a second tube with what looked like a rubber ball attached to it.

After placing the strap around her upper arm and securing it, he squeezed the ball a few times. This made the cuff inflate and tighten. I was amazed to see the mercury in the glass suddenly shoot up and slowly come down. He asked if she'd had days of bedrest or if she had disregarded his advice.

"You told me to forgo my duties at the Albrights and I did that. I resigned immediately."

"What have you been doing with your time? Have you

been resting?" He loosened the strap and placed the machine back on the shelf.

"Not completely, although I have been turning in much earlier in the evenings."

The doctor sighed. "I'm afraid that's not enough. You must understand something. Your pulse is not as strong as it should be and your heart rhythm is still abnormal. And an inspection of your pupils, your hair, and your skin, tells me you are not well." His tone was somber. "I fear you might have the same condition as your aunt and grandmother. If you do, it will affect how you live your life from now on. You will need to be cared for. You will need rest. And there is something else. Something that I honestly wish I didn't have to tell you." He looked at me.

Laura grabbed my hand, tightening her grip. She nodded for him to continue.

"If the result comes back as I think it might, I must advise against having children. Pregnancy would be too strenuous on your heart and so would the labor. It could put you and the child at risk of death."

I caught my breath. Laura screamed. Her wails were so wretched, my whole body constricted. I willed myself not to cry as I placed my arm around her shoulder.

The doctor's mist was murky, and his face was strained. I knew he felt helpless.

Laura cried for several minutes, even as the doctor tried to calm her to down. "This type of stress is not good for you. I'm going to send you home with a mild sedative. It will calm you and help you sleep, which is what your body needs most." He looked at me and gave me a nod, as if to say, "Make sure she does it."

I nodded back.

Laura's face was puffy and her eyes red from crying, but she put on a smile when we walked out. "I'm sorry I carried on that way."

"Don't be." I knew being a mother was all she wanted to be, but as much as my heart ached for Laura, it hurt for Justin too. He might never be a father.

She must have been thinking the same thing because she looked at me. "Justin must not hear of this."

"You're going to keep it from him?" I couldn't imagine her being so deceitful.

She was silent for a long while, then finally, "I will make sure that any further tests are done after the wedding. I'll tell him then."

I was at a loss as to what to say. It was wrong for her not to tell him immediately, but I had to remind myself that no matter how I felt about either of them, their relationship was not my matter. Still, the more I thought about it, the more dishonest it seemed, and it wasn't sitting well at all.

"What is it?" she asked a few moments later. Apparently, I'd been quiet too long.

"I think he should know. Before the wedding. So that maybe he can comfort you."

"He will not hear of this." She glared at me. "I should have never allowed you to hear what Dr. Fisher had to say. You promised you would keep this a secret. I'm holding you to that!"

Her mist was a deep red and I knew it wasn't good for her heart to be so upset.

"Please calm down. I will keep my promise."

She studied me for a moment before softening her stance.

I knew if I didn't change the subject, I might say something else I'd regret, so after a few moments, I asked, "Have you seen Thad since our dinner party?"

"I haven't. Although I'm sure Justin has. Would you like me to ask him?"

"Absolutely not," I blurted out.

A crease formed on her brow. "Why did you say it like that?"

"I'm sorry. I guess I don't want Thad to think I care."

"Do you care?" Her tone was callous.

"I do. Why did you ask it that way?"

She stopped and placed her hands on her hips. "If you do care then why didn't you tell me your sister was a housemaid? I would have made sure you didn't speak of it. And your job at the market isn't temporary. You need that money desperately, don't you? One look at your wardrobe tells me I'm right. And I'm disappointed in you for ruining everything by saying too much. Not only did you embarrass Mrs. Digby, you made me look deceitful for not telling Thad about the market."

My eyes burned. "Why are you saying such cruel things?" I let the tears streak down my face. I wanted her to see how much her words stung.

She stared at me for a moment and then shed tears of her own. "I'm sorry. I … I don't … I just need to get to my room."

I placed my arm around her waist and walked her home.

❦

I KNOCKED on her door a few hours later and asked if she was coming down to dinner.

"Yes. I don't want Mrs. Digby thinking I'm ill." I turned to go. "Wait," she said, grabbing my wrist. "I want to apologize for what I said earlier. It was cruel. I was just surprised to hear your sister is a maid, and it dawned on me that I'd never heard about your parents. Who are they that you must work as a cashier and your sister someone's maid?"

I was struck by her words yet again. I knew she didn't intend to be critical, but I couldn't help feeling her judgement. "Katherine and I lost our mother when we were young. We were brought up by my Grandmother Rose who recently passed away, and my father. He's a tanner in Jefferson City. He doesn't make a lot of money; therefore, Katherine and I do what we must."

"You can understand why I thought differently. Mrs. Digby's boarding house is one of the more expensive places in St. Louis."

"I didn't take the time to inquire about more affordable accommodations before I left Jefferson City. Once I arrived, I knew I couldn't afford to stay, and then I met you and enjoyed your friendship, and I started working at Larsen's which helps cover the cost. And to be honest, I enjoy being there too." The way she looked at me made me think she was condemning me for not only having to work but enjoying it. "What is it?" I wanted to know.

"Thad told Justin he is no longer interested in pursuing a friendship with you."

My insides gripped. Although I anticipated this news, I didn't anticipate hearing it would hurt so much. "When did he say that?"

"The morning after our dinner party."

I closed my eyes. "I'm humiliated."

"We can try again, with someone who won't be as unattainable—"

"*No.*" I said it so sharply it startled us both, but I just couldn't face more judgements.

I turned in early, feeling humiliation and anger festering inside me. I couldn't fathom that a "gentleman" such as Thad could be so coldhearted that he hadn't the decency to tell me himself. Oh, how I wish he would. I'd make him look me in the eyes and explain why.

As I lay there feeling sorry for myself, a thought occurred to me. Perhaps I didn't deserve his love. Or anyone else's for that matter. Who could love a coward?

# Chapter Twenty-Eight

❧

Rebecca asked me to take inventory of the fabric and sewing aisle before she left for lunch. I gladly did it in order to take my mind off Thad, and Katherine, and Laura's health. I took a deep breath to shed my self-pity and turned my full attention to all the colors and textures of the fabrics, and all the pretty buttons and shiny ribbons. I daydreamed about being a seamstress and all the stylish dresses I could make.

*If only I were more talented and fashion mindful like Laura.* The thought triggered my self-pity once again.

My pride was still smarting about Laura's harsh words. Since I arrived in St. Louis, nothing had turned out as I'd hoped, with Thad, with Laura, or with Katherine. And my inappropriate feelings for Justin. Everything in my life was wrong. I suddenly missed Daddy and wondered if I should go back to Jefferson City. But something told me not yet. It hurt too much to think about leaving with Katherine still so angry with me. I had to try one more time.

I came out of my reverie when I heard footfalls on the stairs. When the bell tinkled, I looked around the aisle. It was Nathaniel Malone.

"Howdy, Miss Sarah." As usual, his putrid mist defied his cheerful personality. He placed his hat on his chest. "You sure look mighty pretty on this sweltering blue-sky day."

I forced a smile as I made my way to the register. "How is Mrs. Malone?" Something about Norma didn't feel right.

"A bit under the weather. I told her to stay in bed and I would stop here on my way back from the docks and pick up the crackers she likes. I'm hoping they'll make her feel better."

As he walked toward the dry goods aisle, an image flashed in my mind. A blanket pulled over a body in a dark room. *A dead body?* Suddenly I saw a glimpse of Norma's bruised face and swollen lips. She was crying. *Oh, dear God.* I felt a dizzying rush as I came back to myself. A moment later, Nathaniel came around the corner holding a tin of coffee and a box of digestives.

My hands shook as I rang up the items, and my heart beat so hard, I was sure he could hear it. I forced myself to look at him and smile. "Please tell Norma I hope she feels better," I said as I handed him his change.

He poked the underside of his hat with his finger. "I will surely do that. You have a blessed day."

When I heard him say goodbye to John and head down the steps, I walked back to the fabric aisle and closed my eyes. *What am I supposed to do?* There had to be a reason I connected so easily and so often to this couple. I waited, hoping an answer would come. When nothing did, I breathed deeply to expel the heaviness. *I don't want this connection to Norma.* I had enough to deal with getting Katherine to forgive me and trust me again.

I LEFT EARLY the following morning and headed to John and Rebecca's house. I hoped Katherine would be alone so we could talk or yell or cry or whatever it took to clear things between us. I'd brought Grandma's final letter with me. Maybe it would help Katherine see that Mrs. Bryer's death might have been destined and not strictly my fault as she believed.

"I don't have time," Katherine said when she opened the door. "I've got bed linens to wash and hang."

"It won't take long," I said as she began to close the door. "Please." The door swung open and she stared at me, expressionless. I waited for her to invite me in or move aside, but she didn't. "I have a letter from Grandma Rose that I want you to read."

She stepped aside.

After we sat down at the kitchen table, I pulled the letter out of my handbag and handed it to her. I watched as she read about how Grandma might have misinterpreted her vision of Momma dying at the hands of the doctor. Tears streaked down her face when she read the final line: *There are times we can't change fate, no matter how badly we want to, or how hard we try.*

She placed the letter down. "God, Grandma carried so much guilt. Poor woman. And poor Momma. I never realized how agonizing her death must have been. She hid her pain so well." Her voice cracked and her hands went to her face. Her shoulders shook. "Poor Daddy," she whispered.

I rushed over and hugged her from behind. I was thankful she'd finally glimpsed how much he had suffered all these years, and I said a prayer that she'd finally forgive him. And maybe me too.

"I think Grandma wasn't only referring to what happened when she tried to interfere with Momma's fate," I said as I sat down again. "I think she was also saying that even if you had stopped Mr. Bryer from killing Mrs. Bryer that particular night, it might have happened another night. It would have taken Mrs. Bryer leaving him for good, or him dying, to put an end to it."

Her eyes narrowed. "So, you feel absolutely no responsibility whatsoever?"

"Of course I do. For writing that damned note and for stopping you from doing what you needed to do. But Katherine, there's no way to know if he would have killed her eventually whether we interfered or not."

"That doesn't mean we shouldn't have tried to help her."

"We were too young."

She jerked her head. "Are you saying that we wash our hands of her memory since we were too young? Were we too young to go to the sheriff or tell our teacher or one of our pastors that he might kill her? We knew something like that was fixing to happen and don't you deny it! You felt her pain just like I did."

I had felt her pain. And yes, I was trying to rid myself of my shame by using Grandma's words to clear my conscience. "You're right, Katherine," I whispered. "You're absolutely right." I'd been too worried about getting in trouble to shout it out to whoever might have listened.

*And now Norma.* The thought came unexpectedly and I was struck hard by what it meant. I could help heal the past by helping Norma Malone. But how? I stood up and started pacing.

"What are you doing?"

I stopped and looked at Katherine. "You made me promise not to forget Mildred Bryer or her baby the night before you were taken away. So that's how I make amends to you and to her. I do something in honor of her memory."

"Like what?" Her look was skeptical.

I sat back down. "I realize why I've been having visions and sensations about a couple named Norma and Nathaniel Malone."

I explained to Katherine how my gift had been strengthening, and how I was psychically linked to Norma Malone. I told her what little I knew about the Malones, and every dreadful and exhausting thing I had experienced when I was anywhere near them: seeing the bruises, feeling the fear and wretchedness, sensing the horror of it all. "It leaves me drained. The only way I can describe it is being saturated with sadness."

"What do you plan to do about it?" Katherine asked.

"I ... I'm not sure." Until a few minutes ago, I hadn't planned on doing anything. "What do you think I should do?"

"I think you need to figure out your reason. Would you be doing it for Norma's sake? For the sake of Mildred's memory? Or for the sake of your own guilt? At the moment, I can only assume you're trying to appease your self-loathing."

I turned away. She was hurtful and rude. But she was right. I didn't have an answer.

"Whatever it is, I suggest you figure it out. But you're going to have to do it somewhere else. I have beds to strip and linens to wash." She stood and walked to the door. It was clear she wouldn't respect me until I stopped being so uncertain and insecure about everything in my life.

I walked to the market taking in and releasing deep breaths to help relieve the stress that had been building all morning. She was still disappointed with me and she was right as usual. What did I want? Surely it was to help Norma, wasn't it? But was it? Could I reach out to her as a true friend? No. I couldn't. Because what would Mrs. Digby say if I invited Norma over for lunch? Or what would Laura think if she saw us together? My God, I was a horrible, horrible person to put their snobbery above Norma's need for friendship. And what of Mildred Bryer? If Katherine wasn't still mad at me about her, would I allow myself to think about her? I knew I wouldn't. I'd leave her memory buried in my mind so deep it would never come to the surface again. So, what does that leave me? It leaves me with my selfish desire to win back my sister's love and trust. But even more at this moment, the selfish desire to simply walk away from all the bad memories, difficult tasks, and negative feelings.

"I need your advice," I said as I ascended the market steps.

"Have a seat," John replied, setting his newspaper at his feet.

"I'm thinking about going home."

His brow lifted. "Things not working out here or do you miss your daddy?"

"Both."

John nodded. "Is Jefferson City where you want to be or have things gotten complicated here and it's easier to walk away?"

My stomach turned at his forthrightness. "If I'm being honest, I'm walking away. Because I'm a coward."

John's smile dissipated. "I see. And is that how you want to be referred to or remembered? That when things get hard, you give up?"

"No, sir. It's just that I've never been able to say or do the right thing, especially when it comes to my sister, and I'm not sure I ever will." He stared at me for a minute and I could tell he was seeing things in his mind about me.

"It seems you worry an awful lot about what others think of you. Maybe you should figure out what it is that *you* want instead of trying to be the person you think they want you to be. It's a part of maturity."

"I thought I was grown up the day I left Jefferson City. It seems I'm as naïve as ever."

"Do you think going back to Jefferson City will fix that?"

"No, sir, I don't. I've learned a place can't fix anything. I've got to do that myself."

"Now you're gettin' it. What do you want to fix the most?"

"I don't want to be a coward anymore."

"Then don't be. Shed all those opinions you think are so

important and do what your heart pulls you to do. I told you it will never steer you wrong."

"Yes, you did."

"And just so you know, I'd hate to see you leave."

I placed my hand over my heart and gave him a smile.

# Chapter Twenty-Nine

I sat at the register thinking about what John had told me, about living the life I wanted as opposed to what others, like Mrs. Digby, Laura, or Katherine, expected. I liked the idea of not trying so hard to please everyone. It would hurt me if Katherine never came around, and I wasn't completely sure I'd stop reaching out to her. For now, though, I decided to focus on me.

Suddenly I remembered to check the special-order shelf as I'd done the past several days since Justin and his mother had stopped by. My heart leapt when I saw a shiny white box with gold letters that read *Belgian Dark Chocolate*.

"Shall I call the Conroy household?" I asked Rebecca, trying to sound indifferent.

"I called Mrs. Conroy this morning. She's sending Justin over sometime today."

I looked away before she could see my smile.

When Rebecca went to her office to eat her lunch, I straightened can labels and then swept the floor, all the while trying not to glance at the door or the clock too often. I couldn't stop wondering what time Justin would arrive, hoping against my better judgement that it would be before I left for the day. I hummed a tune as I worked like Grandma Rose used to. I wondered if Katherine hummed while she cleaned.

Two o'clock came quickly and by ten minutes after the hour I decided I'd stalled long enough. I took a breath to dispel my disappointment as I plucked my bonnet off its hook. I said goodbye to John, but as I was about to descend the steps, I saw Justin hurrying up the sidewalk. He broke into a smile.

"I thought I'd missed you," he said, trying to catch his breath.

"Almost. I'm walking home now."

"Can you wait a minute? I'll grab my mother's candy and walk with you."

I was so flustered, my face heated. "Certainly."

I glanced at John, knowing if it were anyone else who had overheard, they would probably think it unbecoming of me to walk home with an engaged gentleman. John simply grinned and winked. *Etiquette be damned*, he seemed to be saying.

I looked down at my dusty shoes and quickly swiped at them with my gloved hand just before Justin stepped out.

We walked in silence for a few moments and I wondered if he was feeling as awkward as I was. Finally, he said, "Tell me about your childhood."

I hesitated, as this wasn't what I expected. *If I'm going to stop trying to be what others want, I must be honest.* To a point. I told him about the most relevant things, like how much we'd loved Steelville, and my grandmother whom I loved more than anyone in the whole world raising me and my sister after my mother's death in Rolla, and my father working hard and doing his best.

I also felt it necessary to question Justin's integrity since I now knew about Thad's. If Justin changed his opinion of me based on how I grew up, then so be it. I told him about me and Katherine tending to farm animals, living on leased land, in leased houses, and being teased by our classmates about being "squatters." I even admitted I worked at Larsen's Market to help pay for my room at Mrs. Digby's.

"I guess you now know I wasn't brought up like you, or Laura, or your other friends."

"What do you mean, exactly?"

"Having wealth and all the advantages that come with it."

"Ah," he said.

Since I couldn't see his mist, I had to rely on his expression to tell me whether I'd offended him. His brows were raised, but his blue eyes and expression were soft.

"I hope you don't judge me too harshly for being born into a prosperous family," he said.

"And I hope you don't judge me too harshly for being born into a less than prosperous one," I replied.

"I'm beginning to understand why I admire you so much. I knew you weren't like anyone I'd met before. I hope you don't think I'm too forward by admitting that I am intrigued by you, from the first moment I saw you. It was at Union Station. Do you remember that?"

"I do. You explained what the allegorical women stand for."

"That's right. Imagine how surprised I was to see it was you weeks later standing at the top of the stairs with Laura. I wondered about the odds of that. I was very happy for Thad, although…" He looked away.

"Thad and I weren't meant for one another and that's all right."

"If I may be honest, I think he's a fool."

It was my turn to look away as my breath became shallow.

When we approached Audubon Street, I asked if he would be coming in to see Laura.

He shook his head. "I'll see her later. I should get this home before they get too hot."

"Of course. It wouldn't do to bring your mother melted chocolates. Please give her my regards." We stared at each other a moment longer than we should have. It was difficult for me to look away because he was, without a doubt, the most captivating man I'd ever met. I forced myself to walk away.

Laura was just coming out of her room when I reached the top of the stairs. She said she was on her way to Justin's. I wished her a nice afternoon, not mentioning I'd just left him. I wondered if he would tell her of our walk. I hoped he wouldn't. I selfishly thought of it as a secret between us. I smiled as I laid on my bed, thinking about all of the complimentary things he said to me and the way he looked at me as if he wanted to say so much more but couldn't.

LAURA'S MIST was a gloomy combination of gray and red when she came home that evening. It was difficult to know if it was due to her health or her emotions. By the way she ignored me, I sensed it was both.

"Eight more days until your wedding," I said, adding cheer to my voice as I spread butter on my bread.

Instead of responding, she looked at Trudy. "Will you please pass the green beans?"

"My, only eight more days until your wedding day," Mrs. Digby said.

"I wish it were only eight more hours," Laura responded. "The waiting is making me miserable."

"How are the arrangements coming along?" Trudy asked.

"Perfectly," Laura replied. "Everything is in order."

Laura continued to focus on the two ladies while disregarding me.

When we'd finished our meal, I followed her out of the room.

"Laura?" She turned and looked at me, her lips thin and tight. "Are you angry with me?"

"As a matter of fact, I am." She waved for me to follow.

I was thankful that whatever she had to say to me, it would not be overheard by the ladies. We went out to the garden and sat on a marble bench under a birch tree.

"I feel like I've been deceived by my fiancé and my friend!"

"What do you mean?"

"I would have appreciated being told that you and he saw each other this afternoon, yet neither of you said a word to me about it. You and I talked when you arrived home. I even told you where I was going, yet you failed to tell me you'd just seen him. It wasn't until Mrs. Conroy offered me a chocolate that she told me Justin had been to the market. I felt like a fool."

"I, uh, I guess neither of us thought it was important. He happened to come as I was leaving. That's the only reason he walked me home. He was only being nice."

She glared at me. "*He walked you home?*"

"I thought that's why you're so upset."

Her face, and her mist, reddened even more. "He didn't tell me that. I thought the two of you only saw each other for a few minutes at the market. I considered you a dear friend! I chose you to escort me to my secret appointments with Dr. Fisher. That should tell you how much I trusted you."

I grabbed her hands. "You can still trust me. And Justin. He was only being a gentleman. I should never have thought it wasn't important enough to tell you."

She stared at me for several seconds as if trying to decide whether or not to believe me. Suddenly, she relaxed. "Thank you," she said. "I'm sorry to have suspected the worst. I'm so irritable these days. I wish my wedding were tomorrow."

I had kept our time together a secret and apparently Justin had tried as well. Did he do it because it meant nothing, or did he know how upset she would be? Or was it because it was a special moment he'd rather not share? Whatever the answer, it was wrong of us because in eight days they would be married. Of all the men in St. Louis, why did I have to fall for *him*?

I went to bed that night feeling every bit as wretched as I was. Despite what John said about prayer not being the answer to put a stop to my feelings for Justin, I prayed for it anyway. *And help me be a better friend, a better sister, a better daughter. A better everything.*

As I began drifting to sleep an image of Norma Malone, bruised and crying, flashed in my mind. It startled me. Suddenly, my mind went blank. My arms and legs wouldn't respond to my will to move them and my eyes refused to open at my command. Fear gripped me as my breath became rapid and shallow. More images flashed, a pathway lined with dead flowers, an outhouse, a screen door. A swift rush swept through my body and I was no longer seeing only pictures in my mind. Part of me was there, an invisible presence inside Norma's house.

*I was there. But how could this be?*

She was in a small kitchen, pulling a pot out of a cabinet. Nathaniel grabbed her arm. He pressed his lips against hers and pried them open with his tongue.

Suddenly it was *my* mouth he was kissing. Somehow a part of me had entered Norma's mind. I was seeing things through her eyes, hearing her thoughts, feeling her pain. The smell of his breath was so foul I could taste it, and the scum on his teeth so thick I could feel it.

"Kiss me like you love it," he demanded.

*But I don't*, I thought as I squeezed my eyes closed and held my breath.

"You're gonna show me how much you love it." He dug his fingers into my upper arm and pulled me to the bedroom.

"Nathaniel, *please*," I begged, trying hard not to cry. I somehow knew he hated it when I, when *Norma*, cried while "making love," as he insisted on calling it.

He forced me onto my stomach with my face in a pillow

and sat on the back of my thighs while he unbuckled his belt. He slipped his trousers down just enough. *God, no! Please!* I screamed in my head. *I don't want to be a part of this*! In an instant, I was once again outside of Norma's body. My relief lasted only a second as she screamed in pain. I looked on in horror as he shoved her head in the pillow and leaned in, pressing the side of his scruffy face against hers. His hot, sickening breath penetrating her nostrils as he groaned.

"Now make me something to eat," he said when he had finished.

I was in her kitchen once again, watching her chop vegetables and meat for a stew. The look on her face and the force with which she was using the knife was as if she was imagining each chop of a carrot was Nathaniel's penis and each slice of beef his heart.

She dumped everything into the broth and opened a cabinet door. I watched her pull out a box of rat poison and hold it over the pot. *You'll go to jail. Put it away Norma, please, before he sees it.* I had no idea if she could sense me or not, but without opening the box she placed it back. She slowly stirred the stew, letting her tears drop into it for flavor.

I felt the rush as I came back to myself. My face and hair were wet from tears. I opened my eyes, thankful to be safe in my own bed. My heart continued to race. *Why is this happening?*

An image of Mildred Bryer with her gray-blue eyes filled my mind, and I remembered Katherine's nightmares before Mildred was murdered. Now I knew they weren't nightmares. They were psychic visitations. Katherine had been psychically linked to Mildred Bryer, just as I now was to Norma Malone.

# Chapter Thirty

I awoke the following morning exhausted and still in disbelief of what had happened the night before. To see and feel the horror Norma went through for just those few moments was enough for me to know I had to help her.

*Grandma Rose, please help me figure out what I should do.*

I lay still and waited, hoping an answer would come. Suddenly an image of cookies popped into my head— cinnamon sugar cookies—the kind Norma said Nathaniel liked. I flipped the covers off and dressed.

I went into the kitchen and asked Martha if we had what I would need to make them. She checked the butter and opened a couple cupboards.

"We do! Shall I make some this afternoon?"

"I'll do it right after breakfast, if you don't mind," I said, thrilled my plan might work.

Martha requested I leave the baking to her, probably due to Mrs. Digby's impertinent remark after the dinner party about how the kitchen was a place for servants, but I insisted, explaining how my sister and I used to help Momma and Grandma Rose bake them for Christmas every year.

When breakfast was over, we prepared three separate

plates of cookies, one to keep at the house for the ladies, and the other two each wrapped in a decorative cloth and tied with a ribbon.

John was sitting behind the counter when I arrived at the market. "You are an angel on Earth," he said when I handed over one of the plates. "These cookies smell delicious. How about some coffee, Rebecca?"

"On one condition." She took the plate from him and untied the ribbon. "You get two. Only two. And I'll bring the rest home for later." She set two cookies on the counter, wrapped the plate back up and walked toward her office.

John winked at me. "She's afraid of sugar belly."

I laughed. "I should have thought of that."

At two o'clock, I told Rebecca my intention for the other plate. "I'd like to do the friendly thing and take these cookies to Norma Malone. Nathaniel came in a couple of days ago and said she was ill." The reason I said anything to her at all was because I needed to know where they lived, and I knew she'd know.

"How kind of you," she said. "They live off of Pernod Road. If you're not up for a long stroll you can catch the trolley part-way." She told me the precise route to take to the rural, south side of town.

I decided to walk the entire way even though it was diffi-cult to ignore the perspiration streaking down my corset, making it damp and even more uncomfortable. I needed time to consider what I would say to get her to accept my friendship.

About forty-five minutes later, I set foot on their road. My mood became heavy, and my hands had started to shake—a combination of nerves and fatigue from holding the plate for so long. Up ahead was a stone pathway. The house was just beyond and it was just as I'd envisioned.

I was relieved to see the wagon was gone and hoped Norma would be alone. Some of the plants were dried out and browning, others still had a touch of color but were drooping, and weeds had begun to intrude between everything. There was a barn several yards away from the house that looked as if it hadn't been used in several years. Its roof was dilapidated and there was no sign or sounds of animals except for a dove cooing in the branches above and a few chickens in a coop. An outhouse had a few boards missing allowing a foul odor to escape.

I held my breath as I hurried past it, taking a breath as I came closer to the house that was desperate for a new coat of paint. I opened the screen door and knocked on the main one, hoping she would be brave enough to answer. After a few moments I knocked again, louder. I heard a female voice on the other side.

"Who's there?"

"It's Sarah, from Larsen's Market. I brought you some cookies."

"I didn't ask for anything," she said.

"I know. Mr. Malone stopped by the other day and said you were ill. I thought maybe you could use a friend."

Silence. Then finally, "I can't pay you for those cookies you brought."

"I'm not expecting you to. It's a gift."

More silence before the latch clicked and the door opened a crack. It was so dark behind her, every drape in the house must have been closed. She squinted at the daylight. Even though I could only see a thin slice of her, I could tell her hair was oily and her eye was bruised.

"I ain't feelin' too good so if you want to leave them right out there, I'd appreciate it."

I bent over and put the plate at my feet. "Is there anything you need?"

"No. I'm sure I'll be feelin' fine real soon. I thank you for your kindness. I should be gettin' back to bed."

"When you start feeling better, maybe you and I can—"

"I'm not sure when that will be," she interrupted. "If you'll excuse me."

As I walked down the porch steps, I heard her snatch up the plate and shut the door.

I walked home discouraged. She didn't trust me. No, of course she wouldn't have opened her door wide and let me in to see the marks on her body and the pain, and perhaps humiliation, in her eyes. I would have to wait for her to come into the market when she was healed enough. If Nathaniel allowed her to heal enough.

❧

THE FOLLOWING DAY, Rebecca was at a Women's Society Officers' lunch and John was on the porch reading a newspaper. I was standing on my toes, dusting the top shelf of canned soups when I heard him say "Howdy." My arm hair prickled. I walked around the aisle to see Nathaniel Malone walking in. I wondered if he'd come to confront me for going to his house uninvited and leaving the plate of cookies. Seeing his face made the awful images of what he'd done to Norma in their bedroom come flooding back. I quickly pushed the memories away.

"Miss Sarah, how're you doing?" he asked.

I gave him a nod and asked about Mrs. Malone.

"She's good. Tending laundry. Told her I'd help her out by doing the market errand on my way to work. A man must take care of a good woman." After a few moments he plopped down a bag of cooking oats and a can of molasses on the counter. "There's another reason I came here," he said, glancing out the window at John who was staring in at us. Nathaniel lowered his voice.

"I'm grateful you were so kind toward my wife, stopping by with those cookies and all, but I'm sure you've noticed she isn't a very sociable woman. As a matter of fact, she was mighty embarrassed you saw her looking the way she did. I tell you, that woman is the clumsiest creature in God's wide world. She was out gardening and accidently stepped on a rake. The handle came right up and hit her square in the eye if you can believe that! Poor woman.

"Now, getting back to my point, she likes to keep to herself mostly, and it makes her uncomfortable when you're nice to her. I do wish she wasn't so shy and had lots of women-friends, I do. That just ain't her way. So, what I'm trying to say is, I think it'd be best if you stop being friendly to her like you do. She'd also appreciate it if you wouldn't stop by like that."

His stare hardened as if he wanted to make his point stronger, but I held his gaze knowing those were his wishes, not hers. "Hmm. That's a shame. I do appreciate you telling me. I don't want to make her uncomfortable."

"I thank you. Like I said, a man needs to take care of a good woman, so I do what I can to make her happy. I'm all she's got."

*You make sure you're all she's got.* Disgust filled me as I punched the prices into the register. "That will be seventy-three cents." I held his stare once again.

He smiled. "Don't misunderstand. I kind of do wish you and she could be friends. It would be real nice to have two pretty ladies sitting at my dinner table sometimes." He poured coins on the counter.

From the corner of my eye, I could see John outside the window, standing up. I scooped up the coins and put them in the till.

"How's things going in here?" John asked as he walked in.

Nathaniel threw a glance over his shoulder and back at me. "Everything is fine," he sang out. He scooped up the oats and molasses in one arm and tipped his hat. "You both have a very blessed day."

John watched Nathaniel make his way down the steps and climb into his wagon before looking at me. "Between you and me, that man ain't right. Some folks are trouble. You might want to steer clear of the Malones."

My heartbeat became erratic. I knew what I knew about them, but I had no idea what John knew. He obviously knew something. "What kind of trouble?"

"You've seen the remnants of that woman's bruises when she comes in here every so often. That should tell you everything you need to know."

"It tells me a lot, you're right. It also makes me wonder if someone should help her somehow." I was suddenly desperate for John's opinion. "I'm seeing visions of them, John, and they're God-awful."

"You don't have to tell me about God-awful visions. I had plenty of those when I was a lawyer. You just need to understand, sometimes meddling in other people's business you wind up hurt yourself."

"So, we should pretend we don't know she's being beaten and violated?"

John pulled the pipe away from his lips. "I get why you feel the way you do, but I'm afraid you're gonna get yourself killed messing with that one. I feel like he's crazier than he lets on. The kind of men who beat on their wives are the kind of men who will have no problem showing a female stranger who's boss."

"I'm not afraid of him," I said.

"It doesn't matter if you are or not. It matters that she is. And what is she supposed to do? Stand up to him? Leave him? How will she afford to live? Are you gonna help take care of her with the few coins you make here?"

"I haven't thought that far. But there has to be something that can be done."

"Maybe, but your good intentions might create a much bigger problem for her. Besides, lots of folks think a man controlling his wife with the back of his hand or a whip or harsh words is acceptable married behavior."

My fists settled on my hips. "*Acceptable married behavior?*"

"Yep. There's women all over St. Louis in her same predicament. I saw plenty of it with my own eyes growing up, and even more when I focused in on those criminal minds. I ain't sayin' it's right, but it happens way more than you want to know. You can't save them all."

His appalling words were having the opposite effect. I was even more determined to protect Norma. "I might not be able to save them all, or even some, but my gut tells me I need to try and save at least one."

"Those aren't the words of a coward." He grinned at me and I realized he hadn't been attempting to dissuade me at all. He'd been subtly urging me to follow my heart.

I LEFT the market and walked home through the park that afternoon, focusing on mist colors. *Sky blue. Sea green. Pale rose. Sunshine yellow.* My attention was suddenly drawn to a pretty shade of pink in the distance where a pair of women were sitting together on a bench. They were conversing as friends do, but the color of their mists told me they meant more to each other. My breath caught when I looked at the women's faces, and I stopped walking.

It was Katherine and another woman. I knew my sister would not be pleased to see me. Just as I decided to go back the way I came, she looked at me. She held her smile, but her mist clouded. I quickly turned and walked away.

*Is my sister in love?* I wasn't sure how I felt about the possibility she might have feelings for a woman. I knew Daddy wouldn't like it one bit. Just one more thing he'd have to worry about as far as not being able to protect her from being judged or hurt by closed-minded people. Momma probably wouldn't have liked it either, for the fact that Katherine wouldn't be giving her any grandchildren. On the other hand, Laura was about to marry a man and wouldn't be giving her mother grandchildren either.

*Love has no place for judgement. Love is pure no matter who it's given to, so long as it brings happiness.* The thought came with the scent of rosewater.

# Chapter Thirty-One

" I 'm getting a donation ready for the Female Hospital," Rebecca said when I walked into the market following day. She was behind the counter placing toiletries and other items into a sack. I offered to help. "My friend Helen is a nurse there. She'll be here shortly to pick it up. You can check off each item." I took the list and a pencil from her and she began calling them off.

Several minutes later, I heard John say, "Hello there, young lady." By the tone of his voice, it sounded as if he knew her well.

I recognized her as soon as she stepped in.

"Helen, this is Sarah. Katherine's sister," Rebecca said.

Helen smiled and walked toward me. Her mist was a splendid green, the color of a healer, which was fitting since she was a nurse. She wasn't as young as I expected, maybe a decade older than me. She was very attractive, with light-brown eyes and fair hair pulled back and twisted into a knot.

"It's nice to meet you, Sarah. I'm a dear friend of Rebecca's. And I know your sister too. We're in the Women's Equality Society."

We chatted for several minutes about nothing of real

importance before she picked up the sack of supplies. She thanked Rebecca for her generous gift and said goodbye to me.

"I'm sure we'll see each other again soon," she said.

*Very soon, I hope.* I missed my sister.

"Helen and I have been best friends, more like sisters, since we were five years old," Rebecca said when she'd gone. "She's an only child, like me."

There were so many things, personal things, I wanted to confirm about her, things I'd sensed but didn't know for sure. "I failed to ask her about her husband and children. I hope she didn't think I was rude not to ask about them."

Rebecca looked at me for a moment and I could tell she was considering her words. "Helen isn't married. She doesn't have the desire to be," she replied.

"I'm sure her work at the Female Hospital keeps her very busy," I said. "All cities should have a female-only hospital. It's very broad-minded of St. Louis."

"That's true. Here's some interesting history, though. About twenty-five years ago, the Female Hospital was called Social Evil Hospital if you can believe that."

I shook my head. "What is social evil?"

"Mainly prostitutes with—" Rebecca looked toward the door to make sure no one was close by. She lowered her voice. "With immorally obtained transferable maladies."

My cheeks heated. "There was an entire hospital for that?"

Rebecca nodded. "That's because St. Louis legalized prostitution at that time. The city loved the tax revenue, but what they didn't love was the undesirable consequence of the profession itself. The women were required to continually pay to be tested for diseases and be medically treated if necessary, in order to be considered legal. The absurdity was that the men who frequented these women were not required to do anything. How does *that* make sense?" She shook her head and laughed. "The legalization only lasted four years and they changed the ludicrous name from 'Social Evil' to 'Female Hospital.' They also changed their focus to providing medical care to any woman of little means."

I laughed. "Sometimes common sense prevails."

❧

AT TWO O'CLOCK, I headed straight to Rebecca's house. When Katherine opened the door and saw me, her shoulders slumped.

I took a deep breath and blurted out, "I'm sorry I didn't tell everyone who would listen about what Donald Bryer was doing to his wife instead of writing that note. And I'm sorry I didn't admit that I was the one who wrote it and should have been the one sent to the asylum and not you. And I miss you. Terribly." Her mist lightened as I talked and I could tell she was suppressing a grin.

She held the door open. "You're just in time."

I gave her a curious look and stepped in. And then I understood. She was polishing silver.

"You can do the forks while I do the spoons and the knives."

"This is, by far, worse than dusting."

"You don't have to stay."

I grabbed a dessert fork and went to work. "How's this?" I asked, holding it up.

"Nicely done. Do another."

"I will if you tell me something."

"What?"

"About Helen."

Katherine raised her eyebrows. "How do you know Helen?"

"She came in the store today. To pick up a donation box."

"Then you know she's Rebecca's best friend."

"I saw you two in the park," I said. "And I know you saw me."

She began aggressively rubbing a stubborn mark on a serving spoon. "We were talking. Why all the suspicion? You and I sat in the same spot when you told me about the note you wrote to Donald Bryer."

I placed the fork down. "Yes, but our mists weren't pink." Her lips tightened and her mist turned hazy. She was closing herself off. I reached my hand across and held hers. "There's no need to get upset. You have feelings for one another, don't you?"

She looked down at our hands. "We do."

"Does Rebecca know?"

Katherine nodded. "She does."

"How … um … gosh, I don't even know how to … to talk about this."

She shot me a look and withdrew her hand from mine. "Then don't."

"I'm not being critical. I promise you. I'd like to understand. That's all."

"Understand what? How a woman can possibly love another woman in a romantic way? If you don't understand, I can't explain it to you."

"I'm worried how you'll be treated if anyone finds out."

"There's no reason to be. Unlike you, I don't care about what others think of me."

"I don't want them to hurt you."

"I can only be hurt by the people I love."

I grasped her hand once again and squeezed it. "If you've found someone to love, and who loves you, then I am happy for you." As she stared at me, her countenance softened. I knew she could see by my mist I was telling the truth.

❧

I THOUGHT about Katherine and Helen as I laid in bed that night, saddened that they would have to always hide their feelings for one another. And then I thought of Justin. I could no more show my feelings for the man I love than Katherine could for Helen.

*Love is love whether it can be openly expressed or not.* Grandma Rose's sentiment echoed in my mind. I repeated it several times. I suddenly wondered about the Malones. Had Nathaniel ever loved Norma or had he always treated her so horribly? Or did the monster residing within that handsome and charming man gradually reveal himself?

I awoke in the night from a disturbing dream. Norma walked into the market and stood before me barefoot and dressed only in a white cotton nightgown. Her skin was as pale as her gown, ghostly, except for several blackish-blue bruises on her arms, face, and neck. Her hand was bandaged. Neither of us said a word, but I heard her voice clearly in my mind. *He's dead.*

The dream stayed with me throughout the following day and I wondered if either Nathaniel, Norma, or both would come to the market. Part of me hoped he would so I'd know she hadn't killed him. By two o'clock, neither of them had come in.

By the time I left the market, the heaviness in my chest was unbearable. I decided to head to the Malones' instead of Mrs. Digby's.

My senses were enhanced the entire way, as if I were keeping psychic watch for any sign of Nathaniel. *Please don't let him be home*, I prayed. I quickened my pace when I turned up their road, all the while looking and listening for his wagon. Thankfully, I didn't feel the nausea or the arm-prickling sensation he tended to cause when he was near. When I was sure he wasn't around, I ran up the steps, pulled open the screen door, and knocked on the front door. After a moment I heard footsteps.

"Who is it?" she asked.

"It's Sarah. From the market. I came to talk to you." My heart pounded in my ears.

"I ain't interested."

"I understand, Norma, but there is something very important I need to tell you. Please. It will only take a moment."

There was silence for so long that I thought she had walked away, and then, "I'm not appropriate for company."

"It doesn't matter. We can even talk through the screen. I don't need to come in." I stepped back and closed the screen door. A few seconds later, the main door opened.

"Make it quick," she said.

I hesitated, trying to think of what I could say to get her to trust me, and just as she was about to close the door, I blurted out, "I know you need help."

Norma closed the door.

"Norma, I know you can hear me, and you don't have to say anything. Please, just listen. Think about my offer to help you before you do something you can't undo, because prison will be no better for you." I waited several seconds. Only silence.

As I stepped off the bottom stair, the door opened.

"Wait," she said.

I turned to look at her, but she had already moved away from the open door. Within seconds, she came out holding a large kitchen cloth, the cloth I had given to her with the cookies a couple of weeks before. Something heavy was wrapped in it. A delightfully sweet smell wafted through.

"Will you take this away? And bury it. Please," she pleaded. Her face was dreadful. There were dark-blue crescents under both eyes. The left one was black all the way around with the eye itself blood red. Her lip was swollen and cut. "Don't open it and don't ask what it is. If you want to help me, you'll do as I ask. And don't say a word to anyone about it."

"I won't," I said.

She scurried back up the stairs.

"Come see me at the market when you're ready to talk," I said. She shut the door and latched it.

I stared down at the cloth bundle. It was warm and smelled sweet and buttery, except I knew this batch contained an ingredient that could kill whoever ate it. I hurried over to the outhouse but the moment I stepped inside I was uneasy. It would be too easy for a critter to crawl down into the hole since there was no way to keep them out.

I left their property looking for someplace I could bury what I held. I headed toward a grove of trees. The ground was moist and covered with decaying leaves, and there were large rocks here and there. I tugged off my gloves, pulled up a rock and watched several sow bugs scurry along. With a large stick, I dug a hole big and deep enough for the bundle. I covered it and piled on several large rocks, praying that would keep any animal from digging it up.

# Chapter Thirty-Two

When I walked in the front door, Mrs. Digby was coming out of the kitchen. Her mist dimmed and she rushed over to me.

"Goodness! Look at your dress. And your shoes! You have mud on them. And your gloves. Martha!"

I thought I could hide my dirty hands in my gloves, but in the process of putting them on, I had soiled them as well. I looked down at the dried mud on my dress where I had knelt down, and I noticed several dried dirt clods had fallen from the bottom of my shoes onto the entry rug. My face flushed. I quickly stepped back onto the porch and swiped at the mud on my dress, and then sat on the bench.

"Martha, please tend to Sarah," I heard Mrs. Digby say.

Martha came outside and helped me unlace and remove my shoes. "May I fetch your house slippers?"

"No. I'll get them."

"All right. Leave these here and I'll clean them."

I tip-toed back in to find Mrs. Digby frowning as she stared at the rug.

"I'm so sorry." I dropped to my knees and began plucking up the clods of dirt.

"Get up and let me," Martha said from the doorway. "Hand me what you have."

I dropped the clods into her open palm and rushed upstairs before Mrs. Digby could ask any questions.

❧

FRESHLY SCRUBBED AND CHANGED, I came downstairs to find Mrs. Digby, Trudy, and Laura in the parlor sipping tea, chatting intently about what on earth could have happened to me. They stopped talking the second I walked in.

"Good afternoon," I said, avoiding the curious stares.

"Are you all right, dear?" Trudy asked.

"Yes. I'm fine. As I was walking home from the market, a large dog jerked away from his mistress's lead and chased me into the woods. There I slipped and fell. Thankfully the woman was able to call it off before it bit me."

The ladies all caught their breath.

"How horrible!" Mrs. Digby said. "Do you know who this woman is? At the very least she must pay for your dress."

I shook my head. "I've never seen her or her dog before, but please don't worry. I'm all right. No real damage done."

"You poor, brave dear," Trudy said. "And you are so forgiving."

"How humiliating it must have been for you to walk home like that! I would have insisted on the woman's name," Laura said.

*Dear God, it's just a dress.* I wondered what their reaction would be if they knew the real reason. "Please. Let's talk about more pleasant things." This false discussion had gone on too long already.

"A much more pleasant topic is that Justin will be joining us for dinner this evening," Mrs. Digby said. "Won't that be nice?"

"Yes," I said, smiling at Laura. I suddenly noticed how

tired and pale she looked and wondered what Mrs. Digby or Trudy must have thought of her appearance.

"He wants to hear about our latest wedding plans," Laura said. "And I'm glad because he's been so preoccupied lately. I thought he might be having second thoughts."

"Surely not," Mrs. Digby said. "I'll bet he's every bit as excited as you are."

"I hope you're right," Laura said.

My heart sank. This beautiful, generous girl did not need me sitting at the dinner table fighting emotions for her fiancé. "I wish I could join you, but I need to write to my father this evening. I hope you don't mind if I take dinner in my room."

Mrs. Digby dropped her smile. "You can write to your father *after* dinner. Laura will be discussing her wedding, and we should all be happy to hear about it." Her tone was sharp.

"Of course," I said. The day had been full of emotion already, and now I had to endure the evening with Justin and Laura.

❧

I WENT DOWN AT PRECISELY six o'clock. I could hear laughter and wedding conversation coming from the dining room where everyone was gathered. Justin stood when I entered, and I gave him a nod and a smile.

"Laura was telling us about the reception," Trudy informed.

For the next several minutes, Laura talked about every intricate detail of a menu she had written down from a New York City magazine. "Father said I'm not to worry about money so I'm following his advice. It's funny. I used to be so lonely as an only child. I realize now that it's a very good thing. I must be the most spoiled daughter in Missouri," she said with a laugh.

"Ah! Does that mean you're thinking of having only one child instead of three?" Mrs. Digby asked with a wide grin.

I looked at Laura, and she at me.

She turned to Mrs. Digby. "We'll see."

"You could always have one and spoil him or her for a few years and then have another," Trudy said.

"And another," Justin said. "And maybe another if my mother has a say."

I inwardly cringed. It was clear she hadn't told him about her heart as I hoped she would. Keeping a secret as important as this one until after they married, a secret that involved his life in so many ways, was downright deceitful.

"I've decided not to rush into having children. I'm not ready to give up being the center of your attention," Laura said with a laugh. "Now let me tell you of all the help we've hired to serve at our reception."

She continued on, clearly not noticing her fiancé tightening his jaw and shifting in his chair, seemingly becoming more and more uncomfortable as she spoke of decadence. I wondered if he was thinking about our conversation the day he walked with me. I had a feeling he was, because I sensed him staring at me and when I would glance at him, he'd look away. I was grateful Laura was too caught up in Mrs. Digby's and Trudy's excitement to notice.

Mrs. Digby took advantage of a momentary lull when Laura placed a piece of roast beef in her mouth. "So, Justin, how is Thaddeus? We've not seen him since the dinner party."

I blushed and stared down at my plate, not wanting to see Justin's discomfort.

"Oh, um, he's been busy preparing for Harvard," he replied.

"Of course," she said.

"You'll see him at our wedding," Laura said to her. "He's not leaving until after that." She looked at me. "Oh, I'm sorry

Sarah. I'm sure you knew Thaddeus will be at our wedding. I hope that doesn't prevent you from wanting to attend."

I knew she meant no harm, but I was embarrassed as everyone looked at me.

"What is this about?" Mrs. Digby asked. "Is he no longer courting Sarah?"

She directed her question at Justin as if I wasn't in the room. At that moment I truly wished I wasn't. He looked at me and then did the gentlemanly thing and kept quiet.

So, I spoke up. "He has not said or sent a word to me since our dinner; therefore, I assume our friendship is over."

"He hasn't said specifically that he doesn't intend to court you?" Mrs. Digby asked.

Her meddling was so irksome, I had to take a breath to calm down. "He doesn't have to. He and I are not compatible and that's perfectly fine."

"Are we certain?" Mrs. Digby asked. "I mean—"

"*Please* let's talk of something else so that we don't continue making Justin uncomfortable," I insisted.

"Justin doesn't mind, do you?" Laura said.

He focused on cutting a piece of fat away from his beef without answering or looking up.

"Well, I do mind," I said.

"Fine. Let me tell you what I'll be packing for our honeymoon in New York," Laura said.

I was never so grateful to hear about how many pairs of shoes, or hats, or all the jewelry she intended to bring or buy while she was there.

After dessert, I declined Laura's request to join her and Justin for a glass of sherry in the parlor. He looked disappointed when I said goodnight. If he only knew how badly I wanted to stay in his presence, he would understand why I had to go.

# Chapter Thirty-Three

I took the trolley to work Monday morning. It had been raining since the previous night, and the streets and walkways were streams of mud. Despite my effort to stay dry, the hem of my dress was damp and discolored, and my shoes were muddy from the walk from the trolley stop. I wasn't surprised John wasn't on the porch when I arrived. I shook my umbrella and stomped my feet before walking inside. Rebecca said that John had decided to stay home due to the weather, and that she had a business owner's lunch meeting to attend.

By twelve forty-five, the clouds gave way to sun, so I grabbed a pail of water and a mop and cleaned up the floor inside the door where muddy tracks had dried. I looked out of the screen door when I heard footfalls coming up the steps. My thoughts immediately scattered.

"Hel-hello," I stuttered when Justin walked in. I placed the mop inside the bucket and leaned it against the wall. My insides gripped as he walked toward me.

A lock of dark hair tumbled into his blue eyes when he took off his hat. He swiped at it and gave me a shy grin as he ran his fingers through his hair.

"What brings you here?"

He glanced around and said, "You."

The floor was unsteady. "Me? What do you mean?"

"I need to talk with you. Is there somewhere we can go?"

"I'm the only one here." I motioned for him to follow me to the register. I walked around the counter and sat on a stool.

His awkwardness as he glanced down and fiddled with his hat made him even more attractive. I quietly waited for him to gather his nerve.

"I wanted to tell you before you heard it from someone else," he finally said.

I slid my shaking hands under me. "Heard what?"

"I've already spoken to my parents, and we've invited Laura's parents over to tell them and Laura this afternoon. Before I do, I wanted you to know … I won't be marrying her."

My stomach clenched. "But … why?"

"I've come to realize that I don't love her."

I reached out to the counter to steady myself. "Justin, are you sure?"

"I am." His look and tone were solemn. "You are the one who made me realize I was marrying her for the wrong reason."

"I made you realize? This is *my* fault?"

"No. Please. I'm not blaming you for anything. I only want you to understand what I've come to understand. I'm aware that I blindly accepted what was expected of me: completing college, getting married, having children. And someday I hope to have all that. Although not now, and not with Laura. Laura is a lovely woman, and she will make someone a wonderful wife. It just won't be me."

I stood, my hands still trembling, my eyes burning. He was about to destroy Laura more than he knew. "Mrs. Digby says love shouldn't be the only reason to marry," I said. "She thinks societal expectations are very important to uphold."

His brow furrowed. "Is that how you feel?"

I shook my head. "No. Although I still don't understand how I made you realize you shouldn't marry her. Was there something I said to you that made you change your mind? I assure you, I didn't do it intentionally."

"You didn't do or say anything. What I told you that day we walked was true. You intrigued me from the first moment I saw you, and there hasn't been one day since that I haven't thought of you. That's why I wanted you to hear about the end of my relationship with Laura from me. The plain truth. Because I have no doubt Laura's explanation will include confusion, anger, and bitterness. All of which I will deserve. But please know, that no matter what you think of me right now, whether you despise me or understand me, I will not change my mind. I don't love her. I realize I never loved her. So, it's the right thing to do, for both her and me. She deserves someone who is truly in love with her."

I couldn't stop my tears. He kindly looked away as I dabbed my eyes with my kerchief and blew my nose. "Justin, this might be too much for her to bear."

"Laura's stronger than you think."

I stared into his eyes as I battled my conscience. If I told him about her weak heart, maybe he would postpone the wedding instead of calling it off. Maybe he would give their engagement more time so he could learn to love her.

"There is something you don't know." Laura was betrayed yet again as I told him about what Dr. Fisher had said about her heart. I explained what I had overheard her doctor say, and how her grandmother and aunt had passed at a young age.

He stared at the ground. When he finally looked up, his face was strained. "She wasn't going to tell me, was she?"

I shook my head. "She didn't want you to worry."

He exhaled and stared out of the window. "I can't ... can't marry someone I don't love out of pity or guilt." His desperation tore at my heart. He placed his hat back on and looked at me. "In case you never want to see me again, I want to thank you. Thank you for helping me see my life more clearly."

*Oh my God, Laura, I'm so sorry.*

I left the market when Rebecca returned and walked reluctant and miserable to the boarding house. I wished John hadn't stayed home so I could go to his house and speak with Katherine in private. I needed to unburden the guilt that was filling me to the point of physical pain. Had I shown too much interest while in Justin's presence? Was this all my fault? Soon Laura would learn her future would not turn out the way she believed it would. All those dreams and plans of her wedding. How could he possibly tell her the news in a way that wouldn't break her already weakened heart?

I gingerly walked up the porch steps and entered the boarding house hoping not to see anyone, but Laura came out of the library just as I stepped inside. She gave me a bright smile.

"I'm leaving for Justin's."

I smiled back. "How are you feeling?" I asked, not sure of what else to say.

"I'm perfect. Rested for most of the day. It's nice to sleep when it's raining. I'm sorry you had to leave in it this morning."

I stared at her, wanting to hug her, knowing her life would too soon be drastically different.

"Is everything all right?" she asked.

"I'm a little tired. I think I'll rest." I hurried upstairs.

After taking off my shoes and shutting the curtains to dim the sunlight, I crawled into bed. If I'd never come to Mrs. Digby's, would Justin have come to his realization on his own? I closed my eyes and slowed my breathing. The length of time it took for my shoulders and neck to finally relax into the pillow made me realize how much my mind and body were exhausted by so many people. Norma, Justin, Laura, Katherine. I drifted off.

Pounding footsteps running up the stairs startled me awake. I wasn't sure how long I'd been asleep. The dim light through the gap in the curtain told me it was possibly early evening. I sat up when Laura's bedroom door slammed. She was sobbing. When I opened my door, I heard Mrs. Digby speaking downstairs.

"My goodness! I don't know what could have happened. Laura was very upset when she came in. She ran upstairs without a word."

"She's been given devastating news," a woman's voice replied.

I stood outside Laura's room, listening to her cries echoing throughout the house. I so badly wanted to comfort her if she'd let me. Before I knocked, I heard a voice from behind.

"Excuse me." I turned and saw a pretty woman with blonde hair the color of Laura's. Her face was tense, and her mist cloudy. She gave me a sharp nod before walking past me. She slipped in and shut the door as Laura yelled for her to go away.

"I will not go away. My daughter is in pain and I insist on holding her. Come here."

I assumed Laura did as she was told because her cries became muffled as if she was sobbing into her mother's chest or shoulder.

"Dr. Fisher is on his way. I asked him to bring a sedative," her mother said.

"Oh, Mother! I wish you hadn't called him."

"We should have been informed of your condition before today," her mother replied.

My stomach dropped. Justin had mentioned her heart condition. I told her she could trust me. What could I say to justify what I had done? Would she understand that I was trying to get him to reconsider?

"I can't believe she told Justin. I hate her!"

"He needed to know. You should have told him immediately."

"How could I, Mother? How could I tell him we would never have children?" Laura's wail became muffled. I pictured her mother rocking her while she cried.

I went to my room fretting, *wishing* I had kept Laura's confidence and not told Justin. How did he explain that he and I saw one another today and I didn't tell her yet again? I had made such a terrible mess of everything.

I was hiding in my room when Dr. Fisher arrived almost an hour later. I paced around, too fidgety to sit still or lay down, and too cowardly to show my face downstairs. I wasn't sure what Mrs. Digby and Trudy knew, but I didn't think my appearance would help matters, especially if Laura's parents knew why she suddenly hated me.

I had to ignore my rumbling stomach as I waited almost another hour for the doctor to examine Laura and consult with her parents afterward. I heard Laura's mother tell Mrs. Digby that since Laura refused to come home with them, she would be back tomorrow. She asked if she could let a room for the next couple of weeks so she could tend to Laura.

When I eventually heard the "good evenings" I'd been waiting for, I opened my door and went to Laura's. Through the door, I heard her whimpering. I took a deep breath and knocked.

"Go away."

"Laura, please, I need to speak with you." I tried to keep my voice low enough not to be heard by Mrs. Digby or Trudy. A moment later the door swung open. Laura glared at me with swollen, red eyes. Her hair was a mess, and her face was pink and blotchy.

"You knew about this when you saw me this afternoon, didn't you?" Before I could answer she screamed, "How dare you! I trusted you and you betrayed me! I hate you!" She slammed the door.

I stood there so stunned I hadn't heard the ladies rushing up the stairs.

"Leave her be," Mrs. Digby said.

I swung around and looked into her angry face. "I'm sorry, I didn't—"

"As of tomorrow, you will find another place to live. Is that clear?"

I felt as if I had been slapped. I glanced at Trudy. She was fighting back tears. I stepped past them and hurried to my room.

It took several hours for me to stop crying and calm down enough to rest. I slept little that night. When I did, I had multiple nightmares, of rocks being thrown at me, of being on trial, of being sent to jail. In between dreams, I prayed for forgiveness for betraying Laura's trust, but it didn't help. The fitful sleep continued until morning.

At dawn, I pulled clothes from the wardrobe and chest of drawers and laid them on the bed. The sight of my expensive gown made tears well up again. How stupid of me to think I deserved any part of this. This house, the dress, or Laura.

A few minutes later there was a slight rap on the door. I opened it to find Martha holding a breakfast tray.

"Here you are," Martha said, placing the tray on the vanity. "I thought you might want some privacy this morning."

"You are so considerate," I said.

She gave me a sorrowful look. "I hate that you have to leave."

I smiled. Not everyone was angry with me. "Me too. I liked it here."

"When you're ready, I'll arrange for your belongings to be delivered to your new place. Do you know where you'll go?"

I shook my head. "Not yet. I'll ring you from the market."

After not eating since the morning before, I was ravenous. When she left, I took a few moments to eat a bowl of oatmeal and plate of scrambled eggs. As I did, I looked around the room. I would miss this place even though I never belonged.

When everything was packed and the room tidied, I brought my dishes downstairs and placed them in the basin. I told Martha I was ready to go. She surprised me by asking if she could give me a hug goodbye.

"I'd like that." As a matter of fact, I needed it.

I gathered my nerve and walked into the dining room. I'd heard Laura crying in her room as I came downstairs so I knew only Mrs. Digby and Trudy were eating there. Trudy smiled when I walked in. Mrs. Digby did not. I lifted my chin and straightened my shoulders and told her my things were packed.

"Mrs. Digby, before I go, I want you to know that I very much appreciated your hospitality. I loved living here. And I'm terribly sorry that I must go this way." I looked away when tears threatened.

"In a way this is my fault," she said. "If only I hadn't assumed you were someone you are not, and dug a little into your background, you would never have come here in the first place. Terrible luck for all of us."

I wanted to tell her, like coincidence, I don't believe in luck.

# Chapter Thirty-Four

It was far too early for me to go to the market, so I took my time walking to John and Rebecca's house instead. I hoped Katherine would be kind and help me figure out how to get control over my emotions. I'd been crying off and on since the previous evening. With so little sleep, my threshold for much of anything was low and I knew I looked as pathetic as I felt.

When she saw how miserable I was, she invited me in. She set a cup of coffee and a pastry before me. "What happened?" she asked.

"Grandma Rose once warned me to think about the consequences before I speak and even though I try, I seem to have messed things up again." I told her what had happened between Laura, and Justin, and me. When I was done, I was in tears again.

Katherine clicked her tongue and shook her head. "Stop crying. It's not your fault he doesn't love her. Now, I've only seen her that moment in the park but from what I recall, she's young and beautiful. She'll fall in love again and this time, hopefully with someone who feels the same for her. For whatever reason, this was meant to happen and you were meant to be a part of it." As she stared at me, her look softened. "You love him, don't you?"

"I do."

"I get a strong sense that he loves you too."

I looked down at my coffee and smiled through my tears.

"Does this mean you'll be staying in St. Louis?" she asked.

I hadn't really thought of anything past this moment. "I'm not ready to leave."

"Then your first intention should be finding a place to live. If you want, I can ask Helen. She'll most likely know of somewhere. She's stopping by here on her way to the hospital. I'll ring you at the market if she has an answer for you."

A FEW HOURS LATER, she had good news.

"There's a boarding home for women near the Female Hospital. Helen says some of the new nurses stay there. They have a room available. She asked them to hold it for you."

The boarding house was located only a few blocks from the hospital and the asylum, in a much more industrial neighborhood than Audubon Street. The slim two-story gray-brick building was not nearly as elaborate as Mrs. Digby's grand porch with white columns, but there were colorful flowerbeds on either side of the front entrance which added a splash of beauty. When a ruby-throated hummingbird swooped down and began feeding from a tubular orange flower, my mood lifted.

Mrs. Callaghan answered the door and I was happy to see she had a soothing light-blue mist, the color of compassion. She also had a lovely Irish accent. She showed me around the first floor that included a cozy parlor with a fireplace, a small reading room with a few bookshelves, a dining room, and private bedrooms for the staff. She introduced me to two servants, Willa and Teresa. I was exhausted, and grateful, when Mrs. Callaghan finally showed me to my room.

"I'll send up your belongings when they arrive," she said, then left me alone.

The floor of worn and scarred wood creaked with each step. I lifted the curtain covering the single window. My solemn smile dissipated completely at the view of the second floor of the building next door. It seemed inches away. I turned back to the room and looked around. The walls were light gray with no adornments, the bed was small with an iron headboard and springs that creaked when I sat down. I tried not to judge my room's sparseness too harshly, but it was diffi-cult not to miss the much larger room I had left behind with heavy curtains, the goose down duvet, the wooden four-poster bed, the plush rugs, and the view of the back garden from the bay window. I reminded myself that lifestyle was never mine. I laid on the squeaky bed and allowed myself to cry just one more time.

Two hours later, I washed up and headed down for dinner. I was curious to meet my new housemates, wondering how different my new life would be. The library and parlor were empty. I heard laughter coming from the kitchen. I went in, pleased to find Mrs. Callaghan helping Teresa and Willa. She was stirring a large pot of what smelled like meat stew. They smiled when I entered.

"Sarah! Come sit. We're telling funny stories," Mrs. Callaghan said.

It seemed ages since I'd laughed.

I sat down while Willa described how she'd left the house that morning with the back of her dress tucked into her slip.

"I walked all the way to the butcher like that," she said.

I was mortified for her.

She looked at me and smiled. "While I was paying for the ham hocks, a young boy tugged on my sleeve and pointed. He said my privates were showing. I almost broke my neck looking back to see if I'd forgotten my drawers."

We burst into laughter, undoubtedly all of us thinking what we would have done if it had been us in Willa's embarrassing spot.

"What did you do?" I asked.

"I gave him a penny and patted him on the head. I thanked him for being braver than the adults standing in line behind me."

"Surely, you adjusted your skirt first," Teresa said.

"No. I wanted those red-faced bastards to squirm a little longer. How dare they allow me to wander around the market like that. The men were too high and mighty, and the ladies too prim and proper to save me from shame."

"There's no shame," Mrs. Callaghan said. "You didn't mean to do it. I'll bet something like that will happen to everyone who had an opportunity to tell ye yet didn't."

"Here's to that," Willa said with a smirk.

I continued to smile, imagining what Mrs. Digby's reaction would have been to Willa's story. I had no doubt that, instead of laughing as loud as Mrs. Callaghan did, she would have been scandalized.

I fell asleep that night feeling lighter than I had in a long time, knowing my unfortunate departure from Mrs. Digby's wasn't so unfortunate after all.

❧

I AMUSED myself at the market the following morning by humming songs from my childhood while filling a jar with colorful gumballs. Their sweet smell triggered memories of heading into town with Momma and Daddy once a month when Katherine and I were young, and getting a penny treat. The thought brought a smile to my lips, which faded when the bell tinkled.

A woman with a veiled hat and gray mist stepped in. She looked around to make sure we were alone before hurrying to the register. It was Norma. Despite the gauzy veil, I could still see her bruises and split lip, but they were healing.

"I wanted to thank you for stopping by the other day," she whispered. "I don't know how you knew to show up. I took it as a sign from God. He sent you as a messenger to stop me from ruining my life." She placed a gloved hand over mine. "And because of that, you have saved my soul from eternal damnation."

I was taken aback. I hadn't really given her soul much thought. "Oh, well—"

"I've been praying for forgiveness real hard since you came," she interrupted. "And I've been asking for the Lord's guidance about how to be the dutiful wife that He and Nathaniel want me to be. I wanted you to know that."

*Oh, God.* "Um, Norma, I know it took courage for you to come here and tell me that, but I didn't come to your house because God personally asked me to, and I didn't go there to help you become a better wife." Even through the gauze, I could see the lines on either side of her mouth deepen as she frowned. "I went there to tell you I know he hurts you. No one deserves to suffer the way you do. I know God would agree with me. I feel like I need to help you."

She straightened her shoulders. I could see her chest heaving as if she was having trouble catching her breath. "Oh … I … uh …"

"I know it's not what you expected, so don't say anything right now. Just keep it to yourself and think about it. When you're ready, come back."

She stared at me for several seconds before turning on her heels.

I was glad I'd told her, certain that the next time he raised his hand toward her, she would give my words serious consideration. Although, if the time came, just how would I help her?

After I left the market, I headed to see Katherine. She'd been civil to me during our last conversation when I told her about Justin and Laura, so I hoped she was softening toward me.

"Sarah?"

I turned toward the female voice who had called me from behind. It was Helen. I waited for her to catch up. "I was on my way to see Katherine," I said. "If she's expecting you, I can come again another time."

"Nonsense!" she said, threading her arm through mine. "It's beyond time the two of you began acting like sisters."

Katherine raised her eyebrows when she opened the door to the two of us with our arms linked. She stepped aside so we could enter.

"We ran into one another, both of us heading to see you," Helen explained. "And I thought it was a wonderful opportunity for you two to finally make peace."

"Yes, and it will make things more comfortable if I'm to join the Women's Equality Society, since we'll be seeing each other more often," I said. Ever since the first morning I woke up at Mrs. Callaghan's, I'd been thinking about it.

"So, you've decided to stay in St. Louis permanently?" Katherine asked.

"Yes. With or without you, St. Louis is where I want to be. And I promise I will not pester you too often. Unless it's regarding something Grandma Rose would have helped me with."

Katherine smiled. "Such as?"

I looked at Helen and hesitated.

"It's all right. Helen knows everything about me."

I was envious, and thankful, that Katherine had found someone she could completely be herself with. "I reached out to Norma Malone," I said.

Helen looked surprised. "You're friends with Norma Malone?"

"Do you know her?" I asked.

Helen nodded. "She was once admitted at the Female Hospital for a fall from a horse. She was pretty battered. A broken arm, a cracked rib, horrible bruises."

I couldn't imagine meek Norma Malone on the back of a horse. Katherine and I looked at one another, and I sensed she was as suspicious of Norma's "fall" as I was.

"You're sure it was a horseback riding accident?" Katherine asked.

Helen looked down at her hands. "That, I can't say. All I know is that her husband explained what had happened, and Norma was right there when he did. And he doted on her constantly. He hardly left her side for a second. Although, part of me wondered if it could have been something else, something more sinister since we see plenty of abused women, especially given how quiet she was around him. But unless it's perfectly clear it's a case of abuse, we're obligated to keep our thoughts to ourselves unless the woman directly asks us for help."

"I know she's being abused. And she knows I know. She's either too frightened or not ready to accept my help," I said.

"Then there's not much you can do," Helen replied.

"She's right," Katherine said. "But tell me, *why* have you decided to reach out to her?"

"Because I know deep in my soul it's the right thing to do. She and I are connected the same way you and Mrs. Bryer were, and I'm not going to turn away from that."

Katherine placed her hand over mine. "I'm proud of you."

I walked home feeling lighter than I had in a very long time. My sister was proud of me.

# Chapter Thirty-Five

A few days later, I walked back to Rebecca's house and attended my first Women's Equality Society meeting.

"Let's have a seat everyone," Rebecca said when the last woman arrived.

I looked around and counted thirty-three women. Each sat wherever she could find a spot. A few, including me, sat with a cushion on the floor. I hadn't sat on the floor since I was young. I was almost giddy at how unpretentious these women were.

The chairwoman, Virginia Satchell, stood and introduced me and two others, the three newest members of the society. She led a discussion about the progress a few of the charter organizations were making in other cities, or the hindrances they had encountered. As she spoke, I could hear clinking as coins were dropped into a cloth bag being passed around.

The discussion eventually shifted to the threats a few of the women received while handing out flyers, hanging posters, or asking for donations. One woman who had been spit on, said, "Regardless of their ignorance and abuse, we will continue our efforts."

The next item on the agenda was a vote about whether to

make a uniform instead of only a sash for each member. After much discussion, the majority voted against a uniform so as "to not contribute to the monotony or standardization of the female gender by making us indistinguishable." Next, there was a call for another shift of volunteers to stuff envelopes, hand out flyers, and solicit donations. Soon, a woman stood and dumped the coin bag onto a table and counted its contents. "Six dollars and sixteen cents," she said.

"Thank you, to those of you who collected these donations. Let's keep up the good work, ladies," Virginia said.

My first duty as a society member was to help hold the banner in our march that upcoming Sunday afternoon. Two others and I would make up the front row, holding on to the six-foot-long banner that announced who we were. We'd begin the procession at two o'clock at Lafayette Park and march for nearly an hour from Park Avenue up Broadway to City Hall where we would hold up hand-painted signs, sing songs, and chant for the right to vote. I'd asked Katherine what good this would do, especially on a Sunday when City Hall was closed, and she said it was the perfect day to do it, because the men would be with their families, after church and before supper, outside and not working. It would be the best time to capture their attention.

I woke up on the day of the march feeling anxious. I knew it was due to the scorn and harassment I was warned we'd receive. Mostly from men but from some women, too. I remembered the day in the park when Laura and Thad had made their opinion of the society known, and all the taunts and heckles the women endured by those who opposed their views.

"Keep your chin up and keep walking," Katherine said as we walked with Rebecca and Helen to meet the rest of the group. "Whatever you do, don't show your anger or your fear. And there's something else I should tell you. Be prepared to be hit with raw eggs and tomatoes."

I stopped walking. "I didn't notice that at the park that day."

"That's because we'd just started. You should've seen us by the time the march ended. But don't worry. You and I have been hit by worse, haven't we?" She gave me a nudge with her elbow and pointed to the crescent-shaped scar on the side of her forehead from a rock all those years ago.

My arm hair prickled as we got closer to our meeting point. Even before I could see the crowd, I could hear it. Several voices chanting, "Back to the home! Back to the kitchen!"

I was thankful to see the police were keeping the opposers at bay, allowing us to get organized. Virginia Satchell held a megaphone and shouted instructions. The atmosphere was circus-like. A few members were wearing britches and riding bicycles on either side of the rest of us who walked. Some held up flags depicting two female hands clasping, symbolizing unity and strength. Others passed out flyers and shouted out an invitation to join the society.

Young and old spending a leisurely day at the park watched us with interest, a few with shouts of support, others with disdain. Neither I nor Katherine needed their voices or actions to make it clear which side they were on, as their mists either brightened or darkened as we approached. It wasn't long before I was hit with my first tomato by an adolescent boy. It splatted against my chest, sending seeds and goo flying onto my neck and face, while the pulp and skin slowly slid down the front of my skirt.

"That's the way!" the boy's father said to him as he ruffled the boy's hair.

"Try and think of it as a badge of honor," the woman next to me said. She'd been hit in the face by one, which caused a spray of slimy seeds to freckle her cheek.

By the time City Hall was in view, I'd been hit by two

tomatoes and one egg. From my side view, I could see yolk dripping from the rim of my hat onto my shoulder.

Once we assembled at City Hall, we held up signs that read: *Equality Now, Equal Education Opportunities for Everyone, We Deserve a Voice! We Deserve to Vote!*, among others. We were instructed to not interact directly with the opposers, and to sing our equality anthem as if they weren't there. It was difficult to do when their shouting drowned out our song, but we held fast and let our collective voices be our shield.

I tried to not only ignore the negativity that was coming from their yelling, but their murky, dark mists as well. If there was ever a crowd where I needed a prayer of protection, it was this one. Thankfully there was more security at City Hall, and no one threw anything at us. When our time was up, we reassembled into our rows and marched back to where we'd started.

As we came to the end of the march, I noticed three young women whose mists were a mix of light and dark, watching us closely. My heart beat out of rhythm when I realized the one with the dark mist was Laura. Her gaze was harsh and the rest of her face expressed disgust. I gave her a smile and a nod. She only shook her head and turned away. It dawned on me how I must have looked drenched in sweat, and covered in tomatoes and raw egg. Shame creeped into my chest at her response to me. Thankfully, it only lasted a moment. I was truly proud of what the Society had done that day, and that I'd been a part of it.

THE FOLLOWING DAY, the postman surprised me with a letter addressed to me, in care of Larsen's Market. It was from Justin.

*Dearest Sarah,*
*I hope this letter finds you well. I first want to tell you how sorry*
*I am for upsetting you with the news of breaking off my engage-*
*ment with Laura that day several weeks ago. I have a feeling she*
*will never forgive me and I certainly don't blame her. I just hope*
*that someday she comes to understand it was for the best.*
*As for you, the loveliest woman I have ever known, I am hoping*
*you do not hate me, and will consider accepting my friendship.*
*With much admiration and sincerity,*
*Justin Conroy*

I READ his letter again the moment I got to my room and held it to my chest when I finished. Would he feel the same once he learned who I truly am? Heaviness filled me as I realized how much more difficult his life would be with me in it.

*Dearest Justin,*
*I was touched to receive your letter. I do not hate you. I wish only*
*the very best for you, and because of that, I feel I should not*
*accept your friendship. It would cause resentment from your*
*friends who might have heard that Laura blames me as much or*
*more than you for what happened. I'm afraid I would not only be*
*considered an outsider, but an instigator.*
*I care about you too much to cause any more pain or trouble, so*
*please forget about me. Before you do, know that I will always be*
*grateful for the kindness you and your mother showed me when I*
*needed it most.*
*With utmost sincerity,*
*Sarah Richardson*

# Chapter Thirty-Six

I looked through the market window when I heard someone running up the stairs. John, who was playing chess with Fred, glanced up at whomever it was and looked back down at the board without acknowledgement. It was unusual for him to ignore a customer. When Norma walked in, I understood. It was his way of respecting her privacy.

She made sure no one else was around before coming to the counter. She was wearing a cape despite the warm day.

"I've thought about what you said, and I think I'm ready to hear you out."

I'd been thinking of what to do if she came. But now that she was here, so many questions and ideas came to me as to how to proceed. "Has he hurt you again?"

She pulled her cape open with one hand, revealing the other heavily bandaged. "Three of my fingers are broken. And it hurts to breathe."

"Goodness! Maybe I should take you to the Female Hospital."

"No! I don't want doctors involved. I don't want anyone involved if we can help it. He's already suspicious."

"Suspicious of what?"

"I told him someone wants to help me. Someone who knows he hurts me. I only said it because he was beatin' me and I thought it would scare him enough to stop. But it only made him madder. He called me a liar. That's when he broke my fingers. He told me I wasn't allowed to leave the house without him ever again. He said if I did, what he did to my fingers will feel like a hug compared to what he'll do to me next." Her voice shook and tears streaked down her face. "He also said he'd start tying me up." She wiped her cheeks with her bandaged hand. "You can help me like you said, right?"

"It's going to take you leaving him and St. Louis for good."

Her lips tightened, but after a moment, she said, "I haven't loved him for a long time. And I'm afraid if I stay, one of us is gonna die."

I knew it was true. "Do you have any family who can safely take you in?"

"I've got a sister he's never met. She lives in St. Claire."

"Would you feel comfortable staying with her for a few days?"

"I would."

"Do you have any money saved up that you can get your hands on?"

She glanced around the store again, then lowered her voice. "I've got almost six dollars hidden in a jar in the garden."

"All right. I need to get things in order. When the time comes to leave, I don't think it's safe for you to take anything of your own. If Nathaniel comes home from work and finds you gone, but none of your clothing or other items missing, that might buy you a little time before he starts to look for you outside of St. Louis."

She shook her head. "I don't have the money to buy new dresses and shoes and everything else I'll need."

"That's something I have to work out, but I promise, I'll take care of that for you. In the meantime you have to keep this from him. Even under extreme circumstances, you can't say a thing. He can't suspect anything at all or we'll both be in danger."

She said she understood and promised to return the next day for more information.

At two o'clock, I rushed over to talk with Katherine. As soon as the door opened, I said, "Norma came in today. She's ready to do whatever I tell her to do. I need your help."

We sat at the dining table and shared our thoughts. After almost an hour, we had a plan that included talking with Helen and Rebecca. I knew Norma wouldn't like it, but I needed their approval to go to the Society's charity closet and get suitable clothes for her. I was also hoping Rebecca would agree to donate toiletries from the market. If so, I would pack everything into my travel bag and give it to Norma. Katherine and I would withdraw money from what little we had in each of our saving accounts, and buy a one-way ticket to Chicago under her real name, and a second one under a different name, to St. Claire. If Nathaniel went looking for her, which he no doubt would, he would think Chicago was her destination and therefore waste time searching for her there.

Katherine informed me that Helen ate dinner at the Larsens' home a couple times a week. She'd be there that very evening. It was the perfect time and place to talk with her and Rebecca.

"I BEAT the tar out of Fred today in chess," John said when he settled at the kitchen table. He drank a cup of coffee while Katherine and I finished preparing supper. "He doesn't like it when I do that. He tends to get grumpy."

"And how do you react when he wins?" I asked as I pulled biscuits out of the oven.

"I don't like it 'cause he gloats. At least I don't gloat. I don't gloat and I don't pout."

"You're a good friend to put up with him," I said.

"He puts up with me too. I guess that's what good friends do."

"What about good friends?" Helen asked as she and Rebecca walked into the kitchen. Katherine lit into a smile.

"The world needs them," John said.

I looked away as thoughts of Laura came to me. But just as suddenly, they were replaced with thoughts of Norma. If there was anyone who needed a good friend, it was her.

When John heard the four of us ladies were going to have a serious discussion over tea afterward, he went out onto the front porch to smoke. I'd invited him to join the conversation, but he winked at me and said, "I'm too old for adventures such as this, but I have faith in whatever decision you come to."

I gathered my nerve as the ladies made themselves comfortable. Other than my family and John who shared my gift, I'd never spoken about it to anyone. I sat on my shaky hands, took in a large breath, and looked at Rebecca. "Do you know how special your father is?"

She laughed. "Of course I do. What does that have to do with you?"

"Do you know *how* special he is?"

Rebecca's smile froze. "Yes."

I stared at her for a few seconds without saying anything.

"Wait. Are you … are you like he is?"

"I am," I said.

"And so am I," Katherine said.

Rebecca looked from me to Katherine to Helen. "Did you know this?"

Helen nodded. "Katherine told me a while ago. It was

difficult for me to believe that I'd met another person like your father. *Two* people, like your father."

Rebecca shifted in her chair. "This is ..." She shook her head. "Does my father know about you both?"

"Yes," I said. "He and I have opened up to one another already." I spent the next half an hour explaining my experiences both psychically and physically with Norma and Nathaniel.

I waited for Rebecca to speak when I'd finished. It took a few moments for her to absorb everything I'd said. Eventually she shook her head. "I feel awful that I've never paid attention to her. That poor woman. Tell me what you need me to do."

"And me," Helen added.

After explaining our initial plan, Helen said, "There's benefits to working at the Hospital. I have access to personal medical documents. I can create one that she can carry with her. It'll have a different name. She'll need to remember to use this new name from now on."

"Couldn't you be fired, or even jailed for that?" Katherine asked.

"If I'm helping save a woman's life, it would be worth it. But don't worry. I won't let either of those happen."

"I can get whatever you need from the market and the charity closet," Rebecca said. "And if you and Katherine can buy the train tickets, I'll give her pocket money."

"So will I," Helen said.

The three of them promised me they wouldn't speak of this to anyone else.

That night I prayed our plan would lead Norma to an unfettered life under a different name, in a different town where she would be safe and unafraid.

The following morning, I handed my empty travel bag to Rebecca and settled behind the register. I hoped Norma would be brave enough to come back to hear the plan.

Rebecca said she would head straight to the charity closet

after closing the market. "And Helen will drop the medical papers off with Katherine sometime today. Norma's new name will be Marney Bogdan. Tell her that if she never wants to see Nathaniel again, she'll have to become Marney Bogdan the moment you hand her the ticket to St. Claire."

With every tick of the clock's minute hand, I became more agitated wondering when Norma would show up, or if she even would. I was unable to concentrate on mundane tasks such as dusting or straightening the shelves. Every time the bell tinkled above the door, and every time it wasn't her, I had to quell my disappointment.

At twelve-twenty, I heard John say "Howdy." The sudden cheer in his tone told me it wouldn't be Norma. I swiped my palms over the front of my skirt and put on a smile, waiting to greet whomever it was. Justin walked in.

He grinned at me as he took off his hat, looking as handsome as I'd ever seen. He glanced over and noticed the top of another customer's head in the next aisle. "I received your letter this morning," he said to me quietly.

I motioned for him to follow me and we walked toward the storage room where Rebecca sat at her desk. "Would you mind if I take a few minutes?" I asked her.

Her brow lifted and I knew she thought Norma had arrived. She looked through the doorway where Justin stood.

"Oh! Of course. I'll handle the register. Take your time." She left us alone.

Justin glanced around the room, tapping his hat against his hand. "I'm afraid I can't abide by your wish to forget about you."

I couldn't contain my smile.

He smiled broadly back. "Your letter also said you care about me, and I wonder how much."

"So much," I said. His proclamation had sounded so bold, and mine, a whisper. It was because of Laura. "Justin, I'm worried about more than just what your friends will think. If

Laura learns we have feelings for one another, I can't imagine what that will do to her."

He stared at me, his blue eyes serious. "I admire your devotion to her, but I was the one who hurt her, so she'll be bitter toward any woman by my side. As far as what others will think, I know you're worried about that. I'm not. If someone decides to end a friendship with me because they don't agree with who I have feelings for, so be it."

I took a breath. "You're risking friendships on someone you don't yet know."

His eyes softened. "The very first moment I saw you at the train station it was as if I'd lost my bearings, as if the floor had shifted and some electrical current had passed between us. Nothing like that has ever happened to me before. I knew at that moment you were someone special. I walked away praying that if it truly meant something, I'd see you again. Imagine what I went through when I saw you step out from behind Laura that night Thad and I came to Mrs. Digby's. It wasn't only the floor shifting that time. It was my whole world. I honestly believe this was meant to be, and it's a feeling I trust. Will you please give us a chance?"

Yes, yes, yes! I wanted to say. Before I could, the bell clinked and my attention was drawn toward the door. I peered around Justin and my smile froze. It was Norma.

I glanced at the travel bag under Rebecca's desk and back at Justin. "I … I don't mean to be rude, but I need to help this customer."

Justin's brow furrowed as he looked over his shoulder. "I thought you were given a few minutes? Surely Rebecca will help her."

My stomach tightened. "This customer has a special order. One I can't explain right now—" Suddenly the bell tinkled again. Another female customer walked in while Norma stood just inside the door, looking like a scared doe.

"Why Mrs. Malone, how nice to see you!" the woman

said. "It's been a while since I've seen you and your husband at church. How is Mr. Malone?"

Rebecca's voice carried from the register. "Mrs. Durrett! I'm so glad you're here." She strode over to the two ladies, looping her arm through Mrs. Durrett's. "I've received a bolt of blue fabric I think you will simply love." She led her toward the fabric aisle.

My heart raced at the sight of Norma's frightened eyes. "I'm so sorry, Justin. Excuse me." I swept past him and went toward her. She opened the screen door and walked out. By the time I reached the porch, she was down the stairs. I went after her. "Norma, please stop."

She turned to me.

"Does Nathaniel work on the docks tomorrow?"

She nodded.

"What time will he leave?"

She thought for a moment. "He works the late morning shift. He should be leaving the house by nine."

"I'll meet you at the train station at ten, directly beneath The Allegorical Window. Do you know where that is? Inside the main entrance?"

She nodded.

"Good. I'll have everything you need. Just grab that hidden money of yours."

Her serious eyes bored through mine. "I will. But tell me why you're doing this for me."

I didn't have a simple answer for her. I was mostly doing it to banish the coward in me. And there was redemption. And guilt. There were so many reasons. Suddenly the truth rose above them all. "You deserve to live a safe and contented life."

She glanced toward the market and then hurried away. I watched her go.

When I turned back, I saw Justin in the distance, walking away in the other direction. I didn't run after him since there wasn't a way to explain why I had abandoned him in the middle of our very serious and delicate conversation.

"Everything all right?" John's face was filled with concern when I mounted the stairs. My nod to him was a lie, and I had no doubt he knew it.

# Chapter Thirty-Seven

I stopped at the market on the way to the train station to fetch the travel bag. Rebecca wished me well and gave me a hug for confidence. Despite the hug, I clutched the bag handle tightly, my nerves in a frenzy. Even though I was thankful we'd come up with an actual plan to get Norma out of St. Louis, I was scattered with so many wonders and worries. I couldn't fathom how I would be an example of confidence and strength she so desperately needed, so I went over the plan in my head as I maneuvered through the crowd: I would buy a ticket to St. Claire under the name Marney Bogdan. I'd give Norma money to buy a ticket to Chicago and she'd sign the travel log with her real name. I'd give her Marney Bogdan's ticket to St. Claire and take the Chicago ticket and destroy it.

*The knothole is only big enough for my soul to slip through.*

I halted my stride. It was Norma's voice I heard. My nerves and pulse were frantic. Was she speaking to me? Please let her be waiting for me at the station, I prayed, and hurried forward.

I was agitated at the number of people walking every-which-way when I approached the station. They reminded me of the ant mounds Katherine and I used to disturb as children.

I looked for Norma outside the doors and then went in, searching every woman's face who happened to be waiting under the arch of the window. She wasn't there. I looked up at the clock, relieved it was ten minutes till ten.

*She'll be here soon*, I told myself.

By ten-fifteen I knew she wasn't coming. Suddenly a sharp pain shot up my arm and my head and I couldn't take in a full breath. I was consumed by a dizzying rush. Images began flashing: a piece of wood with a knothole, bloody scratches, a torn dress, and then total darkness.

*Calm down, calm down, calm down*, I told myself, all the while trying to take a deep breath. *Stop!* I silently screamed. With a rapid *whoosh!* the tension dissipated. What was this knothole and what had she meant that her soul could slip through it? It didn't make sense.

*I can't breathe.* Her voice came to me again.

I rushed out of the station, weaving around so many people who strolled along as if everything was perfect in the world. There wasn't time to tell Katherine or Rebecca where I was going. As I waited for the trolley, my sense of Norma was getting weaker by the moment.

*I'm coming Norma. Please hold on.*

I STEPPED onto the Malone property, staying off the main path so I wouldn't leave footprints. I kept to the tall grass instead, the hem of my dress becoming mucked with dew and dirt. I hid the garment bag behind a large oak with a wide trunk and continued toward the house. The closer I got, the sharper my senses became—my hearing most of all. Beyond the crunch of my shoes on fallen leaves and twigs and the chickens squabbling in the distance, I listened for shouting, or crying, or anything that would tell me what I was about to face.

I came upon the house and hid behind a maple tree. Their wagon was out front with the horse secured to it. Why wasn't Nathaniel at the dock? Had he just returned or not yet left? I shifted back and forth from my left foot to my right. "Please leave," I whispered as the urgency to get to Norma became stronger. The drapes in the two front windows were drawn. I ran toward the side of the house and stooped under a small window. It was open, the curtain blowing in the breeze. I peeked in. The window was above the wash-basin in the kitchen. There were footsteps and I ducked as Nathaniel came into view. Had he seen me? I flattened myself against the side of the house. There was the hollow sound of an empty cup being set down. The footsteps retreated. I listened for conversation, anything, to assure me Norma was all right. I only heard the creak of the floorboards.

When the front door opened, I got as low to the ground as I could and peered around the side of the house. Nathaniel walked down the front steps and went toward the barn. After a minute or so he came back. His face was grim. As he approached the wagon, he glanced around as if he'd heard something or sensed something. I stayed silent and still. The wagon squeaked as he climbed into it.

*Thank God*, I thought as he rode away.

After I could no longer hear the crunching of gravel in the distance, I ran up the stairs, opened the screen door, and knocked. Silence. I knocked again. Nothing. I opened the door. "Norma?" I called out. "Norma, it's Sarah. I came to check on you." There was no response.

I looked out at the road to make sure he was gone. I walked into the darkened house and closed the door. In the kitchen, a coffee cup was next to the washtub on the counter. A dinner pail with a cloth over it was on the table. I rushed to the closed door of the bedroom and opened it. The room was in disarray. Shoes and clothes all over the floor. A horsewhip. A rope. Dark stains on the rumpled bed cover. I got on my hands and knees and looked under the bed. Only a thick layer of dust. I opened the wardrobe. Dresses on one side, trousers and shirts on the other.

"Norma, where are you?" I called out. Silence.

As I walked back into the main room, I heard the clomping of horse hooves and the sound of crunching gravel getting louder through the open kitchen window. Nathaniel was returning. I hurried toward a side window and dashed behind the drapes. I realized the window faced the barn, and I panicked at the thought of him heading into the barn again instead of the house. He walked up the front steps and opened the door.

Through the thin opening in the curtains, I watched as he walked into the kitchen and came out holding the dinner pail. Relief washed over me as he would be on his way, but as he headed toward the front door, he stopped and glanced around as he had done outside.

*Please make him leave*, I pleaded with God.

Instead of leaving, he walked to the bedroom. He opened it and looked around. He turned and studied the living room once again. His jaw was tense, his forehead lines deep. He was clearly disturbed.

*Please go*, I thought.

Finally, he did.

I came out from behind the curtain when the door closed and the screen door slammed shut. I strode over to the front window and watched as he rode away once again. When I could no longer see the wagon, I walked out to the front porch, glancing around for any sign of Norma. *The barn.* I ran down the steps.

The barn was filled with remnants of equipment parts: an old thresher and a combine, an array of rusted farm tools hanging on nails, a worn saddle, a half-bale of hay. And something covered with a faded, dirty quilt. I whipped it off. Underneath was an old wooden trunk with a knothole in the lid. I frantically looked around for a tool or a rock, anything I could get my hands on. I grabbed a claw hammer. I hit the lock with force and immediately heard a whimper. She was inside and she was alive. I hit it again, harder, causing part of the lock to break off. I tugged off my gloves and pried the rest of the lock off with the claw and lifted the lid.

I shook my head, trying to make sense of what I was looking at. Norma's body was contorted in such a gruesome way, it looked as if she was a life-sized doll. A bloody, bruised doll.

"Norma, can you hear me?" I lifted up her head.

Her eyelids flickered and she made gurgling sounds in her throat.

"This is going to hurt, but I have to get you out of here."

I bent forward, pulling her up and into me as I lifted with all my strength. When I got her halfway out, her full weight pressing against me was too much and we tumbled backward. She fell on top of me and I landed on something hard. Pain shot up my back.

"I knew something wasn't right."

I looked toward the voice. Nathaniel stood in the open doorway, his mist blackish red.

I rolled Norma off of me and stood, my chest heaving as I tried to catch my breath.

"How long have you been spying on us, you little bitch? It's a shame you didn't keep yourself out of our business. Now you've put me in a troublesome spot."

I bolted as he lunged at me. He grabbed my skirt and pulled. I heard it rip as I grabbed hold of the combine. He yanked hard and I lost my balance. His arm came around and brought me to the ground. He straddled me, placed his hands around my throat, and began to squeeze. His manhood grew and stiffened the more I struggled. I jerked my knee up as hard as I could. He grimaced. I did it again. This time, both of his hands went to his crotch. I bucked my body, scratching his face as I flailed my arms and legs like a rabid wild animal. I twisted away and shoved him off me with everything I had.

As I got to my feet, he reached out and grabbed my skirt. It ripped even more as I jerked away from his grasp. I looked around for the first thing within reach. He headed toward me raising the claw hammer above him, his face bleeding and mist dark.

I lifted the scythe and brought it down full force on his head.

Blood spattered into my eyes, onto my face and hands, and my dress. I hit him so hard the handle broke off and the blade stuck in his skull. He dropped the hammer, stumbled backward and fell in a sitting position, his head and shoulders slumped forward.

I didn't breathe as I stood still, watching blood pour from his gaping wound and soaking into his shirt, seeping onto his trousers, pooling onto the ground. I bent over, trying to catch my breath, feeling faint.

*God, please forgive me.* I had killed him.

# Chapter Thirty-Eight

Norma moaned. I dropped the broken scythe handle and rushed over to her. Her eyes were fluttering but she couldn't seem to get them open. I grabbed the dirty quilt and laid it on the ground outside the barn and went back for Norma.

I dragged her out, away from the horrific sight, and laid her on the blanket. None of what had happened, or was happening now, seemed real. It was as though I was physically there, doing what I thought needed to be done moment by moment, but my emotions had somehow shut down. I knew it was stopping me from feeling frightened, and perhaps keeping me from realizing how badly my body was hurting too, from the fall we took in the barn, and landing on whatever it was I landed on, and my muscles from struggling with Nathaniel, and hauling Norma's weight.

In the sunlight, I could see the extent of her wounds. She had a gash on her scalp, bruises on her face, rope burn around her neck, and her hands—bloodied fingers with missing fingernails.

I rushed into the house to grab a rag, and back out to the water pump.

As I headed back to Norma, I heard voices. Katherine, Helen, and Rebecca were walking up the path. Katherine stopped, and then ran toward me. I ran to meet her.

"Oh my God! What happened?" she asked, her eyes poring over my face and body. The other two stared with what looked like horror.

I couldn't find the words, so I pointed to Norma. Helen rushed over to her.

"Are *you* all right?" Katherine asked.

I nodded. "Norma needs help."

Rebecca gasped when she saw Norma's condition. Helen was on her knees, placing her ear on Norma's chest. I dabbed the gash on her head with the wet rag.

"Where's Nathaniel?" Katherine asked.

I stood and walked to the barn. The women followed me.

Although I knew what to expect, the sight of him still made my breath catch.

Rebecca too, inhaled sharply. "Oh my God, oh my God, oh my God," she repeated. Her face was white and her mist gray. "How … How did … Oh my God." She hurried out of the barn and vomited.

In a dizzying rush, the reality of what had happened and what I had done hit me. I looked down at my filthy, blood-spattered, torn dress and fell to my knees.

Helen grabbed Nathaniel's wrist and placed her fingers on it. She looked at me. "Are you able to tell us what happened?"

I told them Norma never showed up at the train station as we'd planned, and how I'd heard her pleading voice in my mind. "She was begging for help." I explained everything.

Helen studied my neck. The other two craned theirs to get a look at it. "There are finger marks. And they'll probably get more pronounced in the next couple of hours. You said that after you wrestled free, he came at you with the hammer?"

"He did. And he would have used it. His mist was black and red."

"You were protecting yourself and trying to save Norma's life. You had to do it," Rebecca said.

"She did, but what do we do now?" Katherine asked.

"We need to get Norma to the hospital," I said.

Helen nodded. "Yes. Her injuries are severe."

"What about Nathaniel?" Rebecca asked.

The fear within me expanded. I knew there was only one thing we could do.

"We have to go to the police," I said. My tear ducts burned as I looked at Katherine. She pulled me into her and held me while I cried.

"You had no choice," she whispered.

Something told me it would not be as simple as telling the police the truth.

Helen motioned to Norma. "We need to get her in the wagon."

When I started toward Norma, Katherine grabbed my arm.

"We'll get her in. You need to clean yourself off. You can't be seen like this." I looked down at my torn, blood-splattered dress. "Find something of hers," Katherine said.

After I quickly changed into one of Norma's very faded, too large but clean dresses, Katherine helped me scrub the blood off my face and hands. She searched the chest of drawers and pulled out a scarf to tie around my neck.

Helen held the reins and Rebecca sat up front with her, while Katherine and I sat on either side of Norma in the back, each of us holding her hand. They had placed a bonnet on her head and covered her with a blanket with the hope no one on the road would be able to make out who she was or how bad she looked.

Before we turned onto the main road from the property, I jumped out and retrieved the garment bag. Katherine dug through it until she found the medical papers that Helen had made up. I watched as she ripped them into illegible shreds.

She released them little by little as we made our way toward the hospital.

"How did you know where to find me?" I asked her.

"When you didn't show up at the market, Rebecca called home and told me you hadn't returned from the train station. I'd been feeling uneasy all morning so I knew something was terribly wrong. I called Helen at the hospital right away."

I was so tired, my head felt heavy. Everything still felt like a dream—no, a nightmare. The reality of what I had done kept pulsing through me in waves. Nathaniel was dead. And I killed him. Would I go to prison? Would I be hanged? I closed my eyes, causing tears to run down my cheeks.

Katherine reached over and placed her hand on my shoulder. "I can tell them I did it," she said. Her voice was so low, I wasn't sure if I had heard her correctly.

"What?" I whispered.

She moved closer, covered my ear with her hand and whispered, "I will tell the police I killed him. There's a record of me speaking out against Mr. Bryer during his trial, remember? And my diagnosis from the doctor at the asylum. They will see I was institutionalized. They can assume that's where I belong. At least you won't have to worry about the possibility of jail."

So many memories of her taking my punishments rushed in. I shook my head. "I can't let you do that."

"Why not? I already know what to expect at the asylum. And Helen can visit me. She works close by."

"No. I won't let you do it. You've suffered enough because of me." I grabbed my sister and held her tight. "I love you," I whispered.

As we continued on, the realization that the entire town would soon know, that *Justin* would soon know, that I killed Nathaniel made me nauseous. "There's something I need to do before we go to the police," I said.

Katherine's brow furrowed. "Now?"

"Yes. Get Norma to the hospital." I leaned forward

between Helen and Rebecca. "Will you let me off here? There's something I need to do before I go to the police."

Helen and Rebecca looked at each other. Katherine reached out and placed her hand on Helen's shoulder. Helen slowed and pulled the wagon off to the side where I jumped down.

"Will you tell me where the Conroys live?" I asked Rebecca.

She shook her head. "I don't understand."

"*Please*," I begged.

"They live at number 8 Lindell Boulevard." She looked around to get her bearings. She pointed north. "You'll need to take a trolley."

"Which police station should I go to?"

"The Four Courts, on Twelfth and Clark," Rebecca said.

"I promise I'll be there," I said, then rushed away.

# Chapter Thirty-Nine

Norma's dress was too large and the shoulders kept slipping. When I got off the trolley, I had to hold the skirt up from my shoes so I wouldn't trip on it. I had forgotten my gloves on the barn floor and noticed speckles of dried blood on my wrists and under my nails that we'd failed to wash away. I kept my head down as I made my way to Justin's, in case there were specks of blood still on my face, looking up only to make sure I was still headed in the right direction.

I questioned the reasons I was compelled to tell him what had happened, knowing my confession would make this the very last time I would see him. But, as he'd wanted me to hear the truth directly from him about his feelings for Laura, I wanted him to hear the most awful news of my life directly from me. He would be horrified for certain, and not only about what I'd done, but how close he had come to falling in love with someone who could do such a thing.

I took a breath and rang the bell, praying he would be home, as this would be my only opportunity to speak with him before he would read about it in tomorrow's papers.

A servant opened the door and when I asked to see Justin,

she invited me in. To my dismay, Mrs. Conroy stepped into the hall when she heard my voice.

"Sarah! What a surprise." Her mist was lavender, as usual, beautiful and serene. She didn't seem to take notice of my strained and tired features and my ill-fitting dress, or at least she was kind enough to pretend.

Justin appeared at the top of the stairs. I was relieved he greeted me with a smile, even after I'd left him in the storage room without explanation. "May I speak with you?" I asked.

"Of course," he said, and made his way down the stairs.

I suddenly smelled rosewater, and it occurred to me I should tell him *and* his mother why I was there. I turned to Mrs. Conroy. "May the three of us speak somewhere in private?"

"Certainly," she said.

I followed her to the library with Justin behind us. She and I sat on a settee, while Justin sat across from us in an armchair, leaning forward with his elbows on his knees, his hands clasped together as in prayer. He looked almost as concerned as I felt.

I was about to reveal to the man I loved how I was led to kill another human being. I sat on my hands and inhaled deeply to settle my nerves. Would they believe me as to why it happened or would they think I was mad? I knew it didn't matter either way. There was no time left to reconcile the difference.

"I want to first apologize to you for what happened at the store yesterday," I said to Justin. "When you hear my story, you'll understand. All I ask is for you both to please be patient and listen until I have finished because I don't have much time. Something terrible has happened today, to a married couple. And I was a part of it. That's why I'm here. I wanted to tell you personally, before you hear about it from others and read about it in the papers. It's the only way I can be assured you will know the entire truth."

I chose not to tell them how I knew of Nathaniel's abuse of Norma due to my gift; instead, I disclosed how I too often noticed the bruises she tried but failed to hide and how she confirmed it on the day she showed up at the market with broken fingers.

"She was the woman who rushed out when you were there yesterday," I said to Justin. I explained why she had come to the market in the first place and had acted so bizarrely. "When she didn't show up at the train station, I knew something had happened."

They glanced at one another, distress on both of their faces.

It was clear Justin and his mother were troubled by what I was saying, but I was relieved that while I spoke, neither of them were looking at me as if I were out of my mind. I watched as their expressions changed from curiosity to horror to shock, and when I finished, I extracted the scarf from my neck. Justin ran his hands through his hair as he stood. His mother stared at me with her mouth open. I waited for one of them to speak.

"He did that to you?" Justin asked, pointing to my neck. His tone was filled with anger.

"He did." I looked at Mrs. Conroy whose lower lip trembled as she stared.

"Norma is at the hospital?" she asked when she finally shifted her gaze.

"Yes. With my sister, Helen, and Rebecca. I'm to meet them at the police station. I should be going." I looked at Justin. "I'm so sorry. About everything." Exhaustion and stress caused tears to spill out once again. "I'm sorry that these may be the last words you hear from me, and this sickening incident, your last memory of me."

He knelt in front of me and placed his hand on my knee. "You only did what you had to do." His tone was gentle. "I'll come with you to the police station."

"And so will I," Mrs. Conroy said. "I'll have the carriage brought around."

When she departed, Justin sat next to me and pulled out a handkerchief. "You are incredibly brave," he said as he handed it to me.

I smiled through my tears, relieved that the man I loved, believed me.

I sat between them in the carriage, my thoughts and emotions a tangled mess as I wondered what would become of me. Apparently, Mrs. Conroy sensed my dread.

"If you hadn't been there this morning, Norma Malone would be dead," she said, patting my knee.

"And if you hadn't protected yourself, you most likely would be too," Justin said.

It was true. Had the scythe not been in reach, I would not be sitting in this carriage.

It didn't take long to arrive at the Four Courts. From what I could see through the carriage window, it was an impressive limestone structure the size of couple of city blocks, with carved dormers, arched windows, and an ornate dome. Mrs. Conroy saw my look of awe.

"If one didn't know what business took place within its walls, he or she would think it was a grand theatre." She squeezed my hand. "How I wish it were."

Katherine, Helen, and Rebecca were waiting out front, all three with a look of anguish.

Helen informed us that Norma had severe head trauma, broken bones, maybe even internal injuries. "The doctor confirmed we won't know the extent of it until she is fully examined."

Katherine looked at me. "Are you ready?"

Nausea churned my stomach and my tears would not stop flowing.

Justin grabbed my hands. "We're here for you."

I wasn't sure what happened to them once we told the police why were there. The police chief and another officer led me into a room with a small table and a few chairs, and kept me there for two hours asking question after question about what happened from the moment I woke up that morning.

Katherine, Rebecca, and Helen were in the waiting room when I was finally led out. I looked around for Justin and his mother.

"They were questioned and then asked to leave," Rebecca said. "They're hiring their lawyer for you."

The four of us were taken to a police wagon and driven back to the Malone property. Heaviness and sickness coursed through me the closer we came to it, the image of Nathaniel's cleaved skull and blood-covered body filling my mind.

By the time we returned to the barn, his slumped body was covered in flies, the once red blood now black due to the heat and open air. The sight was so gruesome, two of the police officers gasped and turned their faces away.

I was told several more times to go over what had happened from the moment I awoke, step-by-God-awful-step. I had to walk through the house, explaining I'd been in it that day, in which rooms, and why. My bloody, torn dress was taken as evidence, as was the scythe handle and the hammer, after two artists had finished sketching the horrific scene in the barn and a photographer took several pictures, including a few of me.

I was interrogated again, this time by a detective who asked, "Exactly how did you know Mrs. Malone's life was at stake this morning?"

*I heard her voice in my head telling me her soul was about to slip through the knothole.* My thoughts swirled with what to say as my eyes held his intense gaze.

"Miss Richardson?" he asked.

"I … I just knew."

His brow furrowed at my response.

The women were also interrogated again, each explaining their own version of what they saw and experienced once they had arrived on the Malone property earlier that day. A few hours passed before I realized word had spread around town. Many more people had shown up on the property—the coroner, more police, several newspaper reporters, and several spectators.

By the end of the day, I was too exhausted to be frightened, even when the police said they had no answer when Katherine asked how long it would take to complete the investigation. I wanted nothing more than to lie down in a darkened room and sleep away however long it took in order to escape the fear of waiting, wondering, and worrying what would become of me.

# Chapter Forty

I was told I must not leave my residence during the investigation. Since Mrs. Callaghan didn't know me well enough to feel comfortable with me staying there any longer, I was grateful John and Rebecca agreed to take me in. They had no extra rooms, but Katherine's bed was big enough for the two of us. As when we were young, she and I lay side by side that night. To keep me from mulling over the events of that horrible day, we reminisced about our time in Steelville with Grandma Rose, Momma, and Daddy—a time when we were both too young to know how complicated and harsh the world could be.

Despite my exhaustion, I slept little that night. Dreams woke me several times, of Norma pleading for my help while fighting off a blood-soaked Nathaniel. I calmed myself each time by praying to God to bring peace to my distressed mind.

The following morning, Katherine rode in a hired carriage to retrieve my belongings from Mrs. Callaghan's. It didn't take long for her to return. Through the window, I noticed her mist was turning angry red as she carried a wrapped bundle of my clothes.

"What is it?" I asked when she opened the door.

"Reporters. They were gathered outside Mrs. Callaghan's. They followed me here." She walked over to the window and pulled back the lace curtains. We watched as carriage after carriage began pulling up in front of John and Rebecca's house, catching the attention of pedestrians. Soon several people stood in the yard.

"What should we do?" I asked.

"I'll put in a call to the market," she said.

John came home immediately. He threatened trespassing charges if anyone dared step foot in his yard. He even put a call in to the police.

"Citizens have the right to gather as long as they aren't intruding onto your property," he was told. An officer was eventually sent to disperse the crowd when they began affecting the flow of street traffic.

As we ate dinner that evening, I couldn't express enough how sorry I was that my actions resulted in such a nuisance for John and Rebecca. Both told me it was a minor and, more importantly, a temporary inconvenience and not to worry myself about it.

"They're eager for the truth and soon they'll get it," John said.

The following day, John decided it was best he stay home until things settled down, so Katherine went to help Rebecca at the market. After I'd finished washing and drying the breakfast dishes, John and I sat at the kitchen table drinking coffee.

"You warned me about getting involved with the Malones," I said.

"Yeah, I did get a bad feeling, as if it might change your life, and not for the better."

My throat tightened. "Are you sensing jail for me?"

John stared at his liver-spotted hand wrapped around the mug. My insides knotted the longer he took to answer.

"It's gonna be up to you to make sure that doesn't happen," he finally said.

"How?"

"Don't know exactly. All I can say is, you'll know."

Although I was grateful for the lawyers Justin's parents hired for me, I sensed John might fight harder because he truly cared for me. "I know this is a lot to ask, but would you consider defending me?"

John patted my hand and gave me a tight grin. "You need the best chance you can get. And unfortunately, I'm not the one to give that to you. It's been too long for me. Know that I will be there for you in other ways, don't you worry."

ALTHOUGH NO ONE spoke to the reporters, I was mentioned in the paper daily: *Miss Sarah Richardson was seen performing house-hold chores while she waits,* or *Miss Rebecca Larsen and Miss Katherine Richardson, sister of Sarah Richardson, were seen exiting the Larsen home and heading to Larsen's Market at half-past six this morning.* It baffled me that anyone would be interested in such mundane observations, but I knew what the reporters and the reading public were eagerly awaiting was the moment a police officer would come to the door.

Justin visited me in the evenings, when the reporters had headed home for the day. He'd ask how I was holding up and reminded me how brave I had been, and still was. "I knew you were like no one I'd ever met, and I find myself more and more in awe of you," he said.

I had to restrain myself from rushing over and embracing him.

On the third evening, he brought two gentlemen with him. He introduced them as William Barstow, defense attorney, and Thomas Tanner, co-counsel, the men his parents hired to defend me. I was pleased Mr. Barstow's mist was a deep blue, the color of knowledge and assuredness, while Mr. Tanner's was bright orange, a shade of confidence. Seeing Justin standing beside these decent gentlemen eased my anxiety and filled me with hope.

Mr. Tanner took notes and Justin and John listened, each for the second time, as I recounted to Mr. Barstow the detailed account of what had happened. Afterward, I answered their many questions. Mr. Barstow explained how the investigation was progressing. Part of the delay, he said, was that the police hoped Norma would improve enough to speak in order to corroborate my story or counter it. She'd been in a coma since that horrible day and therefore couldn't explain what had happened to her.

"There seems to be extensive injuries to her neck and throat, bruises that indicate she was choked with both a pair of hands and a rope. She may never recover her ability to speak," Mr. Barstow said. "Her brain may also have been permanently damaged. Therefore, we need to proceed as if we cannot rely on her testimony."

My mood dimmed at the thought of having to be the sole voice of truth.

Two days later, a police officer came to the door. John told him to arrest the reporters for trespassing as a number of them had followed the officer up to the threshold. I watched from the window as the reporters reluctantly stepped back onto the sidewalk, telling each other to "shush" so they could hear what was being said.

I stood beside John as the officer read the written warrant that stated he'd been "commanded to arrest Miss Sarah Richardson for the charge of murder and bring her forthwith to the Four Courts calaboose where she will be held until called before a judge."

Mr. Barstow had warned me a murder charge was the most likely possibility; regardless, I was lightheaded hearing it spoken. I grabbed John's arm.

He placed his hand on mine and looked at me with gentle

eyes. "You'll be all right," he said. "I'll contact Mr. Barstow and let him know."

My insides shook as the officer walked me past the frenzied reporters.

"How do you feel being placed in the hoodlum wagon, Miss Richardson?" someone yelled.

AFTER PROCESSING, which included taking my photograph while I held a chalk slate with my name and the date, I was asked to hand over straight pins and hair pins that could be used as weapons, as well as my boot laces for whatever reason, and then brought to a room to await the arrival of the police matron. She would escort me to the calaboose, "a Spanish word for dungeon," the processor said. "Lucky for you, no one stays in that dreadful place longer than forty-eight hours."

As I waited for the matron, I listened to shouts and screams in the distance. One in particular made me shudder. A woman with awful pain in her voice was begging for liquor. Since there was nothing I could do to help her, I said a prayer for her and one of protection for myself to stop my psychic mind from opening up further and mentally sharing her agony. I thought of Justin to block out the awful noise. How I wished he were with me, easing my worry as he'd done the past several days.

The door finally opened, and a petite older woman walked in. She introduced herself as Mrs. Harris. Her eyes were round and sunken in, her hair dark and wavy, parted down the middle and pinned back. She wore a high-necked dress. Although her look was very serious, her mist was a calming light green.

As I studied her, she studied me from my feet to my dress, to my face and hair. Her scrutiny reminded me of Mrs. Digby.

She relayed to me what she'd been told by the police chief about why I was there.

"He essentially called it a 'passion murder,'" she said.

"I assure you it was neither murder nor passion," I replied. "I had no choice but to defend myself if his wife and I were to live."

She stared at my face for several more seconds. "Regardless, Miss Richardson, you are accused of a felony which means you must stay in the calaboose until your hearing. If Hell exists on earth, this would be it."

My arm hair prickled. "What do you mean?"

"The city's worst criminals are brought there upon arrest. Women in one cell, men in another, only separated by bars, so you'll be in sight of everyone. You'll hear things you may have never heard before, and possibly witness things that only a person with a deviant mind could perform."

I stared, disbelieving. "There isn't a safer place for people like me?"

"Miss Richardson, you are suspected of murder, and so are more than half the people you'll soon meet. Until you've been proven innocent of the charges, you *are* like them."

"I'm innocent," I whispered pathetically.

"Perhaps you are, but there is nothing I can do about it." Her eyes softened and her shoulders relaxed. "If you are pure of heart and mind, they will know and they will harass you for what they consider weakness. So, the only advice I can give you is to do your utmost to stand tall and look them in the eye if it warrants, while at the same time staying in a constant state of prayer. Discreetly, mind you. It will help you appear strong."

Mrs. Harris handed me a thin blanket and escorted me down a hallway and through a door where she acknowledged a guard who stood inside. I said another prayer of protection when the shouts and laughter and screams needled my skin.

The noise quickly settled when we walked in and everyone looked at me. There were several men in a cell on one side of the room, although I didn't look at them long enough to count how many. The only detail that caught my attention, besides the foul stench of vomit, feces, and body odor, was that their mists were a revolting mixture of yellowish-brown, moss green, and gray.

"Come over here, pretty girl!" someone yelled.

On the other side of the room was the women's cell. I held my head up as I approached, as Mrs. Harris had suggested, and looked each of the women in the eyes. There were six of them.

"Please remember your humanity," Mrs. Harris said as her gaze swept over the women.

The guard ushered me in and locked the cell door behind me. As Mrs. Harris walked away, I found myself wishing against hope that she would stay.

The men's jeers and whistles started again. I ignored them and looked at two of the girls who seemed young, thirteen or fourteen years old, and unkempt. One had sores on her face and she scratched her head continually. I knew not to get too close. The other crossed her arms as if she was embracing herself. She stepped back into the corner when I looked at her, as if she wanted to disappear. Her cloudy gray mist told me she was as terribly frightened as I was.

Another woman, who looked to be just older than me, was sitting on the floor with her back against the wall. Her whole body trembled. She stared at my lace-less boots awhile and then asked, "Would you happen to have liquor in there?"

I shook my head.

She drew her knees up under her chin, wrapped her arms around her legs, and returned to rocking and moaning.

Another older, stout woman gave her a sharp rap on the head. "Quiet there!" she hissed, and then turned her angry eyes to me. She was surrounded by murky brownish-red, an indication of uncertainty and resentment. "You the murderess? 'Cause you don't look like a murderess."

"I'm not," I said.

"I saw your picture in the paper. It said you killed that man. Split his skull right down the middle. If that ain't murder, then I don't know what." She clapped her hands in front of her face, before wiping the bloodied guts of a fly on the front of her pinafore.

The thick stench from the slop buckets drifted toward me. A couple of the women laughed as I stepped toward the barred window. It was too high to peer out, but I still tried to catch a waft of fresher air.

"You'll get used to it," one of the women said.

*Dear God, I hope not.*

Only a few slept that night, and I wasn't among them. There were vicious fights in both cells, and the anger hung in the air hours later. Several times, a male with a young-sounding voice begged to be left alone. "*Please* stop," he cried out constantly.

The two younger women near me whimpered, and the painful groans of the woman who'd been begging for liquor got louder until a guard yanked her out of the cell and dragged her from the room. I made myself as small as possible, hugging my knees to my chest and resting my forehead on my knees.

Resentment was building. Getting involved with the Malones might not have been worth what I was possibly facing. The frightening thought that this place could be my future home made the heaviness in my chest more expansive and my bitterness fouler. If only I hadn't pried into Norma's life.

*If you hadn't done what you did, Norma wouldn't be alive. She needed you.* The words came with a scent of rosewater. Grandma Rose was imparting her strength.

I remembered how she'd gone to jail for a few nights in Steelville for making the councilmen angry, and I wondered if her bed had been more comfortable than my blanket on the floor, or the sounds and smell of her cell less appalling.

# Chapter Forty-One

I stood in a courtroom the following afternoon, praying the judge would be merciful. Katherine and Justin were there in the event the judge granted Mr. Barstow's request that I be released on recognizance until my trial. Mr. Barstow warned me not to be too hopeful.

The judge began by reiterating that I had been charged with the murder of Nathaniel Travis Malone. He said my case would be turned over to a state prosecutor, and I would face a grand jury. My trial date would be set within the next six to nine months. "And until that time, Sarah Richardson, you will be held without bail in the Four Courts Women's Holdover."

Katherine gasped as my knees buckled. Mr. Barstow and Mr. Tanner each grabbed me by an arm and held me up. The judge instructed the waiting officer to escort me to the holdover. Mr. Barstow asked if he could be given a few minutes to advise me further, to which the judge agreed. Katherine and Justin followed us to a private consultation room, where the officer waited outside the door. There were only four chairs and a small table so Justin stood behind me, his hands resting on my shoulders. He asked Mr. Barstow why there was no bail.

"Because murder is not a bailable offense," Mr. Barstow responded.

"Even though it was justified?" Katherine asked.

"It's up to us to prove it was."

I clenched handfuls of my skirt to keep my fingernails from piercing my palms. "What if we can't?" I asked.

Mr. Barstow looked at Mr. Tanner. Both men frowned.

"Murder in the second degree, which could mean ten years or more in prison. Or … murder in the first degree, which carries the death penalty," Mr. Tanner said.

If I hadn't already been sitting, I would have collapsed.

Justin knelt beside me and grasped my hands while Mr. Barstow assured me he would do everything in his power to prove it was justifiable.

"You must have faith in the truth, Sarah," Mr. Barstow said.

"The truth is all I have," I replied, pushing away the knowledge that that's all my sister had before she was sent away to the asylum. "Do something for me," I said to Katherine before the guard took me away. "Write to Daddy. Tell him what I've done."

Katherine shook her head. "He doesn't understand us at all, Sarah."

"Please," I said as the guard ushered me out.

I left her, not knowing if she would do what I asked.

&a;

ONCE AGAIN, I waited in Mrs. Harris's office; this time, for her to escort me to the holdover, my home for the next few months. I prayed it would be less vile than what I'd been subjected to in the calaboose because if it was the same, or worse, I'd give in to despair.

She didn't keep me waiting long and asked how I fared overnight.

"I was completely miserable," I said.

"That is what the system hopes for," she responded.

"Why wouldn't they want more sanitary facilities, and less corrupted language and behavior? The guards didn't even attempt to demand civility when fights broke out in *both* cells. And a young man cried all night, begging someone to stop touching him. I prayed to God he wasn't being violated!"

"There's a reason this conduct is ignored. So that those who can be saved, might be."

Her answer was not what I expected. I shook my head. "I don't understand."

"It's a deterrent, Miss Richardson. Hopefully one will not break the law again after they've been introduced to the profane and dangerous life that awaits them in prison."

Sickened by the wretched conditions, so many foul minds, and shocking behavior, I said, "It certainly worked for me. I will never come back here again, I assure you."

She smiled. "I pray not."

"Is it like this in the holdover?"

"No. A safer space has been created for women who must await their trial in custody."

The tension in my neck and shoulders slackened as she spoke.

"You will be housed in a separate part of the jail, away from the men, where there is a matron always on staff. We matrons try and teach decency and humility to women who are amenable to being reformed. You will be allowed an hour per day for creative endeavors, and one hour per day in the jail yard for exercise. You will be given two meals per day. And you will be allowed to request books from the jail library."

"Is there privacy?"

Her brow furrowed. "No, Miss Richardson. It's not economically feasible, nor are such luxuries acceptable. Again, there must be some sort of a deterrent."

At her demand, I surrendered my dress as she handed me

a beige-colored one made of course linen. Although it was cinched at the waist, it hung on me like an over-sized vegetable sack. Felt slippers a size too big, replaced my boots. I had the absurd thought of how Laura would react if she saw me in my new attire. It was the extreme opposite of the silk and lace I had worn in the days of Thaddeus Mitchell.

I followed Mrs. Harris to the women's wing.

"I remind you to stay strong in mind and spirit. Many of the women here can be as profane and threatening as any man." As my stomach churned, she added, "However, there are a few, like you, who should not be here. They are the ones I hold most hope for."

Her warm words surprised me.

"You don't think I should be here?"

"I've been here enough years and have met enough women to know truth from falsehoods. Unfortunately, my sense of character holds no weight in the courtroom."

As we entered a door marked Women's Holdover Hall, I held my head up and jaw tight. Even if I didn't feel brave, I wanted to look as if I were. The hall was a large room with ten cells. Five on one side, five on the other. A wall divided each, and only the front was barred.

Hands—scrawny, broad, smooth, wrinkled—gripped the bars. The memory of walking the path to the asylum came to me, when so many stared from behind the bars of the fence, their mists and whispers mixing and separating like a kaleidoscope. From what I could see from my sideways glances, there were two slop buckets, two cots, and two women in each cell. I prayed my cellmate was as innocent as I was.

One woman laughed as we passed by, another swore, and yet another spat, hitting Mrs. Harris on the arm.

Mrs. Harris stopped and looked at her as she took a kerchief from her pocket and wiped it off. "You've lost your privileges for the next twenty-four hours, Miss Jenson," she said.

The woman turned her back.

We approached the middle of the room where a woman was sitting at a desk. She wore a gray dress buttoned up to her chin. Her black hair had streaks of silver, her mouth and dark eyes severe. I would have thought she was coldhearted, but like Mrs. Harris, her mist was light green.

"This is Sarah," Mrs. Harris said to the woman.

"She's the angel of death," a voice called out from a cell behind us. "Killed that man with a scythe."

Mrs. Harris and the woman in gray ignored the comment.

"And this is Miriam," Mrs. Harris said to me. "She is the hall's matron."

Mrs. Harris gave me a nod before walking away. She turned back. "Twenty-four hours for Miss Jenson."

Miriam nodded and wrote something on her pad of paper. She grabbed the ring of keys attached to her belted waist and motioned for me to follow.

"As you have seen, we have a code of conduct that must be followed. Be respectful of everyone. No spitting, fighting, or threatening. A full list of rules is tacked up in each room. If you fail to conduct yourself properly, you will lose your privileges for twenty-four hours, or, if it warrants, you will be moved to the solitary wing, which is far worse than the calaboose. Your roommate is Sophia." She motioned with her chin to the girl standing alone in the cell.

Sophia had wavy wheat-colored hair. She was tall and clearly with child. Her mist turned a murky shade of envy green the longer she stared at me.

She sat on her cot when I entered, watching me closely. I pretended her scrutiny didn't bother me.

"You're pretty."

I turned to her. "Thank you. So are you," I lied, staring at the inflamed red spots on her chin and forehead, and a smile that revealed a missing tooth. "How old are you?"

"I'm fifteen. I got a baby in me. I ain't even married."

I sat on my cot and looked at her, not sure what to say.

"You kill that man?" she asked.

"Why are you here?" I asked in return, not wanting to explain my actions yet again.

She folded her arms across her chest. "I asked you first."

"I didn't want to."

"How come you did then?"

"I'd be dead now if I hadn't."

"Huh. You and me's twins on that mark."

"How's that?" I asked.

Sophia bit her bottom lip. "I ain't ready to tell you just yet. Got to get to know you first."

"Here you are." Through the bars, Miriam handed me a sheet, a pillow, and a blanket.

Even though they were standard offerings, they held so much comfort.

ROUTINE BECAME MY SOLACE. There was barely time for tedium to set in as the day was broken up every few hours. We were awakened at six every morning and were sitting in the dining hall eating breakfast by six-thirty, back in our cells by seven-fifteen. We were brought to the craft room at nine where we could draw, sew, or write letters.

At noon, we were given a midday snack of bread and milk in our cells. At two we were marched out to the exercise yard where we were encouraged to move our bodies by playing tag or hopscotch, or whatever game our imaginations could invent, as when we were children. I would usually sit alone under the shade of a tree and watch others play.

At four o'clock, we were brought to the music room where volunteers from the Women's Christian Temperance Union gave lessons on the piano, violin, or cello. Although it was noisy, it was also the library. By six in the evening, we were in the dining hall once again, eating our supper that always consisted of a meat, a vegetable, and a bread roll.

Twice a week, at eight o'clock in the evening, we were taken to the showers. I learned quickly that modesty had no place here. By nine o'clock every night it was lights out, whether we were tired or not.

When I couldn't fall sleep, I thought about Sophia—so young and misguided. As she slept, I closed my eyes and concentrated on her, trying to get a sense of how she grew up. Images flashed: a younger sister, a cold mother, a drunken, ill-tempered father.

I did this a few nights in a row, gathering images and feelings and stitching together her undesirable story. Finally, I knew why she was there—the child she was carrying was her father's, and he wanted the evidence of his transgression to disappear. One terrifying night, he attempted just that. Sophia murdered her father to save herself. Instead of him burying the baby, she buried her father.

After piecing Sophia's story together, I wondered if what I'd seen and surmised was correct. I brought it up as subtly as I could as we sat on our beds sipping our milk and eating our bread during midday snack. "Surely they'll give you more food as your pregnancy advances."

She shrugged. "I hope so. But part of me wants this child to starve."

I stared at her. "Why would you say that?"

"It's worse than a bastard. Wouldn't surprise me if it came out with horns and a tail."

"My God, Sophia. The child is innocent."

"Maybe so, but I have kin that had babies together and they ain't right in the head. There's something wrong with 'em." She bit into her lower lip and looked down at her feet.

I was pretty sure she realized she'd said more than she'd intended.

"Anyway, I might as well tell you what happened so you

don't think I'm evil. I killed my daddy 'cause he wouldn't stop hurting me and my little sister. He's the one that made this baby, then he got mad at me 'cause of it. He wanted the baby dead. Killing it meant killing me too so I did what I had to. I hope that son-of-a-bitch burns in Hell for eternity."

I'd read the images correctly and it made me feel ill. This young girl had been through hell only to wind up in a place almost worse.

"Did you tell someone?"

"No. It took some weeks before my secret got out. The cornfield where I buried him gave me away. I guess I was too stupid to realize I couldn't dig up the young cornstalks and replant them on top of him and expect them to grow like nothing happened. When it came time to harvest, the workers spotted the dried-out brown patch in the middle of the field. By then parts of his carcass had been dug up by animals and eaten or whatnot."

"No one wondered where he was?"

"'Course they did. Police asked questions early on when Momma made a missing report. When they asked what I thought, I told them he probably shacked up somewhere with a woman he met at the liquor house. It wasn't until Momma realized I was pregnant that she made sense of what happened. I told her I would do it all over again, I hated him that much. She said I sinned against God by breaking two of His Commandments: Thou shalt not kill and honor thy mother and thy father. She said I had to pay for those sins. She's the one that put me in here."

"I am so terribly sorry, Sophia. For everything you've been through."

She'd had a troubled life due to no fault of her own, and now she was paying a high price for putting a stop to it. I told her I would pray the judge would have mercy on her. She only shrugged and said whatever the outcome, she would be happy knowing her father could never put his hands on her or her sister ever again.

Despite the terrible story my psychic nosiness brought out, I was grateful my gift was improving. Grandma Rose and John had told me it would get stronger as I got older and had more experiences, so I continued to practice connecting to other women's stories. If I received an image and a strong sense of what it meant, I'd find a way to approach the topic. They almost always fell into conversation with me, the friendlier ones anyway, eager as they were to talk about themselves. After a while, it became almost effortless.

Daddy used to say our gifts cost more than we had to spend. I eventually understood he was speaking of what happened to Momma, but they also led Katherine to the asylum and me to this jail cell. On the other hand, I understood Grandma Rose's side of it—that trying to help someone whose life is in danger is more important than the consequences we face because of it. I'd come to realize our gift sometimes presents us with a defining moment: do we embrace humanity to save someone or turn our back on it to save ourselves?

I was no longer questioning my decision to get involved with Norma as I had that awful night in the calaboose. I felt with my entire being that if given another opportunity, even knowing what I'd have to face, I would do it all over again. By heeding my gift, I stopped a monster from walking this earth. He could no longer hurt Norma, or any other woman.

# Chapter Forty-Two

I'd written to Daddy a few days after I'd asked Katherine to, because I sensed she wouldn't. Or if she did, it would most likely lack the benevolent tone he deserved. Telling him where I was, was one of the most difficult things I'd ever done. I apologized for hurting him again and told him I understood if he turned his back on me, even though I didn't think he ever would.

When I received his response, it was clear she hadn't written to him. He was surprised and distressed to know where I was and why. He said that he'd come as soon as he could get away from his job. Since I wasn't sure when that would be, I decided not to mention it to Katherine as it would be a reason for her not to visit me on the one day a week she could.

Many more letters came to me than the other women, mostly from the Equality Society. Those who rarely received letters would ask me to read mine out loud. I'd happily read the ones from the Society who gave me much-needed support. I kept Katherine's and Justin's to myself. Katherine's mostly described the daily happenings at the market, or a conversation she'd had with Helen or John or Rebecca. Every so often, she wrote about a clairvoyant moment she'd had, or a dream she found meaningful—things not meant for others to know.

Justin's letters were poetic. I would read and reread them. They had the ability to absorb me so completely, I'd forget for a moment where I was. He would talk about "someday" which gave me the hope and determination I needed to not give in to despair, because like every woman in the holdover, I lived the same day over and again.

The only occasional difference each day was the weather. Not that it mattered so much, since I was only allowed an hour a day outside. If I was sweltering in the sunshine, savoring a breeze, or enjoying the first chill of the season, I relished that one hour in the exercise yard. I called it the magical hour, because even though I was in a yard surrounded by a wall and in view of the gallows, I breathed fresh air and touched tree bark and grass. I inspected the veins of fallen leaves and watched butterflies dance from one clover flower to the next or one dandelion to the next. I watched grown women who were suddenly no longer thieves, murderers, child abusers, or liars. They were momentarily playing and laughing like innocent children.

While the others played or conversed, I'd sit under an old maple, close my eyes, and listen to the *ti-dee-di-di* of the goldfinch or the soothing *coo-coo-coo* of the dove. I'd hear their song and think about me and Katherine as young girls twirling in the pasture or playing "Name that bird" with Grandma as we plucked clothes from the line. And I thought of Grandma Rose's favorite John Keats poem. I'd read the ode about the nightingale to her so many times before she passed, that part of it stayed with me:

> *Thou light-wingèd Dryad of the trees,*
> *In some melodious plot*
> *Of beechen green, and shadows numberless,*
> *Singest of summer in full-throated ease.*

I imagined myself as one of those birds who neither realized, understood, nor cared that they sat in the branches of a tree that was growing within the walls of a jail yard. For an hour a day I was a bird, untouched by and unconcerned about the human condition of sadness or worry. To a bird, a tree was a tree and its leaves a sanctuary whether growing in an open meadow or within confines made of stone.

"You have a visitor, Sarah," Miriam said.

Justin and Katherine came every week and John and Rebecca had visited a few times, so I wasn't surprised.

I followed Miriam to the exercise yard. There were tables and benches set here and there specifically for visitation day, perfect for holding conversations. I stepped out expecting to see Katherine. Instead, a man stood with his hat in his hands and a cautious smile on his face. I caught my breath and ran toward him. Daddy threw open his arms and hugged me, crying into my hair.

"I got here as quickly as I could. My job held me up," he said, smiling through his tears.

"You're not angry with me, Daddy?" I asked after we'd sat down and discussed what had happened in detail.

He shook his head. "I'm not angry. I'm proud of what you did. You and Katherine are good girls. Always have been, the way you care so much about other people. Your grandmother knew it. I'm sorry I worried more about what others thought. I pray this turns out right."

I forbade myself to think it wouldn't.

"I'll be at your trial. Priscilla, too. I've already talked to my boss about it."

"What about your salary? I can't imagine he'll pay you for that time off."

"You got other things to worry about."

"Oh, Daddy, I don't want you to lose another house because of me."

"Priscilla came into an inheritance and we bought the house out-right. We'll be all right."

"Visitors for Sarah Richardson," a guard yelled out.

I looked over to the door. Justin and Katherine were standing together. Justin smiled and headed toward us. Katherine stood still, her look serious, her mist clouding. Daddy stood, his blue mist turning a shade darker, too.

"She'll be all right," I whispered. "And so will you."

Justin kissed me on the cheek and turned to Daddy. "Justin Conroy, sir."

"Charles Richardson. Sarah's father," he said as he shook Justin's hand. "Sarah's told me about you in her letters. I want to thank you and your parents for supporting my daughter."

His voice strained a little, although I was sure Justin didn't notice. Daddy's splotches began popping up on his neck and face, giving away his distress.

"Justin's a good man, Daddy. Like you," I said. I quickly walked toward Katherine, before she decided to leave. "Please join us."

"I don't know what to say to him," she replied.

"Whatever's in your heart. It won't steer you wrong."

She straightened her shoulders and walked back with me.

Daddy's chest expanded with a deep breath as we walked toward him, his eyes on Katherine. The corner of his lip twitched as he held his smile.

"It's good to see you," he said.

Katherine looked down at her feet. She didn't respond.

Justin ran his fingers through his hair as he looked at me, uncertain.

"This has been a long time coming," I said. "I need the two of you in my life. We've held on to bitterness and anger for far too long. Please, talk to each other. For Grandma Rose, for Momma, and for me."

Katherine kicked a pebble. I took Justin's hand and led him away. We sat under a shade tree and talked while looking in their direction, watching for signs of forgiveness. It finally came when both Daddy and Katherine began to cry and reached for one another. I'm not sure what they said, although it didn't matter. Whatever it was, they needed to say it.

When visiting hours were over, Daddy told me to keep my spirits up and promised when the time came, he would be at my trial every day.

A FEW WEEKS after Daddy's visit, I had a visit from my lawyers who informed me the trial was set for the fifth of December—a month away. It had been almost six months since that terrible day, and Katherine had been keeping me updated on Norma's progress. Her reports validated what my gift showed me when I concentrated on her. She was able to sit up and even stand with support for short amounts of time, but she couldn't control the way her head and hands shook. And she had yet to speak.

As the trial date drew near, I began spending more and more hours a day with Mr. Barstow and Mr. Tanner. At ten o'clock every morning, we would meet.

"This will be a sensational trial," Mr. Barstow warned, "because people are always fascinated by passion murders."

"It *wasn't* a passion murder," I said, my stomach flipping at the thought. "He was an abusive monster who attempted to kill his wife and me."

"Passion encompasses more than love and jealousy," Mr. Barstow said. "The fact that you were compelled to come to the aid of a friend who you determined was at risk of being harmed can be considered a passionate act. That being said, will you explain the depth of your friendship with Norma Malone?"

"I care for her wellbeing and that's all. I hardly know her."

"That doesn't bode well for you, Miss Richardson. Why would anyone put themselves at risk for someone they hardly know?" Mr. Tanner asked.

*Because living with what I saw in my mind and not doing something about it was unacceptable.* "My grandmother used to quote Psalm 82:4: 'Rescue the weak and needy; Deliver them out of the hand of the wicked.' She told us that the highest test of our humanity was to save another life if we're called to do so."

"Even if it means killing someone else?" Mr. Barstow asked.

"If that someone is wicked and attempting to kill me, then yes," I replied.

"You understand the prosecution is going to argue against the notion that Mr. Malone was wicked in order to protect the deceased man's integrity. And without Norma Malone's corroborating testimony, the responsibility is ours to prove he was as wicked as you say," Mr. Barstow said.

I had been praying for months that Norma's ability to speak would return. All I could do was pray harder. Suddenly I remembered something.

"John Larsen has seen bruises on Norma."

Mr. Tanner took note.

# Chapter Forty-Three

*The St. Louis Republic*
*St. Louis, MO, Monday, December 5, 1899*
*Trial News*

*St. Louis City—Proceedings begin to-day in the trial of Miss Sarah Richardson, accused of murdering Nathaniel Malone. Claiming self-defense, Miss Richardson split Mr. Malone's skull with a scythe. Norma Malone, Nathaniel's wife, is convalescing at the Chronic Hospital from wounds she received on or about the day of the murder. It is yet unclear how she obtained these wounds since she cannot speak. The St. Louis Women's Equality Society will be holding a demonstration outside the Four Courts in support of Miss Richardson, who had only become a member weeks before the murder.*

I slept little the night before my trial began. In between praying and calming myself with deep breathing, I reread the letters sent to me from the Women's Equality Society.

"Wife beating has been disregarded for much too long," many of them said. "This trial won't allow it to be ignored any longer." Their words lifted my spirits so much that no matter the outcome, I knew with everything in me, it was worth it.

I was allowed visitors the morning of the first day of my trial. Justin and Katherine came to provide me with moral support, but I was too nervous to completely let go of my worry.

Katherine told me what she knew of the planned demonstration on the courthouse lawn.

"This is their opportunity to not only show support for you, but to emphasize the inequality and mistreatment of women while we have the attention of other cities."

"What cities?" I asked.

"There are reporters here from Chicago, Dallas, Cincinnati, and more," Justin said.

"I don't understand. Why do they care about the death of a dock worker in St. Louis?"

"The suffrage movement is gaining momentum all over the country, and because you belong to an affiliation of it, they're interested to see if you and Norma were truly the victims, or if Nathaniel was," he said.

"We know the truth, Sarah," Katherine said. "For the sake of Mildred Bryer, Norma, and women like them, we need to draw attention to it."

John's words came back to me. *Lots of folks think a man controlling his wife with the back of his hand, or a whip, or harsh words is acceptable married behavior… It happens more than you want to know.*

When Mr. Barstow and Mr. Tanner arrived to escort me to the courthouse, Justin embraced me. "I'll be there every moment."

I clung to him, reluctant to let go. "You're going to hear things that might change your mind about me."

"Have faith in me. In yourself. In *us*," he replied.

Later, as I walked to the courtroom with Mr. Barstow and Mr. Tanner, they told me they had made a stop at the hospital earlier that morning to check on Norma's progress.

"We'll be checking on her every day," Mr. Barstow said. "We haven't given up hope on her. She tries to speak, but her words have no form. It sounds as if she's choking. And she has tremors. Her head and hands shake, sometimes violently. When I tried to get her to hold a pencil, her fingers wouldn't grip it."

"Has anyone told her what happened to Nathaniel?" I asked.

"The police told her, and so have we," Mr. Tanner said. "We also informed her that you are on trial for his murder. I think she understood because she began to cry. The problem is, we can't prove she truly understands."

*She does.* I sensed how frustrated she was, as if she was still locked in that trunk, but now she was locked inside a body that wouldn't cooperate with what she desperately wanted it to do.

If only the judge could see what I could see.

From the many windows, we heard the chants of the boisterous crowd outside getting louder. My fear grew as my senses heightened.

"Sarah Richardson is a man-hater!" I heard some yell.

"Sarah Richardson is a heroine!" others yelled in response.

"There will be a crowd in the hallways too, those who couldn't fit into the courtroom but have permission for one reason or another to wait indoors. Most are reporters," Mr. Barstow said. "There will be an officer walking before us and one behind, while Mr. Tanner and I walk on either side of you."

I took a deep breath as we approached, stifling the effect of so many mists, so many eyes, so much judgement, wonder, or ill will emanating from so many people.

The courtroom was as noisy as the hallways, packed with spectators sitting in a tiered semicircle gallery three rows deep, as well as several men crammed in and around the jury box awaiting selection or dismissal. The windows were shut against the December chill. I was thankful for the ceiling fans, even though they did little to dissipate the smell of so many bodies. It brought back a memory of being in church, sitting shoulder to shoulder wishing for a nosegay or a sachet of lavender. There were two tables in the center of the room facing the judge's bench and witness stand. The table on the left was occupied by three gentlemen who studied me as I walked to the other table and sat down between Mr. Barstow and Mr. Tanner.

Once seated, I dared to look over my shoulder to catch sight of those I loved, to see a bright mist amongst the murky ones and a gentle smile instead of a violating stare.

The first familiar face I saw was John's, then Rebecca, Helen and Katherine. Sitting next to her were Daddy and Priscilla. A few rows away, Justin sat next to his mother and father. Their presence calmed me, until my attention was drawn toward the back of the room where Laura sat next to Mrs. Digby and Trudy Gaines. Based on Laura's and Mrs. Digby's cloudy mists and tight expressions, I was certain they questioned how they could have ever befriended someone like me. When I looked at Trudy, she smiled, her mist a soft blue.

It took the first part of the morning for Mr. Matthews, the lead prosecutor, and my attorney, Mr. Barstow, to choose a jury they were satisfied with. The twelve they settled on were a mix of young and old, none looking too wealthy nor too deprived. Sitting as a group, it was hard for me to distinguish the individual mist colors of these twelve men who would determine my fate. All I could discern in the glance I stole was a grayish cloud with thin streaks here and there of bright and dull blue or green or orange; a convoluted mixture resulting in nothing I could interpret. I thought of asking Katherine to spend some time concentrating on them since she was more skilled and less distracted than I was, but I realized it didn't matter. Whether one man or twelve were purple with empathy or brownish orange with close-mindedness, their moods and thoughts would likely shift moment by moment based on what they were being told.

After a short water break, the room was quieted and we all stood as the judge entered and took his seat. Mr. Matthews began his opening statement.

"Miss Sarah Richardson formed an obsession with Nathaniel and Norma Malone which led her to commit a heinous crime." He read aloud the formal account of what happened that day in the barn. When he finished, he said none of it made sense, especially my answer as to why I went there on that day: because "I just knew" Norma's life was in danger.

"Of course she knew. She knew because she was the one who put Norma Malone's life in danger. Miss Richardson went to the Malone property with the intention of getting rid of the one person standing in the way of her pursuing a romantic relationship with Nathaniel Malone. Why else would a woman who claims not to have known Norma very well take it upon herself to buy her a train ticket out of St. Louis? I will tell you why. Because she was in love with Nathaniel and wanted Norma out of the way. When Norma refused to leave her husband, Sarah Richardson turned on her and beat Norma until she was near death. When Nathaniel came back to retrieve his lunch pail that morning, he must have heard Norma screaming in the barn. A struggle ensued between Nathaniel and Sarah Richardson. Yes, he may have been stronger, but he was no match for the long-handled scythe she used to split his skull in half." Mr. Matthews held up the rusted scythe blade with remnants of dried blood. "She hit him so hard, the handle broke off in her hands. Gentlemen of the jury, Nathaniel Malone died trying to save his wife from the murderess sitting before you."

Movement from the jury drew my attention. A few of them were squirming in their seats, their mists darkening and their features tense as they shifted their gaze from me and watched Mr. Matthews walk over to a covered easel.

"Only someone cold-blooded could accomplish something like this." With a flourish, he lifted the cloth. It was an enlarged photograph of Nathaniel's dead and bloodied body, slumped in a sitting position with the scythe blade embedded in the top of his skull. The jury and audience gasped.

I closed my eyes tight while my heart thudded in my ears. How had I been capable of such a thing?

"You might be wondering how Katherine Richardson, Rebecca Larsen, and Helen McCabe knew to find Sarah Richardson at the Malone property when she didn't show up for work at the market. According to their initial statements, they weren't certain if she'd be there. They simply *assumed* that's where she'd be. Why do you suppose they assumed that? Because they too, knew Sarah Richardson was fixated on this couple. They believed the stories Sarah fed them about her wanting to help 'poor' Mrs. Malone get away from her 'villainous' husband.

"Gentlemen of the jury, I will bring forth witness after witness—from neighbors to fellow church-goers to coworkers —who will testify about his friendly demeanor, his charismatic nature, and his tendency to be the hardest-working man on the docks. They will tell you what a decent citizen he was, and what a loving husband he was to Norma."

After over an hour of exposition, Mr. Matthews concluded. His opening argument filled people's minds with falsehoods which were stated so matter-of-factly, the dense energy in the room closed in.

During the momentary break, I looked for those who loved and supported me, needing reassurance that they still believed in me. My father, Katherine, John, Justin. Rebecca, Mrs. Conroy, Helen. When I looked over my shoulder, they turned their attention to me, and with a nod or a smile, each gave me what I needed.

Mr. Barstow stood for his opening statement. "Your Honor, and gentlemen of the jury, I am going to make my speech after the prosecution rests. Until then, know that what Mr. Matthews described is better suited for one of those crime novels that are popular today. His story doesn't apply here because there were three crucial decisions Sarah Richardson made on the day of Nathaniel Malone's death; decisions that a cold-blooded murderess would not make. First, she helped escort Norma Malone to the hospital. Second, she went to the home of one of St. Louis's prominent families and told them what happened. And third, she insisted on making a statement to the police afterward. I encourage you to keep these facts in mind while the prosecution proceeds."

The stream of witnesses began that afternoon, starting with the two officers who took my initial confession, followed by the officers who investigated the crime scene, the photographer and artists who captured images of the body and the property, as well as the coroner and doctors who examined the body. They described in gory detail what they had seen that day, and how the horrific image of Nathaniel's bloody body still caused them nightmares, these professional men who have seen nearly everything a human could do to another.

I shuddered, wondering how their admissions must be impacting not only the jury, but Justin and his parents.

In the following days, the prosecution called more witnesses, men who had worked with Nathaniel, including the dock foreman who spoke of Nathaniel's impeccable work ethic. He and others depicted Nathaniel as selfless, professional, reliable, and personable. A few of them said that on rare occasions when the topic of family came up, Nathaniel told them how much he loved his wife and how blessed he was to have married her.

My only spark of hope came during Mr. Barstow's cross-examination. He asked if they had ever seen Norma in person. Only a few said they'd seen her from a distance at church or some other place around town.

"After all the years you knew and worked with Nathaniel, he never introduced his wife that he claimed to love so much?" Not one of them could say yes.

The prosecution called on several members of their church. Everyone testified about how shocked they were to hear that a man as friendly and God-fearing as Nathaniel could have met with such a violent end. "He was always smiling and so cheerful," many said.

During cross-examination, Mr. Barstow asked what they thought of Norma's personality.

"Timid," "shy," or "withdrawn," they said.

He looked around the courtroom. "It's curious that their personalities were so different. I wonder if she doesn't feel comfortable in public. Or perhaps she didn't feel comfortable around Nathaniel."

Mr. Matthews objected.

AT THE END of every day, my tense muscles ached and my mind was exhausted from the non-stop praise for Nathaniel's character by people who had never observed his true nature the way I had. At one point, Mr. Tanner passed me a note from Justin that told me how it was only a short time before the jury would be educated about the other side that made up Nathaniel Malone. I tried my best to stay strong, but on the fourth morning, I was dismayed all over again.

Laura took the stand. My stomach knotted as her mist clouded at the sight of me. Perspiration formed on my forehead as I listened to her tell everyone how distrusting she came to be of me and how disloyal I had been as a friend. She said I had betrayed her confidence by telling her fiancé of a very private matter I had promised to keep secret.

*I told him about your weak heart so he wouldn't leave you,* I thought in vain.

Then she surprised me by voicing suspicions about my feelings for Justin.

"Sarah failed to tell me that she and my fiancé—I mean my *former* fiancé—Justin Conroy ran into one another on a couple of occasions and even walked home together. If Sarah had been a true friend with nothing to hide, she would have said something."

"Is it true your fiancé broke off your engagement after he met Sarah Richardson?" Mr. Matthews asked.

"Yes, sir."

"Was it because Sarah lured him away from you?"

Laura lifted her chin and stared at me. "She might have tried, but I know Justin would never choose a woman of her … her class."

Although I was hurt, it was hard for me to be angry with her for saying such spiteful things because I knew she was the one in misery.

Mrs. Digby was called to the stand as the prosecution's final witness. Mr. Matthews started by asking for her initial thoughts after learning I had killed Nathaniel Malone.

"Shocked, of course, and then disturbed that I had welcomed her into my home."

"Did you ever have reason to question Miss Richardson's integrity?"

"A few times," she said, and explained how she felt misled about who I had presented myself to be in my introduction letter. "I was under the assumption she was the grand-daughter of Percival Richardson, and that was the sole reason I accepted her. When I discovered she wasn't at all related to him, it caused me extreme embarrassment." She continued to tell of the night Laura severed our friendship due to her anger and mistrust of me, and how Mrs. Digby told me to leave the very next day. "And there is something that nags at me to this day. Something I wish I had paid more attention to."

"What is that, Mrs. Digby?"

She told about an inquiry I'd made during church services one day, when I asked what she knew about Nathaniel and Norma Malone. She said she found it odd that I would be interested in the couple, since they didn't seem to have anything in common with me. "And one more thing I feel obligated to say," she said. "Sarah remarked on how handsome Nathaniel was."

I gripped my skirt with my fists. It was she who mentioned his attractiveness. I had merely agreed.

AT THE END of the day, the prosecution finally rested their case. I was never so relieved. I'd sat through four emotionally fatiguing and demeaning days, suffering through the prosecution's attempt at convincing the jury—and everyone else—that I was the one with the devious character, and I'd killed a decent man in a passionate rage.

# Chapter Forty-Four

Miriam fetched me a little earlier than she had the past several days. Mr. Barstow and Mr. Tanner wanted to spend extra time preparing me for the second half of the trial. That the jury would now hear the truth dispelled some of the gloom that had enveloped me. It lightened even more when Mr. Tanner said he had promising news about Norma.

"She took a few steps. She was being helped by two nurses, but she walked. She's also able to hold her own spoon. We're hoping she'll be able to hold a pencil and write soon."

"Is there any chance she might get well enough in the next few days to testify?" It was doubtful, I knew.

Mr. Tanner's mist dimmed. "It's not likely, but we'll keep checking in."

Mr. Barstow's opening remarks directed the jury's attention away from Norma and Nathaniel and turned the focus on me. He told them about how and where I grew up, and the love I had for my family to the point of leaving Jefferson City to be near my sister. He pointed to where Katherine, Justin, and the rest of my supporters sat and said, "The reason these good citizens are here today is because they believe in Sarah Richardson." He pulled a piece of paper out of his vest pocket. "These words were spoken by Mr. John Larsen. Many of you know him. He's been the owner of Larsen's Market for thirty years. His daughter Rebecca hired Sarah Richardson days after Sarah moved to town. I asked Mr. Larsen what he thought of Sarah, and he said this: 'She is a young woman uncertain about her place in the world yet, as young people tend to be, but she's one of the most selfless and kind-hearted women I've ever met.'"

Compassion filled me when I heard his words, because I knew John had the ability to see things in me that no one else could.

"As we proceed, I fully believe you will learn for yourselves that Sarah Richardson truly is a kind-hearted woman and not the murderess the prosecution has made her out to be. Now, if you'll recall, on the first day of the trial I told you to keep three things in mind; three crucial choices Miss Richardson made after Nathaniel was killed—decisions that are not made by a cold-blooded killer.

"Decision number one: she joined her sister Katherine, Miss Larsen, and Miss McCabe as they brought Norma Malone to the hospital. Sarah Richardson could have made excuses to let them do it and used the train ticket she'd bought Norma and headed out of town, but she did not. Not only did she go along, she held Norma's hand all the way there.

"Decision number two: When they arrived at the hospital, she was compelled to tell Justin Conroy and his mother what had happened for reasons you will soon learn. She told the ladies to get Norma medical assistance right away, and that she would meet them at the Four Courts Police Headquarters. She then went straight to the prominent Conroy residence to explain what had occurred that morning. At this point, again, she could have gone to Union Station and used that train ticket, but she didn't.

"Decision number three: Miss Richardson went straight to the police after meeting with Mrs. Conroy and her son Justin.

"Gentlemen, do these decisions sound like they were made by a murderess? Not to me. To me it sounds like a scared young woman who wanted Norma to live, and who wanted the Conroys and the police to know the truth about the nightmare she and Norma Malone had been through. And what Sarah Richardson had been through was a fight for her life."

He showed the jury an enlarged photograph of the large finger-shaped bruises around my neck. He then walked over to the blood-splattered dress I'd been wearing that hung on display in the corner of the room. He pointed to the tears, explaining how it was ripped when Nathaniel yanked me toward him.

Mr. Barstow said he would prove that I was performing a noble act on that dreadful morning by trying to help Norma Malone escape a life of hell, and if I hadn't defended myself against Nathaniel Malone, Norma and I would both be dead.

Katherine was called as the first witness for the defense. Mr. Barstow asked her how many times I had come to her with stories of Norma Malone's abuse, and how she and I had come up with a plan to help Norma leave Nathaniel.

After her lengthy explanation, Mr. Matthews stood for cross-examination. He asked if she'd ever met Norma Malone.

"No, sir."

"Have you ever seen Norma Malone?"

"No, sir."

"Then why did you agree to involve yourself in the plan?"

"Because I love my sister. And I believe her."

Mr. Matthews looked at the jury. The smirk on his face made my stomach churn.

"You hear that, gentlemen? She believes her because she is

her sister. That's it. No proof necessary. Her sister could say she saw a cow jump over the moon and Katherine Richardson would say 'all right.'"

"Objection!" Mr. Barstow yelled over the laughter.

"Moving on," Mr. Matthews said. "Will you describe to the jury the part you played in the 1896 trial of Donald Bryer in Jefferson City?" The judge overruled Mr. Barstow's objection. "And if you can't recall, I have the story right here." He held up a newspaper and proceeded to read aloud how Katherine had stormed into the courtroom and accused Mr. Bryer of abusing, then murdering his wife. "Will you tell the jury the outcome of Mr. Bryer's trial, Miss Richardson?"

She narrowed her eyes at him, her mist turning a deep red. "He was found not guilty."

"And what was *your* outcome, Miss Richardson? What happened to you afterward?"

My thoughts immediately went to Daddy, wondering how awful he must feel hearing Mr. Matthews's tone and insinuations.

"I was appalled that the judge and jury could be so ignorant and blind," she replied.

"Since you won't tell the jury what happened to you, I will. You were sent to the lunatic asylum right here in St. Louis, isn't that right?" Before she could answer, Mr. Matthews went on, "You tried to sully the reputation of Donald Bryer in front of the entire town of Jefferson City and you failed, didn't you?"

"Objection, Your Honor," Mr. Barstow said. "What Katherine Richardson did in the past or where she resided has nothing to do with why we are here today."

"I disagree," Mr. Matthews said.

"Explain, Mr. Matthews," the judge responded.

"Sarah Richardson seems to be following in her older sister's footsteps. When Katherine Richardson was released from the asylum, she joined the St. Louis Women's Equality

Society. It's a society of women that is detrimental to the traditional American family. Listen to their disruptive chanting outside this very minute."

He walked over to the window and cupped his hand around his ear for effect.

I wanted so badly to yell out what they were saying outside: "Justice for Sarah! Justice for Sarah!"

Mr. Matthews continued. "This society's goal is to destroy the holy union between husbands and wives; wives who the Bible says should submit to their husbands. And guess what, gentlemen of the jury? Sarah Richardson joined this society of women as well, weeks before she killed Nathaniel Malone."

My insides gripped tighter with every appalling intimation this man made. There were mumbling and whispers throughout the gallery until the judge demanded quiet. I turned and looked at Rebecca and Helen. Their anger-red mists matched Katherine's.

# Chapter Forty-Five

Mr. Barstow showed me a newspaper article in the *Republic* the following morning: "*Does the Women's Equality Society want to bring men to their knees?*"

As we neared the courtroom, I heard the Society's women outside, chanting louder than ever: "We want equality and respect!"

"They might cause more harm than good," Mr. Barstow said, his brow furrowed. "The judge is against the suffrage movement, and I'm sure many on the jury are as well."

My heart sank. He wanted their voices stifled for my benefit. "They're speaking out against the inferences made in the news article. Let them be," I said.

JOHN WAS CALLED to the witness stand. He looked right at me with a wink and smile. My confidant, my advisor, my friend. His mist was orange, the color of confidence. I thought of how Trudy Gaines must be feeling seeing John up there. Although she sat with Laura and Mrs. Digby, I turned to look at her. I couldn't help myself. Her eyes caught mine and she gave me a nod and a warm smile. She shifted her gaze back to John. Her mist was soft pink, full of love and serenity. I wondered if he noticed.

Mr. Barstow asked John if he knew either Nathaniel or Norma Malone.

"They've been customers of my market since the day they moved here," he said.

"So, we can assume you've spoken directly to both of them?"

"Yes, sir."

"And what is your impression of Mrs. Malone?"

"Like the church ladies said. Timid, skittish."

"And what about Mr. Malone."

John sat quiet for a moment. I knew he was trying to articulate a convincing way to say he didn't care much for him.

"I guess I would say he was a talkative fella."

"Would you call him friendly?"

"Some might, sure."

"Some? Not you?"

"I always got the sense he was disingenuous," he said.

"Mr. Larsen, can you give us a precise example as to why you feel Mr. Malone was disingenuous?" Mr. Barstow asked.

"I guess I'd have to say his friendly words did little to detract from the bruises I'd see on his wife's face."

There were gasps and murmurs in the gallery until the gavel was brought down.

"Tell us more about those bruises on Norma Malone you saw with your own eyes."

"They'd be faded, like they were a few days old every time, and she'd tried to hide them, either with a veiled hat or the face powder the ladies like to use sometimes."

"What makes you think they were old bruises?"

"They'd be turning green and yella. I'm sure you've had a shiner before. You know how it goes after a few days."

"Yes, sir, I do," Mr. Barstow said. "Did you ever witness Nathaniel hitting Norma?"

"No, sir. Even so, I recognize the results."

"What exactly do you mean by that?"

"I've known a few abused women in all my years. My aunt. My cousin's wife. My momma's dear friend. My own sister. And more. Too many to be proud of the male gender. I came to recognize how these women responded to people, how they tried to hide their fear and shame, and their bruises."

"Do you feel you're a good judge of character, Mr. Larsen?" Mr. Barstow asked.

John looked directly at Mr. Matthews. "I know I am."

I, too, looked at Mr. Matthews and watched as his mist turned a dull shade of purplish-brown, a shade of self-doubt. When it came time for cross-examination, I stifled a grin when Mr. Matthews said he had no questions.

After John was released from the stand, Helen was called. She was asked about the time, the year before, when Norma had gone to the Female Hospital with injuries she'd obtained from taking a fall from a horse.

"As the nurse who attended her, is it your professional opinion that her broken arm, cracked rib, facial lacerations, and bruises were a result of this accident?" Mr. Barstow asked.

"It's possible, yes."

"Is it also possible these injuries could have been a result of being beaten by someone?"

"Yes, sir. That is also a possibility," she replied.

"Was Norma Malone ever asked about that possibility?"

"No, sir. Mr. Malone explained in detail what had happened with the horse. Mrs. Malone was right there when he gave the report. At the time, I felt like I should question her in private, away from Mr. Malone. I asked the doctor if I could, but he said there was no need."

"Why did you feel like you should?" Mr. Barstow asked.

"To make sure it was the truth, because I didn't like the way Mr. Malone took over every conversation. He never allowed her to speak for herself. He acted like she was too fragile to talk or think too much."

"Apparently the doctor did not agree with you?"

"That's right. After everything that's happened though, I wish I had followed my gut."

"Thank you, Miss McCabe," Mr. Barstow said.

Mr. Matthews quickly stood. "You are a member of the Women's Equality Society, Miss McCabe, is that correct?"

"Yes, sir."

Mr. Matthews paused, wrapping his fingers around his chin as if he was thinking. "Explain something to me. Just because a man doted on his wife, you became suspicious. Could it be possible you're not familiar with what true love between a man and woman looks like?"

Mr. Barstow's chair scraped the floor as he stood and yelled, "Objection!"

The judge immediately sustained.

"All right, Miss McCabe, are you saying your patients' family members are not to be believed?"

"No, sir. I'm saying I won't be accepting only one person's explanation from now on if my instincts tell me otherwise."

Mr. Matthews's gaze narrowed. "That's interesting, Miss McCabe, because if I recall correctly, those in the medical field are supposed to suspend personal bias, judgement, or prejudice and simply do their duty as dictated by medical science, or have you forgotten that?"

"There is a very real possibility, Mr. Matthews, if I had followed my instincts—instincts that have been honed by working with female patients as long as I have—that maybe we wouldn't be here today."

"If instincts could be proven with an X-ray or a thermometer I'd say perhaps, Miss McCabe, but I guess we'll never know. That's all I have, Your Honor."

I looked over at the jury, wondering if any of them believed in the power and validity of instincts. Based on their critical expressions and murky mists, it didn't seem so.

Justin was called as the final witness of the day. I thought of his last letter as he walked to the stand, where he said he longed for the day when the two of us could finally sit in a room together and not guard our feelings and words about one another so closely. "We have yet to let our hearts do all the speaking for us," he'd said. Suddenly my thoughts went to Laura. I could feel her in the gallery, watching Justin intently. I sensed from her a mixture of both sadness and love at the sight of him.

Mr. Barstow addressed the jury. "The Conroy family has lived in St. Louis for generations. They are held in high regard in their upper-class social circle. I will remind you that Miss Richardson went straight to the home of Bartholomew and Janece Conroy to speak with their son Justin after traveling with Norma Malone to the hospital. Finding both Janece and Justin home, Miss Richardson told them both what had occurred that morning." He turned to Justin and asked what his relationship was to me.

"We're friends for now."

"Is friendship the only feeling you have toward Miss Richardson?"

"No. I have romantic feelings for her."

Laura gasped and then whimpered. Justin looked to where she sat in the gallery. I, too, turned to look at her but quickly turned back. I hoped he wouldn't notice the looks of animosity directed at the both of us coming from the spectators who apparently sympathized with her.

"Has Miss Richardson expressed those feelings toward you?"

"She has," he said.

"That doesn't bode well for Mr. Matthews's accusation

that Sarah Richardson killed Nathaniel Malone in a passionate, jealous rage does it?"

"No, sir, it does not."

"So that we're clear about this, Mr. Conroy, did you and Miss Richardson express your feelings to one another while you were engaged to Miss Laura Woodard?"

"We did not. It was after I broke off the engagement that I revealed my true feelings to Miss Richardson."

"So, Sarah Richardson did not pursue you first, or purposely break up the two of you?"

"No, sir. I came to the conclusion on my own that I didn't have the love one should have for the person they are engaged to marry. I broke it off with Miss Woodard so that she might find someone who truly loves her."

There was a rustling behind me. I turned and saw Laura and Mrs. Digby standing up. Trudy Gaines looked dismayed. She shook her head when Mrs. Digby motioned for her to get up. Mrs. Digby's mouth tightened and she turned on her heels. The judge slammed the gavel as she and Laura made their way to the aisle where a guard met them and escorted them to the door.

The judge scowled at the disruption. "Do not return to this courtroom," he warned.

Laura glanced over her shoulder. Her angry, teary eyes met mine before she hurried out. I didn't think it was possible, but it seemed she hated me even more.

Mr. Barstow continued. "Mr. Conroy, had Miss Richardson ever spoken to you about Nathaniel or Norma Malone before that dreadful day she showed up at your parents' home?"

"No, sir. Although I saw Norma Malone at Larsen's Market the day before it happened."

"Why were you at Larsen's Market?"

Justin explained that he'd come as a response to my letter.

He described how Norma looked uncomfortable, and how it wasn't long before she rushed out and I went after her.

"Did Miss Richardson explain to you why she ran after Mrs. Malone?"

"I didn't give her a chance. I left. Clearly there was something private and important between them that wasn't my business."

"Did you ever find out why?"

"Yes, sir. When Sarah, I mean Miss Richardson, came to my parents' house to tell us what had happened at the Malones'. She said Norma had come to the market the day before to get Miss Richardson's help to leave Mr. Malone for good."

"So, Miss Richardson told you that she had been trying to help Mrs. Malone leave her relationship with Mr. Malone?"

"Yes, sir." Justin said. "She told me and my mother about her attempts to help Mrs. Malone. She said it was because her husband continually beat her."

Mr. Barstow asked Justin more about my confession to him, and then asked if he'd seen any physical marks on me.

"Yes, sir. She had finger marks on her neck that were turning from deep red to blue."

"Were these the marks you are referring to?" Mr. Barstow asked, pointing to the photograph of my bruised neck.

"Yes, sir."

"Did she say how she came to have those marks?"

"She said Nathaniel Malone did that to her."

Mr. Barstow thanked Justin. As Mr. Barstow sat down, Mr. Matthews stood.

"How long have you and Miss Richardson been courting?"

Justin looked at me. "Our courtship has not yet been officially established."

"And why is that? Are you waiting for something specific?"

"We want to take it slow out of respect for Miss Woodard. It's the proper thing to do."

"You've already broken that poor woman's heart. Whether you wait or not, nothing's going to fix that."

The judge sustained Mr. Barstow's objection.

"All right, Mr. Conroy, you said Miss Richardson told you and your mother everything about Mr. and Mrs. Malone's marriage. Everything she *thought* she knew, anyway, is that right?"

"Yes, sir."

"And you took her word for it?"

"Yes. I believed her."

"Forgive me, Mr. Conroy. You're telling me your love interest shows up on your doorstep and admits to killing a man in a most ghastly way, and you don't think twice about her ability to do such a thing?"

"Of course, I thought about it. I haven't stopped thinking about it for a second. And when I heard that Norma Malone was no longer in a coma, my mother and I went to visit her at the hospital. We asked her if she knows what happened to her—"

"I'm gonna stop you right there, Mr. Conroy," Mr. Matthews interrupted.

Mr. Barstow leaned over and whispered in my ear. "Did you know about that?"

I shook my head. I was as surprised as Mr. Barstow at this news. I was thankful they had, for I knew they would be reassured that what I had told them was the truth.

"Let me get this straight," Mr. Matthews continued. "You and your mother went to see Norma Malone to find out if Miss Richardson was telling the truth? In other words, you didn't believe her story?"

"That's not what I said. I believe Sarah. We just thought that maybe Mrs. Malone could tell you herself that it wasn't murder."

"That's the defense team's job to question Mrs. Malone, Mr. Conroy, not yours."

"I know. I was … so helpless." Justin looked at me. If he could see my mist at that moment, I'm certain he would have seen the brightest shade of pink.

Mr. Barstow stood. "I'd like to discuss this with you and Mr. Matthews in private, Your Honor."

The judge agreed and ordered a ten-minute recess. The lawyers followed the judge into his chamber.

When the lawyers and the judge emerged, Mr. Matthews looked smug and Mr. Barstow looked perturbed. Clearly things had not gone our way.

Mr. Barstow passed a note to Mr. Tanner who read it and immediately passed it to me. *He won't allow Justin's meeting with Norma to be relayed. Until the judge questions Norma himself, she is considered an unreliable source.*

My spirits plummeted.

"Mr. Matthews, are you finished questioning this witness?" the judge asked.

"I am."

"Mr. Barstow, are you finished with your witness?"

"No, sir. I'd like clarification on one more thing." He walked over to Justin. "What reason did Miss Richardson give as to why she came to you before she went to the police?"

"Just what you said yesterday. She wanted me to hear it directly from her, before we read about it in the newspapers or heard it from someone else, to ensure I heard the entire truth."

"What happened after she told you everything?"

"She insisted on going to the police."

"Thank you, Mr. Conroy," Mr. Barstow said.

Justin's eyes met mine as he stepped down, and I caught my breath. I saw pink mist surrounding him. It only lasted a brief second, but for the first time, I was able to see his colors.

# Chapter Forty-Six

As the three of us walked back to the counsel rooms, I could see Mr. Barstow's and Mr. Tanner's mists becoming cloudy.

"You're frightened," I said.

Mr. Barstow looked at me. His eyes were gentle. "I'm not sure the jury understood how significant John Larsen's and Helen McCabe's statements are. And I'm definitely not happy the judge didn't allow Justin to tell us what he learned from Norma Malone."

"Will you interview Justin and his mother privately?" I asked, hopeful that they had been able to obtain some useful information.

"It won't make a difference. The judge was adamant that whatever Norma Malone might have communicated to them, it's not admissible."

I was listless. "What do we do?"

"Mr. Tanner and I are meeting the judge and Mr. Matthews where Norma Malone is convalescing. We're hoping she'll somehow be able to relay her story."

"And if she can't?"

"It'll be up to you to finally convince the jury of the truth," Mr. Barstow said.

They told me they would be back later that afternoon.

I decided not to psychically connect with Norma during the wait. It would be pointless because what she was thinking was not necessarily what she was capable of expressing. No matter how urgently her brain wanted to get her message out, her voice might not obey.

Miriam came to my cell after two hours and escorted me to a counsel room where Mr. Barstow and Mr. Tanner waited. My arm hair prickled as I approached the door.

As I suspected, their mists were cloudy and their looks grim. They both stood when I entered. "I assume the answer is no," I said, sitting.

"You are correct," Mr. Barstow said. "The judge asked Norma if she knew who had caused her physical harm and she nodded. She tried to talk, but her words had no distinct form. It was hard to determine if she even understood what had been asked. So, I gave her a piece of paper and a pencil. Her hands shook so violently she had trouble holding them. She got frustrated when she couldn't draw a straight line and began stabbing the paper with the pencil. I believe she was overly eager to answer. In her excited state, she became overwhelmed. The judge said he could not comprehend anything she was attempting to communicate, and it was clear we were upsetting her with our questions. He won't accept her as a reliable witness."

"What if you showed her a picture of Nathaniel, and one of me, and asked her to point to who hurt her?" I asked.

"We thought of that. The judge said it would prove nothing since the doctor confirmed there is no way to tell at this point in her recovery if she is truly mentally and physiologically capable of understanding what is being asked."

I slumped in the chair.

"Before you get on the stand tomorrow, we need to go over

a few things," Mr. Tanner said, opening the file before him. He ran his finger down a page of text. "One thing we still need to clarify is how you knew to be at the Malone property at that critical moment. Because one of the weakest parts of your argument was your reply of 'I just knew.' Will you tell us what you meant by that?"

*How do I explain?* I breathed deeply to calm myself. Suddenly I smelled rosewater and an image of a key formed in my mind followed by a warm feeling of peace. It was time.

"Will you allow me to show you how I knew?" They looked at me curiously, then nodded. I told them to sit quiet and still. I closed my eyes and concentrated as hard as I could on Mr. Barstow. After several seconds, I told him of the images I saw in my mind, of him as a young boy, kneeling over a black Labrador. "She's hurt. You're crying, begging the dog to stay with you. She's … she's bleeding. Her side is gaping open. You can't save her."

I opened my eyes and looked at Mr. Barstow. His mist was sadness-gray and his eyes glistened. "How on earth?"

"She's right? She saw you and your dog?" Mr. Tanner asked.

Mr. Barstow continued to stare at me as he answered Mr. Tanner's question. "Ella was my dog's name. A wild boar gored her." He shifted in his chair. "Not sure what the statistics are on lucky guesses, so perhaps we should try this again. Try it on Mr. Tanner."

I closed my eyes again, pushing aside the irksome thought of being a part of a circus freakshow. I concentrated on Mr. Tanner. I spoke of the images that flashed, of a younger him reading a book in a hayloft, then smoke, and fire. He'd drifted off while reading. The book slipped from his hands and hit the lantern. "The breaking of the glass startled you awake, but it was too late. The fire spread quickly." I didn't speak of the animals that died because of it.

"This is incredible," Mr. Tanner said, his mist was gray as

well, and his face pale. "I was fortunate to get out. Broke my leg jumping. Burned my father's barn to the ground. To this day I can't bring myself to even look at the cover of *The Adventures of Tom Sawyer.*"

Mr. Barstow continued to stare at me as he sat back. He placed his hands behind his head and blew out a slow, long breath. "I can't believe it. I mean, I believe it because what you've said is all true, but I can't get over how you're able to know this stuff."

"So, start at the beginning and tell us exactly what you saw in the life of Nathaniel and Norma Malone that brought you there on that very day," Mr. Tanner said.

I spent the next hour and a half relaying everything I had ever sensed and saw in my mind, psychically, emotionally, and physically, from the first moment I saw them in church until I heard Norma's voice in my mind saying the knothole was big enough for her soul to slip through. Both men took notes, writing as fast and as much as they could to capture the details. And when I was done with my story of the Malones, I told them about Katherine and the Bryers.

"If I hadn't heeded my gift, Norma would have met the same fate as Mrs. Bryer."

The gentlemen stared at me for a few moments, absorbing everything I'd revealed.

"Remarkable," Mr. Barstow finally said. "For the sake of absolute certainty, tell me something else that only I would know."

I closed my eyes and waited for an image to form. When it did, I looked at him. "Your mother's wedding ring sits in a silver box under a pile of folded shirts in your wardrobe."

"Is she right?" Mr. Tanner asked.

"She is," Mr. Barstow said.

Mr. Tanner smiled. "You said this trial would be sensational."

"I did. Now I'm at a loss as to what we do with it. The

judge isn't going to allow mysticism in his courtroom." Mr. Barstow looked at me. "We'd be putting your life at stake by claiming you have psychic powers."

My chest constricted. "Even if it's the absolute truth?"

Mr. Barstow wiped his sweaty brow. "It's too much of a risk. The papers will sensationalize your clairvoyant claim even more because they love that kind of stuff, and it will cause a frenzy in the community. We'll be reported in every newspaper in every city in the country and they won't be impartial. They'll call you a charlatan or a witch." He shook his head vigorously. "No. We're going to have to stick with what *physically* happened. You noticed bruises on Mrs. Malone and you wanted to help her. She admitted to you she wanted to leave her husband due to his abuse on the day she showed up with broken fingers. You came up with a plan to help her leave. On the day and time you agreed upon meeting at the station, she didn't show up so you went to their property to find out why. You found her nearly dead, stuffed in a trunk. Nathaniel came home unexpectedly to retrieve a forgotten lunch pail and found you in the barn with Norma. He attacked you and you defended yourself. *Those* are the facts."

"Except the part where you said I went to their property 'to find out why.' I already knew why. In my police statement I said I knew why."

"I won't mention your statement," he said.

"Mr. Matthews already has. And he might again."

"If he does," he said, straightening his papers, "you'll explain that since she'd been abused before, you thought it might have happened again."

It was the truth, except I didn't think it might have, I absolutely knew.

# Chapter Forty-Seven

I tried to have faith the following morning after praying all night that Mr. Barstow was right about sticking to only what physically happened, but my insides shuddered. I couldn't shake the doubt that retelling my story would be enough to save me. I needed Norma there to tell her story.

As the jurors filled the jury box, I watched as the spectators filled the gallery. I craved the encouragement of my loved ones on this day. I noticed an empty chair next to Katherine.

"*Helen?*" I mouthed to my sister. She simply smiled at me.

A moment later, the main doors opened and I caught my breath. Helen and another nurse were walking on either side of Norma, their hands on her for support. Norma was walking with a cane.

"Oh my God. She's here," I whispered. Mr. Barstow and Mr. Tanner turned.

"Well, look at that," Mr. Barstow said.

I looked at Katherine. Her nod told me it had been her idea. "*Thank you,*" I mouthed.

After the judge was seated, Mr. Barstow stood. "Your Honor, I'd like to call Norma Malone to the witness stand."

"I object, Your Honor," Mr. Matthews shouted.

The judge stared at Norma, obviously considering it. "Mrs. Malone, are you here on your own volition?"

She straightened her shoulders and lifted her chin. She nodded.

"I'll allow it," he said.

"Wait, Your Honor. You determined she isn't a reliable witness," Mr. Matthews said.

"We won't know that for certain until she proves it. Therefore, I will allow Mrs. Malone to testify if she agrees."

Norma was already making her way toward us. Helen and the nurse helped her to where Mr. Barstow waited to assist her to the witness stand.

"Can you speak to us?" the judge asked when she sat.

She shook her head.

The judge raised his eyebrows and looked at Mr. Barstow.

"Mrs. Malone," Mr. Barstow said. "Can you tap your cane on the floor twice for yes, and stay perfectly still if the answer is no?" She nodded and tapped her cane twice.

The judge nodded as well. "Proceed, Mr. Barstow."

"Mrs. Malone, do you know this woman?" He pointed at me. She tapped twice. "Do you trust this woman?" She tapped twice. "Has this woman ever hurt you?" She remained still. "Do you know who hurt you?" She tapped twice. "Did I hurt you?" She remained still. "Did this man hurt you?" He pointed to Mr. Matthews. She remained still. "Did your husband, Nathaniel Malone, hurt you?" She tapped twice. "In all the years you knew Nathaniel, did he hurt you only one time?" She remained silent. "Did he hurt you often?" She tapped twice. "Do you remember anything about the day you were injured? The same day Nathaniel died?" She tapped twice. "Did Nathaniel hurt you on that day?" She tapped twice. "I have only one more question for you, Mrs. Malone. When he hurt you on that day, did you fear for your life?" She tapped twice, loudly.

There were murmurs in the gallery as Mr. Matthews stood up.

"Mrs. Malone, I am awful glad you're well enough to join us today, and I don't want to cause you any more trauma by making you relive that day you may or may not remember, so I will respectfully pass on any questions. But I will tell the judge and jury that the testimony you gave still does not explain how Miss Richardson knew you were supposedly in danger and why she made it a priority to go to your house instead of Larsen's Market where she was expected to work."

"Mr. Barstow?" The judge said.

Mr. Barstow walked over to Norma. "You may step down, Mrs. Malone," he said as he reached out his hand to help her. He walked her to where the nurse and Helen stood waiting to escort her to her seat.

"Gentlemen of the jury," Mr. Barstow began, "I'm grateful we had the unexpected privilege of hearing from Mrs. Norma Malone herself. I hope you will give her answers serious and thoughtful consideration." He motioned toward me. "I now call Miss Sarah Richardson to the stand."

*Help me stay strong. Help me stay calm. Help me have faith that the truth will prevail.* I sat in the witness box.

Mr. Barstow addressed the audience. "Despite that Sarah Richardson and Norma Malone didn't know each other well, they had a very special bond. One based on empathy and human decency. When Miss Richardson noticed Mrs. Malone's timid behavior and her bruises, she was compelled to do what she could to help the poor woman." He turned to me. "Tell us about the day Mrs. Malone came to the market with bandages on her hand."

For nearly an hour we went back and forth, he asking me questions or telling me to elaborate on certain instances. We went over and over crucial events, events that held the most weight against Nathaniel's character. When there was nothing left to describe or reiterate, Mr. Barstow sat down. I tried to ignore the gnawing in my chest telling me my testimony had not been strong enough.

"It seems it's up to me to ask the question we still don't know the answer to," Mr. Matthews said as he walked over to me. "Miss Richardson, did Norma Malone invite you over to her house on the day you killed Nathaniel?"

"No, sir."

"Then why did you go over there?"

"Because she didn't show up at the train station."

"What if she had simply changed her mind, or was delayed for some reason? Why is it that instead of going to work at the market, you went all the way to the Malone property?"

"He'd hurt her before, so of course I would think he might have done it again."

"Oh, so now you *thought* she *might* have been in trouble. That's interesting because in your police statement you said, and I quote, 'I just knew.'" He stared at the jury for a moment before turning to me. "Miss Richardson, none of the actions you claim happened on that day make sense, and do you know why? Because you admitted not knowing Norma Malone very well, yet you risked your own safety by interfering in a marriage you didn't know anything about, you took money out of your own bank account to buy train tickets for a woman you aren't even friends with, and then you murdered a man you didn't know."

The judge overruled Mr. Barstow's objection.

"And all of that because you *thought* she *might* be in trouble."

I tried to control the rush of flustered emotion as everything in me was screaming to tell him why I had to go there. I glanced at those who knew about my gift and believed in me, Daddy, John, Katherine. Suddenly I smelled rosewater, and I knew Grandma Rose was with me in my darkest moment. I looked at Justin. Would he continue to love me? *You must love yourself more.* I exhaled a long, slow breath. It was my gift that brought me to this moment, and I had to trust it would set me free.

I looked at Mr. Matthews and straightened my shoulders. "I knew she was in trouble because she was mentally pleading to me for help. I heard her voice in my mind."

The entire courtroom erupted—the spectators, the jury. Mr. Barstow and Mr. Tanner looked at me, panic-stricken. The judge slammed his gavel repeatedly.

Mr. Matthews stared at me for several seconds and then looked at the judge. "Your Honor, I believe Miss Richardson truly is following in her sister's footsteps. Her mental state needs to be evaluated at the asylum."

"Objection!" Mr. Barstow yelled. "Your Honor, I assure you Sarah Richardson does not need to be evaluated."

The judge stared at me, and then turned to Mr. Barstow. "Why are you so certain?"

I could see perspiration forming on Mr. Barstow's upper lip and hairline. His face and neck were red. I spoke up before he could. "I have an ability, Your Honor. It's called clair-voyance."

There were gasps and comments and whispers from the gallery. Mr. Matthews laughed until his face turned red. I had to quell my rising anger knowing he was doing it for show, especially when he wiped his eyes with his handkerchief.

"Your Honor, I think we should all be presented with this clairvoyant ability. I'd like Miss Richardson to explain it," Mr. Matthews said.

The judge looked at me. "Lying in court is considered perjury, Miss Richardson."

"I'm not lying. I can prove it," I said.

If the spectators had rocks, I'm certain they would have thrown them. They threw words instead—fraud, witch, and liar.

I closed my eyes and covered my ears as the judge

slammed his gavel again and again. He demanded the gallery be cleared out.

I looked at Justin as he stood to leave. I wanted him to look at me so I could see he wasn't distressed or appalled. I watched as he and his parents melded into the withdrawing crowd. As far as I could tell, he didn't look back.

"This courtroom is to be treated with the utmost respect, Miss Richardson, not a fortune teller's parlor." He looked at the jury. "We will reconvene at two o'clock, gentlemen, so that Mr. Barstow and Mr. Tanner may reconsider their defense."

Mr. Barstow's jaw tensed and his mist darkened as he stared at the judge.

We walked back to the counsel room in silence.

As we sat, I looked out the window into the exercise yard. I could see the gallows. I tried not to give in to the growing dread in my chest.

"I had to," I said, before they asked why.

"The reaction of the judge, and everyone else for that matter, was *exactly* what I was afraid of," Mr. Barstow said, his tone sharp.

"He wants us to change our approach," Mr. Tanner said. "I'm not sure there's anything we can do to gain back our credibility."

We sat in silence, absorbing what Mr. Tanner had said. In my desperation to save myself, I'd achieved the opposite. Oddly, instead of feeling defeated, I was elated. What did I have to lose? "Then I continue with my approach," I said. "I can prove that what I said was the absolute truth. I won't tell the judge his fortune, I'll tell of his past. Something he holds close. Something only he knows."

"No. We can't do that," Mr. Barstow said. "Because even if what you tell him is true, he might get angry or humiliated if you speak of his private life in the courtroom. He'll want to punish you for that."

"I won't speak it. I'll write it. He can tear it up or burn it or whatever he feels necessary."

"Won't it be considered evidence?" Mr. Tanner asked Mr. Barstow.

"That will be up to him," Mr. Barstow replied, still staring at me. "Sarah, your disclosure has already put our defense in serious jeopardy. You need to fully understand that your psychic revelation about the judge may end up sending you to the asylum."

I stared at Mr. Barstow. "Then so be it."

# Chapter Forty-Eight

As we came near the courtroom, the shouts of the crowd outside the building were louder than ever with screams of "hang the charlatan," "she's a liar," and "burn the witch," as Mr. Barstow had warned. I said a prayer of protection as the men hurried me through the halls. It was a relief that only a couple of guards stood outside the courtroom. The judge must have insisted that everyone who was not permitted in the courtroom not be permitted in the building either.

"Are you ready?" Mr. Barstow asked when we approached the doors.

"I am." And I truly was, because whether I succeeded or failed in my efforts, I would have done everything I possibly could.

I scanned the fifty or so people sitting in the gallery when I walked in. Norma was sitting between Katherine and Helen. I saw Justin and when his eyes locked onto mine, he placed his hand over his heart. A rush of relief overcame the fear I'd had of him abandoning me. John gave me a smile and a nod as he placed his hand over his heart as Justin had done. Daddy too, covered his heart, as did Priscilla, and Katherine, Helen, and Rebecca. And Norma. I realized it was their sign to me to have faith and stay strong. The awful anxiety that had been binding my insides slackened. *Thank you, God, for these wonderful people.*

"If any one of you says a word, you will be held in contempt," the judge said to the audience. "Mr. Barstow, is the defendant prepared to give her testimony?"

"Yes, Your Honor," he said.

I was sworn in for the second time and took my seat.

"Your Honor, and gentlemen of the jury, you heard Miss Richardson's testimony earlier, that many found to be peculiar, or to some, even unbelievable. I have to admit, your skepticism is understandable. But I witnessed her clairvoyance first-hand, as did Mr. Tanner, and I am not overreacting when I say we were astonished with her accuracy."

Mr. Barstow turned to the judge. "Miss Richardson is not a fortune-teller. Nor is she insane. She is an average young woman who happens to have inherited a God-given psychic gift handed down from her grandmother. She doesn't use this gift to make a profit or to create a sensation as fortune-tellers do. If it had been up to her, she would have kept this special ability a secret for her entire life. It wasn't until she felt Norma Malone's hidden pain so acutely, and saw her abuse so vividly in her mind, that she was compelled to reach out to her. I understand you want this courtroom treated with respect. Your Honor, I believe that includes giving a defendant who is on trial for her life respect as well. Miss Richardson should be given the opportunity to prove to you she is telling the truth."

The judge looked from Mr. Barstow to me and back again. "How do you propose she proves herself?"

Mr. Barstow reached his hand out to Mr. Tanner who handed him a pad of paper and a pencil. "She will write down a private moment in your past that only you know about. Only you will see it."

The judge shifted in his seat. "My private life has no relevance to this case."

"Your Honor, it's the only way you will believe she has the ability to see into the life of others, like Norma Malone."

The judge's face was grim. "All right. What do I need to do?"

"Sit quietly while she writes."

The judge nodded.

"Gentlemen of the jury, I want to show that this pad of paper is completely blank." He held it up in front of the men, flipping pages back and forth until they were satisfied.

As Mr. Barstow walked toward me, I looked at Katherine and John for encouragement. They each placed their hand over their heart. I looked at the judge for a moment, closed my eyes, and concentrated. My pulse was so fast it was causing images to flash one after another, with no coherence. *Please help me, Grandma Rose.* I took a deep breath and slowly released it.

Just as I smelled rosewater, the images began to slow down, and, as if I was watching a play, I could see the judge as a young man. Maybe twelve years old. Where was he? The area was not familiar to me. Rocky coastline. Somewhere in the Northeast. He was distressed. Why? A woman. A neighbor woman. She was older, married. A mother of three young children. Was he in love with her? He thought he was. Her name … Ophelia … He helped her with chores while her husband was at work. She had feelings for him too. Inappropriate feelings. She acted on them. Several times. He wanted to stop. What if his parents found out? He was ashamed. He never told a soul.

I opened my eyes and wrote as quickly as I could before the sensations faded completely, all the while hoping the judge wouldn't condemn me for bringing up such an uncomfortable —and shameful—part of his past.

When I finished writing, I hesitated to hand it over. There

had to be a reason this particular memory was shown to me. Something was missing. Something important. And then I understood. I quickly jotted down: *It wasn't your fault. You were a boy. She was the adult. Forgive yourself.*

I folded the paper and gave it to the bailiff who handed it to the judge.

"Before you open it, Your Honor," Mr. Barstow said, "all I ask is that you read it with the knowledge that Miss Richardson's fate is based on the contents of this piece of paper. When you are done, please, say either 'true' or 'false.'"

The judge gave Mr. Barstow a grim nod and opened it.

I stared at the judge as he read, watching his mist turn cloudy and dim. After several moments, he folded the paper and placed his hand on it. He looked at me, his eyes sorrowful.

"It is the truth," he said.

There were gasps and whispers once again from the gallery and looks of shock on many faces. The judge hit his gavel.

When the gallery quieted, he said, "I will not make the contents of this public for the sake of my privacy, just let it be known that the person who is mentioned in this note lived in another part of the country and has been dead for several years. There is no way Miss Richardson could have been told what she described here." He turned his attention to me. "Miss Richardson, I believe the jury should hear more about the connection you have with Norma Malone."

"Yes, sir," I said, and took a breath. I told the story of my unusual gift, my strange abilities, my extraordinary life. The judge called for order when the crowd mumbled, and I continued on, undeterred by the air becoming more oppressive due to the astonishment and excitement of the audience and jury. I left out no details as I gave example after example of my clairvoyant and clairsentient moments of Norma, knowing my words were the only thing that could save me.

When I finished, there was a moment of stunned silence, and then our attention was drawn to the gallery. Norma Malone was standing and nodding. *Yes, yes, yes.*

Chapter Forty-Nine

My not guilty verdict was followed by pandemonium, far greater than the circus of Donald Bryer's trial. The crowds nearly swallowed me and my lawyers alive as we left the courthouse. Reporters from the gallery crammed beside us, asking me what revelation I'd had about the judge. I repeated the words Grandma Rose had said to me when I asked her the same question so many years ago: "That's between him and me." Accusations of casting spells and bewitching the judge and jury were shouted by several members of the crowd, as were cheers of support from the Women's Equality Society.

I'd wanted to say goodbye to Mrs. Harris, Miriam, Sophia and a few other women in the holdover, but Mr. Barstow suggested that if I wanted to get away from the chaos, I better exercise my right to freedom immediately. "There will be time another day for farewells," he said. I'd even hoped to celebrate with everyone at a dinner at the Conroys', but we quickly realized that until the fervor died down, we'd all be prisoners in our own homes.

For days after the trial, reporters and curiosity seekers gathered in front of John and Rebecca's home, the market, and the Conroys' home as well. The operator switchboards were overwhelmed with calls from reporters and busybodies asking to be connected to the Larsen and Conroy households, which the papers reported was causing a call disruption for important matters such as police business.

The interest in Nathaniel's story had shifted, and now everyone only wanted proof of my psychic abilities. The offers to be interviewed by newspaper reporters and magazines kept coming, several a day, some from other cities.

It wasn't until the evening of the third day that Justin was able to get a call through to me. Although we knew our conversation was far from private, it didn't keep us from expressing our longing to finally see one another outside of the Four Courts. He admitted to being continually asked if I'd given him a love potion, or if I'd cast some kind of love spell. I worried he would tire of it all, but he assured me he wouldn't allow anything to change the way he felt about me.

John and Rebecca had to make a rule and post it outside the market: "If you step inside, you must buy something." Too many people were taking up the limited space to ask questions that John and Rebecca weren't willing to answer.

Mercifully, interest began to wane after several weeks. There came a day when no one was lurking outside, and no operator rang to connect an incoming call from a reporter. People still came to the market, hoping to see me. It was clear I could no longer work there, much to my dismay. I realized it would be some time before I'd be able to work anywhere in public, so I continued living at John and Rebecca's, taking over the cooking and cleaning as Katherine had done. She moved into Helen's home after taking over my job at the market.

"Just two spinsters dividing the cost of living," she'd said with a smile.

When things calmed down, my courtship with Justin became official. Four times a week, he either came to visit me or sent a carriage to bring me to his parents' home. Daddy and Priscilla came back to St. Louis to visit and spent a couple evenings having dinner at the Conroys' who were kind enough to extend the invitation to John, Rebecca, Katherine, and Helen.

Mrs. Conroy talked to us about the Women's Equality Society during those dinners, and one day she asked to attend a meeting with me. I was thrilled. When I asked Justin what he thought about it, he agreed.

"It's overdue," he said. "Every adult citizen of this country should have the same privileges, rights, and freedoms that I have."

I hugged him for that.

It was weeks before I made it back to the holdover. Sophia's trial was delayed until she gave birth. Mrs. Harris said there would be a woman from the Christian Women's Temperance Union present at the birth who would help place Sophia's child in an orphanage. I was relieved to hear it, but more relieved when she said that the union, who had campaigned for harsher punishments for incest and rape, as well as age-of-consent legislation, had organized more than one hundred members to show up at Sophia's trial to support her.

# Chapter Fifty

J ohn and I sat in the parlor after dinner, watching the
flames in the fireplace change from orange to blue to
iridescent.

"I had a visitor at the market today," he said.
"Gertrude Gaines stopped in."

"What did she say?"

"She said, 'I'm sorry.'"

"And what did you say?"

"No need to be."

It was obvious John had been to the barber the day Trudy
came for dinner, as he was freshly groomed and smelled like
spring. And he wore a suit. Rebecca and I welcomed her in, as
John waited his turn to greet her.

"Gertrude, it's lovely to see you," he said, lifting her gloved
hand and kissing it.

"And you, John," she said.

As we ate, Trudy confided in us that her friendship with
Mrs. Digby had become strained during the trial, so much

that she moved out of the boarding house and moved in with her daughter.

"I wasn't going to give in to her way of thinking. I knew in my heart you were innocent," she said to me. She then looked at John. "And there was you. I was no longer going to allow her to influence my feelings for anyone."

At the end of the evening, Rebecca and I watched as John walked Trudy out to the waiting carriage. As they said good-bye, they clutched each other's hands like loving friends.

*THERE'S no reason for me and Priscilla to be in Jefferson City when our girls are in St. Louis,* Daddy's letter had said. *And I'm bringing something for you both.* Katherine and I were delighted. He was coming here for an interview.

Helen was at work at the hospital on the day he was to meet the two of us, so I went early to help Katherine prepare a lunch consisting of ham sandwiches, a fruit plate, and raspberry tarts.

"Does he know how you and Helen feel about one another?" It was a sensitive topic, though an important one. I wanted her to be able to live as authentically as I now did.

She stopped arranging the fruit. "I told him the first evening he came here. He asked if I had 'a fellow' and I told him I never would. I didn't care what his response would be. If he couldn't love me because of who I love, then I would've said goodbye to him again." She walked over to the dish cabinet and brought out three plates. "I could tell it bothered him because his mist turned gray and the lines on his face deepened." She laughed. "His neck and face turned splotchy, do you remember how it always happened when he was embarrassed or upset?"

"I absolutely remember."

"I didn't even try to help him through his uneasiness. I sat there and waited for him to think about it and say whatever it was he needed to."

"What did he say?"

"He said his first thought was how I might get mistreated because of it, the same fear you had about what other people think. And then he said, 'To Hell with them,' and that his only wish is for me to be happy. I know he was telling the truth because his mist turned bright blue. And he was very friendly to Helen when he met her afterward. She likes Daddy."

I was relieved. All those years he'd lived with the guilt of what he'd done to Katherine had taught him what truly matters.

We opened the door to Daddy's knock to see his mist sky blue and his smile as warm as the sun. There were two chests at his feet; the chests he had hand-carved and painted for us, and Grandma Rose had filled so long ago.

The three of us sat in the parlor after lunch, sipping coffee and nibbling on the tarts.

"I've thought about these hope chests throughout the years," Katherine said.

"I've taken good care of them, waiting for a day like this. Unfortunately, the keys have been misplaced. I'm afraid we'll have to break into them," Daddy said.

Katherine left the room, returning moments later with an ice pick. "This might work." She walked over to the one with the S painted on top of it. "Let's do Sarah's first."

I leaned forward, watching closely as she moved the pick around in the lock. Finally, I heard a click. I placed a cushion on the floor and sat beside my chest, Katherine and Daddy looking on. One by one, I took out the individually wrapped items: doilies, a lace table cloth, baby blankets, baby clothes—one for a boy and one for a girl. A box of silver coins, a pair of amethyst earrings, and finally, something soft and large at the very bottom. I stood up and pulled it out with care. I unwrapped the outer protective cloth and caught my breath at the sight. It was Grandma Rose's wedding dress.

"It's beautiful!" I said, laughing like a young girl. It was like Christmas morning.

Katherine knelt down at her open chest and pulled out a hand-sewn quilt, a sweater, a scarf and pair of mittens, all knitted by Grandma. She then pulled out a jewelry box. She silently read the note that was inside it, and then looked at me. "She knew."

I looked at Daddy, who was as perplexed as I was. "Knew what?" I asked.

Katherine showed us the contents of the jewelry box. There were two identical gold bracelets. "Her note says, 'For you, and the woman you love.'" She placed it down and went back to the chest. "There's one more letter in here." She pulled it out and tore it open.

"Read it out loud," I said.

*My Dearest Katherine,*

*I wish I could be with you on the day you open this, though I know it is not meant to be. I thought of you often, wished you the very best, and sent so much love to you since we've been apart. Every one of these gifts are from my heart to yours. There is one more that doesn't fit in this chest. It is at the First National Bank of Missouri in St. Louis. Go there and inquire about an account in your name. I set it up weeks after you were sent away, and by now, it should have accrued a nice amount of interest. My hope is that you and Sarah will use the money and your God-given gifts to help women. Women like Mildred Bryer.*

*I knew her plight became your destiny, and Sarah's, the night you tried to save her life. She would be so proud of the women I am certain the two of you have become.*

*With all my love,*

*Grandma Rose*

I reached my hand toward Katherine and she reached back. We held on tight and smiled at one another. Yes, women like Mildred and Norma *were* our destiny.

❧

IT TOOK A COUPLE OF MONTHS, but Katherine and I found the perfect house with the money Grandma Rose had given her. Justin's father had offered to hire help for all the restoration work that needed to be done. We kindly refused, explaining we wanted it to be tended to with loving hands, as Grandma Rose would have wanted. He apologized for his "insensitivity," as he called it, and then asked if he could help.

Katherine, Helen, and I cleaned and painted the interior, while Daddy, Justin, and Mr. Conroy made repairs and painted the exterior. Mrs. Conroy helped us when it came time to decorate and plant the flower garden.

A hand-painted sign that read *Mildred's Boarding House for Women* hung on a post. The words were bright green, a chain of daisies made a border, and a yellow butterfly was painted in the lower left corner. The butterfly was in memory of Mildred's unborn child.

When the work was complete, we all stood in front, looking at the stone walkway bordered with mix of pink and yellow plants: coneflowers, primroses, milkweeds, and others, leading up to the porch steps. The steps and the porch were painted white, as were the columns on either side of the entry. The house itself was a narrow two-story made of yellow brick with painted white wood trim windows. And there was a porch swing, the same type of swing we had when we were young, in Rolla.

As I stared at the lovely house, my heart swelled with pride for my sister. *Thank you, Grandma Rose.* The first guest Katherine and Helen moved into their home was Norma Malone.

TEN MONTHS after our courtship became official, Justin and I were married in my sister and Helen's home. The wedding was a very small affair attended by his parents, Katherine, Helen, Daddy, Priscilla, Trudy, John, Rebecca, and Norma.

I proudly wore Grandma Rose's simple linen and lace wedding dress and cake and coffee were served after the ceremony. It was nothing at all compared to the "royal event" Justin almost had with Laura, but he assured me it was the happiest day of his life. It certainly was mine.

# Epilogue

*May 1905*

I sat on the market porch, rocking our eighteen-month-old son, Steven James, asleep in my arms. Justin stood next to me. We were chatting with "great grandpa" John while our four-year-old daughter, Victoria Rose, sat cross-legged at Justin's feet with a coloring book in her lap. She was using a green crayon for the leaves of a tree.

John named all the birds he'd seen now that warm weather was settling in.

"My mother loved birds," I said. "And so did my grandmother. They taught me and my sister to name them by sight or sound."

"You have a favorite?" John asked.

"I do, although it's not a songbird. It's the hummingbird. I love their squeaky chatter, the whir of their wings, and their inquisitive nature. They are so intelligent for being so small. What I love most are their gorgeous colors. Their feathers are shades we don't see anywhere else, and when the sun hits them, they shimmer, shine, almost glow."

"Like some people," John said.

"Indeed," I replied, nodding toward Justin.

"Wait. I thought you couldn't see my colors," he said.

"I can't, but I have no doubt they're as lovely as a hummingbird's."

"You're blue, Daddy," Victoria said.

We all looked at her. "What did you say?" I asked.

"He's blue, Momma. Like the sky."

I turned to John. He tapped his nose and grinned.

# Acknowledgments

When I was a little girl, I would cry every morning before school because I was shy and terribly afraid. Afraid of the students, afraid of the teachers, afraid to learn new things. Thankfully, I grew out of it. Mostly. When I turned fifty, I had a big decision to make. I had been writing short stories for years, but if I wanted my dream of writing and publishing a novel to come true, I had to step out of my comfort zone and immerse myself in a writing community. I researched MFA programs, and one in particular caught my attention.

I was enthusiastic when I was accepted and when I packed my bag for the first ten-day residency, but when it came time to actually leave my husband and get on a plane to travel across the country, my level of anxiety and uncertainty was so high, I had to ask myself if it was worth it. Let me tell you—it was so worth it. If I'd given in to my insecurities, I never would have met the wonderful people on my list who helped me become a stronger writer.

Thank you to all of my Newport MFA cohorts, most especially Leah Bogdan DeCesare and Marney McNall. You are my writing soul sisters and invaluable critique partners. Every page of this novel has your essence. Thank you for keeping me on track, for being brutally honest, and for your support, enthusiasm, and dear friendship.

Thank you to the creator of The Newport MFA, Ann Hood, and my Creative Writing faculty mentors: Tim Weed, Danielle Trussoni, Bill Roorbach, and Allen Kurzweil.

Thank you to developmental and diagnostic editor Abigail K. Perry whose advice changed the trajectory of the novel and made it much more compelling. Thank you to editors Katie Reed and Marci Clark. Thank you to Lee Ann Ward and Writing Away Refuge.

Thank you to beta-readers Sharon Kurtzman, Geradline Maschio, Ph.D., Judith Fisher, Ph.D., Victoria Fortune, and Manda Newlin. Thank you to Joan Fernandez who introduced me to the Women Fiction Writer Association Historical Fiction Affinity Group, and who put me in touch with Dennis Northcott, Associate Archivist for Reference for the Missouri Historical Society Library and Research Center. Dennis provided resources for the St. Louis Four Courts, which led me to read about Mrs. Louisa Harris, the first police matron in St. Louis. I found her so fascinating, I had to include her in the book.

Thank you to Holly Kammier, Jessica Hammett, and everyone at Acorn Publishing, LLC. It has been a wonderful experience working with you!

Thank you to my entire family whom I love and adore. And finally, thank you to my love of many lifetimes, my husband Steve. You have never given up hope, nor would you ever let me. You have always encouraged, supported, and believed in me. I thank God for you every day.

# About the Author

*Photo by Nina Pak*

Raquel Y. Levitt holds an MFA in Creative Writing and a Master's degree in English. Her short stories have been published in various anthologies and literary journals and reflect her passion for writing about strong women finding their voice and their power. She is a world traveler, an amateur nature photographer, and a collector of cool rocks. Raquel and her husband live, work, and play in the Texas Hill Country and Montana's Bitterroot Valley. *The Seer* is her debut novel.

www.ingramcontent.com/pod-product-compliance
Lightning Source LLC
Chambersburg PA
CBHW030137310726